QUASPECK

Also by Eric Gabriel Lehman

Waterboys

QUASPECK

a novel by

ERIC GABRIEL LEHMAN

MERCURY HOUSE
San Francisco

This is a work of fiction. Names, characters, places, and incidents either are the product of the author's imagination or are used fictitiously. Any resemblance to actual events, locales, or persons, living or dead, is entirely coincidental.

Copyright © 1993 by Eric Gabriel Lehman. "Rikki Don't Lose that Number," words and music by Walter Becker and Donald Fagen, © copyright 1974 by MCA Music Publishing, a division of MCA Inc., New York, NY 10019. Used by permission. All rights reserved.

Published in the United States by
Mercury House
San Francisco, California

All rights reserved, including, without limitation, the right of the publisher to sell directly to end users of this and other Mercury House books. No part of this book may be reproduced in any form or by any electronic or mechanical means, including information storage and retrieval systems, without permission in writing from the publisher, except by a reviewer who may quote brief passages in a review.

United States Constitution, First Amendment: Congress shall make no law respecting an establishment of religion, or prohibiting the free exercise thereof; or abridging the freedom of speech, or of the press; or the right of the people peaceably to assemble, and to petition the Government for a redress of grievances.

Mercury House and colophon are registered trademarks
of Mercury House, Incorporated

Printed on acid-free paper
Manufactured in the United States of America

Library of Congress Cataloging-in-Publication Data
Lehman, Eric Gabriel, 1954–
  Quaspeck : a novel / by Eric Gabriel Lehman.
    p. cm.
  ISBN 1-56279-036-6
  I. Title.
PS3562.E42825Q37   1993
813'.54—dc20

                                     92-42343
                                          CIP

5   4   3   2   1

for Lisa Dunn

Part One

I

C<small>EE KEPT CALLING</small> *for him to stop. Her voice billowed up behind him. But Jason was running too fast. The road swung up under his bare feet. The asphalt was as hot as a cookie sheet straight from the oven. He tried to run to the other side but the headlights had slipped over a rise in the road and caught him, holding him still in fright like a raccoon. Get back, Cee shouted, but she'd disappeared far behind. Jason's knees went soft, he fell, tasted asphalt. The car was almost upon him; he had to stop it. He swung his head, ready to butt the car like a goat—*

Jason sprang up in bed into a cloud of cold air. Chill sucked at his back and found the dampness across his chest. Two floors below, deep within the warm heart of the house, his father's new alarm had gone off, a stubborn, ominous buzz. The old Baby Ben was better; it ticked, and its alarm started with a tingly clatter, a marching mouse band with tiny cymbals. Then the tingling petered out, as if the band had turned a corner. His own clock said five-fifty-nine. He didn't have to be up to go to school for another two hours and could even sleep later, since Richie's Mustang was faster than the bus.

Hey, Early Bird! How come you're always up so early?

He leaned back on his elbows. Each time he breathed, a double row of muscle corded his bare stomach like a snake's rattle. He breathed in and out, his stomach rippled, the rattle shook. He ran his hand along the muscle padding his shoulders and then over the warm bulge of his upper arm. Today he'd do an extra tough workout with Richie on account of Nina. She liked guys with muscles, Richie said. He promised to take him to Nina's after the gym. Then Jason would get to do it, finally. At least that's what Richie said.

Richie Castro had just transferred to Jason's school that September, and they'd become friends. He was two years older than Jason, popular and self-confident. He told people he was Italian so they wouldn't make jokes about Fidel Castro; with his dark hair and eyes maybe he was. He wore his shirts with the sleeves rolled up just above the bicep, tight enough to raise a blue vein over the muscle. He kept his head tilted to the side when he talked to someone, as though impatient or bored. The lower part of his face looked older, hardened by a jaw beginning to square. Guys respected him. Girls liked him, and even those who didn't—smart ones from nearby Saint Ursula's never seemed to—enjoyed telling him to get lost. His model was his older brother, Nelson, a full-grown version of Richie, with a prison record and a child he'd fathered out of wedlock. Richie was especially proud of how Nelson had tricked the woman by putting a needle through the rubber he'd used with her. It was Nelson who'd first brought Richie to Nina.

Richie went to Nina when he had the money, once a month or so, in the afternoon. Jason's heart thumped to hear him talk about her. Guys were always telling getting-laid stories at school, their voices thick with triumph. But Jason really believed Richie's accounts. "She likes me," he said, his eyes narrowing with satisfaction.

Jason assumed that Nina was simply a prostitute. Richie certainly gave her money. He'd check his wallet before leaving the gym, counting out the bills with deliberate slowness, as if to figure out how many minutes of pleasure each would buy. But Richie was genuinely fond of her; she seemed more like a girlfriend who took money for her favors.

Jason leapt out of bed and pulled off his underwear. He always did his exercises naked. His mother once walked in on him. "What in God's name are you doing, rolling around in your birthday suit on the floor?" He began his squat thrusts, then rested, belly on the floor, heart knocking against the prickly carpet. His father's alarm had shut off. For a time after the crash he heard almost everything that went on in the house—a match being struck, Cee's puff on the cigarettes she wasn't supposed to have, the squeak when his mother rubbed polish off her nails. Some time after his hearing returned to normal, the blinking started.

His father's heavy tread began tracing a heavy line from the bedroom to the kitchen. Jason used to think that his father was too big for the house. Everything shrunk in his hands: forks and knives, his razor and his comb.

I don't know what the hell happened to him, Theresa, but he ain't the same anymore.

Winters, Jason went downstairs, waded through the layer of cold air in the kitchen, and spooned the bitter-smelling instant coffee into his father's cup. He ferried a kettleful of water to the stove and reached for the Ohio Blue Tips. His father lumbered into the kitchen, bulky in his work boots, sweater, and overhauls.

He ain't the same anymore.

The air felt damp, oily, as though it might rain. Jason turned over onto his back and crooked his arms behind his head, releasing sour funk from under his arms. He began his sit-ups. His thigh muscles pulled to the surface like cables, his thing lopped from side to side.

—twenty, twenty-one. In the second his head swung backward, the windows slid into view, squares of daylight his father had cut into the ceiling, without curtains or shades, too high up for him to see anything but sky. Nights, when he was younger, he was afraid to fall asleep, in case the windows broke and the night poured in. He'd stay awake listening to Cee and Carl talking in Carl's room. Carl's voice was low and whistling: "I can't ac-sssept that. That goesss againssst what I believe in, can't you sssee?" Cee's voice pillowed around his. The next day at school, Jason would be drowsy. The spaces between the blue lines on his paper teased him, as though hiding what was there. He held the paper up to the light, searching through the cloudy masses of pulp for hidden words. Or else he'd draw. The ink was dark and cool-looking. Even if he was caught and the paper snatched away, his pen kept on, dragging against the wood of the desk like a train derailed.

Did you read the note his teacher sent home, Theresa?

He needs time to adjust.

Any eight-year-old in his right mind knows better than to walk down the middle of a road.

—forty-five, forty-six. His limbs pumped like pistons, and his muscles gave off heat. Fifty-three, fifty-four—

A whine and shudder rose from the pipes as his father turned on the hot water in the bathroom.

—sixty-nine, seventy—

"Theresa!"

His mother's slippered footsteps, headed for the bathroom to rub his father down with Ben-Gay. Cee's clock radio used to go off around this time, a metal flower one floor below, WENE in Binghamton, New York, Rock on 1430 AM. She'd pull off her nightgown, scratch herself—arms, shoulders, belly, legs—everything pink and shiny, scritch-scritch. "God-deayam," she said whenever she couldn't find something. "God-deayam." Sometimes she'd sneak into his room and surprise him. "Outtabed, Puttyhead." Nights when he couldn't sleep he crept into her bed and slumped against her wide back. She smelled of damp grass and candy because of what she smeared on her face. She let him touch her titty once while they were at Quaspeck. It felt like the corner of a pillow.

You're too old to be running to your sister at night, Jason. Your sister is becoming a young lady and a young lady's privacy is very important. Your father built that nice room for you . . .

Carl's room was opposite Cee's. He slept in one corner of his bed, stiff as a book. He was skinny and looked as if he were held together by string. He used to remind Jason of a giant ant with glasses. Jason shared Carl's room until the attic was done over. Carl made him sleep on the side of the room away from the heating vent. Jason got back by waiting until Carl went to take a piss, then banging on the door to scare him so he'd whizz on the floor.

Cee and Carl were two, Jason used to think. A pair, boy and girl, dog-Carl and cat-Cee, together, a room for each, as if everything had been planned out perfect. Even their names started with the same letter. Jason was one, alone. There wasn't even enough room for him; that's why he'd been stuck under the roof.

—ninety-nine, hundred. Jason fell onto his back and felt himself uncoiling.

How come you never put the light on, Dad?

Costs money. Besides, I know where everything is.

How did your hands get like that?

From work. Yours'll look that way too when you start working.

Jason turned over onto his stomach to start his push-ups, his favorite. With each drop (back straight, don't rush) he imagined himself lowered onto a faceless female torso that offered an explosion of breasts for the press of his taut pectorals. He would try to place Nina below him, except he'd never seen her, and knew only that she was black. What tantalized him far more than breasts was what it must be like to lower his thing into the warm, wet chute between a woman's legs.

One, two—

Heavy drops of rain began rattling on the roof. Damn, if it kept on raining it meant they couldn't go to Nina's. She never let Richie come over when it rained. She was superstitious and believed that when it rained the heavens were wide open and God saw everything.

—eleven, twelve—

What're you building today?

Office building foundation.

What's that?

It's what this damned house doesn't have, and what makes it so damp.

Can I come with you?

What about school?

No school today. Holiday.

Remember what I told you about going to those Quaspeck houses. You never know when they might fall down.

—thirty-nine, forty—

Outside, the rain had grown harder. Nina probably wasn't going to let them do it today for sure. But even if the sun was shining and there wasn't a cloud in the goddamn sky, Richie could think of a reason not to take Jason along.

—forty-nine, fifty!

A knock at the door startled him. He flopped down hard.

"Jason?"

"Wait!"

"I'm not coming in. I just wanted to give you your allowance." A bill emerged from under the door. "I can only give you five today. Your mother will give you the rest by the end of the week."

Jason picked it up. It smelled of Ben-Gay.

Five dollars, he thought. Nina charged ten.

The weather stayed bad all day, and the rattle of the rain against the school windows seemed to be Nina telling Jason, Not today, not today. But as it turned out, he and Richie stayed in the gym longer than usual, and afterward Jason felt too tired to do anything except go straight home.

The kitchen was empty when he got there, and the living room dark. His mother was stepping out of the bedroom into the hallway as he neared the stairs.

"Is that Jason?" his father called out from behind the door.

"What's going on?" Jason asked his mother.

She led him away from the door and spoke as if passing on a terrible secret. "Your father's been laid off," she said.

JASON HAD BEGUN working out because of Richie. Richie went to an after-school recreation program in a complex next to the new county office building. "You can come, too, Blink," he said. Blink was Richie's nickname for Jason. Other kids made fun of the occasional flutter of his eyes, and it made him mad, but not Richie. While he shed his school clothes and jumped a little rope, Jason carried out the weights. Before Richie did any lifting, he pulled on his leather cycler's gloves. He never touched a bar with bare hands: germs.

Jason strapped on a pair of twenties for a start. Richie approached the barbells and stood feet apart. He took a breath and closed his eyes, appealing to his private god. The first weights seemed to pull up into the air as if on strings. Soon he was calling for another pair of twenties, then forty on each side. The shiny bar rose elegantly in his grasp until it reached his shoulders. Muscles massed beneath his skin like an army called to combat, and veins hardened up and down his neck. Then he paused, his chest glistening, the spark of his gold cross like water struck by sunlight. He took another deep breath and heaved the bar up until his arms were completely outstretched over his head and the weights hung in the air, proud and perilous. His lips petaled into a dark, pulpy ring, his eyes burned with what appeared to be exquisite pain. He let the bar back down, but only as far as his chest, and then pressed it up once more with a raw grunt. Jason stood close by, breathing Richie's rich scent. He imagined Richie's power pressing deep into his heart, a power all the more alluring, since Jason never saw it being used for anything but lifting weights. Then the bar would be lowered, like a great machine come out of the sky to land with a rattle.

"Don't you ever feel like boxing sometimes?" Jason would ask. "You could take all the guys here, no problem." But Richie shook his head no.

"Then why do you do all this?"

Richie grinned. "Women. And if a man doesn't screw he gets nervous," he would explain. "It's like steam pushing up the lid of a pot. You know what I mean, Blink?"

He did and he didn't.

Jason watched as Richie shouldered his way into conversation with girls. If they acted aloof, his voice wrestled theirs soft until the color rose in their faces. There was something that smoldered at Richie's core. It pushed up from deep within him, it was what made his eyes look heavy, and what darkened his lips.

Richie said he liked going to Nina's best after working out, because that's when he felt nice and tough. He'd shower and pull on his clothes, buoyant with anticipation. They walked as far as Endicott Street, where the monument stood on a traffic island. He'd give Jason a farewell pat on the shoulder and head in the direction of the bus station, Nina's neighborhood. Jason followed with his eyes, tensed with a yearning he couldn't name.

One day, feeling especially listless after Richie had gone, Jason crossed over to the little island. A square column of grey stone rose on a mound in the middle. A plaque was bolted to the base, blackened to near-illegibility and crusted with dried mud. It commemorated a victory of the colonists against the Quaspeck Indians in seventeen-hundred-something. It made him think of something in a book Cee once showed him, but he couldn't remember what. He ran his fingers over the dirty bronze letters, as if that might tell him more, then headed back to the sidewalk, trying to remember what the book had said. Something about the Indians coming onto the settlers' ship—

A sudden screech of brakes startled him, and he sprang up from the road back onto the grass. A car's chrome radiator gleamed with danger, inches away.

"Why don't you look where you're going?" the driver said, raising an angry fist out of the window.

"LET'S SEE WHAT you can do," Richie said one day, sweating after several heavy lifts.

Jason never had much interest in sports. He tired easily and might grow dizzy. He waved Richie away, but Richie was already unlocking some of the weights from his bar. "Do some running in place to get yourself warmed up." Jason just stared at him. "Hey, what are you waiting for?"

Jason began; his sneakers stamped against the floor, one-two, one-two, until the blood sang through his temples.

"Ready?"

Jason reached down for the steel bar, still warm from Richie's grip.

"Hands the other way around," Richie said. "Knuckles facing the floor. Works your biceps better that way. Hey, wait a minute." He pulled off his gloves and gave them to Jason.

The leather was damp and held the shape of Richie's hands. Jason heaved the bar up as high as his chest, then his wrists trembled and his fingers turned to paper. The weights came down with a clatter.

"Take a breath and try it again," Richie said, patient.

The next time Jason only got it up as far as his waist.

"It's my hands," he said. "They can't hold good."

"You gotta lift with your legs, not with your hands. Don't lean forward so much. Keep your shoulders back and think of bringing the weight down through your hips. Try it again." He planted himself right in front of Jason.

Jason went for the weights.

"Easy does it, that's it, get that weight going through you, not against you."

"I can't hold on anymore," Jason cried. "I'm gonna drop them."

"No you ain't," Richie hissed. "If you do I'll kick your ass."

Pain threaded through Jason's arms. "Richie—"

"You hold that fucker until I tell you to let her down." Richie stepped closer. His glance locked into Jason's.

"I can't—"

"You better."

Jason held the bar where it was.

"Good, very good," Richie said with a pleased growl in his voice. "Now you can let it down. But I better not hear you doing it."

They began working out together, both of them shirtless, and Jason wearing Richie's old gloves, which he'd let Jason keep. "Looking good, Blink," Richie sang as Jason attempted fifty pounds. "Getting tough."

Richie took Jason to parties and let him come along when Richie and Nelson went for drives in Nelson's Corvette. Nelson hardly seemed to notice him. One evening, in Nelson's living room, a few empty bottles of beer on the coffee table before them, Nelson asked him whether he'd been to Nina's yet. Jason shook his head no.

"Go on, take him, Richie," Nelson said, stretching his long legs out in front of him. His hand disappeared under his shirt to scratch his hairy belly. "That woman taught me all I know," he said with a dark smile. "Let her get your friend here started." His hand lingered under his shirt contentedly.

Jason began to think of nothing else, and badgered Richie to let him come with him to Nina's. Richie never would. Maybe he wants to have her all to himself, Jason thought, burning each time Richie refused him. Or maybe he wants to have something over me. Yeah, that was it: Jason was getting better all the time, so Richie wanted to keep his edge.

"You promised you'd take me," Jason said as they reached the traffic circle one afternoon. "Even Nelson said you should." He saw Richie's arm flexed with the weight of his gym bag and imagined the drive coursing through his body. Jason yearned to pounce on Richie and tear it from him.

"I will," Richie said. But he'd already turned toward the bus station, impatient to be gone.

2

Cee entered the washroom, a towel over her shoulder, a drawstring toiletry bag dangling from her fingers. Sinks lined one wall like statuary. The cleaning woman's disinfectant hung in the air, a stern presence.

Soon the washroom would ring with the sounds of women at the sinks spitting out toothpaste and frantically brushing their hair, each mirror the frame of a disjointed movie. Cee always tried to get in early so that she could shower alone; the three stalls were no more than curtained-off sections of what had been a common shower when the floor housed men. Cee'd just slipped into the middle section and turned on the water when laughter broke against the tiled walls.

"That you, Jackie?"

"No, Pat, it's Cee."

"Hiya," said Judy.

Pat and Judy lived in the room next to Cee's. Judy had a doll-like voice and the penetrating good nature of women who organize welcome wagons for newcomers to the subdivision. Pat was more serious, a geology major. They began showering, and their talk coursed back and forth freely. Cee felt like she was sitting between two friends in a movie.

"You won't believe what happened last night," Judy said.

Maybe not, Cee thought, a little irritated, but now they'd get to hear all about it.

Cee felt like an outsider on the floor. Most of the other women had met the previous year. And at least half of them were from New York City—which often meant Longguyland. For many, Buffalo was an outpost of Merrick or Bethpage. Just the other day Cee'd overheard someone say that they had never been downtown in two years at the university.

". . . and we have a paper due next week for Psych," Judy continued.

Why was it people from New York talked so loudly?

Judy and Pat were friendly to Cee; all the women on the floor were. (Out of pity for the lonely, fat girl in room 906?) Cee toked on the occasional communal joint, she went to the floor meetings and get-acquainted party. But she couldn't really throw herself into what the housing office referred to in its orientation brochure as Residential Life. So many of her floormates seemed to have a reason for being in college. There were the serious students like Pat, and those like Judy who enjoyed mingling. The pre-meds and pre-laws wanted to become M.D.s and J.D.s. Socially committed women picketed in front of the administration to expand the university's day-care facilities. But Cee?

Her freshman-year classes had been factory-sized, the professor an amplified voice rising from deep within the lecture hall, a ghoulish face in the glow of an overhead projector. Introduction to Psychology—she called it "Mass Psychology"—was less an introduction to the subject than a screen to prevent too many people from majoring in it. Spanish consisted of memorizing dialogues, and the English of her South American TA sounded as if she'd memorized the appropriate English dialogue the night before. All things considered, the thrill, as B. B. King might have put it, was gone.

That first year she'd had grown close with Fran, her roommate, who, like Cee, missed as many classes as she could without being forced to drop them. They took to spending their afternoons in the food co-op, peacefully measuring out bags of soybeans or else listening to co-op members debate whether to sell local—but inorganically grown—carrots instead of the organic kind "from strangers." Fran eventually left for California. Her parting words to Cee were, "You gotta get physical."

"By the way, did you really stop taking the pill?" Judy asked.

"Since the beginning of the semester."

"Doesn't that . . . inhibit you?"

There it was again—sex. The subject was never far from the surface. It hovered over their floor like the very steam in the shower stalls. *Sexum gratia sexus*—slippery, odiferous intercourse, one-nighters, fucking, was never discussed. Questions of need, fulfillment, and energy were, couched in the context of a relationship or the politically correct issue of reproductive rights, and debated with the seriousness of suffragettes. Cee wondered what kind of exalted species of men these women found to bed—surely none of the oily-skinned undergraduates, dripping with hormones. She wasn't sure how much of this dialectic of sex was bullshit but reckoned the figure to hover around fifty percent.

If sex was never far from the women's talk, then neither were boyfriends: Michael from Clement Hall, Lenny who lived off-campus, Ray who hitched in every weekend from Jamestown, and Phil, the rarest of finds, a Buffalonian, "but no pig," his girlfriend was quick to clarify, as if to differentiate him from the hordes of unenlightened natives. These men might surprise Cee in the bathroom early in the morning, emerging from a toilet stall—having left the seat up, of course—and still fiddling with their underwear or, if they had none on, smiling sheepishly, a hand cupped to their privates like hairy Botticelli *Venus*es.

Cee reached for the soap. She felt attracted to men, but her interest was dulled with mistrust. Clothed, men were clumsy mysteries. But shirtless on a summer day, their shape not soft with disuse, they possessed an exquisite rhythm of tautness and elongations. Their beauty could do harm, but it enticed.

Still, a visit to a male floor of her coed dorm was a descent into a little-boy underworld. Shopping carts stolen from the A&P were jettisoned out of the windows to crash like clumsy biplanes on the front lawn. A favorite trick was to arrange for as many toilets as possible to be flushed throughout the dorm simultaneously, releasing tides of water into the hallways. On especially cold nights, the men on the top floor—was it accidental that it had been assigned to men?—sealed the doors to the bathroom, steaming it to sauna proportions with torrents of hot water from the showers, then opened one window a crack, causing the hot air to be sucked out, condensed and, so they claimed, turned to snow by the time it reached the ground. As if Buffalo didn't get enough snow.

"A diaphragm seems safer to me," Pat was saying.

"Yeah, but it's so . . . unspontaneous. What about you, Cee?" Judy asked.

Cee dropped the soap. "Wh-what do you mean?"

"Judy's playing Dr. Joyce Brothers with you," Pat explained. "She wants to know what method of contraception you prefer."

Cee retrieved the soap. "Maybe I'm a lesbian."

Silence.

Well, that would teach them to ask personal questions in an inappropriate setting.

Cee didn't really think she was a . . . dyke, but up until then she'd had sex exactly once, in her senior year of high school. One and a half times, if you included the guy who'd sprayed her thigh with his seed before getting any deeper during the Watkins Glen music festival. Her official deflowerer—it sounded like defoliater—was Malcolm Brack, one of the loose band of outcasts to which Cee belonged. Malcolm was very tall and not unattractive but shy to the point of near-invisibility. He wore his hair chopped off just below his ears, which made him resemble a hungry peasant. He had an after-school job at an animal hospital and wanted to become a vet. Of all the people she knew who claimed to be vegetarians, he was the only one who never, never ate meat.

Cee and her friends were sitting all the way in the back of the balcony of the funky Emerald Theater one Friday watching one of the head movies they showed at midnight. They'd already passed a couple of joints back and forth. Cee could hardly keep her eyes open for the movie—what was the name of it? At some point she noticed Malcolm sitting beside her, as wasted as she, the orange tip of yet another joint held her way. She toked on it, wondering whether Malcolm had been there all along. Before she could make up her mind, his hand landed on her knee and began migrating toward her . . . lap. She remembered thinking, How incongruous: the hand of Malcolm Brack between my legs, between anybody's legs, even his own. Malcolm simply seemed too skinny to have a functioning sexuality.

She grew uneasy, but was too curious—or stoned—to move. He cantilevered over to her and sealed his mouth against hers, all the while his hand fought with her zipper. "Is it okay?" he whispered. "Is it okay?" The rest happened very quickly—or perhaps very, very slowly, she couldn't be sure which. She gave a moment's obligatory thought to birth control, murmuring a word or two about whether he had "something for it," but too late, he'd already begun angling her legs over the seat's metal sides as though anchoring them in a gynecologist's stirrups. He folded himself into position. The shock of his entry—Malcolm turned out to be skinny in all but one respect—made her scream. She buried her mouth in his leather jacket. (What kind of vegetarian wears a leather jacket? she thought.) He pushed farther in, a little too fast, setting off a biting pain, which lessened but never went away completely. Malcolm persisted, a leathery bat fluttering between her legs —who was that woman who got fucked by a swan? Like a ship steaming into port too quickly, Malcolm bypassed the faint signal of pleasure the lighthouse of her clitoris was emitting. She reached up under his shirt where his back's bony machinery churned below his skin. His leather jacket crinkled with each thrust, the ancient seat creaked, they made what seemed an unignorable racket. His breath began howling in her ears, and just as her pain subsided—or had she grown used to it?—he retreated. Did that mean he'd come? She couldn't bear to ask. As she pulled her pants back up she noticed that the seats around them were empty; her friends had discreetly moved forward. Which meant that everyone knew what had happened.

"Hey, Cee, you okay?" Judy said.

"I'm scrubbing away at my ring around the collar."

Now what was the name of that movie? She remembered only one thing about it: The final scene was of a sunset that went on forever.

She brought the soap between her legs; she loved sudsing her muff. Just below it was her favorite part of her body, the stretch of skin that was impossibly soft; a secret, maidenly place. She brought the soap over her breasts and across her belly in long, luxurious strokes. Her skin was white and smooth; a swansdown beauty she was, perfect for the seventeenth century. Her nipples were soon erect, exceptionally sensitive. She kneaded her palms into her arms and biceps. Why, she had muscles! She imagined herself as a discus throwerette ready to toss a bar of Dial.

Her fingers lingered near her breasts. This June would be five years since her mother's operation. If they found nothing by then, she'd be okay. Not cured; you were never cured of cancer. But out of danger. It was Carl who had revealed the secret of her mother's operation when no one was supposed to know, Carl the precocious Elder Sibling, the boy-scientist, who'd thrown frightening words like *mammography* and *carcinoma* at her. Her mother had left the hospital looking old, as if they'd cut away some precious, womanly essence along with the poison.

Cee worked the soap into the cheeks of her ass. In the past year alone, it seemed, she'd gotten fatter. No, not fatter. Bigger. She'd always been fat, um, big. Was it because of the unsold pastries her mother brought home from the bakery where she worked? Carl and Jason ate more of the black and whites than she did, but they stayed slim. As a child she didn't think she was uglier than the other girls, just more delicate, more prone to the falls and scrapes of jump rope and roller skating. She learned the golden rule of the overweight: take your time. She developed a gravity and calm that drew her schoolmates to her for counsel.

That had all changed with a single remark, made one day by Mickey Grazer, a bucktoothed wiseguy in her sixth grade class with borderline grades, the type of kid who knew how to run the movie projector but little else. The ice-cream truck was waiting opposite the school after dismissal one stifling hot day. Everyone made a run for it, dimes in their hands. Cee forgot the golden rule and ran, too. She tripped and fell. "Hey, look at Big Bertha!" Mickey shouted.

Everyone heard.

She looked up, winded, her knees capped with pain and her head ringing as if made of metal. People pointed, and the glare of sun fused them into a single, hideous laugh. His utterance, like a first inkling about sex, was unforgettable. It swiftly divided the world into two camps: those like her and those not, the ugly and the attractive. The lines had been drawn since time began, and her side was losing. Simpleton though he was, Mickey had only repeated the obvious.

Then came the precautions. She wore camouflaging skirts to school even after the dress code changed to allow pants. She broiled in jeans during the summer, shunning the tentlike shifts other fat, hippie-type girls wore. She never pinned up her long hair: That emphasized the bulk of her shoulders. Too much makeup made fat girls look like kewpie dolls, she knew, and she never, never went without a bra.

Why had she been fat? Before Mickey, her explanation had a convincing simplicity: She was different. But as she grew older—and bigger—it seemed her body was responding to what had nothing to do with beauty or ugliness but her need for protection, for keeping what was fragile out of danger, safe behind a fortress of flesh. It had to do with touching, with being touched. Or not being touched. Her girlfriend Jeanine had been raped while hitchhiking and said that the worst thing about it was the sensation of something foreign lodged inside her that persisted for weeks and weeks afterward. Cee understood immediately. She hated crowds and avoided concerts and demonstrations that threatened to thrust her into the anonymous press of strangers.

And here were Pat and Judy, gabbing away in a common shower room about what they placed inside their vaginas. Amazing.

The water turned ice cold.

"Hey!" Pat shouted.

Judy let out a scream. "I've got a head full of shampoo!"

Cee had just finishing rinsing off and stepped free of the sudden cold. The boys were playing Waterworks again, no doubt.

That morning she'd meant to make her English class: Women on the Edge of Time—Kate Chopin, Margaret Atwood, Isak Dinesen, Nadine Gordimer, Doris Lessing, and, of course, Marge Piercy. But once in her room, so quiet after her shower, it was hard to leave it. Her eyes fell on the empty bed and a heaviness overcame her.

She'd arrived on campus that fall, anxious to see Fran again—they'd arranged to room together—but Fran wasn't there. It was nice being able to spread her things out, dance naked to the radio, and let the butts pile up in the ashtray, yet she resisted taking over the whole room, sure that Fran would show up any day. Another week passed, registration drew to a close, and Fran still wasn't there. The sight of the unoccupied bed made Cee feel like the floor spinster.

She put water on the hot plate for coffee. Her eyes fell on the two framed photographs she'd hung up. The first was of herself, taken accidentally as she cleaned the lens of her Konica. The second was of Jason on the front lawn. He never understood that lawns were just for show. He lay on his back, shirtless, a garden statue toppled to the ground, with a shapeless torso and a belly soft as cake batter. It was taken before he'd begun that weight lifting, of course. When had that been? When had Jason hardened so much that his very thoughts had become thick and opaque?

The accident resulted in a mild concussion but no organic brain damage. His doctors can't rule out possible learning disabilities, speech pathology, and memory loss. His prognosis, however, is good.

That means that Jason isn't going to be a zombie, right, Carl?

She visited him in the hospital every day after school. His head was wrapped in a gauze helmet that extended to below his eyes, and his hands lay placidly at his sides. Cee told him who she was, she read to him, and he seemed to understand, but he spoke little, as if his bandages not only darkened his vision but silenced him. Doesn't he know who I am? Cee asked herself. Or is he angry at me because of what happened? She played the defendant in her own cross-examination: He only got hit on the head; head, not brain—that would have meant brain damage. An injury to the head wasn't serious. People got headaches, they bumped their heads and got lumps, no big deal. The chilly chrome bed rail and stiff-lipped porcelain sink faced her like the members of a pitiless jury.

Once Jason was discharged from the hospital Cee kept on the lookout for signs of damage. ("The possibility of reduced motor skills, dyslexia, and loss of memory," Carl reeled off.) Jason's speech drifted in and out of what other people said to him, like a foreigner's. His gaze wandered around the room, as if he were trying to figure out where he was. He began blinking, a kind of stutter of the eyes.

Her mother was flustered by Jason's strangeness, or maybe her job at the bakery left her too tired for yet another round of motherhood. Jason was too fragile for Walter to tumble around in the backyard with, and too young for thirteen-year-old Carl. Perhaps because of the accident, Cee came to think of Jason as her child.

Her father converted the attic into Jason's room but at first he resisted being moved into it. It was too far away, he said, up a hidden flight of attic stairs. Cee understood. It was almost as if his parents wanted to banish Jason, she thought, giving him the room no one else wanted, a forgotten place that paint and carpeting couldn't change. She granted Jason refuge in her room. "Let's run away," he whispered to her one night, nestled beside her. "We can go back to Quaspeck and live there."

The water came to a boil and she made coffee. She recalled the afternoons he'd return from school in tears after kids taunted him with, "Retard, retard!" She held him, a hot, fluttering bird that had fallen into her arms with a broken wing. He was sent to a special school in Binghamton, and his teachers reported improvement, but for Cee he slowly became faceless and dull, sanded smooth, so that no part of him would catch or jam against anyone else.

She drank her coffee. Was Jason angry at what had happened to him? she wondered. Did he think he'd been punished for something he'd done?

There was another question: Did he blame her for what happened?

The bells of Hayes Hall began ringing the hour.

She went to the window. Down below, walkways framed plots of withered grass. Like the city, the campus had been laid out according to someone's grand notion: a stately main building complete with cupola, a Greek temple library with wide steps. But the aluminum Quonset huts—provisional classroom space—put up later gave the campus the feeling of a mobile home park.

The coffee was strong and good. She'd been going to fewer and fewer classes. She'd gather up spiral notebook and pen but get as far as the fountain in front of the student union. There she'd sit watching the dogs splash around while freaks threw Frisbees. The bells would peal out the lost time in fifteen-minute intervals, and another lecture would pass by unattended. She'd duck inside the union to get the latest leaflets about saving the whales or the formation of an all-black republic in the South. A delegation of religious Jewish men in dark suits, complete with beanies and curling forelocks, wrangled with the feminists or the Gay Liberation Front. The Vietnam Veterans Against the War were an unsmiling lot. Once Cee picked up a leaflet explaining the amnesty law, but she hurried away, not wanting to get into a conversation with the man behind the table, who was in a wheelchair.

She heard more bells. Hadn't she waited all her life to go to college? After the Pablum of high school, college was supposed be a cloisterlike compound of columned buildings, where you read important things instead of textbooks issued in September and collected in June. Yet here she was, books, bells, and even a couple of columns, and she could hardly bring herself to leave the dorm.

Just what had Fran meant by "get physical"?

Cee pulled out a thin volume from her row of books, *Where We Live*, about Thompson City, compliments of the Susquehanna Savings and Loan Association. She'd read it with Jason when he was a little boy. He would run his fingers over the pictures of the Indians, tracing their headdresses, the stripes on their faces, their sleek, Chinese-looking hair. She opened to a picture of the Quaspeck Indians waiting on the shore with arms outstretched, as a large ship with many sails approached. Wigwams—or were they tepees?—formed a circle on the edge of the river. She leafed ahead, stopping at a drawing of the Indians, now looking savage, as they took tomahawks to men in long black coats—the settlers. She read the accompanying text.

> The cordial relations between the Indians and whites did not last long after the first English ships sailed up the Susquehanna River. At some point after the settlers' boat had docked, an Indian living in the village of Quaspeck climbed aboard out of curiosity and was thereafter accused of taking some clothing and a mirror as souvenirs. A mate of the ship spied him as he attempted to leave and shot him dead. The missing items were recovered. When a second Indian boarded the ship to extract vengeance for the murder of his tribesman, the cook lopped off his head with a sword, signaling the beginning of a series of bloody encounters between the natives and the European settlers.

The next page showed Thompson City's first settlement, then called New Chelsea. The Indians had vanished along with their tepees, and in their place was a neatly arranged hamlet, complete with a school, a quarry, and an icehouse. Later, everything was abandoned when the river flooded its banks. The flood, occurring on Easter Sunday in 1754, was seen as proof of Indian deviltry, since the river had never risen so high before.

Still another page showed the Quaspeck Youth Village, erected by the WPA on the shores of Davis Lake during the depression, built to resemble the early settlement. Jason was so fascinated by the story of the Indians that he convinced her to take him there. She hesitated; Quaspeck was dangerous. Bums prowled around there. An escaped convict once hid out in one of the WPA cabins.

Cee finally agreed to go with him one day in early spring, not long before the accident. The old cabins were as black as tombstones. The shingles of the houses were warped and their windows boarded up. The remains of a cobblestone road, like corn with missing kernels, led toward the lake. Cee forgot that the cabins were no older than her parents. She imagined the houses whitewashed, their windows curtained, women in long skirts with baskets of groceries, dogs barking, the clop of hooves, and the school flying its American flag, just as it had been in that book. Then she blinked and saw everything as it was, ruined and black, as though the picture had been replaced by its negative.

We could live here, Cee. Just you and me.

They went to Quaspeck often, in secret, since her father had forbidden them to go there. On hot summer days Cee took off her shirt and sat in the sun.

Thanks to you your brother's an idiot, Celia.

Cee decided to check her mailbox. She got dressed. Maybe she'd go to the music library a little later.

Greaser's Palace, she thought as the elevator doors closed. That was the name of the movie playing that night at the Emerald.

A letter from the Housing Office was waiting for her. She'd been assigned a new roommate, Stephanie Polite, who was due to move in within the next week.

3

O NE DAY CEE returned to find a trio of strangers in her room. A middle-aged black woman looked up from smoothing the sheets on the other bed. A youngish black man wearing a leather jacket sat in Cee's chair, smoking a cigarette. His leg shook with impatience, as though he were the taxi driver who'd brought their luggage upstairs and now wanted to be off. In the middle of it all, loaded down with an armful of shirts, stood her new roommate, a younger, thinner version of the woman making the bed, with a delicate, oval face.

"I'm Stephanie. You must be Cee." Stephanie smiled bravely. "Sorry about the mess. This is my mother."

The woman extended a weary hand for Cee to shake. "Pleased to meet you," she said with but a moment's smile before her face tightened. "Stephanie, go and hang those shirts up and help me pull this bed out so I can tuck the sheet in on the other side. Hand me that pillowcase, will you, Horace?"

"You know what my name is," he said, frowning as he picked up a stiff square from a stack of bed linen. A gold chain shone around his neck. His watch threw off hard crescents of reflection.

"And get off the girl's chair," Mrs. Polite said, shaking open the pillowcase with a snap.

He glowered at Cee as she walked by and set her books down. She felt as if she'd stumbled into someone's living room.

Stephanie asked her mother whether it would be all right to hang up her sweaters, since all her dresser drawers were full.

"Fine, as long as you grow three inches when they get stretched out," her mother answered with a shake of her head.

"My lowest drawer is empty," Cee said. "You can use it, if you want."

"Can I? Thanks."

"Where's the bathroom around here?" Horace said.

Stephanie looked to Cee for help.

"The men's bathroom is one floor down," Cee said, with emphasis.

"You remember what I told you about him," Mrs. Polite said to Stephanie after the door closed. "I don't want him coming up here." When she was finished she shoved the bed back to the wall with her knee, as if to make her point. She turned to Cee. "You just starting out, too?"

"I'm a sophomore."

"That's good. Maybe you can show my girl around and keep her out of trouble." She smiled.

The man returned. "You two almost finished? I didn't plan on spending my whole day off here."

"Just let me get these put away, Race," Stephanie said. She grabbed a handful of panties from a suitcase. "Cee, which drawer did you—"

Race collided with Stephanie, and the panties landed on the floor like a stack of paper.

"Shit!" Stephanie said, shooting a guilty glance at her mother.

"Why can't you stay out of the way?" her mother said to the man sharply.

He glared at her. "I'll be waiting downstairs," he said, and then stormed out.

"That man!" Mrs. Polite said.

STEPHANIE POLITE WAS assigned to Cee's room as part of a program to house inner-city students on campus. She came from one of Buffalo's toughest areas, the Fruit Belt (Cherry Street, Orange Street). Cee guessed she had rarely ventured out of her neighborhood and, when she did, it certainly wasn't to go to North Buffalo, where the university was, with its food co-op and stores selling ceramic mugs and flimsy clothing from India. She sensed that the two of them were as different as—she cringed at the comparison—night and day. For Stephanie, just starting out, college meant goals and plans and her diploma, "a ticket out of the ghetto," as an ad for a black scholarship fund put it.

Cee yearned for Fran to return. (No way, Fran had written from somewhere in Oregon.) When Fran went to bed she stripped naked, no matter who happened to be in the room; Stephanie fled to a bathroom cubicle. Fran lived in a relaxed chaos; Stephanie's side of the room was painfully neat. Fran would bark at Cee when she was in her morning exercise phase. "Come on, girl, get those bazumbas moving!" Instead, the day began with Stephanie before the mirror, mascara brush in hand. Her tight jeans lifted and separated her backside as a bra might breasts. Cee watched with a mixture of aversion and fascination before crawling out of bed and into her overalls and flannel shirt.

"THAT'S CARL, my older brother," Cee said as they sat looking at her collection of photographs one evening. It had been Carl's senior year in high school, and he'd gone to a march after the Kent State shootings. He held his sign like a standard borne to a mountain summit. His wild, frizzy hair flamed from his head, and her unsteady shutter hand gave his face an angelic shadow. The year before, he'd snuck away to the big anti-war demo in Washington, then tramped into the house late, waking everyone up, especially their father, who'd forbidden the trip. He'd burst into her room smelling of cold and dope and peanut butter, and presented her with a doorstop stolen from a government building: a souvenir.

Stephanie reached for another picture. "Who's this?"

"My younger brother."

It was one of many she'd taken of Jason in the backyard from her bedroom window. More shots followed of Jason walking along the shore of Davis Lake, his eyes fixed ahead, as though he were about to walk into the water.

"You sure have lots of pictures of him. Is your father dead?" she asked.

"No," Cee said. "Why?"

"I haven't seen any pictures of him. My father, he died in the bathtub. I walked in one day after school and there he was. He must have been in there a long time. His skin was already dry and all the water had drained out."

"Stephanie, that must have been terrible for you." Cee couldn't remember ever having seen her father naked. When they went swimming, the sight of his body, so broad and bare, surprised her, as if it belonged to a stranger and not to the man who fixed the water heater or took them shopping.

Stephanie continued matter-of-factly, "He just looked like someone without any clothes on lying in the bathtub." She reached for a print of Cee's mother. Cee had surprised Theresa as she did the dishes, and her look of annoyance seemed to say that she wished she'd been able to fix herself up beforehand.

"Sometimes my mom don't know when to mind her own business," Stephanie said, addressing the picture.

Stephanie never mentioned that Horace person. Would she now? But no, she picked up a picture Cee had taken of herself nude.

Stephanie giggled. "You look so— Oh, I'm sorry," she said, returning the picture.

Cee held it protectively. "Yes, I suppose I do."

Several nights later, just after they both got into bed and turned out the lights, Stephanie said, "I'll be going back home tomorrow."

"Back home?"

"Just for the weekend. My mother needs help with the house. And I'd like to see Race. We're engaged. He loves me, I know he does. But sometimes we have problems. He's older than me, he already has a good job with the phone company, he don't see why I got to go and break my head to get a college degree. But he's all right."

Cee sensed Stephanie waiting for her reaction, but she said nothing. She hadn't liked what she'd seen of Race.

"He has his ways, that's all," Stephanie concluded.

Just then the sounds of people having sex began filtering through the wall from the next room.

Stephanie giggled. "Do you hear that?"

"It's Judy and Glen," Cee said.

"Doesn't it bother you?"

"It bothers me that Glen pees in the urinals of our bathroom because he says they're for male guests."

"I can't believe that they're just doing it like that, right here—"

"Judy wants everybody to know how uninhibited she is."

"All the girls here do it, don't they?"

It sounded like something Cee's grandmother might say. "It's not exactly an undergraduate core requirement," she joked.

Stephanie remained serious. "When my mother found out that men lived in this building she almost didn't let me come here."

Stephanie was probably no more than a year younger than she, Cee thought. Yet she felt she had to shield Stephanie from Judy's moaning. On the other hand, Race hardly seemed like the type to be content to hold hands in the movies. Maybe Stephanie hoped to stave off his advances until marriage, for her mother's sake.

"Oh, Glen, yeah . . ."

"My, my," Stephanie said.

CEE AND STEPHANIE were in the same section of Introduction to Sociology ("Mass Sociology") and often went for coffee together afterward. Stephanie's heels struck the terrazzo floor, piercing the midday din of the union. People looked, drawn by the clatter, or by the sight of a slender, well-dressed black woman beside the generously proportioned white woman in her overalls.

"Freedom for the People of Chile." Stephanie read a sign over one of the tables. "Those guys don't look like they come from Chile."

"They want to show their support."

"You don't really think it makes a difference, do you?"

They entered the cafeteria.

"Those kind of people remind me of the social workers they used to send over to our house to make sure my mother wasn't spending too much on the wrong things. Why don't people just learn to mind their own business?"

"Last year I worked with a group supporting the rights of American Indians," Cee said.

"Like I said, those guys don't come from Chile, and you sure don't look like no Indian." Her voice had a bitter ring to it.

"How do you like the dorm?" Cee asked when they'd sat down with their coffee.

"Some of the girls are a little silly, but it's better than living at home. My mother sure can get close sometimes."

A tall black man approached their table with a tray. He looked Stephanie up and down and seemed on the verge of saying something when he caught Cee's glare and continued on his way.

Stephanie giggled.

"Doesn't that drive you crazy?" Cee said.

"I got nothing against men," she said, sipping her coffee.

Stephanie's speech seemed especially sloppy just then. No, Cee thought, she hadn't minded the man staring at her. On the contrary.

"Do you have a boyfriend?" Stephanie's eyes shot her way.

"Um, no," Cee stammered.

Stephanie's lips tightened.

Afterward Cee headed for the library. People were huddled before the dry basin of the fountain in dark bundles of clothing. The way things were going in September, she might have been there too. Strangely enough, Stephanie was part of why she wasn't. Stephanie worked hard, as if pursuing her degree on a dare, which she probably was, considering Race. Cee had begun taking her classes seriously, as if to keep up with her. And Cee had begun to like her. But what was she supposed to make of their talk in the cafeteria? Stephanie seemed angry at her for not having a boyfriend. Cee felt as if she'd failed some kind of test. Be careful, she told herself.

The next time they met for coffee Stephanie had a copy of Frantz Fanon's *Wretched of the Earth* with her.

"It's for my Black Studies class," she explained, idly leafing through it. "All this black liberation stuff just isn't for me. Black people should have the same rights as anybody else, but I'm no militant." She giggled. "Just because someone's black doesn't mean they're Martin Luther King or Malcolm X."

They talked about their families. Stephanie's sounded as strapped for funds as hers. "But you dress so well," Cee said.

"No one has to know how much I got in my bank account from the way I look. People are poor because they don't want to work."

"My father doesn't have a job," Cee said. "He wants to work but he can't. He blames himself for being out of work. He was brought up to believe that everyone could earn a living in this country if they wanted to. America can't be wrong, so he thinks something must be the matter with him."

"All I can say is, being poor is bad news. I don't have to be rich, but not poor. Middle class is fine with me."

"I'm not afraid of being poor."

"Is that why you dress like you do?" A trace of derision clung to the question.

Cee looked startled. "I dress this way because I don't want anyone telling me how I'm supposed to look."

"You turn everything into something political."

"How come the university thought up this program to get inner-city students into the dorms? That's political too, isn't it?"

Stephanie looked hurt. Living in the dorm wasn't an "issue" for Stephanie, it was an adventure, and Cee had belittled it. Without really wanting to she'd had gotten back at Stephanie for the comment about her clothing. Now she wished she could apologize but feared that would only make it worse. For a moment neither spoke.

"I don't know about why the university does anything," Stephanie said, "but I know why I'm in the dorms. I wanted to see how all those nice white kids live. I wanted to hear them talk about how their fathers are doctors or dentists or whatever. Nobody I grew up with ever talked about that because nobody's father was a doctor or a dentist. I want to keep track of how things are other places. As soon as I get my degree I'm going to have all that, too."

Her eyes drifted to a table full of women.

"You know how I can tell that the girls living in our dorm got fathers with nice cars? They're the ones who play poor and rip stuff off."

Cee'd heard women from the dorm boasting about their latest haul: nice cheese, a shirt, a paperback.

It occurred to her that Stephanie had used the word *white* in her presence for the first time.

"Do you think I'm like . . . them?"

Stephanie thought about it. "Well, you do seem . . . a little different." She picked up the book. "*The Wretched of the Earth,*" she read. "Not me."

She pronounced *wretched* as the past tense of *retch*.

STEPHANIE BEGAN GOING home every weekend. Cee would return to find her bed made, her desk cleared, and a trace of her fragile, flowery scent in the air. Cee liked having the room to herself on the weekends, even if word did get around that Stephanie's bed was available to crash in, should the need, in the words of one pundit, arise. Stephanie would return Sunday evening, somber, as if regretting her lost study time. She changed into her work jeans—those with the barely frayed cuffs—and pored over her books for an hour or two.

Cee's side of the dresser looked spartan as a cadet's with its box of tissues, hairbrush, and vial of patchouli oil. Stephanie's array of gold-capped tubes and shiny little bottles sparkled like a shop display. Cee picked up a tube of lipstick, so elegant in her hand, so deliberately "feminine." Did Stephanie have two sets of makeup—one for here and one for downtown? Cee opened a tube of lipstick and began applying the oily color, feeling like a naughty girl who'd rummaged through her mother's handbag. What would Stephanie say if she knew?

Probably that you put it on way too thick, she thought, glancing at herself in the mirror.

She reached into Stephanie's top drawer for a Q-tip. A spark of pain met her finger, and she yanked it out. What was that? She opened the drawer wider: one of those disposable "lady" razors.

That Sunday Cee returned to the room to find Stephanie on the phone. "Race," she murmured, "don't say that." She was crying.

Cee busied herself on her side of the room, trying to be inconspicuous.

"Race? Race?" Stephanie whispered, as if he'd hung up on her.

When Cee woke up the next morning Stephanie wasn't at the mirror. The clock said ten-thirty. Without Stephanie's early-morning activity, Cee had overslept and missed her Poli-Sci class. She looked over and saw that Stephanie was still in bed.

"How am I supposed to know what time it is if you don't do your face?" she joked.

Stephanie lay still. "I don't feel like doing much of anything," she said.

Cee sat up, remembering that she'd planned to go to a photography exhibition in the public library on Lafayette Square that afternoon.

"Why don't you come with me?" Cee said. "We can play hookey together."

Stephanie brightened. Cee took her camera, and they hopped onto a downtown bus. Main Street was endlessly drab, as if the ugliest Main Streets from all America had been laid out end to end. Stretches of the city looked only partially occupied. The sight of so many black faces downtown made her feel like a visitor to an African republic or, worse, a preserve where only blacks were welcome. The Marine Midland building peered down coldly on it all.

At the Main Place Mall Cee bought waterproofing for her boots, and they stopped at a store selling cosmetics for black women where Stephanie chose a lipstick in a shade called *Terra-cotta*. Just before leaving the mall Cee saw a record store and was tempted to browse inside.

"What's the use?" she decided. "I don't even have a record player."

"My house is about ten minutes from here," Stephanie remarked when they were back outside.

"Feel like popping home?"

Stephanie shook her head. "I was there yesterday. That'll last me for a while."

"I'd like to see where you live," Cee said. Would she talk about her phone call with Race?

Stephanie looked uncomfortable. "Maybe some other time."

Cee remembered that she'd brought her camera. "How about if I take a couple of pictures of you?"

"No, no—" But she was smiling.

Cee already had the camera out of her backpack. "Stand there, next to the bus stop sign. You know what those letters mean?" she said, adjusting the lens.

"You mean NFT? Niagara Frontier Transit. My mother called it the Not Fast Trolley—hey!"

Cee snapped the shutter. "Look that way."

"Why?"

She snapped it again.

"Cee, you better not show these to anyone."

Click.

"There," Cee said, replacing the lens cap. "That didn't hurt, now did it?" She slipped the camera into her backpack. "You should feel honored. Those were my first pictures of the semester."

It had begun to grow dark, and the streets seemed deserted. Church bells made Cee think of the photography exhibition, which they'd completely forgotten about. The brightly lit windows of a hi-fi store caught her attention.

"Speaking of not having a stereo," she said, leading them over to the window. "What do you think of that one with the radio for four hundred dollars?"

"Fine with me. I'll ask Race to bring up my records."

Cee's spirit darkened.

When they reached the corner of Ferry Street Stephanie said she was hungry, so they went into an Arthur Treacher's fish and chips. The order girl, a black teenager, was dressed in the official brightly colored Arthur Treacher outfit, fit for a cartoon character. She was wiping a counter that didn't look dirty. She took their money and rang up their orders in a single, bored flow of motion.

"There's something I have to ask you," Stephanie said when they'd sat down. Her face hardened. "Do you like men?" Before Cee could say anything, Stephanie said, "Race thinks you don't. He thinks you one of those women who go after other women."

"How does he know? He's only met me once."

"He says you look that way."

"I look that way," Cee repeated.

Stephanie grew flustered. "Well?"

Cee felt challenged. "Maybe."

Stephanie's hand hit the table. "I think you just making something intellectual out of it. You don't like giving plain answers." She took an angry stab at a french fry.

"Would it make a difference one way or the other?"

Stephanie dragged the french fry through ketchup. "Let me tell you something. I seen a lot of weird people at that school since I been there, black people, too. When I decided to go to UB Race said, 'What you doing going up there with all them freaks?' And maybe he's right."

"Even if everybody at UB was a freak," Cee began, "whatever that means, what does it have to do with me?" Asshole Race, she thought.

"He said I didn't belong there."

"How does Race"—she would have loved to call him Horace—"know so much about UB? I think that he's jealous of you. He's scared you might start having ideas about things he doesn't understand. He's scared you might find a new boyfriend, too."

Stephanie fiddled with her plastic fork. "If he knew I was downtown and didn't stop by he'd be real angry."

They finished eating and headed back to the bus stop. The lights of downtown created an illusion of big-city nightlife, of crowds hustling from supper clubs to theaters, people hopping in and out of taxis, horns honking. But at this time of night, downtown Buffalo was a well-lit ghost town. Its only signs of life were fast-food huts plunked down in vacant lots.

Back in the dorm Cee spotted a poster for a festival of women's culture and a stack of schedules.

Cee took two of the schedules and gave Stephanie one. "Think you might want to check it out? It's on the weekend, but maybe you could come up for the day."

They walked to the elevator. "Cee, you really want to come by where I live?"

"Yes."

Stephanie smiled.

SOME OF THE WOMEN in her English class had planned to go to an all-woman version of *Oedipus Rex*, renamed *Oedipa Regina*, part of the festival, and Cee went too. The play brought applause at Oedipa's murder of her father, Laius, and whoops of delight when Oedipa made it with Jocasta.

They all decided to head for the women's dance afterward in the union. The Fillmore Room swam in murky red light, and a women's funk band saturated the room with heavy, stinging music. The women in the class soon filtered away into the thick crowd, and Cee and Marlene, her instructor, found themselves together. They headed for the beer line. Marlene was short, with dark eyes and long dark hair. She looked a little uncomfortable there, like an animal disturbed by noise and light, and she retained her sober, classroom demeanor. Maybe she doesn't go out much, Cee thought.

"Where to?" Marlene asked, holding her wobbly plastic tumbler of beer. Cee pointed to a less hectic corner at the far end of the room.

Marlene talked about the play, but Cee found it hard to concentrate. Her gaze drifted around the room, overwhelmed by the crowd of women dancing, being rowdy, and pressing together. It was exhilarating but so new to her that she was glad to have Marlene there, a tranquil vantage point from which she could survey the scene.

"What made you take my class?" Marlene asked suddenly.

"Maybe the course title, 'Women at the Edge of Time.' Sometimes I feel like I'm that kind of a woman. Someone who doesn't quite belong to one particular . . . genre."

"Genre?"

"You probably think that's just undergraduate drivel."

"No. I think most people want to not belong in some way."

"Not my roommate. She's black. She dresses nicely. She's planning on getting married. She wants to belong something fierce. Maybe not belonging is a privilege."

Marlene looked interested.

Cee tried to piece together her next sentence, but Marlene seemed to be studying her, and it made her nervous. Before she could answer, a samba band began playing. Hoots and shouts rose up in the room, and a samba line latched together. As it snaked past them, hands hooked onto Cee and Marlene, and they let themselves be pulled along. She felt Marlene gripping her waist with tentative hands as the line lurched through the room.

"I really should get home," Marlene said, out of breath and smiling after the line broke up. "But let me give you my number. Maybe we can go for coffee and talk some more. Where it's a little quieter." Cee pulled out her program for Marlene to write on, and she was gone.

Next morning Cee slept late, made coffee, got back into bed, and read for the rest of the afternoon. Later, she tried to decide whether to go to a slide show entitled "Buffalo Gals: Feminist Local History" or to a coffeehouse of Appalachian women's music. She opted for the coffeehouse and was about to leave when the door opened. It was Stephanie.

"Am I late?" she said, out of breath. "I tried to get here as soon as I could."

Cee hugged her.

"I wasn't going to come, but this morning, me and Race had another fight about me going to UB and living in the dorms, and I said to him, 'That's it. I don't have to spend the rest of my weekend listening to this.' On the way up on the bus I reached into my bag and there was that schedule."

They went to the rathskeller after the concert.

"You're worried about you and Race, aren't you?"

"He's really mad now, that's for sure." She shook her head angrily. "Men think they have to hold women tight. That's the problem. Race thinks he can make me love him if he holds on tight enough. But he's wrong."

Later that week Cee bought the stereo and decided to celebrate with a little party. She arranged to bring it home when she knew Stephanie would be in class, a surprise. She bought some wine and munchies, and rounded up her floormates. Stephanie returned to find the room full of women and cloudy with dope. They ordered up a couple of pizzas. When Judy introduced herself to Stephanie, Stephanie shot Cee an embarrassed smile.

"That was real nice," Stephanie said, flopping down onto her bed after everyone had gone.

Cee poured out two cups of wine. "Here," she said, sitting down next to Stephanie. "To the stereo."

"To the stereo."

"And to us," Cee added.

Stephanie looked away shyly. "Sure is a mess here," she said, surveying the bottles, cups, and empty pizza boxes. "Too bad we don't have no girl here to come clean up. Whoops!" She put her hand over her mouth in mock embarrassment. Then she broke out giggling. Her eyes fell on the picture of Cee and Jason. "Hey, what happened to my pictures," she asked, "the ones you took of me downtown?"

"They're still in the camera. But I could take some more of you now to finish the roll off."

Stephanie grinned devilishly. "Or else I could take some of you!"

Cee went for the camera. "You ever use one of these guys?"

"Wait. Before we get started, can you do me a favor? There's something I've been dying to do since I moved in here."

Cee looked at her, pleasantly confused.

Stephanie pulled a chair over to the dresser and motioned for Cee to sit down. "I want to make you up."

Stephanie surveyed her tubes and jars like a dentist selecting the proper drill, then applied eye shadow, liner, blush, and lipstick to Cee's face. Her touch was light but sure, like Theresa's reassuring dab of ointment when Cee hurt herself.

Stephanie stepped back and examined Cee's face critically. The blush on one cheek was smoothed out with her thumb, and her left brow got a little more pencil. "There," Stephanie said at last. "Have a look."

She'd given Cee's blue eyes an iridescent, azure shadow. The black pencil framed them. Blush gave the roundness of her cheeks shape. Her lips were a moody red.

"Now I'm almost as pretty as you, Stephanie."

Cee handed her the camera. "Here's the shutter release. Turn this to focus."

She sat down, and the shutter slid open and closed several times.

"Hope I did it right," Stephanie said, returning the camera. She yawned. "Suddenly I feel so wasted. That wine really got to me."

"Don't go to sleep yet. You promised I could take some shots of you. Wait until I come back from the bathroom."

Stephanie had just gotten undressed when Cee returned.

"Oooh," she said, frantically trying to slip into her nightgown. She pulled it over her head clumsily, and her arms caught in the sleeves. Something tore. Stephanie tried punching her arm through a sleeve, and a seam ripped open. She stood with her back to Cee, the nightgown twisted around the upper half of her body, exposing the shining globes of her backside.

Cee came over. "Hold still," she said, shading her voice with concern to conceal her delight.

"Let me get the nightgown from the bottom," Cee said, grabbing hold of the hem and lifting until the nightgown peeled off her.

And then Stephanie stood there, naked.

"Don't bother with that one, it's all ripped," Stephanie said, stamping her foot. "There's another nightgown in the drawer."

"You're very pretty," Cee whispered.

"Hurry up with that, will you?" She snatched the nightgown from Cee's hands, thrust her arms into it, and threw herself under the covers.

"It was a nice party," Stephanie said, calm once more when they were both in bed, and the lights were out. "But there are some strange people on this floor. I talked with someone who eats only raw fruits and vegetables."

"Sounds like Meg from 915."

"I'm glad you're my roommate," Stephanie said after a pause.

Cee warmed.

"Thanksgiving's coming up," Stephanie said.

"I wish it weren't. I sure don't feel like going home. Not for Christmas, either."

"Maybe I could ask my mother about you coming over for Christmas."

"Really?"

"My brothers are going to visit my uncle in Atlanta, it'll be just my momma and me. She said she likes you."

"What about Race?"

"Don't you worry bout him. I'll set him straight."

STEPHANIE WAS CURLED UP into a corner of her bed, the phone pulled close, and her study jeans over her chair, as though the call had come just as she was about to change. She was crying. After she hung up, Cee approached her cautiously.

"Stephanie?" she said, sitting down at the edge of the bed, inches from Stephanie's tiny feet in their gauze of panty hose.

Race was pressuring her to give up school and get married, Stephanie explained. He said she had to choose, and he wasn't going to wait forever until she decided.

"I'm afraid of losing him," she said.

"Don't be."

She'd spoken without thinking. Stephanie's sudden, angry look told her she'd made a mistake. Yet wasn't that what she'd wanted to say all along—that Race didn't seem worth the trouble?

"You're saying that because you don't have a boyfriend," Stephanie declared with sudden sharpness. "And you sound like you don't want one, neither."

Cee choked with surprise. "You yourself said Race was holding on to you too tightly."

"If you've never had a man, then you don't know what it is to lose one." She pulled to the other side of the bed.

"Who said I never—"

"The way you looked when that guy came over to our table that day in the cafeteria."

"I didn't like the way he was sizing you up."

"And those farmer pants. I think you wear them on purpose, just to keep men away from you."

"We've already talked about the pants," Cee said, getting up. It wasn't until she went to light a cigarette that she noticed how her hands shook.

RACE BEGAN COMING up to the room several evenings a week. He brought over a small TV, and they'd curl up in front of it with a bottle of red wine. It meant Cee had to tramp to the library in all weather if she wanted to get any work done.

So this had been Stephanie's reaction to Race's conditions, Cee thought, pulling on her coat to go to the library one evening. She glanced at Stephanie, sitting next to Race on the bed, her face held in the glare of the screen.

"Don't forget about the quiz in Soc tomorrow," she said as she left.

Stephanie flashed her a worried look.

Sociology, Cee thought, stepping into the cold: She didn't have to bother studying it, she was living it. She repeated the promise she had made to herself when Race first started coming over: Under no circumstances would she vacate the room should Race want to spend the night.

Race was still in the room when Cee returned. She dumped her books down, making as much noise as she could, then kicked her heavy winter boots off so that they hit the floor like bricks. She gathered her bathroom things and headed out of the room but in her haste her foot caught on the television cord strung across the room. The set fell with a dense crash and the picture fizzled out.

"What the fuck did you do?" Race said, springing up. He put the set back on the dresser, plugged it in, but nothing happened. "You busted my TV!"

"I'm sorry," Cee said. Annoyance hardened her voice. She turned to Stephanie. "I didn't mean to—"

"You gonna pay for that!" Race said.

"Maybe you can get it fixed, Race," Stephanie said, weary, not knowing whose side to take. "Let your brother have a look at it."

"If she had watched where she was going instead of charging around the room like a goddamn elephant—"

"Race!"

He pulled up close to Cee, his eyes flashing with points of heat. She was afraid that he might hit her, until a tiny voice inside her piped, "Cee, you're a head taller than he is."

"I think it's time for you to leave," she said to him.

4

It was a little past four when Richie and Jason reached the bus station.

"You sure it's okay that I'm coming?" Jason asked.

"I already told you it's okay, so quit asking me."

They walked a little farther, then Jason said, "Maybe she'll only have time to do it with you. Maybe she'll be too tired for the both of us."

"Nina's never too tired for that. What's the matter, Blink? Don't you want to do it? You've been bugging me about letting you come along all this time, and now—"

"Sure I want to do it."

Richie shook his head. "I knew it. You're scared. You never did it before, admit it."

Jason's face steamed with shame.

"Hey, Blink, take it easy. Here, chew on this." He gave Jason a Tic-Tac. "Nina don't like it when she smells liquor. Nina has a thing about drinking ever since one of her kids was runned over by a drunk driver."

They'd shared a pocket flask of cheap bourbon, which Richie had finagled out of Petersen's Liquors. He said it would help Jason relax, but a few slugs had left Jason dizzy. Now his head ached, as though the hot sun had brought the alcohol in his brain to a boil. He popped the candy into his mouth but spit it back out.

"What's the matter?"

"Tastes terrible mixed with the whiskey."

"Suit yourself," Richie said. "If she don't let you, it's your fault."

"Hey, Richie, that kid of hers who was run over—you think he was killed right away or did it take a long time for him to die?"

"How the hell should I know? God, you're weird sometimes."

Nina's house was low and covered with shingles that were supposed to resemble bricks. The hallway smelled of damp, and the railing gave when Jason held it. Richie had to knock for a long time before anyone answered. The door opened only wide enough for Jason to see a pair of eyes behind a taut length of chain.

"You're late, Junior," a woman said with a mouthful of food as she went to undo the chain.

Jason was anxious to see what a whore looked like but was swiftly disappointed. She was older than he'd expected. She wore a bathrobe but she'd made her face up as though she were going out. Her hair swirled on top of her head, held stiffly in place with pins except for a few spiky stray strands. Crumbs clung to her lower lip. If he'd seen her on the street he would have simply thought: Negro woman. Yet merely knowing what she was about to do with Richie made her exotic, even dangerous. His gaze settled on her ears, perhaps because they were so small.

"You know you gotta be out of here before six," she was saying.

Richie leaned over, put his hands on her shoulders, and gave her a heavy kiss. "Sorry I'm late."

"Who's that?" she said, pulling away as she noticed Jason.

"Friend."

Nina glared at Jason. "What he looking at? Hey, you. Ain't you never seen a woman before?"

"This is Jason, he's a friend of mine. I thought maybe . . . you could—"

Her voice grew sharp. "I could what, double-date?" She put a hand on her hip. "I don't need any new customers. And I don't got all the time in the world."

Richie fired Jason an I-knew-it-was-a-bad-idea look.

"You got some nerve, is all I can say."

"Just this once."

She motioned for them to come in. "Don't pull this again," she said, locking the door. She turned to Jason. "What was your name again? Hey, wake up. I asked you what your name was."

Jason told her.

"How old are you?"

"Sixteen."

"You don't look no more than twelve."

"You wait in the living room," Richie said to him.

"Who are you to be telling people where to go in my house?" She turned to Jason. "You look a little pale. How come you blinking?"

"He always blinks," Richie said.

"You want to go first?"

"Hey, what's the big idea?" said Richie.

Nina kept smiling at him. "You're cute, Joseph," she said, stroking Jason's cheek.

"It's Jason. That's okay. Richie can go first."

"Well, have a seat then. This won't take long, if I know Junior."

Richie started for the bedroom. She yanked him back by the arm and pulled him close. "You been drinking, ain't you. Ain't you?" Richie looked away. "I done told you I don't want you coming in here after you been drinking." She released him. "Go and rinse out your mouth with Listerine. Go on, go!" He slunk away. She looked at Jason. "You know him long?"

"Couple of months."

She gave his biceps a squeeze. "You look like a nice boy. What's someone like you doing hanging round with the likes of him?"

Richie was back before he could answer. He headed for the bedroom, Nina followed, and the door closed.

The living room held a coffee table, club chairs, and a record player on a stand. A soap opera was on TV, and an open box of vanilla wafers lay on the sofa. In one corner there was a narrow bed, along with a dresser and a small bookcase: a room within a room. A photograph of a Negro kid about his own age wearing glasses hung on the wall. Jason approached the desk. A load of schoolbooks had been dumped on it. He picked one up. *Our World.* He knew that book from the year before. Pictures of different kinds of people were on the cover: a Chinese woman, an Eskimo, an old man wearing a turban. "Property of Thompson City High School," he read on the inside cover, and penned into the book form pasted below it: "Reginald Franklin. Class 10–6. Sept. 74." He looked up at the picture, then back down to the name written in the book, then toward Nina's closed bedroom door. Her son, he thought. His mother. Jason put the book away, eager to get it out of his hands.

The lumpy sofa swallowed him as he sat down. He was about to take a vanilla wafer, thought of the crumbs on Nina's lips, and didn't. Sweet-smelling exhaust fed the room through a half-open window as a bus pulled into the station. Another bus started up, the luggage hatch slammed shut, and the bus pulled out. Jason watched until it turned out of sight. He wondered what it would be like to be on it, driving all the way down Front Street until Thompson City thinned out to just road and fields. The fumes were making him drowsy. He closed his eyes. The bus station sounded like an ocean. He let himself coast on it. Nina was speaking to Richie, but the drone of the buses clouded over what she said. Jason crept toward the bedroom door.

"You can't because you been drinking, that's why," Nina was saying.

"Wait," Richie pleaded. "Just gimme a little more time."

"I ain't *got* more time. My boy's coming home at six, I gotta make supper."

"I don't know what's wrong today. Maybe it's because of him waiting out there. I knew this would happen, that's why I never wanted him to come along."

"What he got to do with it? You can't get it up, plain and simple, so let me see your ten dollars and get your little friend in here. Go on, get your pants on."

Richie threw open the door. "What the hell you doing, you Peeping Tom!" he shouted, as Jason jumped back.

"Sure as hell didn't see much," Nina muttered.

"I knew I shouldn't't'a brought you!"

"Okay, your turn, Joseph," Nina called from inside the room.

Jason walked in and shut the door. Nina waited under a thin sheet. The room was barely large enough for the bed, which lay in suggestive dimness behind the drawn curtains. Jason recognized Richie's sweat in the air. Piercing through it were the tines of a second, sharper odor, hers, masked by a flowery tissue of deodorant. Nina smiled; a glint of silver showed from inside her mouth.

"Well, well. Like I said, you sure are nice-looking. We gonna have some fun now, ain't we?"

She was too thickly built to be pretty, but her smile warmed him. She folded the sheet down to reveal her breasts, heavy with pouting nipples. Exposed, she looked larger than before.

"Come on closer."

He advanced to the edge of the bed. Gently, she eased him down and slid a warm arm around his neck.

"It's okay, honey. You gonna be fine." She kissed him on the forehead, her mouth trailing the bitter cherry of her lipstick.

Jason caught sight of a picture on the dresser, another kid.

"Who's that?" he asked, alarmed.

"That's my son Albert. He was seven years old there. Hey, don't be looking at him."

The one who was killed?

She turned Jason's face toward her. "What's the matter, you scared? How come you blinking so much?"

Run over.

"Oh, you poor thing." She reached down under his shirt. "It's your first time, right?"

Jason felt Richie in the next room.

"Well, let's get your clothes off." She pulled his T-shirt over his head. It felt funny having someone else undressing him.

"You don't have to worry," she said. "Maybe you think you not a he-man like Junior out there but that don't mean you ain't got what you got." She draped his shirt over the back of a chair carefully, as his mother might. "Come on, do the rest. What'd you say your name was?"

"Jason."

"That sure is a nice name. If I had another boy maybe I'd name him Jason, too. But I won't be having no more. It's all I can do to keep up with Reggie. Let me tell you, it ain't easy raising children when you alone. Reggie's daddy died in Korea. Don't you even ask me what he was doing there. The telegram they sent me sure didn't say. You ain't got your pants off yet? You want to do it with them on? Then hurry up."

"Wait," said Jason.

Nina looked at him.

"He's gonna come home soon?"

"Who?"

"That boy in the picture. In the other room."

She laughed. "Reggie? Oh no. He's out working in the A&P. Now come on. Maybe you scared, but we ain't got all day. At least I don't."

"You sure he won't come in here?"

"How come you so worried about him, you think he'll shoot you? Listen, all I'm doing here is trying to make sure my boy has enough of what he needs. Is that so bad? And I get mighty lonely sometimes. I already told you I ain't got no man no more. And I am too old to go out looking for one, neither. Men won't give you no second glance if you ain't something out of a magazine." Her voice lowered, and she turned her head to the side. "You think I'm pretty?"

Jason swallowed. "Oh, y-y-yes. You're very pretty."

"Why, thank you. You know, sometimes it's nice being with a young man." She ran her hand over Jason's belly. "Nice and smooth, smooth like a baby. Now take off your clothes like I told you, so I can see the rest of you."

Jason unzipped his zipper and stepped out of his pants. His hands shook, his underpants roped around his legs as he struggled to get them off. He kept his back toward her. He wasn't hard. He was afraid to have her see. He felt her, heavy and wet, behind him. Goddamn, he was finally with a naked woman and he was supposed to be hard, so why wasn't he? He thought of the lumpy sofa with the box of vanilla wafers, about Reggie Franklin, Class 10–6, Thompson City High School.

"Hey," she whispered. He let himself be turned around. She sat on the edge of the bed, her face level with his crotch. She cupped his bare backside with her warm hands. "I bet you wanted the girls to do this with you," she said in a dusky voice. Then her head dropped and the wet silk of her lips and tongue gloved his dick. Her mouth was alive, and he grew within it. Yeah, hard, get hard. He thought of Richie, naked, his ass rising and falling as he humped, his back muscles straining. Jason was getting stiffer. Nina hummed with pleasure. When she pulled away, Jason's penis sprang free, glazed with her spittle.

"You good now, little one," Nina said. "Now let's just give your friend a raincoat," she said, reaching for the Trojans on the night table.

She quickly tore open the package and began slipping on the watery condom, but his dick shrank before it was halfway on. Nina looked up at him as though he'd just played a joke on her.

"I'm sorry," he said, stepping back.

Nina sighed and stood up. "You don't have to be sorry," she said, grabbing her bathrobe from the chair. "Just gimme ten dollars, and we all settled. Now hurry up, I got things to do."

Jason pulled his pants back up and reached into his pocket, took out a crumpled five-dollar bill and some change.

Nina took the money, fingering the change, waiting.

He gave her a helpless look. "That's all I got."

She threw the coins to the floor. "What? First Junior comes here and wants twofers. Then he can't get it up. You come in next and you no better. I do what I can, and you don't even have the decency to give me my due. Maybe Junior didn't tell you but it ain't five dollars and small change you got to pay me, it's ten." She knotted her bathrobe tight. "You both get me worked up and then don't even treat me right. I swear some of you people truly ain't worth the time of day. Now get out, you blinking idiot!"

Jason threw the door open. Nina stormed out behind him. "Junior, where'd you get this number from?"

"What happened?"

"I ain't got time to play psychiatrist. I gotta get supper on the table for my son. At least he's normal. Which is more than I can say for Pretty Boy over there."

"Let's go," Richie said to Jason. He went for the door. Nina planted herself in front of him.

"You brought Pretty Boy here, so you treatin'." She held out her hand. "He coughed up five dollars. You paying the rest."

"No way!"

She grabbed the collar of his jacket and pulled him toward her. "I don't give a good goddamn what you think of me, but it'll be a cold day in hell before I let any one of you cheat me, a cold day!" She pushed him against the wall. He pulled out his wallet, took out a few bills, and threw them at her.

Jason heard someone coming up the stairs.

"You pick those up and give them to me, do you hear? In my hand!"

"The hell I will." Richie went to leave.

She blocked the way. "I said pick them up." Her eyes grew wild.

The sound of footfalls on the steps grew louder. Nina's head turned as if just hearing it. "Lord Jesus, what's he doing back so early?"

Richie tried to push Nina away. She yanked her knee hard between the legs. Richie let out a hollow gasp and fell away. She flung herself against the door, terrified. Jason grabbed the money and pressed it into Nina's hand.

A key turned in the lock.

"Let me out of here," said Richie.

"Shut up, you," she said, still against the door. Her eyes closed for a moment, as if she wished she were somewhere else.

"Let me the fuck out of here, you bitch!"

"Hey Mom, open up, it's me," came the voice from outside.

Nina didn't move. The key jiggled in the lock.

"Jesus," Nina muttered, crumpling the bills into her fist. She stepped away from the door and let it open.

The boy Jason had seen in the photograph in the living room stood before them. He looked at Jason, at Richie.

"Mom?" he said, as if waiting for an explanation.

"Get out, you two," Nina said hoarsely from behind the door. "And I don't ever want to see you again, never."

Richie stampeded out of the apartment. Jason followed. He tried to keep his eyes steeled to the ground but felt his glance being pried upward, until his eyes were forced to meet Reggie's, burning with shame, with rage.

Richie was walking down the street when Jason got outside. "Hey, Richie, wait up!" he called.

"Get the fuck away from me. I don't want to see your blinking face again, either."

"But Richie—"

"And you better keep away from the gym, too, if you know what's good for you." He punctuated his threat with a clenched fist.

Jason attempted to sputter an explanation, but Richie broke away. Jason stood there, looking back at the lighted windows of Nina's house. He thought he heard voices and tried to make out what they were saying, but just then another bus pulled out, and the street filled with the churn of its noise and exhaust.

5

"Melissa! get back here! Melissa!"

The mountain rang with the tense echo of Carl's voice. The little three-year-old pushed ahead as if not having heard, moving down the path with the stiff-legged crush of a tiny giant. Her yellow hair, purple overalls, and bright blue jacket glowed against the November gloom of the woods. The dull morning light fell through a sieve of bare branches. The woods looked lean and vacant.

"Don't worry," Cee said, injecting an extra measure of patience into her voice. "She can't get lost. You could spot her a mile away in what she's wearing—"

"For chrissakes! Melissa!"

Her face spun around as if her shoulders had been yanked. She shouted back a syllable of annoyance, her mouth an impatient curl.

Carl noticed Cee looking at him. "Please watch out, Melissa," he said, adjusting his voice.

"When you scream at her like that you remind me of my father."

"Maybe that's because I'm a father, too," he said, somewhat harshly.

Cee touched his arm. "Don't worry, I'm keeping an eye on her, Carl."

Cee saw him looking down, regretting his outburst. The whole time they'd been out walking Carl hadn't let Melissa alone for a minute. He warned her about tree roots and low-lying branches. He kept her from running too far ahead, even though she showed every sign of knowing the way.

"Is the bookstore still being hassled by the cops?" Cee asked. The store, where Carl worked, specialized in leftist politics and history. It was considered a nest of radicals and had been searched and ransacked by the police on the pretense of looking for drugs.

He shook his head no.

Cee sighed. Whenever they saw each other after a long break they needed some warm-up before the talk flowed. Today it was taking especially long. Just after Cee drove up from Thompson City, she'd been excited to see Carl. But his moodiness leadened her spirits, and it seemed as if Melissa alone pulled them along the path.

Another difficult Gajewski man, she thought. She'd already had two whole days of them. Her unemployed father remained plugged into his chair watching television. Drapes drawn, the living room lay in perpetual twilight. Jason huffed and puffed in his room with his weights but hardly spoke. After the Thanksgiving dinner father and son took over the living room to watch the Army-Navy game while the womenfolk did the dishes.

She wished Elaine were here.

"Don't people usually get the Friday after Thanksgiving off?" she asked.

"Not if you work on a newspaper."

Cee doubted that Carl had many close connections to people other than Elaine. His letters were dry and reflexive. "I'm dealing with the contradictions of living collectively and struggling to free myself of the bourgeois need for my own space," he wrote soon after moving into the house. Which probably meant that his housemates were getting on his nerves. She'd scan the political verbiage for news of Elaine or Melissa, of the wind generator, or, for chrissakes, of the wild goat that had showed up the summer before—anything that hinted at life on a mountain. But he might as well have been living in a basement for all he mentioned his surroundings.

How he'd changed! Alone in their dour family, Carl had been the talker, the professor on the lecture circuit. He was always organizing pranks, getting caught, and talking his way out of punishment. "You gab as much as a woman," his father said, cutting him off at supper. To break Carl of his chatter Walter initiated him into the forced silence of fishing trips. Carl returned sunburned and subdued, appalled by having to thread live worms onto a gleaming hook, releasing a fluid he knew was blood, even if his father claimed that worms had none. The fishing trips broke Carl's ebullience and, as if to reward his taciturnity, Walter presented him with a microscope. Carl spent hours bent over it, his room quiet as a chapel. He announced that he wanted to become a biologist.

Then came Vietnam. Carl joined the Anti-War Mobilization. He hung the walls of his room with maps of Southeast Asia, and came home hoarse and bleary-eyed from the cold, after distributing leaflets at shopping centers. "The people in this town are morons," he'd say, gesticulating with an ink-stained hand. "They really believe the crap they see on TV." He soon abandoned his plans of becoming a biologist: Biologists helped the pharmaceutical industry develop chemical warfare.

Cee loved the house Carl had moved into. She and her high school friend Jeanine would hitch up, laden with whatever Cee'd liberated from the fascist Safeway. They stuck out their thumbs, imagining they were depression hobos fleeing the dustbowl. The front room of the house was always full of people sitting in the buttery glow of kerosene lamps under a cabbage cloud of dope.

The house, simple and roughly shingled, two rambling floors under a peaked roof, had once belonged to a fundamentalist Christian sect, an outpost of the Burned-Over District, those counties of northern New York State caught in the frenzied religious revival of the mid-nineteenth century. Right after people from the Mobilization squatted it, the mood in the house was heady as the main square of a capital city following a revolution. It became a way station for those headed West or coming back East or in transit between spiritual planes. It was a seminary of the possible, an unweeded resort, the kind of place *Life* magazine might sensationalize as a "commune." Cee awoke mornings and stepped over a sea of bodies jackknifed in sleeping bags, while figures floated through T'ai Chi outside. People came who ate no meat or no dairy products or only what grew in the local biotope. Pots steamed with bitter-smelling medicinal teas, and women performed rituals to the Mother Goddess, ululating as they boiled their menstrual sponges. If people really got high enough—or if enough Marxist-Leninists were on hand—the house got cleaned. Otherwise, things got done very organically, which meant, usually by accident and mostly not at all.

A truck rumbled down the road.

"There goes Junior," Carl said.

Junior and his mother were their closest neighbors. Junior was a mechanic. His mother was religious and wouldn't let him keep beer in the refrigerator, so he stowed cases of Bud under his bed and drank the beer warm.

"Is his mother still giving you guys trouble?" She'd filed numerous complaints with the county to get them evicted.

"Not in a while. Last winter she needed to get a prescription filled in town. Junior's pickup was in the shop. I drove down in Elaine's car and got it."

"Isn't he a little old to be living with his mother? He must be at least thirty-five."

"He's the only child; he feels responsible for her. But sometimes she makes him want to drive his truck right off the mountain."

Melissa headed for the turnoff to Quaspeck Lake, shouting as if about to blaze the trail herself. The lake took its name from the Indians who'd sought refuge on the mountain after being expelled from the rich lowlands by white settlers. It was really a large pond, a glacial crater fed by rain, a small wonder twelve hundred feet above sea level. The Burned-Over fundamentalists had done their baptizing in it.

"How about a rest?" Cee said, when they reached the lake. "I'm out of shape."

They found a large rock to sit on. The water was slate grey under a creamy haze of clouds.

"The Indians who settled here after being chased up from the town were mystified by a body of water so high up," Carl said.

They watched Melissa make her way along the tightrope of a log.

"Her hair is really too long," Carl said. Earlier it had caught in a branch and pulled painfully before Carl could free her.

"I don't think she'd want to have it cut."

Melissa obviously loved her hair, its color an unexpected gift from dark-haired parents. She fingered it like modeling clay or swung it like an elephant's trunk. Cee remembered her own long hair: a soft privacy around her shoulders. Carl's seemed more of a burden, something to confine within a rubber band and banish behind his head. His scalp showed through, pale and waxy, an old man's, even though he was only twenty-two.

"This was where Melissa's naming ceremony was held, right?" Cee asked.

She had not been baptized. Friends assembled, assigned a mantra to her, presented Carl and Elaine with Melissa's zodiac chart, and offered hand-sewn clothing. Elaine strewed her cradle with raspberry and red clover, herbs helpful to women's healing. Cee had gazed at the tiny red face nestled in blankets, amazed to see her brother's face imprinted on it; Carl was a child himself.

"Has Dad ever seen Melissa?"

Carl hadn't asked his father to the naming ceremony. Only his mother came.

He stiffened. "You know he hasn't."

"I thought you might have changed your mind in the meantime."

"No. I don't think that I will. And I don't want to talk about it."

Cee dug her hands into her pockets as though they'd been slapped. A bird skimmed the surface of the lake. Melissa splashed water after it.

"How's Elaine these days?"

"Busy, as always. She works four days a week at the paper and does her shift in the day-care center." He picked up a twig and began digging with it in the ground. "I think she feels a little trapped here," he said. "She talks of training to become a midwife. It would mean her going to Syracuse."

He and Elaine had stopped having sex during the past winter. The cold weather had been part of it; they slept with Melissa downstairs to save money on wood. Yet nothing changed when Melissa went back in her own room.

"We've grown apart from one another, he continued. "Sometimes I want to touch her . . . but I can't, I just can't. She says I've become distant."

Melissa ran over to them, a wooden stake in her hand.

"Shit," said Carl, taking it from her. "Know what that is? It's what surveyors use to mark off areas to be measured. That means they've already been snooping around."

"Who's 'they'?"

"The developers. I'll give you the whole sad story when we get back to the house. Come on, let's go. I'm getting cold."

"Wait, let me get a shot of the two of you by the lake." She reached inside her backpack. Carl stood behind Melissa, his hands clutching her shoulders. For a moment it looked as if he meant to hide behind her, as if she were a shield to protect him.

"You remember how we had the whole second floor of the house to ourselves, before Jason was born?" Cee asked as they headed back.

It had been their private preserve. Their parents entered it as rulers visiting a distant province, apprehensive of the locals. Cee and Carl had pretended it was a castle on a hill, towering above the lower city of the first floor, below the parapets of the attic. But their world on the second floor disintegrated as Carl grew older. His circle of friends excluded girls, and he shot up in a matter of months, as if to make the change permanent. Cee missed him, and was secretly glad that his body stayed boyishly hairless, that no more than a cap of fuzz sprouted on his chin, and that his voice perched stubbornly high. Toward his senior year of high school they grew closer once more.

"You remember that poster I had, with information about what happened in the world year by year?" Carl asked.

"It showed that 1776 was not only the year of the American Revolution but also when Gibbon wrote *The Decline and Fall of the Roman Empire*, Hoffmann wrote *The Tales of Hoffmann*, Mozart composed the *Haffner* Serenade, and Cook went to the Pacific for the third time," Cee recited.

"You get an A plus."

Her voice lowered. "I also remember how we used to go into each other's room to sleep. We brought books with us. You told me about Vietnam. You were the first person I ever heard who used words like *imperialism* and *genocide*. I was so impressed."

"I probably heard them at the Mobilization office the day before."

"Oh, Carl," she said, warmed by their closeness once more. She threaded her arm through his, a cable in the middle of his jacket sleeve.

Around that time Cee had realized that her feelings for Carl went beyond the safe, reflex affection of brother and sister. She yearned to probe the source of his being as a chemist might atoms and molecules. She knew it wasn't sex that she wanted from him, but what else brought men and women together as tightly as they? Once she told Jeanine that Carl's eyes were like pale, blue glass. Jeanine had shot her a funny look.

"Mom told me to tell you that she wishes she could see Melissa more often."

"What are you suggesting? A weekly visit to Grandma on Sunday? Sorry, but if you haven't noticed, I don't exactly have that kind of relationship with my family."

"You're taking out your feelings about Dad on Mom, and that's not fair. She doesn't feel free to do what she wants because of him. And I still don't understand what harm it would do for Dad to see Melissa."

"First, it would mean me going to see him. And second, Melissa stands for everything he hates about me—the way I live, what I believe in."

"Melissa doesn't stand for anything."

"You used to understand why I cut myself off from them. What happened?"

"Maybe seeing Dad the way he is has made me reconsider things —no job, his health not terrific."

Carl looked away, as if to signal a change of subject. "What's Jason up to these days?"

"Still going to the vocational school. He's also into body building. You wouldn't recognize him: thick arms, a neck like a tree. Dad's become real buddy-buddy with him. I overheard him telling Jason that he was putting his faith in him, whatever that's supposed to mean."

"Jason Gajewski, the future of America," Carl said. "He was always so scary. I never knew what was going on behind those blinking eyes of his. He was like a child raised by wolves."

Melissa pushed in between them. Cee ran her hand through Melissa's hair. "If your Dad wasn't so stubborn you could have had an all-American Thanksgiving dinner with the Gajewski family yesterday. Hey Carl, remember those Thanksgivings when you ate oatmeal to show contempt for meat-eating—"

"It was in opposition to a holiday that commemorated swindling Native Americans out of their land. Speaking of Thanksgiving, did Dad thank the wonderful American government for making him unemployed?"

"He's so disheartened that he's stopped looking for work. He sits and watches the news on television with Jason and tells him how the communists are taking over the world."

They'd reached the house.

"How late can you stay?"

"Not too. I promised Jeanine I'd go out with her later."

Melissa grabbed Cee's arm to keep her from going up the steps. "Shoo," she shouted. "Shoo!"

"Not today, Melissa, it's too cold."

"Oh, come on, Carl. You probably haven't gone down the chute with her in ages. Now's the best time, there are so many dead leaves." She took Melissa's hand. "Aunt Cee will take you down. See you later, Carl."

The chute was a furrow in the earth that once carried a wooden conduit from the lake all the way down to houses in the town and by force of gravity—and to the envy of the rest of the county—right into kitchens. It was considered a local engineering marvel for its time but was abandoned once the town switched to well water. The wooden conduit had long since rotted away, but the furrow remained, a perfect bobsled run. The sled—a piece of sheet metal strung with rope handles—hung on a tree.

"Okay, kid," Cee said, setting the sled on the edge of the path. "I'm not going to let you lose out on any fun because of your old fuddy-duddy daddy." Cee lowered herself onto the metal—ooh, it was cold!—then held out her hand to Melissa. "All aboard." Melissa wedged between her legs, warm and bony. Cee lurched forward to get them going, and they pushed off with a scrape. The first drop was the steepest and scariest, where a great hand had scooped out a side of the mountain. The wind hit her face in cold blocks. Melissa sat bolt upright, fearless. Cee was relieved when the chute leveled off near the bottom. They hit a rock and tumbled into a dune of dead leaves, falling over each other and laughing. The chute came to a halt just before the road. There, rooted like a gnarled tree before them, Junior's mother stood, scowling.

Carl wokked up some vegetables and millet. They ate in the kitchen before the large window overlooking the valley. Melissa churned her millet into paste with her spoon, while holding a babbling conversation with the doll Cee had brought her, baby-sized and sexless, swiped from the nursery school run by the education department.

In two years, the house had changed from a freak dormitory to the settled domain of a family. The ancient wringer washer still rusted on the porch beside a legless sofa. But the living room floor had been sanded and varnished to a honey-brown, the pots and pans were stored in Carl's cabinets, instead of hanging from nails, and the seesaw of a table sat squarely on the floor.

Legs crossed, and without the deceptive bulk of clothing, Carl appeared nearly weightless. The sleeves of his sweater hung from his wrists like a monk's robe. Cee recalled how he had looked naked, sunning by the lake, how his flesh clung to his frame with the barest putty of fat, the curls of black hair in tense patches at his nipples and navel. Now he seemed even thinner.

Cee poured herself more tea, noticing the teapot, a graceful oval glazed pearly black: Elaine's work. It was good to see her presence in that kitchen, which otherwise seemed so full of Carl. At first Cee hadn't liked Elaine, a Jewish woman from New York, with muscular arms and legs—and a faint mustache—who didn't shave her legs or pits. She was one of several of pungent-smelling women going around barefoot in peasant skirts during the early days of the house. But Elaine was different, the only one among them who held down a normal job.

She quit school, learned typesetting, and did paste-up and mechanicals before getting her job at the newspaper. Compared to Carl, bloodless and nearly neuter, Elaine was lush and sensual. "I like you," she'd told Cee some time after they'd met. "You're like Carl but I don't need a can opener to get to know you."

"It's a little nippy here," Cee said, rubbing her arms.

"I should have a look at the oil burner," Carl mumbled.

"Tell me about the developers."

"People have been eyeing this house since we squatted it, but the Burned-Overs left no title deed behind to designate an heir, so after the congregation broke up, the property hung in limbo. We always assumed the county would offer us a lease. What could they do with a mountain except turn it into some kind of reserve? We figured we'd be able to stay on as caretakers. Then this rich fucker from Rochester by the name of Larrabee announces that he wants to build vacation homes here. I didn't think it would ever come to anything because of the recession. But he's promised jobs, and the county wants them real bad. We formed the Mountain Coalition to get the area declared a county recreation area. But times are tight. A third of the county is out of work."

"Won't the jobs be temporary?"

"Larrabee's not just talking about houses. He also wants to put in a hotel, a golf club, a restaurant."

"Who's going to buy a vacation home in the middle of a recession?"

"Corporate vice-presidents. Rich Arabs. Rock stars. The same people who'll stay in the hotel, I guess. I didn't tell you the best part: It's going to be called Quaspeck Village."

"Who says we Americans have no sense of history."

"This is what Dad has been waiting for—the chance to see me thrown out of my own house. Don't you remember how he threatened to sic the draft board on me because I refused to register?"

"He wouldn't have done it anyway."

Carl began clearing the table. "Walter Gajewski, the man with the Stars and Stripes tattooed on his brain? I wouldn't have put it past him. But he got back at me another way. You know those trust fund accounts of ours? Right after I moved out of the house he took the lousy couple of thousand that was in mine and put it into Jason's. He said that if his house wasn't good enough for me, then neither was his money. Jason hadn't run away and forgotten his family, he said. Never mind that he hardly said a goddamn word to him after the accident!" He threw a fistful of silverware into the sink.

Melissa gave a worried whimper.

Cee put her arms around her. "He did that because he was hurt, Carl."

"Why make excuses for him? Doesn't it piss *you* off that you didn't get the money? He might have split it between you and Jason. But no—you're just the daughter. Jason is his son, the bearer of the fucking family name!"

"Cawl, Cawl," cried Melissa.

"It's all right, sweetheart," Cee said, stroking her arm. "And anyway, I don't need your money," she said softly.

"But I sure did, especially right after Melissa was born. You know about her infection last year? It was partly because of the dampness of the house. You think it's cold now, you should have been here before we finished insulating. If I'd had that money we could have done it earlier, and maybe she wouldn't have gotten sick."

"Does Mom know about what Dad did with the money?"

"I guess, but what could she do? Both our trust funds were in his name."

Melissa seated the doll at the edge of the table so that its legs dangled.

"By the way, you think that guy Junior might join forces with you to fight the developer?" Cee asked. "He'd get thrown off the mountain, too, if the land got sold, right?"

"Junior's not the joining-forces type. He has his own problems. One night he came up here totally ripped, fresh from a fight with his mother. She had told him it was time he grew up and made something of himself. He blamed her for holding him down and said he never wanted to see her again. She said that was fine with her, since he wasn't her son anyway. It seems his real mother died after he was born."

"We saw her at the bottom of the chute, standing there like the Wicked Witch of the West." Melissa pressed next to Cee, the doll in her arms. Cee kissed Melissa's forehead. "How does it feel to be a mother?" Cee asked her. "No free time left for yourself, huh?"

Carl watched them. "I wonder if I've made the right choice," he said somewhat somberly. "Doing this whole house number. Not going to college. Living here." He looked at Melissa. "When I see her, I see the choices I've made, the things I've thrown over. It scares me."

"What's to be scared of? She's a great kid," Cee said, poking Melissa's nose with one of the doll's hands.

"Sometimes when she looks at me I think she's saying, 'Okay, you took a chance, and you better not blow it.'"

"Carl, she doesn't care about your politics. She just wants you to love her."

"What you said before about me reminding you of Dad, well, Melissa does makes me feel like . . . him. Something inside makes me want to keep her in line. It's frightening."

"What frightens you is that she loves you so much, Carl. Imagine that." She leaned over to Melissa. "Does your old ex-hippie daddy love you enough, huh, does he?" Cee pressed her mouth against Melissa's scalp and breathed in its woody smell.

"You feel like getting high by any chance?" Carl asked.

"I was thinking of taking a little snooze before heading back to the old homestead."

Cee went upstairs. Melissa followed. "You just want to keep me awake, don't you?" Cee said, hoisting Melissa into the air and onto her shoulders. Melissa's laugh faded up the stairs.

Carl rolled himself a joint, put on his parka, and headed for the belfry, his favorite part of the house. Its bell was long gone, leaving just enough space for a chair, and the squatters had replaced the cross on the belfry's roof with a revolving yin-yang. He lit the joint and toked, shielding the joint from intermittent gusts of wind. Indian Mountain was the highest point in the county; on a good day he might see the new county office building in Binghamton. Today clouds obscured all but a narrow radius of trees, as if nothing existed beyond the house: no developer, no father, nothing.

Because I said so.

Another toke.

It was his father's favorite reason for everything. But it wasn't a reason, it meant he had nothing better to say. It showed he wasn't trying to understand, just boss around, which was simpler. Trying to make someone understand meant talking, but talk was invisible, nothing you could put your hands on or keep quiet. People like his father were suspicious of anything you couldn't pick up or throw down.

Carl had always tried to understand things, to discern an order in them. Wasn't that why he cherished his microscope so? Its lenses rendered things that at first seemed random and opaque clear and orderly. He scraped the inside of his mouth and coaxed sperm from his penis, collecting secrets, which he'd seal with balsam onto a slide and then try to unravel. A cell was an exquisite organization. Nature seemed accidental until you got either close enough or far enough away.

One day Jason had smashed those slides, turning the floor of Carl's room into a terrible mosaic of broken glass. Why? Carl doubted that Jason himself knew. It was just another of his outbursts, as fast and unexpected as a downpour of summer rain. Carl left Jason with a welt across his arm and Walter, in turn, had taken the strap to Carl. Later, smarting with pain, Carl picked up one of the few undamaged slides and slipped it into position under the objective with trembling hands. He hastily turned the knob, needing more than anything to resolve the blur into clarity. But he turned too far, there was a snap, and the objective crushed the slide into confusion.

Carl didn't go to school for days after that, and forgot about antiwar work. His dreams were loud with faces shattering and falling into chaos like a kaleidoscope gone awry. Carl put the microscope away for good. He decided that the world was made up of two types of people: those who sought reason and those who didn't. The first might do useful things. The others destroyed. The rule carried a cruel corollary along with it: Those who sought to understand were invariably weaker than and defenseless against those who did not.

Carl took another toke. The dope was weak and left no more than a finger of warmth in his brain. But Jason hadn't been a madman, just an extremely messed-up kid. Cee revealed Jason's reason for smashing the slides: "You ignore him, Carl." It was as simple as that. Jason hoped Carl might love him. Carl wouldn't.

Carl snubbed out the joint between his fingers and tossed it away. He'd already withdrawn so much from Elaine. He'd told Cee more in the past afternoon than he had told Elaine in the past year.

Elaine.

He'd been spared the up-and-down search for love. He and Elaine had flowed into each other's lives easily. The house had been part of it, much of it. It provided them with enough work and dope and enough mountain to run around on, so that each evening they came together, fresh and newly eager.

Elaine had taught him so much. She never worried whether she talked too much, and that freed his tongue of Walter's clamp. Before Elaine, Carl would come with an adolescent's haste or else have to grind away interminably. Her hands and mouth lavished attention his body had never known before. She writhed like a python, singing as she came.

But not since Melissa got sick.

He recalled the terrible night that past winter when Melissa's temperature had climbed to 104. They had no telephone, so they couldn't call Dr. Willets. They bundled Melissa up and drove to the doctor's house at three in the morning in a snowstorm, praying that they'd stay on the road, praying that Dr. Willets would be there and able to help. Icy winds jostled the car like the tongues of a jealous god demanding Melissa's sacrifice. "If we'd had a phone we might have been able to ask the doctor to come to us," Elaine had muttered, pulling Melissa close. "But no, you refused to have a phone for ideological reasons . . ."

Carl had waited in the kitchen. Mrs. Willets sat in her bathrobe, her hands clasped over his. Carl looked at the yellowed walls, the framed prints of dogs, the rack of mugs. The woman's warm hands reminded him of feeling Melissa's heartbeat nestled deep within Elaine's body before she was born.

The doctor gave Melissa penicillin. They stayed the night in the doctor's warm house, and Melissa's fever broke. Before the month was out their telephone was hooked up. It cost several hundred dollars to run a line from Junior's house. Carl borrowed money from someone in the bookstore to pay for it. Elaine seemed satisfied.

But a rift had opened between them.

Some weeks ago, a woman named Brigid began working at the bookstore. She was sweet and demure, and very earnest. One night he and Brigid stayed late at the store to paint shelves and had a couple of beers at the Mill Tavern. Brigid looked up to him as one of the early squatters of the house. She was full of questions. Her openness and her curiosity touched him. Several days later, he visited her in the afternoon, and they made love.

"Cawl!"

Melissa was calling to him from the attic. She placed her foot on the bottom rung of the ladder, but couldn't hoist herself up. He carried her up and bundled her in his parka.

"One day all of this may or may not be yours," he said, gesturing dramatically. Then he brought his lips to her milky cheek and kissed and kissed.

Elaine surprised Cee just as she rose from her nap. Cee threw her arms around her and sank into a citrus-scented thickness of sweaters and scarves.

"What are you doing back so early?" Cee said. "Carl said you didn't get out of work until after five. I was ready to go back to Thompson City."

Elaine frowned. "I told Carl we'd have a shorter day on account of Thanksgiving. Sometimes I wonder if we speak the same language. It's so good to see you again. When was the last time? During the summer? Hungry?" She persuaded Cee to stay for supper. Cee called up Jeanine to say she wouldn't be driving back until the morning.

"This place is so cold," Elaine said, grabbing a flannel shirt from a hook near the door. "The oil burner has been on the blink for days. Melissa catches colds almost as easily as breathing. Where is she? Where's Carl?"

"I think they're up in the belfry," Cee said. After the moody afternoon with Carl, Elaine's energy was bracing.

"I guess that means he didn't get around to fixing the oil burner today, either."

"Don't be so hard on him."

Elaine gave her an exhausted look. "I know this sounds horrible, but I've found that the best way to get a response out of Carl is to demand one." She went over to the shelves of glass jars containing grains and beans. "Bulgur, brown rice, millet—the joys of being a vegetarian are endless," she said, shaking her head. "God, I don't feel like cooking. How about swiss chard with some kind of cheese sauce on top?"

"Actually, I had my heart set on leftover turkey..."

They had supper. Carl cut Melissa's food into little pieces and helped her eat. Elaine watched, supervising, looking impatient, as if expecting him to foul up in some way. They hardly spoke to one another directly but seemed to speak more through Melissa than to each other.

With Melissa asleep, they sat with mugs of tea, bundled in sweaters. Carl smoked a half a joint, looking transfixed by the plumes of smoke. Elaine put her feet up on a chair and leaned back, letting her long hair fall in thick torrents over her shoulder. Without Melissa the kitchen was very quiet.

"What have you been up to since you've been home?" Elaine said at last.

Cee told them about going with her mother to the welfare office on Wednesday. The evening before, they'd waited until Walter and Jason were asleep to spread all the social services papers, household bills, and shopping receipts out on the kitchen table, poring over them like a pair of forgers, trying to organize them in some fashion. The next morning they left the house at six-thirty, to be among the first when the office opened at nine. Bundled in a shapeless winter coat of several seasons ago, with a kerchief around her head, Cee's mother looked as if she were on a train in Eastern Europe journeying toward the next market town with her basketful of eggs. Theresa, who'd always dressed so carefully, now wanted to look as badly off as she could.

They shuffled around in the hall with the others. A poster on the wall listed The Golden Rules of Shopping (never shop when you're hungry, don't bring little children along if possible . . .). Another reminded its audience to eat from the Four Basic Food Groups each day. (Did her mother know that peanut butter was in the same group as meat? Would that make it any easier to serve it at supper instead of a pork chop?) Restlessness muddied the morning calm: Everyone there was competing for the same prize.

The doors opened. People filed into the warm room, meekly grateful for the heat and a chance to sit down. Theresa's caseworker was a woman whose house might have been within blocks of theirs, but who seemed to live in another world, the world of people with secure jobs. The interview was mercifully short, perhaps because it was the day before the holiday. The woman looked over their bills, did some tallying on a pocket calculator, then showed her mother where to sign, informing her that their benefits would remain at the same level.

"I didn't realize your folks were getting welfare," Elaine said. "Did you, Carl?"

Carl shook his head numbly. "Jesus," he mumbled.

6

Cee pulled up to her parents' house and parked. There it was, a box poised on cinderblock stilts to avoid the cost of a basement, built with her father's VA loan in a Susquehanna River town with a sheen to it like an old pair of pants. Their lawn sprouted grass that neither grew nor died but just got dirty. The narrow driveway was the dry moat separating this undersized castle from the next. A flagstone front pathway—costly, but too hot for bare feet in the summer—was all that distinguished the house from the others with their walks of colored concrete. Carl had refused to help lay the stones, saying, with characteristic near-humor, that he was no prisoner on a chain gang.

She went in through the back door. (No one ever used the front entrance, flagstone path or no.) Her eyes fell on the *G* that her father had carved into the wooden cabinet below the sink, painted black.

"Where were you?" Her mother met her in the downstairs hall.

"I decided to stay over at Carl's."

"You could have at least called."

Her mother had seemed edgy toward her the whole time Cee was there, she thought, giving her chores, complaining about Cee's cigarette smoking. She said she was sorry and went upstairs to shower. The unheated second floor was chilly. She peeked into Carl's room. It was almost empty, now that Jason had Carl's desk and chair, and seemed dismantled, as if cleansed of painful memories. Cee recalled the nights when she and Carl did their most important talking there. In the four years since Carl had moved out, the house had slipped into a dusty silence, with nobody to stir the dust up. His name hadn't been mentioned once the whole time she'd been home, as though pruned from the family tree.

She'd read somewhere that after seven years no more dust could collect on any given surface. Another three years and they'd be all set.

Cee stepped into the shower. It was hard to think of her own father as having joined the faceless ranks of the unemployed, the nonworking, the idle. Walter Gajewski, one-time builder of shopping centers and insurance company headquarters, one of those mythic, muscled men toiling on the mural in the main post office downtown, jaws set, tools in hand, as they threw up bridges and plowed fields, proud and sweatless in their overalls, loving America and never thinking of leaving it, asking what they might do for their country... and now watching soap operas in the middle of the afternoon.

He'd once been so proud of his hands: a ten-fingered workshop he was the foreman of. His house and car had convinced him of the powerful sorcery of work. But the sorcery had failed, and now his wife arranged the magic with the help of the social services office. And, like the parent who puts a quarter under the pillow in place of a child's tooth, she strove to keep its secret from him.

Cee dried off and slipped into her bathrobe, bracing herself for the hallway. Upstairs Jason's strained counting meant that he was working out again. She peeked in through the door. The sight of him heaving a barbell before a full-length mirror in his underwear was almost funny; she associated weight lifting with grinning men on the back covers of comics. His newly won bulk made him look ready to burst. His mouth fumed, the sweat from his eyes looked like tears, and the glazed, devoted expression he wore seemed almost religious.

"Hey!" The weights fell abruptly as his eyes met hers, and he kicked the door closed.

In the afternoon Cee and Theresa made *chrust*.

Cee poured flour in the bowl while her mother got out a skillet. *Chrust*, Cee thought, bow-ties of deep-fried carbohydrate, one of the few things besides her last name and a painted wooden plaque of the Black Madonna above the kitchen table that reminded her that she had Polish grandparents.

"How come you brought home a pumpkin pie from the bakery this year, Mom?" Cee asked.

A conversation starter, just like her and Carl yesterday.

"Didn't you like it?"

"It was great. But we never used to have pumpkin pie. Just *chrust*."

"Your brother's already eaten most of it. I guess that's a good sign."

"He needs it for his all-American muscles."

"That weight lifting keeps him out of trouble, Cee."

Cee began shaping the *chrust*. Dutiful daughter, she thought, in the kitchen, helping to make these unhealthy pastries that had let her peasant ancestors forget their hunger. And her mother: a woman with modest features and clear skin, who'd kept her figure, but who'd reached middle age without ever having been pretty.

When Cee was thirteen, Theresa began drawing Cee into her confidence. They went shopping together. "Nobody else has to be around when you get underwear," she told Cee. They were frequently in her parents' bedroom, alone, leaning against the dresser, talking. The top of the dresser was her mother's private place, adorned with a married woman's treasures: flasks of perfume, a jewelry box, and her sepia wedding portrait, iconlike on a square of Polish linen. It was in her bedroom that Theresa had asked Cee what she and Carl were doing the night she found them together in his bed. Her mother fiddled nervously with a brooch the whole time. "That's no place to have a talk ... with your brother."

Around that time she began complaining to Cee about her aches and pains, her monthly cramps. You are your mother's daughter, she seemed to be telling Cee. I am passing my woman's wisdom on to you, entrusting you with a secret, and the secret is: It's damned hard to be a woman but don't you ever let on because men don't like women who gripe.

It was also the time when her tumor had been diagnosed as malignant.

"Is everything all right with your, I mean, did Dr. Kraus . . ."

"Everything's fine," her mother said, impatient with Cee's indirectness. "We've begun the countdown until the summer. Are you ready to start frying?"

When the *chrust* were drained, dusted with sugar, and set out on a platter to cool, Cee and her mother cleaned up and had coffee. Cee was about to reach for a cigarette but stopped when her mother asked how Carl was doing.

Finally someone had mentioned his name.

She wondered how much her mother knew about the developer Larrabee, about Melissa's sickness, about Carl and Elaine not getting along. Carl always kept bad news about the house from his mother to keep it from leaking to his father.

Cee said that Carl was fine.

Her mother gave her an exasperated look. "I suppose I shouldn't have asked. I know that you and your brother have signed a pact of secrecy." Before Cee could protest, Theresa started talking about Elaine. "I was relieved when I first met her. She's a good girl, no nonsense. I thought she might make Carl . . . I don't know, simpler, more down-to-earth."

"Carl is never going to be simple, Mom."

"I don't mean simple-minded. But he's hard, so hard. It started with politics, then the draft. It was all more than a belief for him, it was a defense. Beliefs make a person strong; Carl's made him bitter. And then your father made it worse by throwing him out of the house."

"I never heard you talk about it that way."

"Well, that's what happened, didn't it? I can say it now, even if I couldn't then."

"Carl would have gone anyway. He was just looking for an out."

"He might not have cut himself off from us the way he did. I was so angry with your father for taking my son away from me. But I couldn't run after Carl. I didn't even know where he was."

Cee looked down. "Were you angry at me for not telling you that he'd gone up to the house? You must have known that I knew."

"I also knew that you wouldn't tell me. But I didn't think that much about finding him because . . . I blamed myself for his leaving."

"It was Carl's decision to go."

"What kinds of decisions do eighteen-year-olds make?" She set her cup down loudly. "They do whatever their parents don't want them to do, and the smart ones like Carl figure out reasons to explain it. But that's not a decision."

"Carl didn't want to register, and nothing you could have done would have changed his mind."

Her mother sighed, regretting having brought up the subject.

"Do you think the vocational school will be good for Jason?" Cee asked.

Theresa stared straight ahead, as if Jason stood before her. "I don't know what'll be good for Jason. I'm just happy that he and your father are getting along better now."

"If you call that getting along. I call it brainwashing. So he'll forget how Dad used to hardly talk to him."

"Jason was a very difficult child, Cee." Theresa's voice grew agitated. "You never wanted to see that. You treated him like the underdog."

"I was trying to help him, which is more than most people in this family did, especially Dad."

"What did you want me to do, divorce him? Like those women I read about in magazines who leave their husband and children and go off to meditate? There's nothing you can tell me about your father that I don't know."

"Dad carries on like he's a caliph. He always has."

"Look at him now, Cee. Your father was always someone who had to prove himself."

"All men do. That's their problem."

"What do you expect from a man with a bad heart who hated being a sickly kid, always being told he couldn't do this or that in case he overworked himself?"

"That still doesn't give him the right to take it out on Jason," she said, trying to control her voice. "Or on you."

"Who else would listen to him? It might sound strange to you, but it's his way of showing love."

Cee glanced at the G carved below the sink. At that moment it reminded her of the brand on an animal's hide. "Is it true that Dad transferred the money in Carl's trust fund to Jason's?"

Theresa looked away, as if embarrassed. "I tried to stop him, but he's the signator for the account. He did it without thinking; he was enraged . . . broken. He never in his wildest dreams believed Carl would really leave." Her voice lowered. "Promise me you won't talk to him about it. Not now. It's been hard enough with you being here. You make him think about Carl. He's knows you were up to see him."

Cee saw the folds at the corners of her mother's mouth and felt a light thump on her heart. "But couldn't you at least speak to him about it? Carl really needs the money."

"I know this might sound strange, but I think your father is waiting for Carl to come and ask for it," Theresa said softly. She put her hand on Cee's arm. "If you can keep a secret, I'll tell you something. I might have a job soon. I took the civil service exam in September and did fine. A woman from social services called and said the county might be hiring. It won't be more than typing and filing. Women's work, you know."

"That's wonderful! But what about your job in the bakery?"

"They can find someone else to tie the string around the cake boxes."

Walter walked in.

"How come you're sitting in the dark?" he said, snapping on the light.

Everyone went with Cee to the bus station. She had been firm about taking the late bus Saturday night instead of staying another night. The bus coming from New York was delayed. Cee panicked; unforeseen complications made her father nervous. She told her parents to go home but they insisted on waiting. Everyone stood in silence during the last ten minutes, as though already having used up what they had to say. It occurred to Cee that she'd be doing this again in another six weeks, at the end of Christmas break.

When the bus pulled up. Cee hugged her mother and then let her father kiss her on the cheek. Jason seemed to hesitate saying good-bye, as though feeling bad that he'd hardly spoken to her. Finally he offered her a meaty hand to shake. She got on and settled into her seat. The bag of food her mother had packed rode between her legs. When the bus pulled out she reached down for a *chrust* and bit into the crispy mantle, showering her lap with powdered sugar.

The bus swung into the Buffalo Greyhound station, and the doors hissed open. In novels, she'd read of the echoing tumult of train stations in Europe, cathedrals for farewells and homecomings. The Greyhound terminal had the feel of a police station, brightly lit and grimy. People waiting for midnight runs to New York and Montreal killed time before coin television sets. Nearby sat the luggageless and the poorly dressed who weren't going anywhere, just keeping warm. Outside, the corner of Main and Chippewa was like a midway, sleazy and yellow from the flashing marquee of Shea's Buffalo.

She was nervous about seeing Stephanie again after the incident with Race. She and Stephanie had carefully avoided each other for the next few days.

Stephanie wasn't there when she got back to the room.

She didn't show up the next day, or the next.

Well, this was strange, Cee thought, coming home the third evening. She smelled food and realized she was hungry. People were hauling pots of water from the bathroom to cook with, like women filling their buckets at the village well. Cooking seemed irrevocably female, even if she knew her own mother disliked it even more than housekeeping. "Cleaning is cleaning," Theresa would say, "but cooking means cooking and cleaning." The early dark outside the window reminded her of beef stew suppers, potato soup, boiled sausage. Should she open a can of something and heat it up or go to the basement snack bar?

It occurred to her that she was hoping Stephanie would show up so that they might talk.

Stephanie turned the key to the room just as Cee awoke the next morning.

"Hello," Cee said, rubbing her eyes. "What time is it?"

"After eleven."

Cee bolted up in bed. Stephanie went about, taking things out of her carrying bag and putting them into drawers.

"How have you been?" said Cee.

"Fine." Stephanie yanked a sweater out of the bag, threw it down on the bed, slapped the arms over, and then folded it together roughly, as if to teach the garment a lesson. When she went to put the sweater in a drawer, the folding came undone. She cursed and threw it back onto the bed.

"Is everything okay?"

Stephanie swung around to face her. "I just want to tell you one thing. I don't want you saying nothing bad about my man, ever, you hear?" She dumped some books into her shoulder bag, and left.

The next few days they were careful whenever they were together. The floor grew somber as exam week approached, and the lounge filled with people studying late into the night. Cee had three finals plus a paper for English. The Sociology and Poli-Sci exams were both multiple choice, no problem. The paper would take time but didn't have to be longer than ten pages. She'd have to cram for Psych, though. But anytime she opened a book, Stephanie's stern warning about Race clouded her concentration. She'd spoken to Cee as though they were strangers, even enemies.

Later that week Cee asked her what was going on. "You've been ignoring me," she said. "I already told you that I'm sorry about the television set, but it was an accident—"

"I got things on my mind," Stephanie answered, hanging up her coat. She began rearranging the notebooks on her desk. It reminded Cee of the way her mother would start clearing the table whenever an argument erupted. Stephanie went for her towel to go wash.

"Wait," said Cee, touching her on the shoulder.

Stephanie spun around, as though Cee had stung her. "Listen. I'm not like you, you gotta understand that." She grabbed her toiletry bag.

"What's that supposed to mean?"

"You know what I'm talking about." Her eyes flickered with anger, yet she seemed frightened.

"You're so sure." Cee heard the tremor in her own voice. "But it sounds like Race talking."

Stephanie looked away.

"What else did he say about me?"

"He said he didn't like me hanging out with you," she said slowly.

Cee swallowed. "And what do you think?"

Stephanie fussed with her toiletry bag, as though anxious to leave the room.

Cee turned around, sure that a single word would start her crying. Stephanie left. Cee got undressed and crawled into bed. Stephanie was punishing her for liking her and for growing attached to her. What was harder—being queer, or someone else accusing you of it? But that wasn't the issue, no matter what Race thought. She heard Stephanie coming in and pulled the blanket tighter around her. What did Race have to do with them, someone Cee hardly knew, who had no business butting in: a man.

Cee managed to get some studying done in the days that followed but Stephanie's distance hurt, and Cee felt her momentum diminishing. She read passages from her psychology book over and over again, highlighting with sloppy strokes until whole pages glowed poison green. The paralysis of the beginning of the term began setting in, and all her old doubts about school returned. A warm spell enhanced her September mood. She took up her old post by the fountain. One day, following the arc of a Frisbee over the dry fountain as the bells of Hayes Hall rang out another hour, she came to the conclusion that the very best thing she could do was to take a vacation from being a student. What would she do instead? Find a job and get an apartment, in that order, she hoped.

She took incompletes in all her courses except English; she'd write the paper. (She had her topic picked out: "A Trapped Woman: Edna Pontellier in Kate Chopin's *The Awakening*.") Each day, instead of studying, she scanned the *Courier-Express* want ads. A veterinarian needed a secretary. Giving appointments for sick dachshunds seemed at least as meaningful as memorizing Maslow's hierarchy of needs. But the job had already been filled, and the druggist looking for someone to drive his delivery van wanted a guy.

It turned cold again. Cee returned to the dorm chilled to the bone after trudging through the first snowstorm of the season. The door was locked. From inside she heard music. Cee turned her key and opened the door. The curtains were drawn and the room was thick with the sweet smell of dope. She went to switch on the light.

"Leave it," snarled a man's voice.

Her hand pulled back, as if the switch had delivered a shock. Race hiked the covers over his naked backside. Stephanie lay half-buried beneath him, no more than her face and a slender arm visible. Their eyes met for a second before Stephanie turned to the wall.

"Close the door and get out," Race said.

Cee waited for Stephanie to turn around and say something.

"Hey!" the man shouted.

"Stephanie!" Cee implored.

"Get out, bitch!" Race sat up, the blanket around him fell away, revealing the dark bulk of his torso. His eyes shot to the pile of his clothes on the chair.

"It's my room," Cee said, shaken by equal parts of fright and rage. "You don't belong here."

"Just go," said Stephanie dryly, without turning around.

Cee turned on the light.

Stephanie gave a shriek of surprise and covered herself. Race cursed, straddled Stephanie's prone form, and lunged for his pants, but he tumbled out of bed, falling with a hard thud of flesh on the tile floor. He made a crazed scramble for Cee, one hand cupped between his legs. She ran out of the room and headed for the fire exit. Halfway down the first flight of steps she burst into tears. The sound of her crying boomed through the concrete stairway. By the time she reached the ground, her head was hot and spinning. She leaned against the wall, weeping. The door opened.

"You okay?" A black man was leaning over her.

She gasped, then she realized it was Kenny, the man who worked behind the lobby desk.

Without thinking, Cee reached into her pocket to make sure she still had her room key.

"I'm all right," Cee said, letting him help her up. She walked outside.

A heavy snow had fallen, and the brightly lit dorms towered over it like a base station on the South Pole. The people she passed were muffled silent and unidentifiable under their parkas and scarves. She found herself heading down Bailey Avenue past the dark plain of the golf course. Whose idea was it to have a golf course in such a climate? she thought, her rage shifting to the first thing she saw. And what was a golf course doing next to a university, anyway? Cee imagined golfers in their ridiculous white shoes pulling their stupid, little carts across the lawn as students rioted on the other side of the street.

Cee wondered what Stephanie was doing at that moment. Still in bed? Showering? She was definitely the type to scald herself after sex. No doubt Race blamed Stephanie for what happened, saying she had no business going to that school anyway. He'd use the incident to persuade her to move in with him. Dumb Stephanie might just fall for it.

Cee shivered. Goddamn! She was out here freezing her ass off, wondering what the two of them were doing in her nice, warm room. She was ready to turn back, but she stopped. She couldn't face the sight of them in that bed one more time. She didn't even want to go back there to sleep that night. She kept on walking.

Why had they been there and not at his house? Surely not because he suddenly had the urge to fuck in a dorm. Maybe Stephanie felt she had to make it up to him after the busted TV. Or else it had been her way of letting Cee know once and for all what she, Stephanie, was. And what she wasn't. Maybe Stephanie thought Cee wanted to change her. In her eyes Cee was no better than one of those meddlesome social workers. Stephanie needed to get things clear in her mind again. She'd brought in Race to help her.

Cee headed for the union. The tables stacked with political leaflets were gone; even the revolutionaries were studying. From the other end she heard music: the folk dancers. Exams or no, they were there, leaping into the air, although fewer than usual. The lively music and twirling couples made Cee think of peasants celebrating the winter solstice. It reminded her of the time her parents took her to a party at the Polish National Home, where they'd dance together, so light-footed and joyous. Cee came upon a poster left over from the women's festival.

Change Stephanie from what? Into what?

She and Race were mercifully gone by the time Cee returned. The bed had been made as carefully as always. The room was chilly; Stephanie had thought to air out the place.

There was a knock. It was Pat.

"Oh God," Cee said, about to cry once more.

Pat held her. "What happened? I wasn't here. Judy said she heard you arguing with someone in your room, and then the door slammed. She knocked on your door afterward and heard people in there, but no one answered."

Cee told her what had happened.

"That's really gross," Pat said. Her eyes fell to Stephanie's side of the bureau. "She uses all that stuff?"

"It makes her pretty, or haven't you noticed?" Cee pulled out one of Stephanie's perfumed tissues and blew her nose. "You think we can go to your room? I don't feel like being here right now."

"No problem. You can even sleep there. Judy's with her boyfriend."

THE DORM GREW quiet as a monastery as exam week began. Cee chain-smoked and drank beer as she tried to crank out her English paper, but the incident with Race still plagued her. Stephanie stayed away for most of the next week, and her absence only made things worse. If she'd been there, they might have talked about what happened. Cee slept poorly. Whenever she switched off the lights the darkness coalesced into a man's naked form, ridiculing her, frightening her.

She began to worry about what she would do in two weeks when the term was over. She still had no job and no apartment and had already notified the housing office that she was moving out. Going home was out of the question. What about staying with Carl and Elaine? No, it was too close to home, too cold, and being around Carl and Elaine had been too depressing.

She filled out application forms in offices and stores in every mall she could reach by bus. The forms demanded a life history for work a child could do. Did anybody care that she'd been a speech therapist's assistant two summers ago? Her pen halted at "Position Desired": a "position," no mere job, and one worth desiring at that. But she wouldn't desire any position at all if she could find someone else to pay her bills. Once she was tempted to fill the blank with "Company President"; weren't Americans brought up to believe that they could become president?

Several days later she went to the room and found all of Stephanie's things gone. Her bed had been stripped, and the closet and drawers were empty. Some makeup had been left behind, as if she'd been in a hurry to pack.

Cee looked around the room. Something wasn't right.

Her stereo. Gone.

She walked to the corner and stood there as if to be sure that the stereo was no longer there.

Her camera?

She flung open the closet door, and pushed through her clothing. Thank God, it still hung on its nail in the back. She noticed a scattering of torn paper on her desk: the pictures Cee had taken of Stephanie that day downtown. She picked up a ragged rectangle. A tear left a half of Stephanie's surprised smile and cut away some of the bus stop sign, leaving the letters NF. Not funny, Cee thought. No friend. Nicely fucked-up.

She fell into a chair and lit a cigarette, staring at the rips in the paper until they resembled the slashes of a knife. She began idly rearranging the pieces, as if to reconstruct Stephanie in different ways: Stephanie the serious woman, Stephanie the activist, Stephanie the true friend, all the things she hadn't been. Had Race seen the pictures and torn them up in a rage? Or had they fallen into Stephanie's hands during her rushed exodus, triggering old doubts about him she wished to forget? *Race thinks he can make me love him if he holds on tight enough.*

Cee was certain that it was Race's idea to lift the stereo. He had a car. He was friends with one of the night security guards. Most important, he had a score to settle with Cee. She considered reporting the loss to campus security, but figured that the stereo was already downtown, plugged in, and blasting Barry White. Cee thought of telling Stephanie's mother. She hadn't liked Race, either. Cee flipped through the phone book in the booth downstairs. There was a Polite listed on Peach Street. Amalia Polite. Cee dialed.

"Hello?"

It was Stephanie. Cee hung up. She returned to her room, empty as it had been in the beginning of the term.

Cee left more application forms in more offices. She almost went into an Arthur Treacher's with a Help Wanted sign in the window, but nothing could make her put on one of those uniforms. Looking for a place to live seemed equally hopeless. Students were graduating, but their rooms had already been taken by transfers from other schools.

And what was she even doing looking for an apartment when she had no job to pay the rent? She escaped from the cold for a while by going to see *Chinatown*. She bought popcorn, sank into a seat and watched Faye Dunaway and Jack Nicholson walking around in summer clothes in the desert heat of Los Angeles.

By the end of the week the strained quiet in the dorm gave way to restlessness, as people began to talk of standby flights and ski trips. Slowly the floor emptied. Fewer women were in the bathroom mornings when Cee went to wash. The building was due to close in a matter of days. A steady stream of cars and taxis lined up in front of the union, their trunks open for suitcases.

Who could she crash with until she found a place of her own? There weren't many possibilities. Pat had mentioned going winter camping in the Adirondacks with a friend. Judy, an unlikely alternative in any case, would be with her parents in Florida. Fran's last postcard came from San Francisco. For some reason Marlene came to mind. She'd given Cee her number the night of the women's dance and suggested going for coffee; Cee had felt too intimidated to take up her offer. Maybe she knew of someone with a couch to spare. But when she looked for Marlene's telephone number she couldn't find it.

The afternoon before the dorms closed, Pat came to say good-bye. "Too bad you're going," she said. She glanced at Stephanie's stripped mattress. "What are you going to do now?"

Cee could almost feel the point of the question sinking into her chest. "I'll be staying with friends until I find a place of my own," she said, wishing it were so.

Later that evening the telephone rang, echoing in the half-empty room.

"Mom!"

"I was wondering when you'll be home."

"I'm ... not sure."

"Cee, you sound worried."

"Exams." Cee found herself staring in the direction of the empty corner. She had never told her mother she'd bought a stereo so there was no point mentioning it being stolen. "How come you're speaking so softly? I can hardly hear you."

"I don't want your father to know I'm calling. Long distance, you know." There was a pause. "He still hasn't found any work. He's feeling even worse than when you were here, what with Christmas coming up."

Her mother sounded terrible. She really wants to see me, Cee thought. Her eyes fell to the makeup Stephanie had left behind, and she felt a spurt of anger. Makeup was nothing but a greasy ploy to attract men. Women were divorcing their husbands or becoming electrical engineers but the Stephanies of the world were dutifully buying their Maybelline for men like Race.

"You're still thinking of going to work, aren't you, Mom?"

"Of course. Why do you ask? What's wrong? You sound so . . . sad."

Cee said nothing.

"You're not thinking of hitching home, are you?"

"No." That was certainly true.

"If you're worried about Christmas presents, well, don't be, okay? I know you don't have a lot—"

Cee heard the simple tenderness of her mother's voice, soft as *chrust* dough, so soothing after Stephanie and Race. She thought she would start to cry any minute. She'd been dreading having to tell her mother that she wouldn't be home for Christmas. She'd meant to put it in a letter but wanted to wait until she had found a place to live. She had to get off the phone fast. Her eyes were already growing hot.

"Okay," she said, "I won't worry about presents. I should go study for my finals."

"It was nice seeing you Thanksgiving," her mother said, almost shyly. "But I wasn't in the best of spirits."

"It was okay, Mom." Cee didn't think she could hold out much longer.

"I hope we'll have a little more time to talk during Christmas."

Cee pursed her lips, closed her eyes, and breathed deeply to keep the tears back. "Yes."

After she hung up, everything inside her broke loose. Enraged, she started throwing things into her trunk. She had to get out of here. The room was poisoned by Stephanie and Race. Another moment in it would wreck her. The trunk was half full when she came across her Kate Chopin book. She began thumbing through the pages. Passages slashed with fervent underlining flipped by, the margins crammed with urgently written notes. After reading a few pages she felt calmer. She reached for a sheet of typing paper, cranked it into her Smith-Corona portable, and typed:

A Trapped Woman: Edna Pontellier
in Kate Chopin's *The Awakening*

The title looked confident on the fresh paper. She began typing and didn't stop until she'd covered three pages. She read them. The opening paragraphs meandered from thought to thought like a diary entry, but then her ideas began pulling together. Pleased, she made coffee and continued, filling another seven pages by the time it began to grow light outside. Then she stopped and looked with satisfaction at the stack of curling paper beside the typewriter. She lit a cigarette and read what she'd written. The woman she described, Edna, was twenty-eight and lived in New Orleans at the turn of the century. But by the end of the paper it was clear Cee'd written about someone else: her own mother, trying to free herself from the marriage that had held her fast for as long as Edna was old. She set the pages down, satisfied.

In an instant of clarity she recalled where she'd scribbled Marlene's number: on the theater program. Cee dug it out of her shoebox of keepsakes. There it was, two lines of shaky script at the bottom of the program (Marlene had leaned against Cee's back to write). Could Cee bring herself to call? It was eight in the morning. Perhaps she could tell Marlene that she'd finished her paper and wanted to show it to her. They'd have coffee, Cee would explain her situation. Marlene had lived in Buffalo as an undergraduate; she was sure to know someone Cee could stay with. It was Cee's only chance. She lit a cigarette and dialed. The phone rang. It kept ringing. No one answered.

She switched on the little radio she kept on her desk. (At least Race had left that.) The news came on. A terrorist bombing in Northern Ireland. Alexander Haig talking about the security of West Germany. The weather: There was a fifty-fifty chance of a white Christmas.

She picked up *The Awakening* again and riffled through the pages. Her eye caught passages heavy with underlining.

> Edna began to feel like one who awakens gradually out of a dream, a delicious, grotesque, impossible dream, to feel again the realities pressing into her soul. . . . She felt as if a mist had been lifted from her eyes, enabling her to look upon and comprehend the significance of life, that monster made up of beauty and brutality.

Cee set the book down and turned to her own text. A second, closer reading made her work seem like nothing more than the confused ramblings of someone careening on a caffeine buzz. Compared with Chopin's Edna, Theresa came off as a frustrated housewife. Cee tore the pages in half and let them flutter to the floor around her. She lay down on the bed, exhausted, but ringing with restlessness. She'd have given anything to listen to some music now.

The Hayes Hall clock said almost ten. The dorms were officially closing at twelve. Two hours. What then?

It seemed that she would just have to go home.

She envisioned getting on the bus with her trunk. Walter and Theresa would be smiling as the bus pulled in at Thompson City, and a half-hour later she'd be back in her old room, dumping clothing back into the dresser waiting for her. She'd plunk her toothbrush into the holder beside Jason's, as though she'd never left. No, no . . .

The floor was completely quiet. It occurred to her that she might be the last one in the building. She envisioned each of the floors, room after room, empty. She noticed that her two framed photographs remained on the wall, people from another time, now barely recognizable: she, painfully, perhaps deliberately, naive, and Jason, softly receptive. She almost felt like flinging the pictures to the floor. Instead she took them down, folded them in newspaper and found a secure place for them in the trunk.

Staying up all night made her want to take a shower. She undressed and put on her bathrobe, but when she went for her toiletry bag she saw she'd run out of shampoo. Had Stephanie left any? Cee rummaged through her roommate's top drawer, found tampons and a disposable razor. She held it by its pink plastic handle, the blade shining, not yet used.

She caught sight of herself in the mirror and set the razor down. Her bathrobe parted, and a chill caressed the exposed strip of her flesh. The heat had already been turned off. It meant they wanted her out of there, they were waiting for her to go, good-bye, good riddance. She put her hands to her face, then slid them down until they reached her breasts. She cupped them and lifted their warm weight, as if to make an offering to whatever deity might be appeased into helping her. Her skin was very smooth, very white. Her girth filled it, spilling out beyond the frame of the mirror, so much flesh that no one wanted. She went for the razor again. Jackson Browne came on the radio. "Doctor, my eyes have seen the years . . ."

Why did she feel so alone?

Just because she had no one to call in Buffalo who might give her a place to crash, no one except her English instructor, a person she hardly knew and who couldn't be reached anyway? Or because Fran was in California, Pat was going winter camping, and Judy would be in Florida?

If you're worried about Christmas presents . . .

Her thoughts grew looser, swinging wider and wider apart like couples dancing out of control. Was it on account of not having a job and her money running out that she felt the way she did?

Or because of Stephanie? No, no way, not because of a wimp like her . . .

On the radio, Jackson Browne was asking his doctor whether he'd left his eyes open too long. She understood what he meant. Seeing hurt. Sometimes it was easier to look the other way. She studied her reflection as she held the razor against her wrist—no, no, against her skin, she thought, as if to correct herself. She wasn't going to do anything rash, she just wanted to see how it felt. The metal was cool, hard, decisive; it was masculine, nothing like the silly pink plastic of the handle, with its flowers, pink, the color of the rubber gloves her mother put on to wash windows. Cee closed her eyes, then pressed the blade into her flesh ever so gently—

Did she really have a reason to do it?

Did she have a reason not to?

I hope we'll have a little more time to talk during Christmas.

Oh, Mom—

This is probably very dangerous, she thought. And stupid. So she was going to put the razor down. She was going to put the razor back where she found it, right along with the rest of the shit that Stephanie left behind. But not yet. The blade's hint of pain tempted her, it dared her. It made her want to see how much she could take. She pressed some more. The chill of the blade deepened to a sting, yet the pain seemed to come not from the razor but from her alone, from her body's stubborn resistance. Relax, she told herself, relax. She could never accept things as they were; hadn't that always been her problem? She was forever hurling herself against anything that seemed immovable and unwilling to change: her father, her brothers, Stephanie, the world, the whole goddamn world. Relax . . .

She kept on pressing.

The pounding bass of the music began to sound a warning. She felt herself slowly opening up to the razor's persistence, and a moment later, something broke free. She opened her eyes to see her fingers gloved by a bright red syrup, which striped her skin like a candy cane. The music grew larger around her, a machine fueled by her blood. Blood, she thought, already dizzy. Women were made of it; men, of stone. Women die a little each month. They die in order to live, die in order to live . . .

The voice on the radio stretched and slowed, as though played at the wrong speed. She slowed with it. Her legs started going weak, and she fell. A blow to her side knocked her alert for a moment before she sank into numbness. A calm spread inside her like a drop of ink blossoming effortlessly in water. Knocks on the door, the beat of a wooden drum, began to sound.

Part Two

1

I AM A WOMAN returned from the dead, Cee thought, waking up in her bed in the emergency room of Meyer Memorial Hospital.

A maintenance man had gone up to Cee's floor to find out why her name wasn't on the checkout sheet. He'd heard the radio, knocked, and when no one answered, opened the door with a passkey. He found Cee stretched out on the floor, bleeding, and got an emergency team to trundle her off to Meyer Memorial. He gave them the theater program with Marlene's number, which he'd found beside the telephone, because he thought it might be important.

"You came," Cee whispered, when she saw Marlene's face beside her bed.

"Cee," said Marlene. She looked down with controlled horror at the baseball mitt's thickness of bandages around Cee's left hand, unable to connect the person in the hospital bed with the one who'd pulled her along the samba line. "Are you okay?"

"I'm still weak," Cee whispered. "Weak and stupid."

"The woman at the desk says she's been trying to reach the school to get your parents' telephone number, but all the offices are closed for the holidays. She asked me if I was a relative—"

"Don't let them tell my parents."

Marlene looked worried. "I can't lie to them—"

"Tell them something, tell them anything. But if they call my mother and tell her what happened, she'll go out of her mind."

When it came time for Cee to be discharged, she said she needed a place to stay, and Marlene offered to put her up.

"Are you sure it's okay?" Cee asked as they walked to the parking lot.

"Actually I could use some company," Marlene confided. Her roommate was gone for the holidays, she explained. Joel, her boyfriend, had recently moved back into his old apartment, and it looked like quits. "I was just getting ready for a long, lonely winter break."

Cee noticed Marlene glancing down at Cee's bandage uncomfortably.

As soon as Cee was settled in Marlene's house she called her parents to let them know that she wouldn't be coming down for the holidays.

"What happened?" Theresa's voice was fragile with worry, as if she could see the bandage.

"I just felt it would be better if I stayed up here," Cee answered, not knowing what else to say. She heard her mother gripping the receiver tighter.

"Where are you?"

"At a friend's."

There was a pause. "I knew something was the matter the last time I spoke with you."

"There's nothing wrong!" Cee said, exasperated that her mother saw through her explanation so easily. Cee knew she had to come up with something more substantial. "I dropped out of school and I have to start looking for a job."

"Oh," her mother said, muted with surprise.

Cee slept through the rest of the day and awoke early the next morning to the humid sweetness of baking. Marlene was just about to set a tray of breakfast muffins on the table when Cee walked into the kitchen. With her hair pulled back tightly, wearing a corduroy shirt, and tending to her muffins, Marlene resembled a frontier woman. She brought plates and glasses to the table, moving about the kitchen with quick efficiency.

"They look wonderful," Cee said, reaching for a muffin with her good hand. The bandaged hand rested on the table like the paw of a dog poised for scraps.

"How are you feeling?"

"Glad to be here, mostly." Cee sensed that Marlene wanted to talk about the . . . incident. Cee couldn't, not yet. She kept hearing a voice inside her that said, You must have known that someone from the dorm would eventually come around to see that everyone was out. A picture of Virginia Woolf that hung above the sink glowered down at her, as if to mock her botched suicide.

MARLENE HAD NO Christmas tree, and Christmas Day was no different from the day before, except that Cee found a small gift-wrapped package on her breakfast plate, a book: *A Room of One's Own*.

Right after breakfast Marlene disappeared into her room to work: no holiday for her. Her parents lived in Seattle, she explained, which was too far away for a Christmas jaunt. A little later Cee heard her at the typewriter, pounding the keys with uncommon strength. Cee read a little of her new book. Around two, she decided to go for a walk.

The sunlight was already yellowing when Cee left the house. Snow frosted each of the lawns she passed as if it were a cake. Buffalo looked best under snow. With little or no traffic on the streets and the stores closed, the city felt more or less at peace. A white Christmas on the Niagara Frontier, she thought.

Her steelshank boots made a pleasing crunch in the snow. The boots belonged to Joel; Cee had no others, since her steamer trunk full of clothing had been locked up by campus security, and she wouldn't be able to get it until after the holiday. Judging from the size of the boots, Joel was a giant. She'd also borrowed a fiery red sweater of his, which peeked out from the bottom of her parka. His jeans fit her like the baggiest of breeches; she'd looked like a street waif in the mirror.

The ache in her side where she'd hit the edge of her dorm bed had begun to come alive in the cold. She thought back to that terrible morning, thankful that someone had rescued her, thankful again that someone else had taken her in. She'd read of people being resuscitated and later reporting that they'd hovered above their dying selves, peering down as the doctors pumped them back to life. She recalled feeling very chilly, as though the razor cut had let in the cold air of the dorm room. Yes, she was thankful. She came upon a church. How easy it would be to wander in, dab on the water, kneel down, and switch on the automatic pilot. No doubt her mother had been to midnight mass the night before and prayed for Cee's safety.

The streets were practically empty. In house after house colored lights flickered behind filmy curtains. Everyone was Doing Christmas.

She imagined the turkey, gleaming as if varnished, the sweet potatoes under a cloudy marshmallow heaven. Tomorrow the curbside would be heaped with packaging, mixing with snow to form cliffs of dirty papier-mâché.

Her first Christmas away from home.

Christmas Day her mother's face took on a saintly patina in the steamy kitchen. She wore a good dress under her apron, like a woman in a television commercial dolled up to scrub floors. Her mother's presents —her father never gift-shopped—were usually out of sync with Cee: a frilly blouse a secretary might wear, a hand mirror, V-neck sweaters. Had the gifts been poor choices or hints?

It was almost three. Where to go while the last bit of sun still shone in the sky? Sunlight was a precious commodity in Buffalo. She wandered under the old trees of Buffalo State Hospital. She came upon a pine bush and tore off a branch to arrange in Marlene's living room. It was Christmas, after all.

CEE WAS EXPECTED to report to Meyer Memorial Hospital to talk with a counselor for an hour each day, part of a deal worked out with the hospital in return for not notifying her parents about what she'd done. The Meyer's buildings were strewn along the expressway as if the city hadn't known what else to do with them. A border of blue ceramic bas reliefs ran above the windows of the psych wing. Each disc bore the figure of a baby in swaddling clothes. The baby appeared dead, as if strangled by its blankets. Inside, the building reminded Cee of the social services office back home: scuffed, grey tile floors, walls the obligatory beige or sea-foam green, the colors poor people would have on their flag if they ever decided to found their own nation.

Dr. Lux, her counselor, wore the dark suits of Mormon missionaries, nerdy black-framed eyeglasses, and a bulky college ring. The first two sessions Cee'd hardly spoken; she simply stared at the white clump of her bandage as if it were a sick pet and Lux were the vet. She resented being blackmailed into coming. Talking about yourself was something for her old floormate Judy, but it didn't appeal to Cee. What annoyed her most of all was how little Lux said. She expected a kind of psychological pep talk from him, convincing her that she had all the reasons in the world to want to live, and so on. Instead he observed her, speaking with the same caution as Marlene, as though worried that at any minute Cee might take a razor to her other wrist.

"How come there are pictures of babies being strangled all around this building?" Cee said before the end of the second session, trying to provoke him.

"If you mean the ceramic reliefs," he said, his words italicized by a hint of annoyance, "they're copies of the tondi of Luca della Robbia around the Ospedale in Florence." He looked at his watch. "Before we get through another session in silence, do you think you might tell me why you did what you did to your wrist, Miss Gajewski?"

"Because I was too happy to live."

"Would you mind answering seriously?"

"Ask me serious questions."

"I take that to mean that you did it because you were not very happy. Did the razor have any significance?"

"It was all I had."

"It belonged to your roommate—" He glanced at her file. "Stephanie Polite. "Did she have anything to do with your actions?"

"Isn't it time for me to go already, Doc?"

That was how far they got. By the third session she knew that if she didn't start talking as soon as she got there the silence would knot around her like those blankets. And she wanted to speak. She yearned to scream out that she'd put her trust in a brainless shit like Stephanie who then betrayed her just when she really needed to feel close to someone. She also wanted to say that most men were assholes, and that perhaps black men had problems of their own. But something stopped her from saying all that. It would mean conceding that she'd failed at winning and keeping Stephanie's friendship. The proof of her failure was obvious, even if Cee realized how helpless Stephanie was against Race. As for talking to Lux, there was something else wrapped tightly about her heart: She felt ashamed of what she'd done.

"I have a little rule," he said at last. "If a patient doesn't tell me what they're thinking, then after a certain time I have the right to guess."

"Go ahead."

"Maybe it had to do with love."

Cee waited.

"But it wasn't reciprocated. Perhaps your suicide attempt was supposed to finish off what the person you cared for had started. They hurt you, they made you feel worthless, so you were determined to hurt yourself. But you're no fool. Maybe you inflicted a wound in order to heal it." He wrote something in her folder.

Inflicting a wound in order to heal it. Something about that struck her. From that perspective her actions became understandable, even necessary. She was about to say something, but he'd already closed the folder.

"You're done," he said.

THE NEXT DAY her bandages came off, revealing an angry, purple seam where her hand and arm met. On the way home she picked up a *Courier*. Buffalo General Hospital had placed a large ad in the classified section. She arranged an interview, and a week later she found herself newly employed as an Emergency Room Secretary Trainee.

Cee returned in the evening and knocked on the door to Marlene's room with a bottle of wine to celebrate. The room was barely large enough for her desk and double bed, fine for a small person like Marlene, but how did she fit this Paul Bunyan Joel in? The night of the dance Marlene had seemed somewhat helpless, but at her desk in her small room full of books and papers, she was secure and sovereign. She went for glasses, and they toasted. Marlene congratulated her, yet she seemed distracted. Joel had called that afternoon to invite her to a little bash, a combination New Year's Eve and going-away party. "He's moving to New York," Marlene said, staring into her glass. He'd been on the waiting list for the Columbia doctoral program, and they'd called to tell him he'd been accepted for the spring. "He could have gone in the fall, if he'd wanted." She set down the glass. "I know why he's going. He wants a clean break." Cee saw Marlene looking at the jeans Cee had on.

"Were you worried about how things stood with Joel the night we went to the women's dance?" she asked.

Marlene's eyes widened in surprise. "How did you know? That was when he said that he'd definitely go to New York if Columbia took him." She took another sip of wine. "Now that I think of it, you could probably move into Joel's apartment. Come with me to the party and ask him." She smiled. "Don't you think you could use a belt for those jeans?"

MOST OF THE PEOPLE at the party were English grad students or French grad students, people Cee didn't know and who looked hard to approach. Aggressively dissonant jazz tore from the stereo, so no one danced. But there was lots of dope, and she wound up getting very stoned.

Cee was surprised when she met Joel. She'd expected someone like Marlene, but he turned out to be a good-natured bear of a man—and big, as she'd expected—who clearly enjoyed having the tiny apartment crammed with people. His face had an inviting softness to it, framed with woolly hair and a beard. He seemed excited to be going to New York. When she asked him about the apartment, he said that someone was already interested in it. "But I could let you have it as a favor to Marlene," he said. Cee thanked him, but couldn't help wondering whether he had a guilty conscience about leaving Marlene and wanted to make it up to her in some way.

Someone had brought a roman candle, and just before midnight, they went out back to light it. The candle zipped into the air and shed a menacing red glow on the untouched snow of the yard. Firecrackers were breaking in the sky all over the city, spiking the cold air with sulfur. Cee saw Joel and Marlene kissing. She disappeared into his arms, and they held each other for what seemed a long time.

Even though Marlene had said that they no longer slept together, Cee wondered whether Joel might come home with Marlene for a going-away tryst. It seemed that whenever Cee turned her head, Joel and Marlene were sitting together. As the night wore on, Cee's dope-logic flowered, fueled by the stinging image of Stephanie and Race. Cee grew afraid: The prospect of being on the other side of a thin wall separating her from other people's passion was too much to bear. But when Marlene was ready to leave, Joel kissed her once more and then said good-bye.

On the way home the cold air cleared Cee's head, and she confessed what she'd been thinking.

"Ridiculous," Marlene said.

What was she referring to—the idea that Joel would come home with her, or that Cee had thought up such a thing? Either way Cee could tell that she'd said the wrong thing.

2

For the first couple of weeks after the incident at Nina's Jason was careful to avoid their old corner of the locker room when he went to the gym. He would change, nervously listening for Richie's step over the hollow bang of the lockers, and then he'd gather his gloves and towel and head for the gym, afraid Richie would see him there and be furious that Jason had defied his ban. But weeks went by and Richie didn't show.

Without Richie, Jason discovered how much he enjoyed the weight room, especially after the battering noise of the vocational high school, where everyone always seemed to be shouting. He grew friendly with the other guys and went with them to the nearby Wendy's afterward. The talk almost always turned to girls. He'd busy himself with his burger or drink his Coke, careful to have a wicked laugh ready when someone reached the meat of his story. He had to give a story, too. His ten embarrassing minutes with Nina might be transformed into triumph—especially because Nina was black—but what could he say the next time his turn came around? He hit upon a surefire topic that always changed the subject: car repair.

Jason searched for Richie at school, but didn't see him. Had his family moved away? Had he switched schools? Someone in metal shop told him: Richie had dropped out and was working in a lumber yard in Binghamton.

JASON CHECKED his mother's list once more, grabbed a carton of milk from the dairy section, then steered his cart toward the checkout line, minutes before closing time. Way up ahead, the cashier girl blew a wayward curl from her face, punching the register keys with fury, eager to finish. Jason noticed someone leaning against the glass outside. The jacket with the green collar looked familiar. He strained to get a better view.

It was him.

By the time Jason left the store, Richie was nowhere to be seen, but just as he was about to get into his car, Richie's Mustang pulled up near the entrance to the supermarket. The lights inside the store began to go out. The cashier girl emerged. She was getting in with him! As soon as they drove off, Jason followed.

The traffic was heavy, and he almost lost them near Floral Park Cemetery. It was already dark, but Richie's car had a busted taillight so it wasn't hard trailing him. The dashboard clock said a quarter to six. His mother was expecting him to be home any minute. But Jason had to know where they were going. He didn't have to wait long to find out. Richie made a right onto Fitch. At River Road he turned off again.

Jason panicked. If he turned off, too, they were bound to notice, since there were so few cars on that stretch of road. Jason slowed, and pulled over to the side, growing more anxious. He hadn't been down here since the accident. He'd even avoided Fitch, knowing where it led. Richie's red-and-white taillights kept crawling farther down the road, growing fainter. Jason saw the car stop. He imagined them getting out, going to one of the houses, and closing the door. Richie would pull off his clothes and then he would get her—

The lights of Richie's car went off, and night filled the road like a shade pulled against Jason's prying eyes.

OWEN, ONE of the guys who lifted weights, knew of a party. He picked Jason up. Two guys from the weight room were already sitting in the backseat. One of them pressed a beer into Jason's hand, and they were off.

A girl with an oily face in a floor-length batik skirt answered the door. "And who are you?" she asked, a hand on her hip.

"Friend of Tony," Owen said.

The girl made a face and held the door without letting them in. "Did he say you could come?" Owen shook his head yes, and she released her hold on the door.

"Hey, Tony!" she shouted over the crowd. "Who said you could invite people to my party?"

It was a big house, and full. Colored light bulbs had been screwed into the lamps in the living room. Empty beer cans clanked underfoot. Jason took one or two hefty tokes of a joint passed his way and began investigating. Most of the people seemed to be from Thompson City High, and he didn't know them. Any time the girl who opened the door caught sight of him she looked away, as if to emphasize that he wasn't one of her friends. It didn't bother him. There was plenty to eat and drink, and Jason was feeling fine. He stumbled into a room lit by a single candle at a far end of the house where the music hardly penetrated. Several people sat around a water pipe. The ember of dope in the tiny cup glowed, and the water bubbled in the glass each time someone toked. Jason noticed Owen sitting across from him, grinning, his eyes shiny. The next thing he knew, Owen was getting up lifting the girl next to him into the air with his hands around her waist. She clucked in mock terror as he hoisted her up to the ceiling, but then looked down at him with dreamy surprise.

"Don't you dare try that with me," said a girl who sat near Jason. She smiled at him, and the candle's flicker slid across her very round cheeks.

The dope had relaxed him, and he felt playful. "Why not? Bend your elbows," he said to her.

"No," she laughed.

He did it for her, then pushed himself into a crouch, slid his hands around the points of her elbows, and lifted her as he stood up.

"Put me down," she gently protested, rising all the time. By the time Jason's arms were outstretched, she'd almost reached the ceiling. Jason saw Owen watching. She let her head fall back as if she were floating, and the tips of her hair fell lightly on Jason's face.

When they were sitting again she whispered, "You must be strong if you can pick up someone as heavy as me." Her round cheeks pressed close, looking almost liquid. They smoked some more. Jason was conscious of her leg pressing against his. He saw Owen put his arm around the girl he'd lifted up and, as if that were his cue, Jason reached over and kissed the girl beside him. Her mouth was small and tight, flavored with the grassy taste of dope. She moved closer, he felt surrounded by her, and then a shudder of panic rippled through him. He pulled away. Some more dope, he thought. But the pipe was empty. Maybe something to drink, something hard. He'd seen a bottle of tequila going around—

He told the girl he had to go to the bathroom, which was true, and her round cheeks seemed to sink. On the way back to the room he ran into a guy he knew from the vocational school, they talked, and he had something to eat in the kitchen. By the time Jason returned to the room everyone had left. The pipe stood, abandoned. He felt relieved and headed for the colored wasteland of the living room, trying to find Owen. He was ready to leave. Owen wasn't there. Jason wandered from room to room, until he found himself upstairs. There was a door like the one that led to his attic room. He opened it and felt for where the light switch should have been but his fingers rubbed against the raw wood of beams. Stairs led up around a curve, the sounds of the party sank farther and farther below, and soon he stood under a dome of near-darkness. He stood still, as though another step might set off an alarm. Whispers rose in one corner like wind trapped in an alleyway. Something shifted. The jittery edge of a girl's voice hooked into the air. "Someone's here, wait—"

Jason's eyes adjusted to the darkness; rubbery outlines of naked limbs grew before him, heaving and pushing like a turbine. Jason stepped closer: the curve of an ass, layers of legs. A guy's face turned, as though Jason had called his name—Owen, with the girl he'd lifted up.

Jason felt a strike to his chest. He retreated down the steps and out of the house, still breathing the dusty air of the attic. When he got home he sat in the living room for a long time, staring through the front window, seeing Owen clearer and clearer in the glass, as though the attic had been brightly lit. His face turned toward Jason, smiling in slippery satisfaction. Something in Jason tore loose. He pushed up from where he sat and and put his fist through the window.

"AREN'T YOU the one who likes to pick people up by their elbows?" the girl working at the Wendy's said. Her hair was pulled back the way his mother did when cleaning house.

"You were at that party, too?"

"Yes. You want a cheeseburger with double onions and a small orange soda?"

He looked at her, growing more confused.

"It's what you always order, isn't it?"

He would notice her looking at him after that. He learned her name was Marcy, and he hoped she might speak to him again, but she never did more than grin. Still, someone noticing him was enjoyable, and it emboldened him to wait for her in the back of the Wendy's after her shift. He expected her to be pleasantly surprised, but the look on her face made him feel like he'd walked in on her in the girls' bathroom. She let out a surprised whoop, then walked away, leaving him to scurry between the garbage containers to catch up.

"But you always look at me," he called after her.

"I wasn't looking at you," she said without turning around. "I was studying the proportions of your face, that's all."

"My proportions?" Jason said.

"Yes," she said, stopping at last. "They're so . . . feral," she said, then continued on her way.

Jason felt as if she'd dropped a boulder in his path. He spent the whole walk home pondering her comment. Looking up the word in the dictionary when he got home only made things worse.

The next time he saw her at the counter he flashed her a nervous smile and apologized and asked her if she wanted to go to the movies.

She thought for a minute. "What about a little hike, instead? This Saturday."

She packed them a lunch. They drove to Upper Lisle Park. She walked briskly, not saying much, and Jason had to struggle to keep up with her. He wondered whether she'd begun to regret the outing. When they reached the Whitney Point Reservoir, she pulled out her sketch pad.

"The problem with bodies of water like this is getting them to really *sit* in the landscape," she said. Her pencil moved swiftly across the paper, as if she were sculpting it. Jason sat, hungry and cold. He dug his bandaged hand deep into his pocket. On days like this the stitches felt like tiny bites. She turned the pad so that he could see the finished drawing.

"It's nice," he said. Then he went to kiss her.

She smiled and gently eased him back. "That's okay, Jason. You don't have to pretend we're boyfriend and girlfriend." She spoke calmly, even affectionately and slipped the pad back into her bag. "I'm hungry. What'll you have, chicken salad or tuna?"

AS LONG AS his hand remained bandaged he couldn't work out. Afternoons he would come over to Marcy's house and watch her paint. An easel stood in one corner of her room. She worked wearing an old shirt of her father's over her clothes.

"Why don't you paint in the basement?" Jason had asked. "You wouldn't smell up the room that way."

She laughed. "In the basement? How could I paint in the basement? There's no light."

Jason pointed to her high-intensity lamp.

"Not that kind of light, natural light." And she laughed some more.

Jason asked her to paint a picture of him.

"Oh no," she said. "I couldn't do that, I'm not ready to paint the human figure yet."

That was Marcy all over. She never said anything straight out; she didn't say, I'm not ready to paint people or, there's not enough light in the basement. It had to be "the human figure" or "natural light."

She asked Jason one day if she could watch him working out when his hand had healed.

The idea struck Jason as strange. "The weight room's just for guys," he said.

"I don't want to lift weights, I just want to draw."

"But you can't come into the locker room, Marcy."

"There must be another entrance to the gym somewhere," she said, and the confident look in her eyes convinced Jason that there must be one, even if he'd never seen it.

As soon as the doctor said it was all right for Jason to use his hand, Jason went with Marcy to see Mr. Skinner, the director of the gym, and, sure enough, he took her down a corridor that led to the weight room from the back end of the building. By the time Jason emerged from the locker room, she'd settled herself in a chair and was calmly taking out her pencils. Owen made a crack or two about her, but the sight of her opening a large sketch pad sobered him.

"Don't watch me," she said to Jason, sharpening a pencil. "Just go about your routine as always."

Jason prepared his weights and began. All the while, her eyes shuttled from him to her sketchbook. He smiled, but her studious glance never faltered. He was conscious of being nearly naked before her. He noticed the other guys watching. After a while she moved her stool and began sketching them, too. Owen beamed with childish delight, struggling to lift a load that was clearly too heavy for him.

They came over to inspect the work at the end of the session. Marcy flipped over the pages, revealing the faceless, roughly drawn figures.

"That ain't me," Owen quickly protested.

"I wasn't drawing a picture of you," Marcy said, reddening. "I was just making some studies." She was about to slap the sketch pad shut, but Jason inserted his finger into it.

"Where's the . . . the study you made of me?"

Her face softened, pleased that he'd used the correct terminology. She opened to pages bearing heavy, black slashes and half-circles—muscles?—attempted several times, and looking like eclipsed moons. Jason tried to find himself on the paper. He was aware of being alone with her, of her nearness, and of the energy coiled in his bare arms.

"Marcy," he said, kissing her.

She let out a whimper of surprise, but didn't resist him as before. The sketchbook jabbed Jason in the belly, but when he tried to push it away he found that Marcy held it tight.

"Closing time!"

Mr. Skinner's voice boomed across the room. They pulled apart; the sketch pad hit the floor with an accusatory thwap.

3

It was almost ten-thirty in the evening. Cee woke from a nap she hadn't intended to take, and gulped down a thick potion of hot water and instant coffee as she zipped herself into her uniform smock. She dumped a hairbrush, an orange, and *Martha Quest* into her shoulder bag, threw on her parka, and ran. Her clogs pummeled the wooden steps. She still wasn't used to her new routine. She'd become a working woman, a career girl, as people used to say, which brought to mind images of pert young women in skirts and sweaters and heels. She couldn't remember the last time she'd worn a skirt. And heels! Clop, clop went her clogs. Don, her landlord and the owner of the grocery downstairs, would no doubt make some wiseass remark about the charge of the light brigade the next time she went in for her Old Golds. She'd mention his revving up his Harley-Davidson in front of her windows at nine o'clock on a Saturday morning.

She caught a glimpse of herself in the mirror. Good thing she had her brush along, and she could use some blush, too. Durkin, her head nurse, had suggested a bit of mascara and pencil for her. "You have such pretty eyes," she'd said. Cee was suspicious: People frequently complimented fat women on their eyes. She wanted to please Durkin so she jostled among the high school girls in Discount Drug for liner, mascara, and eyebrow pencil.

"Hey, look! It's Lady Madonna."

Don's rednecky friends, cowboy boots, leather jackets, and all, headed into the store, their clubhouse. "Isn't it past your bedtime, boys?" she shot back without stopping. Drugs had turned them into fossils at the age of twenty-five. Victor, a former member of this charmed circle, had showed up for work one day at Bethlehem stoned out of his mind on bad dope and fallen into a vat of molten steel.

The night sky shone as if lacquered. The frame houses on the block, set snugly behind hedges, might have lined the lane of an English town. Was that why the nearby streets were named Fairfax, Middlesex, and Bedford? Cee loved the three small rooms Joel had bequeathed to her, a welcome relief from the dorm's cinderblock corridors straight out of *1984*. A cold wind whipped up from under the viaduct, carrying with it the flat smell of dirty snow. Railroad tracks scored the city, but in her two years of living in Buffalo Cee had never seen a single train. At night, though, just before the ten o'clock news, she heard them, ghosts of the city's past, lumbering by, a hundred cars at a time, like a string of escaped slaves headed for Canada.

Caffeine had begun rattling her bones. Time to play Find the Car, she thought, scanning the street for Ruby, her newly purchased but not-completely-paid-for used burgundy Karmann Ghia. Ruby was cramped like most foreign cars, and it took muscles of iron to turn the wheel. But even if a Karmann Ghia was only a souped-up VW, it was better than one of her father's clunky Pontiacs. ("I'd never drive anything but a General Motors car," her father said, fond of formulating such principles.) How utterly wonderful it was to have a car! It smoothed out Buffalo's rough edges, and wove it together, potholes and all. She hated walking. Walking tired her, it was slow, and, as she knew from experience, it was something overweight people couldn't do well above a certain speed. Cee would drive to one of the appalling suburban malls instead of shopping at the Tops nearby. And when she had no place in particular to drive to, she went for a drive.

Growing up, she'd watched Yellowbirds and Whisperjets in television commercials taking off on the hour, but her family stayed put. The occasional Sunday visit to relatives had them back home by nightfall, more ordeal than pleasure. Her father firmly believed that drivers who talked behind the wheel caused accidents, so the trips felt like tense, drawn-out elevator rides. Carl was annoyed at not being able to read, since it made him carsick. Jason sat anchored between Cee and Carl, his face glazed with fright anytime he rode in a car after the accident.

Where was Ruby? Cee panicked. Her three-month trial period in the emergency room had just begun, but she'd been late twice already. Durkin said once more meant a that's-all-folks. Which would be bad news. Cee'd managed the impossible by finding a job in one of the unemployment capitals of America. She needed that job, any job. And she liked working in the ER, a miniature hospital set at high speed. She pictured Durkin's cold smile waiting for her that night. If you let me slide this time, Mrs. Durkin, I will never be late again, Cee vowed, like the scrawled lines of a grade-school punishment. I will never be late again, I will never be late again, I will never—

The moment she caught sight of Ruby's dog-profile she ran, her uniform swishing as her thighs rubbed together. The sweat on her face chilled to crystal and cramp chiseled into her chest. She grabbed the door handle as though it were a rescue ring.

"Don't you pull anything now," she warned Ruby as she got in. Lately the starter had been acting up. She turned the ignition key, praying for the engine to turn over. Her nervous grip on the wheel pulled the veins of her wrists taut, and a gristly line of scar tissue rose in relief. Durkin had spotted it on Cee's first night on duty, and Cee had feared the worst. It didn't take a nurse to figure out how a person got such a scar. Would Durkin want someone like that working with her? The engine turned over, she swerved onto Main Street, then drove like a maniac until a red light stopped her at Amherst and Delevan. Cold, blue floodlights shone down on the vast, empty intersection. The surrounding streets were deserted. It felt as though she were about to cross the border of a dictatorship.

Farther downtown she passed a bus lumbering by, nearly empty. An American flag flew from someone's porch. It brought to mind mornings in public school when she stood, sour-mouthed and sleepy, beside her desk, hand folded onto her chest under George Washington's watchful gaze. Without having to look she could describe the house flying that flag: two sturdy wooden stories, a porch that was never used, a front room with a gas fireplace, also never used. It was a house built by people eager for children and responsibility, planted into the dirt of a neighborhood its owner expected to raise a family and grow old in, before he decided to put the place up for sale and flee to the suburbs.

Cee slid into the ER, expecting to fall into Durkin's searchlight glance. But the ER looked almost deserted. A curtain had been pulled around one of the beds, and behind it the controlled rush of voices meant someone was being coded. A moment later Durkin emerged. She glanced at her watch and gave Cee a paper cup holding a syringe imbedded in ice.

"I want it stat," she snarled. "And we'll talk later. Oh, Holy Mother of God, what now?"

Just outside, brakes screeched to a halt down the ramp. The doors to the ER flew open, an ambulance's flashing lights spilled inside.

Cee ran for the elevator, heading for the blood gas lab, still in her coat, bag swinging from her shoulder. When she returned, a man was huddled on the bench in the hall, wearing the rumpled clothes of someone who'd dressed in a hurry. He sprang up when he saw her.

"Is he okay?" he asked.

Cee thought he meant the person they were coding. "I don't know," she said, half because she didn't and half because she wasn't supposed to give out that kind of information.

The ER rang with the shouts of the new admit. "Here," she said, handing Durkin the lab slip.

Durkin took it without looking at her. "What's his story?" she asked Anne, one of the nurses.

"Internal bleeding, gastrointestinal. I saw tracks on his arms, so it might be substance abuse, too. He got some fresh frozen plasma for the bleeding."

"Do we have a place to send him to?"

"No one'll take him without a history," she said.

"Didn't they find any ID on him?"

She looked down. "He was nude."

"Give me a fucking Percodan," the new admit cried.

Durkin shook her head, glanced at the results of the gas, then returned it to Cee. "Chart this. And here." She handed Cee a folder mounted on a clipboard. "Go over to that loudmouth and see if you can get at least the top part from him. But take your coat off first."

Durkin was too impatient to be polite, and Cee had been put off by her until she got used to the ER, which valued speed over manners. The ER nurses respected Durkin, and together they tolerated an invasion of medical students and residents on the unit every six weeks, as a cloister might tolerate a garrison quartered in their midst. Cee had quickly learned to dislike most of these students: arrogant young men—the most recent batch wasn't coed—who were extraordinarily pleased at their status of doctors-to-be.

Cee folded the curtain back. There lay a small, slender man, looking nearly flat under the sheet. His lips were a muddy red. He had dark, syrupy eyes, and his skin was the color of milk. Veins webbed his forearms. He looked like a child asleep on the sofa during a visit to relatives.

"You're no doctor," he snapped, shattering the illusion. "I want a doctor."

"I have to ask you some questions."

"You want to know what's wrong?" he said, glaring at her. "I'll tell you what's wrong. I got an ass full of glass. Anything else you want to know?"

"Your name, address, telephone number—"

He rattled off the information.

"Not so fast," said Cee. "Occupation?"

His eyes narrowed. "Professional queer."

Her pen stopped. "You really want me to write that?"

"You can write whatever the fuck you want—"

The curtain parted. Anne walked in and smiled at Cee. "It's okay. I'll do the rest of it." Cee put the folder down onto the nightstand and left.

"Mr. Gizzi?" she heard Anne begin in a soft voice. Cee held back a chuckle; Anne, quiet and serious, had trained at a Catholic nursing college.

Later, when she processed his report, Cee shuddered to reread it: "William Gizzi, white homosexual male, 23 years old. Profession: unemployed. Place of Residence: 73 Virginia Street, Buffalo, New York 14201. Int. bleeding caused by"—she'd read the next words at least three times—"p. inserting a light bulb into rectum which cracked." She thought of the man's frail, white body, the skin, which had looked soft enough for a fingernail to scrape, then imagined darts of glass imbedded in the watery tissue of his—she couldn't believe that someone would actually do that. Under "Person(s) to notify in case of emergency," Stanley MacIntyre had been written.

The man sitting in the hall? She got up and peeked out through the swinging door. He was still there, hunched over, his face buried in his hands. Gizzi had quieted down, but his cries began anew when the residents and medical students began working on him.

Cee was kept busy until her break, all the while fearing Durkin's finger crooked to summon her to the back room, where she'd hear the fatal words of dismissal. Just before her break, one of the medical students who'd come from Gizzi's bed made a joke about a sixty-watt dildo. He saw Cee looking his way and and winked at her.

"What the hell is that supposed to mean?" she asked, surprised at her own reaction. Perhaps it was the wink, which seemed to say, "You and me, we're normal, but him . . ."

Durkin appeared. The medical student gave a guilty shrug and hurried away.

"Don't let any of those turkeys get to you, okay?" she said, then leaned closer. "You don't know him, do you?" she asked, nodding toward Gizzi's bed.

Cee shook her head.

Durkin looked relieved. "Poor frigging junkie," she said.

Before going on her break, Cee peeked in at him again. He'd been given a shot for pain; now he slept. A second pack of fresh frozen plasma hung somberly above his bed. Quiet, he looked like a child once more.

"Where are you going?" Durkin asked, as Cee was about to leave through the ER ramp.

"Just to the corner and back."

"Be careful. We don't want to lose you." Then she added, "We're short tonight," and winked.

The brightly lit hospital parking lot looked like a military installation. There wasn't a soul to be seen. People didn't go for evening strolls in Buffalo as they did in movie musicals, where lovers took a turn through the park and wound up dancing on the benches. (Only in *West Side Story* did the dancers get jumped just like real life.) Buffalo had been built along a lake, a river, and a canal, eager for commerce, but the waterways had been abandoned for a windy moat of expressways, which she heard as a faint, persistent rustle of traffic.

Cee checked her watch. Ten minutes left. She'd remembered the night of Jason's accident. She'd been eleven years old. She went to the hospital straight from school and stayed until visiting hours were over. Her father had already left. Jason lay in the relentless sleep of a coma. Oxygen hissed through the nasal canula like a drug responsible for his stupor. His lips were gently parted, as if waiting for a kiss. She and her mother had gone for a walk. The giant hospital building hummed beside them. Their steps seemed to measure the time remaining until Jason's verdict would be delivered: death, or some unmendable corruption of life.

"What a beautiful child Jason was," her mother said. "His skin, his hair, even softer than yours. A very beautiful child. We hadn't planned on him. He was so different from the two of you. Sometimes he didn't seem like my child at all. He came at a time of life when things had begun . . . slipping away from me. Your father was never an easy man to love and I was never very . . . passionate. Jason was so amazed at being alive. After he was born, something disappeared between your father and I, as if Jason had taken it with him."

A broken bottle lay on the curb, its ragged crown glittering in the streetlight. Cee thought of Gizzi and shivered. She turned back. Just before reaching the emergency ramp she heard a scream—a woman's scream, shrill with terror. It seemed to come from just beyond the parking lot.

Cee ran into the ER to tell Durkin and asked whether they should report it to the police.

Durkin shook her head and gave Cee's shoulder a good-natured pat. "It wouldn't make a damn bit of difference. That neighborhood's full of screams just like that one," she said.

SEVERAL NIGHTS LATER, on the way back from her break she went to pick up a chart from a station in the new wing.

"Hey, aren't you the number from the ER?" a voice behind her said.

William Gizzi sat on the couch in the lounge under a cloud of cigarette smoke, thumbing through a magazine. The gown sheathed the bony packet of his body loosely. His limbs bent at sharp angles; he looked collapsible. "If I knew company was coming I would have changed into something more festive."

Cee glanced at her watch. The ER was slow that night. Just a couple of minutes, she told herself. She sat down and took out her cigarettes. "How are you?" she asked.

He squirmed in his seat. "It's still a little hard to get any eggs to hatch. Mind if I—" He motioned to her pack. "I don't usually approach strange women for cigarettes but I've already filched two smokes from the night nurse, which I shouldn't have, since cigarettes don't grow on trees, well, they *do*, in a way, but the poor girl has a young child to support because she was once foolish and in love—"

"I'm Cee," she said.

"Pleased to meet you. I'm Billy."

"I know. The professional queer." Her eyes fell on his lilac-colored house shoes, the upholstered-looking kind her grandmother wore.

"What do you think?" he said, lifting one foot up, exposing a length of white, hairless shin. "They were a present—"

"From a Stanley MacIntyre, by any chance?"

He wagged an accusing finger at her. "You are one clever little girl."

He had the high, penetrating voice of a cartoon mouse, flattened by the local twang ("Buffalo born and bled," he would tell her later). She'd known men like him in her high school, or at least she'd known of them. Everyone had; boys like Billy weren't allowed to escape notice. Tiny Fred Marks, for instance, with his china-doll face, whispery voice, and feathery hands. Or Andrew Smits, with his headful of teased hair and tight pants like a Caucasian Little Richard.

Billy yawned. "I am absurdly tired. But I can't sleep."

"How come you don't ask for something?"

"Then I would have missed your visit. And that would have been a pity. Well, actually, they did give me something. But it didn't work. I've always been this way. I come from a long line of insomniacs. They say insomnia is a sign of deep spiritual conflict." He accented "spiritual" on the second syllable.

"What is that supposed to mean?"

"It means I'm the nervous type."

She rose to go.

"I hope to be receiving visitors for as long as I'm here," he said, extracting another cigarette from her pack.

She gave him a light. "I can see why."

"I WENT TO Canisius College for a while," Billy was saying the next time she dropped in on him. "It's where all good repressed Catholic boys go."

Billy had spent his days ferrying from the college chapel to the college library toilet and back to the chapel—the first to assuage his spirit, the second his glands, and the third his conscience. He claimed that theology majors were always the best: so terribly ardent and twisted with guilt, staring straight ahead, stoic as saints on a pyre, while Billy undid their zippers.

He dropped out and waitered at the Spain but was fired for throwing water in a customer's face. ("For effect, a very Noel Cowardy thing to do.") He tutored a ninth-grader in math until the boy's mother returned home unexpectedly to find them both with their pants down. ("She didn't go for my line about me being the school nurse.") The mother was ready to press charges, until the father appeared, took one look at Billy, with whom he'd tricked the week before, slipped him a fifty-dollar bill, and told him to get his little butt out of that house.

One day, visiting him after her shift was over, Cee asked about the light bulb.

"Oh, that. Let's not get into that."

"I'm curious to know why a person, why someone would—"

"Why? Why?" He threw his hand up in the air. "For love, of course. Why else? Do you think it was *fun?*"

"You said you were a professional queer. Maybe the sign of true professionals is that they wing things like that."

Billy clucked his tongue. "Even professional queers fall in love."

"I would have thought that was something for amateurs."

"You are indeed the clever girl I took you for. And because you are,

I'll do what I rarely find it necessary to do: give a straight answer. But first I must tell you about the obscure object of my desire, Stanley MacIntyre, age thirty-nine, married, father of two wonderful children, a boy, Seth, thirteen, and a girl, Anita, eleven, place of residence, Scarborough, Province of Ontario, Dominion of Canada. We have what may be called an intimate relationship. I have a weakness for married men just slipping past their prime. Call it my need for a father figure. Owing to the transient nature of most homosexual relationships, I presumed that Stanley was destined for a short shelf life. We met only when he came to Buffalo on business. I was interested, but I kept my dance card open. Then one day Stanley brought a little something for us over the border." He took a toke from an imaginary joint. "Now hash makes me, how shall I put it, romantic. Loosens up the muscles, if you know what I mean. And we smoked our way through all of it. That night sealed my fate. And, if I am any judge of human character," he said with gravity, "his as well."

"What's a businessman doing smoking hash?"

"The same thing he's doing getting off watching a queen like me model my newest Salvation Army frock. I might be his worst fear but I'm also his best fantasy. He'd sell his mother to have the nerve to walk down Allen Street in an A-line, as I have been known to do. It's that classic dilemma: He's queer, but instead of sitting back, spreading his legs, and enjoying it, he marries—a *woman*—and reproduces. His evil urges remain, of course, but he's too scared to indulge them on home turf, so he crosses the longest unguarded border in the world to commit sodomy."

"What does he do for a living?"

Billy lowered his eyes and shook his head. "The boy sells . . . insulation. Building insulation."

"He's really married? I mean, you said he and you—"

"If I had a chin for every queer with a wife and kids, I could sing Wagner. He won't kiss me, of course. That would be too faggy, no no nonononno*no!* When we fuck it's in the dark—and with the TV on. He says it relaxes him and makes him feel at home, so you can imagine what sex with wifey is like."

"But the light bulb—"

"I'm getting to that. We were in bed one night—he always rents a room at the Towne House, whose decor makes my mother's living room look tasteful. We have this routine. We shower. Separately, of course. When we're both squeaky clean, he shuts out the lights, switches on the TV, turns it up loud, and we slip under the covers. I'm in my birthday suit, he's in his pajamas. Pajamas! Pa*ja*mas! Checks, plaids, stripes, fleurs-de-fucking-lis—he has them all. With the exception of rubber sheets, is there anything less hot than pajamas?

"We smoke some hash. Then he starts talking shop. Fiberglass insulation versus the new ecological material coming onto the market. How the asbestos industry is hurting. Next he starts in about his little boy pitching a no-hitter in the neighborhood softball league. Funny, I thought Canadians played soccer, like the English. Anyway, soon I start feeling his leg sliding up against mine. He does it very discreetly, as though someone else were in the room who might notice. He goes right on talking and makes like even he doesn't notice. Most important, I'm supposed to make like I don't notice, either. Suddenly, somewhere in between fiberglass and softball, he pulls my face down to his crotch. I blow him and get him hard, he throws me over on my stomach, stuffs his dick up my ass, and pumps up and down until he comes. I know when he's about to come because he reaches for the remote control to make the TV louder to cover his heavy breathing."

Cee looked to see if the secretary was listening.

"He's still new at the game, you see, which lends a certain deathless passion to it all. Me, I've known what I wanted since I was fifteen and spent the evenings of my middle teen years in the parking lot behind the Greyhound bus station getting it. There I encountered a veritable procession of Stanleys, each one behind the wheel of a Ford or other fine car, beer bellies under their polyester shirts like sausage in casing. I'd sidle up to one, he'd roll down his window and come up with something scintillating like, 'What's a kid your age doing up so late?' or, from those for whom gas prices were no object, 'Feel like going for a ride?'"

"But the light bulb?"

"Yes, yes, of course, dear. But you really you won't be able to appreciate it without a little background. So, where was I? Oh yes. The Greyhound parking lot. I met two types of men: the throwers and the sitters. The throwers threw themselves at me. Their lips and tongues felt like a plate of noodles in my face. They'd grab my dick, do one thing or the other with it, then before you could say Peter Pan, they'd spray and make haste for the Kleenex. I was lucky to get a piece of the action at all. The sitters, now, they sat. Sort of like Lincoln up there in the memorial. They opened their legs and, child labor laws or no, they expected me to work. I should add that, as a rule I wasn't doing this for the money, but when someone offered to pay, don't think I refused, like a Boy Scout doing a good turn."

"Did it make you feel funny to take money?"

"Of course not. I was performing a valuable public service. Their wives would have been grateful to me if they knew I was satisfying their husbands' filthy urges so that they wouldn't have to get their own—uh—hands dirty. I relieved the stress of some of the leading figures in the local business and political community. They should have installed me in the bathroom of the Buffalo chamber of commerce, with a secretary to make appointments."

"I guess I'm not going to find out about the light bulb after all," Cee said.

"Wait, I just about to come to that. Now Stanley and I have been seeing each other for almost a year. But what have I gotten from him? Do I get to hear words of love, so soft and tender? Does he tell me he loves me? No. Does he as much as hint at his affection for me? Also no. Instead I get to hear about insulation. So the other night in the motel I decided to teach the Royal Canadian Mountie a lesson. I waited until he began reaching for the remote control, when his passion was about to reach its mighty peak. Then I uncoupled myself and *voilà*, coitus interruptus. I switched on the light as his confused member sank behind the cheerful stripes of his pajama bottoms.

"He was about to protest but I cut him off. 'The only thing I want to hear from you is that you love me,' I told him. He looked at me as though I had just read his death sentence. 'You heard me,' I said. He asked what had gotten into me all of a sudden. 'All of a sudden?' I said. 'Do you call a year all of a sudden?' He made for the bathroom but I told him to stay put. 'You never even look at me when we screw,' I said. 'Why not? Because you're ashamed, aren't you? It grosses you out that you're queerer than a three-dollar bill. But y'are, Blanche, y'are.'

"You should have seen the look on well-bred Stanley MacIntyre's face! He'd motored down for his weekly orgasm and clearly hadn't counted on a day of reckoning. 'I'm still waiting to hear what you have to say,' I told him. 'If I hear nothing from you I will be forced to do something drastic.' I actually didn't know what I would do, I figured I'd just scare him. When he began getting dressed I knew I had to put up or shut up. I was about to grab the lamp and throw it at him. Instead something—call it divine inspiration—made me unscrew the bulb. It was hot. I juggled it back and forth. He got scared and stopped dressing. 'What are you doing?' he said. I turned myself around, crouched down into doggy position, my ass facing him. I spread my legs and started bringing those sixty watts up to my moneymaker. The narrow end in first, of course.

"Stanley started shouting in that wonderfully clear Canadian English of his, 'If you don't stop I'm going to run out of here, and you can do what you want.' I brought the hot tip of the bulb closer until it seared my skin. Then I gritted my teeth and began easing it in. He looked away. 'What's the matter,' I said. 'Can't take a little kinkiness?' That bulb was already in past the metal part. He begged for me to stop. 'I will,' I said, 'but only on one condition and you know what that is.' 'You're only doing this because you're high,' he said. 'Wrong,' I said. 'Why do I have to be crazy or stoned to want to hear that you love me? We've been coming to this motel room for a year, and every time we fuck you talk about insulation. I don't want to hear about insulation. I don't want to hear about your wonderful little son or your wonderful little wife and her wonderful zinnias growing in her garden. I want you to tell me you love me, goddamn it! Now go on! Tell me! And if you don't I'm going to make it so you won't be able to fuck me ever again. What do you think of that? I'm going to screw this bulb into my socket until it blows a fuse!' 'Billy,' he said, 'please stop.' 'Say it, Stanley,' I told him, 'say it!' But he didn't. I closed my eyes, said a Hail Mary, and shoved that fucker in hard. I got it in almost half way before it—"

"Okay, okay," Cee said. "That's enough." She reached for another cigarette, and offered him one. For a minute or so they sat smoking in silence. She was sure that the floor secretary had overheard him. She sensed that Billy had wanted her to.

"Do you really love Stanley?" she asked at last.

"Love," Billy said, with a trace of bitterness. "Yeah I love him. Otherwise I wouldn't put up with such a closet case." He thought for a moment. "Maybe that's what attracts me to him."

"Has he come to visit you here?"

Billy pointed to the house shoes. "To bring me these. I could have cried when I saw him. You must understand what a big step this is for him, being in public with me and risking a promising future in insulation. As it is, our names are linked for all eternity in the records of the Buffalo Police Department, since his name's on the report."

A few days later Cee went up to Billy's floor and discovered that he'd been discharged.

"Since yesterday," the floor secretary told her, somewhat coldly, as though glad that he was gone.

He didn't even have the decency to let me know, she thought, heading for the elevator. He'd also wormed five bucks out of her the last time she'd visited him. God, she hated moochers. She punched the elevator button. Just before the doors opened she glanced back at the sofa in the lounge as though hoping that Billy might have materialized by then.

4

*T*wo weeks later, Billy showed up at the ER in the middle of Cee's shift.

Durkin recognized him immediately. "How's your love life, dearie?" she asked.

"What are you doing here?" Cee whispered, feeling her face redden.

"I'm the new gynecologist."

His good humor was hard to take. "Why in hell didn't you let me know you were going to be discharged?"

"They didn't give me any advance notice. As soon as I told them I could shit okay they booted me out." Dressed in street clothes instead of shapeless hospital garb he looked springy as a boxer.

"I should get back to work," Cee said.

"Oh yeah? It looks pretty quiet around here." His voice carried through the entire unit. "Let's go out and play sometime. What are you doing later?"

"I work until seven."

"I'll meet you a quarter after, in the Dog House."

After Billy left, Cee knew Durkin could be depended on to make some commentary.

"I'm going to central supply to pick up some more charge slips," Cee announced, springing up from her chair.

Billy didn't show. Cee was livid. But a week or so later, after work she found him waiting in the parking lot.

"Surprise!" Billy said.

"Jesus, you scared me."

He wore a baseball cap and a bomber jacket opened to a T-shirt printed with "Buffalo, City of No Illusions." In the bluish morning light his eyes appeared especially dark under their thick ridge of brow.

He went to take her shopping bag. "Carry your books?"

"Know what I hate more than anything? Unreliability. It makes me feel as if I'm being taken advantage of. And by the way, where's the five dollars I loaned you?"

To her surprise he fumbled in his pocket and produced a crumpled bill.

She took it from him and started toward the car.

"Let's go for a ride," he said.

"I'm not in the mood for excursions. I've had a very rough night." She unlocked the car door and got in. He stood on the other side, the message on his T-shirt pressed against the window. Why did she think he was teasing her? she thought, thrusting her key into the ignition, determined to drive away. Then she stalled.

There was a knock on the glass. Billy held up the shopping bag.

She leaned over and opened the window.

"I want you to know I got up early especially because of you," he said, handing her the bag.

"And I want *you* to know I felt like an idiot asking the floor secretary where you were, waiting for you at the Dog House, and then being disappointed when you didn't come."

"Will you give me a lift anyway?"

She gave a resigned sigh and opened the door. Soon they were on the thruway, headed north. "You know my take on you so far? I think you've gotten used to sponging off people and making sure they don't catch up with you. You've forgotten how it is to be with someone just because you like them. I didn't have to come up and visit you all those times, you know."

"I know—"

"And you didn't have to tell me you were going to meet me if you knew you weren't going to—"

"I forgot," he said meekly.

"It sucks that you forgot."

He held up an instructive finger. "I feel compelled to inform you that the use of the word 'suck' in that context is homophobic—"

"Fuck you!"

"How come you're so worked up?"

"Let's just say that I've become a little sensitive about people I thought were half-decent suddenly acting shitty to me."

"I only stood you up once. One itty-bitty time." He shot her a hopeful smile.

"Did you understand what I just said to you?"

"Yes, ma'am." He fidgeted in his seat. "That's some mean traffic in the other lane. Imagine, even Buffalo has a rush hour."

"By the way," she said, softening. "Is everything okay with you? Down there, I mean."

"It only hurts when I cry, I mean, when I shit. No, really, I made a remarkable recovery. The docs said I had a deep fissure but that it would heal. They used me as an audiovisual aid. They took me to this room, made me lie stomach-down on what looked like a big sled. Next thing I knew they were cranking my head down and my ass up to get a bird's-eye view. I overheard one saying that I had no business taking up space in a hospital." He paused. "One thing's for certain: I won't be able to engage in anal intercourse for a while. I can't wait to tell Stanley."

"You mean you haven't seen him since you were in the hospital?"

Billy shook his head.

"One of the nurse's aides asked me if you were my boyfriend."

"Did you tell her I was?"

"No."

"Why not? You should have. These people need to be shook up every so often. It keeps them from being too pleased with themselves."

"What do you mean, 'These people'?"

"Breeders."

Cee had to think for a moment before she realized what he meant. "I'm a breeder, too, Billy."

He grinned slyly. "Are you sure? You ever done it with a girl?"

Cee swallowed.

"But I'll bet you've done it with a boy, heh, heh."

"I don't think it's any of your business—"

"So how do you know for sure you're a genuine one-hundred-percent hetero-sexual? Maybe deep down inside of you there's a bull dyke waiting to be born." His eyes widened. "Unless you're chicken—"

She swerved off the highway at the next exit, terminating the conversation with a high-pitched shriek of rubber. "I think I need some coffee. Where the hell are we?"

"In Tonawanda," Billy said, grabbing the arm rest. "Why'd you turn off like that?"

"Because I goddamn wanted to!"

They found a diner and pulled in. It was painfully cheerful. The menus were as large as choir folios, in oversized type that seemed to be for the marginally literate. Their placemats were printed with a little quiz about Buffalo: something to keep kids occupied until their junior portions came.

"Isn't it wonderfully down-home here?" Billy said.

She could see why Billy liked it; the diner was a parody of itself. He seemed to like parodies. Wasn't that why he'd been so happy to get those house shoes, why he was dressed like the all-American boy, bomber jacket, baseball cap, and all? Cee held up the menu so that it blocked him from view. She was beginning to regret this outing. The conversation in the car had left her feeling taunted. Billy obviously divvied up the world into two camps, one straight, one not. Although he claimed to hate the doctors for what they thought of him, Cee sensed that Billy actually relished their disapproval.

The waitress appeared, a pretty girl with a bright, singing voice. "What'll it be, gang?"

"French toast and sausages for me," said Billy. "Wait." He leaned over to Cee. "You paying?"

Cee gave him an exasperated look.

"Better make that just coffee."

"Me too," said Cee.

"Something wrong?" said Billy after the waitress had left. "You're frowning."

"Am I paying?" she muttered, shaking her head as she lit a cigarette.

Billy was about to reach over to her pack of cigarettes but didn't.

"Let's see if you can answer this," he said, reading from the placemat. "Which American president was assassinated in Buffalo?"

"You don't have to entertain me."

"I don't think I am." He sighed. "Maybe it was a mistake for me to come to see you," he said, pushing away the placemat. "Anyway, the answer is William McKinley."

She let her forehead rest against her hand. "Tonight they brought a woman into the ER who'd been raped," she said. "She couldn't have been more than twenty; a tiny, tiny woman. When they rolled her in on the cart, her eyes were open wide, as if she was still watching it happen. She'd been raped more than once, probably by more than one man. Then she'd been knifed. You would assume that she'd been knifed afterward; who'd want to fuck a woman covered with blood, right? But surprise, she'd been raped before and after. And, for all I know, during. So why did they knife her? They'd already gotten what they wanted from her."

The waitress appeared with cups and a carafe of coffee. "Here you go, guys," she said, pouring. She tore off the check and set it down with a smile. "Have a nice day."

Cee opened a packet of Sweet'N Low. "I'll tell you why. Because they hated her. Men hate women. They force them into being pigs, and then they hate them for it. If the woman refuses to be a pig, men hate her for that too. If a woman happens to get off on being a pig, men hate her even more. The cops found the woman with her clothing on; her pants were pulled down just enough to get at her. It wouldn't have mattered if she was the ugliest woman in the world. She wasn't more than a hole for them to stick their pricks into.

"The night they brought you in, I went outside for a walk during my break and I heard a woman's scream. Who knows what happened to her? She didn't even make it to the hospital." She drank her coffee. "I think I could kill a man if I knew he'd raped a woman."

They drove back to Buffalo.

"You have a lot of nerve getting on my case about who I sleep with," Cee said. "It didn't matter to those rapists what that woman did in bed, for instance."

"Whoa, horsie! Are you trying to make a comparison between me and them?"

"You have no right to dictate the terms of anyone's sexuality."

"Who was dictating? I was just fact-finding."

"You were trying to get my goat."

"A little."

"Well, don't. Not after I've had a night like the one I had." She turned off the highway.

"Hey, why'd you do that? We could have kept going straight."

"I thought this was—oh, shit. Where are we now?"

"On 198."

"I'll get off at Main."

But they were already past that exit.

"You might as well just take 33 to the end now," Billy said.

"You made me miss my turnoff!"

"Well you gotta give me credit. I don't provoke anyone half-assed."

It was almost nine. The cars in their lane had slowed to a crawl; they'd joined the traffic headed for the city. The band of cars ahead gleamed like a flow of quicksilver.

"Just what I need," Cee said. "I'm so tired I can hardly keep my eyes open."

The roadway had dipped below the level of the street. Up on either side, houses clung to the rim.

"Before they built this highway there was a big green park in the middle of the street. It was so pretty, people used to have their weddings in it. I grew up around here."

"Where?"

"There," he said, pointing. "In that nondescript white house with the uninspired forest green trim, indiscernible from all the others."

She yanked the wheel, the car lurched to the right, they drove along the shoulder, and a moment later they were headed up the exit ramp.

"Tell me, do you always drive like you're in a demolition derby?"

"I want to see the Billy Gizzi birthplace."

"Take the next right," he said glumly. "But I'm staying in the car." He shrank down in his seat.

Cee double parked in front of the house. "Where was your room?"

"Right up there." He pointed to a curtained window. "Captain God and my mother slept in the back." Billy stared at the dashboard.

"Who?"

"My father, the retired air force sergeant. Captain God. We rented the upstairs to the Nowaks. Adam Nowak, the son, had a dong like a salami."

"The traffic is so loud."

"Most of these houses are owned by blacks now. They're used to urban inconvenience."

"Did people really have weddings there?" she said, pointing to the highway.

"Sure. My parents, too. I saw pictures. My father was in uniform. I guess there really must be something about a man in a uniform. I can't figure out why my mother would have married him otherwise. Can we go now?" His voice was stiff with discomfort.

"So I gather that you're not crazy about your father, right?"

"Maybe because he wasn't too crazy about me. Maybe because he treated me like an aberration and kicked me out of the house in the middle of the afternoon. It wasn't quite as dramatic as kicking me out in the middle of the night, I grant you, but it served its purpose." His voice had begun to thicken. "I was eighteen, in my first and last year at Canisius. My mother discovered me in a compromising position with the television repairman in that bedroom up there. I begged Mom not to report the incident to Captain God. She fretted about it for a week before breaking under the weight of her Catholic conscience. The sight of her son, her only son, her only child, on his back with his legs up in the air—like a woman, as she put it—and mounted by a brute of a repairman, the same son who'd been a Cub Scout and then a choirboy and who'd worked and saved enough money on his paper route to buy the very same television set the repairman had come to fix, had been too much for her to bear alone, she explained to me tearfully afterward."

"So she told him?"

"She told him, and he booted me out. I tracked down the repairman and stayed with him for a bit, and after that I lived with one of the four Canisius students who dared to live off-campus. Then I met Vincent, an older Negro gentleman who took me under his wing. We lived together in his rooms on Cherry Street which, as you know, is located in the heart of the Negro Quarter. He taught me a simple lesson: There is no reason to let anyone tell you that you don't know what's best for you. So now you've heard the story of the revolt of the father against the son. Can we go now?"

He brooded for the rest of the ride. When they reached Main he said, "That's fine," and opened the door, ready to spring out.

"Hey!" she said, grabbing hold of his jacket.

He turned to her. His face looked weathered.

"Feel like getting together again?"

He shrugged. "Name a place."

"The CPG. Friday at ten."

"Oh, I get it," he said, smiling faintly. "Cultural exchange." The Central Park Grill was a straight bar.

Cee drove home. Who is this strange person, she thought, this confused cat that bit and purred almost at the same time? Something about him appealed to her. But being with him felt like stepping into an open house where she hardly knew what lay in wait behind the stairs.

SINCE THE CPG was not a gay bar, Billy would not ordinarily have gone there, he explained to Cee, somewhat loudly, as they walked in. But, as he conceded, at least the CPG wasn't one of those straight pickup parlors on Elmwood Avenue crammed with Buff State's *jeunesse dorée*. And he was unlikely to run into someone he owed money to. There were several of those, he said.

"Are you so hard up for cash?" she said, after they'd ordered beers.

"For investment capital, you might say."

"What do you invest in?"

"Mornings, I invest in breakfast. Afternoons, lunch. And evenings, supper."

"I guess I should feel honored that you paid me back," Cee said. "Why do you keep borrowing money if you're broke?"

"Because I'm lonely and I want people to call me up. Anyway, the real reason I agreed to meet you here is because of the urinals. They're grottoes, built for a race of giants. One look at them and you'll wish you had a penis, pardon my Freud."

Their beers came. "How do you get by if you're so strapped for funds?" Cee asked.

It was a long story, he said. He finagled monthly SSI checks by putting on a little show in the office. After his stint as a tutor, he delivered lunches to shut-ins, which included an ancient Nazi, several grizzled Chippewa Street ex-prostitutes, and a man who claimed to have been the escort of J. Edgar Hoover. Billy supplemented his income with what he called political economy—shoplifting.

"I hit Stanley up for some of that pretty Canadian money every so often. Vincent used to contribute to the cause, too. Anything else you want to know will have to wait until I return from the little boy's room. Maybe I'll find a frog prince squatting near one of those wonderful urinals."

Being with Billy gave Cee the feeling of being tugged along by a moving vehicle. It was hard for her to imagine him bringing elderly people their meals. It was easier to imagine him chucking them out of their wheelchairs.

"No frogs," he reported, returning. "Merely some girl I once tricked with from Canisius."

"A girl?"

"Well, not a real one, of course."

"I'm not sure how I feel about this 'girl' talk of yours."

"Puh-leeze don't turn on the feminist number. I know that whenever you hear certain words like *girl*, a voice in your head says, 'Not girl, *woman*.' I've heard all that from my dear friend Kal, a real woman just like yourself. It would be one thing if I were a man saying something like that. But I'm not a man."

Cee gave him a give-me-a-break look.

"Do I look like a man to you?"

People at the next table turned around.

"Yes," she said, lowering her voice.

"Well, you're wrong. I'm a fag." He inhaled thick, deliberate drags of his cigarette.

It got quieter.

"You're still a man," Cee said, almost whispering.

"No. I'm a fag."

Cee motioned with her eyes toward the next table.

"Honey, I don't care if they print 'Billy Gizzi Sucks Cock' on the front page of the *Buffalo Evening News*."

"Shut the fuck up," someone yelled.

"Jesus," said Cee, miserable.

"See why I don't like coming to these places? They make me feel like I'm a walking freak show."

"If you didn't go around advertising . . ."

"Why should I hide? I be who I be, as Vincent says."

Cee slumped down with her arms around her beer. "I think you want people to hate you. You do things just so they will."

"You don't have to tell people to hate queers, they do it by themselves, like that guy over there—"

"He just wanted to drink his beer in peace. And frankly, so do I."

"I can go," said Billy.

"Can the poor, put-upon number. Tell me about this Kal."

Billy brightened. "Kal, aka Ms. Katharine Lund, is, as she so picturesquely puts it, a woman-loving woman. We've known each other since she was a man-loving woman. I even lived with the happy couple for a year or two. She was all set to be a respectable, mindless housewife, complete with kidlet, before I helped her opt for Sappho. Now she's going to night school to become a medical technician."

"When do I get to meet her?"

"When you're lucky. She is one very busy girl, working as she does full-time to overthrow the patriarchy." He snubbed out his cigarette. "Say, do you remember when I stood you up that time?" The sting left his voice. "Well, I have a confession to make. I hadn't forgotten about our date at the Dog House. I didn't come on purpose. Actually, I did come. I went there and waited across the street until I saw you turning the corner. But at the last moment I split. I was afraid."

"You were afraid . . . of me?"

He nodded. "Because I like you. And because I thought you liked me. Most people don't. They find me abrasive, obnoxious, belligerent. I get on people's nerves."

"Well you are, and you do."

"Your nerves, too?"

"A little. But I come from a long line of quiet people, so maybe I'm not used to your . . . style yet."

"I didn't think you'd want to see me after I got on your case on the way out to the diner." Billy thought for a moment. "I was being bad on purpose that time. I wanted to see how far I could get before you told me to fuck off."

"You weren't going to get much farther. Tell me, if this is how you act with people you like, how are you otherwise?"

He grinned devilishly. "Less than friendly."

They began seeing each other once a week or so, sometimes at the CPG, sometimes at places Billy referred to as taverns: Lockport dives, the Red Ball in Tonawanda where the piano player sang dirty songs, or dreary neighborhood bars in East Buffalo. Billy would invariably flirt with a local and come close to getting his head handed to him.

"I can't believe you even know these places," Cee said, driving home one night. "I thought you only went to gay bars."

"I go to gay bars to see and be seen by gays. I go to these places to be seen by straights. That's called politics."

He was always surprising her with little gifts, bought or otherwise procured. When Cee announced that she wanted to fix up her apartment, he peeled off layer upon layer of old wallpaper, pulled up the brittle, old linoleum, and carried trash bags of it all downstairs. His strength amazed her. (Ever since she fell in the dorm, Cee's back punished her when she lifted anything heavy.) Slowly, they grew closer. He'd appear at her door with doughnuts from the twenty-four-hour place or wonderfully greasy chicken wings. Late at night, after they'd had a little dope, he'd become quiet and reflective, the way Cee imagined he might have been as a choirboy in robe and stiff black shoes.

He told her about a big fight his mother had had with his father, how she'd thrown clothing into a suitcase, crying and cursing, packed him into the car, and driven off in the middle of the night to his Aunt Ida's in Akron, Ohio. It had been a wild adventure. Billy slept in the car, shivering, since the heater didn't work and his mother had forgotten blankets. He felt like a fugitive on the run from his father; he loved it. But Captain God soon tracked them down. Phone calls went back and forth all during the weekend, Aunt Ida complained about her phone bill, and by Sunday morning they were back on I-90, heading east.

Other nights he talked about Stanley, usually in the form of a monologue, since what could Cee say? Billy would cross-examine himself with the heartlessness of a chief prosecutor. What am I doing with a building insulation salesman who is, truth to tell, neither good-looking nor a great conversationalist? How can I expect him to give up house, sheepdog, and offspring for me, even if I do give such good head...

He told her about his first romance, Lewis Bley, an eighth-grade friend. They'd charge home right after the dismissal bell, barely able to wait until they got to Lewis's room to pull off their school clothes and climb naked over each other. There was Leonard Masten, star of the Bennett High School track team, with muscular legs that begged to be tongued. They'd meet in a far corner of the football field, and Leonard obliged. One afternoon, for no reason Billy could fathom, except that Leonard had grown to like what Billy did a little too much for his own self-image, Leonard arranged to meet Billy as usual and, just as Billy knelt down, he was jumped by a ring of Leonard's friends who punched him silly. Leonard delivered the coup de grace: the kick of a spike-soled track shoe in Billy's face.

"So that's where you got that scar," Cee said, motioning to the little indentation on his left cheek.

"Speaking of scars," he said, pointing to her wrist with a knowing nod. "Cut yourself with your Girl Scout penknife?"

"If you know, then why are you asking?"

Cee felt a tightness in her chest. She'd been careful talking about herself, since anything was putty in Billy's sarcastic hands. The little she'd let out about Carl and Jason she'd phrased with painful care.

Billy noticed her reaction. "Sorry," he said.

One of his favorite exploits was visiting the trucks parked on the wasteland at the foot of Main Street under the Pulaski Skyway. The cabs of the trucks were like little motel rooms, complete with sleeping compartments behind the front seats. Unlike the men at the bus station, the truck drivers didn't make any bones about what they wanted.

"I go to the trucks as a churchgoer might go to mass: for the sake of humility and purification," he explained.

Humility she understood. But purification?

"Sex with strangers leaves you clean," he explained. "It's sex without expectation. It's pure need gratified."

"And you still want that, I mean, even now that you have Stanley?"

Billy laughed. "Did you think I was going to save myself for our wedding night?"

"It sounds so obsessive. It doesn't even sound like fun."

"*Fun?* We're grown-ups. Grown-ups aren't supposed to have fun."

"You're about as grown up as Donald Duck. And sorry for being dumb, but I figured that if you were in love with Stanley, as you claim to be, you wouldn't be interested in anyone else. Or at least not so many others."

"It wasn't interest I was talking about. It's fascination. Most of those truck drivers are part-time mongoloids. For all I know, they might have a Playboy centerfold tacked up on the wall over my head as they mount me. But I need to have someone fuck my brains out or choke me with their cocks to purge myself of years of being told that it's filthy, disgusting, and wrong. Those nights under the skyway might not be made of romance, but they're honest."

"Honest?"

There wasn't time to explain. Billy had just seen a "creditor" sitting at the bar, and they made a hasty exit.

"Which one was he?" Cee asked when they were outside.

"The one all the way at the end with the fringed leather jacket and the lean and hungry look."

On her days off Cee sometimes went to the restaurant of the Statler where Billy had begun working the lunch shift. In his black pants, white shirt, and black bow tie, he looked dressed for a grade school assembly day. He brought her a Bloody Mary, and then she'd watch him taking the orders of businessmen from Toronto or from the downtown office buildings.

"See the man with the thick-rimmed black glasses at the table on your left? I know him from next door," he whispered as he slipped Cee a plate of hors d'oeuvres. Next door meant the bus station.

Cee observed the man. A wedding band shone on his finger. Strands of grey hair were carefully arranged over a pink-speckled dome. When the others at his table talked of their wives, he would no doubt talk of his, she thought. Cee imagined their house in Williamsville, the print of waterfowl above the dining room table, the built-in kitchen. He'd have an excuse for leaving the house later in the evening.

She left feeling some of Billy's anger. She recalled Carl and his friends up at the house lazing on the porch as they analyzed the military-industrial complex or pitted one brand of oppression against the other—women's, Native Americans', the working class's—all the while guzzling sangria and stuffing themselves with organic popcorn. Where had their philosophy ripened? In the suburbs. And Billy's? Under the Pulaski Skyway.

Yet it didn't seem as if Billy wished to be anyone other than who he was. Like the proverbial pearl left after the oyster's irritation, Billy emerged from his tribulations hard and shining. The old Nazi he delivered food to got an undetectable dose of laxative with his chicken salad each day. When someone went after Billy with a knife under the Skyway, and a cop happened by, Billy pressed charges, even though it meant giving his name. He had an onion's worth of layers, each one stung as she peeled it away. And peel she did. The labyrinth of Billy's commentaries, snide remarks, and parodies was a test designed to shake off all but the cleverest, who would then be worthy of his continued attention.

What did a blow job have to do with honesty?

She thought of what Billy did with the light bulb. You couldn't get more honest than that.

CEE FELT LIKE having a snack before heading off to work and went down to Don's. She bought as little there as possible. His prices were outrageous, and most nights two of Don's mangy high school friends held court there. They didn't seem especially close anymore, but Don tolerated them as long as they didn't mooch. There was Curt, blond-haired, short, and broad; his Fu Manchu mustache looked as if he'd pasted it onto his doughy babyface. Luke was his exact opposite, tall, and with a rock musician's thinness. His cheekbones pressed into his sallow face as though it hurt. He showed signs of once having been good-looking, but years of chemically induced nirvana had left a yellow film over his eyes, and they seemed adrift in their own murky sea.

"Don't start that again," Don was saying to Luke as Cee came in. "You know as well as I do why Vic died. He died because he was dumb enough to show up at work tripping out of his mind." He flashed her a look which said, At least someone normal is here now.

"That shows how much you know," Luke said, stabbing the air with his cigarette. "My brother Vic was smoking dope before you even knew which end of a joint to light. He could always hold his dope. He died because someone slipped him bad stuff." He took a swig from his can of beer.

Curt nodded his head in silent agreement, staring down, as though a mourner at Vic's burial.

Cee took a bottle of orange juice from the cooler.

"You have to be crazy to show up at work at a steel plant with a head full of acid," Don said.

"It was the only way to get through a day's work at that place," Curt shouted back.

"You know what I think, Don?" Luke said angrily. "I think you're blaming Vic for what happened. Yeah, that's right," he said, agreeing with himself. "You sound like you're fucking blaming Vic for what fucking happened!"

"The guy fell into a vat of molten steel," Curt said solemnly. "I heard they didn't even try to pull him out."

"Bad acid can fry anybody's brain," Luke said with authority. "And that cocksucker knew it was bad, but he didn't care. He just wanted to get his bucks for it."

No one took themselves as seriously as a head, Cee thought, selecting a pint of Breyer's maple walnut from the frozen food case. How many late-night dope-induced lectures had she heard given by some frowzy prophet who'd landed at the house? Yet although it was hard to take Luke seriously, he had a desperate streak to him that frightened her.

"That cocksucker," echoed Curt like a Greek chorus.

Cee went farther and came to a halt in front of the snack section. Cheese Doodles! God, she hadn't had some of that crap in she didn't know how long. At some point she'd promised herself never to eat things like Cheese Doodles anymore, especially when she was alone; it was depressing and unhealthy. But you only lived once. She reached for the bag, thinking, Here I go, about to consume a million-point-three calories.

"Vic is gone," Don was saying. "No amount of explaining is going to bring him back."

Curt and Luke fell silent, like parishioners hit with a weight of scripture. Cee was conscious of the crinkle the Cheese Doodles bag made as she carried it.

"Maybe he is," Luke said, his voice rising after a dramatic pause. "Maybe he is. But I'll be damned if I let that cocksucker get away with what he did."

"And what happened to Vic is just the tail end of a long line of shit that guy has pulled," added Curt.

Cee realized what she needed to make her picnic complete: chocolate syrup for the ice cream. She'd heat it up and make a pseudo-hot-fudge sundae, yes, indeedy! She passed Curt on his way to take a can of Schaefer beer from the cooler. Up closc he looked like an aged infant.

"You remember the rule, Curt," Don's voiced pursued him from the front of the store. "Pay first, drink later."

"Aw, come on, Don." He winked at Cee.

"Hey!" Don's voice boomed.

Luke pulled out a bill and slapped it on the counter. "Here, for chrissakes!"

Curt returned up front, popped open the beer, and drank. "Remember the time he busted you, down under the Skyway? It must have been a payoff deal. You said the cop car came out of nowhere. When your goddamn dealer busts you, you can't get much lower than that."

Cee was about to head for the counter but stopped. Why did that story sound familiar?

"And then what he and that bitch did to you that night—"

"You don't have to go into it," Luke said.

"But it was pretty nasty. I didn't think people would stoop to anything so low—" He seemed anxious to elaborate.

"Yeah, Curt. I know. So let's drop it."

Curt took another swallow. "Okay. But I'll never forget when you first told me—"

Luke lifted his can and brought it down against the counter with an echoing crack. "I said drop it, you fucking pygmy!"

The store fell silent, except for the crinkle of the Cheese Doodles bag.

Cee made her way to the counter. "Pack of OGs, please," Cee said.

Luke eyed her with annoyance, as though she'd intruded. "I heard you clomping all the way down the street the other night," he said.

She took the bag Don had packed for her. "Well, I guess you have very good hearing," she answered, avoiding Luke's glance.

Upstairs she put on some music—Joel had left her his old record player—lit a cigarette, and made herself a sundae. The men in Don's looked as though they wouldn't be able to keep from falling into a vat of molten steel, with or without the acid. She'd known people in high school who were into the big H. Their eyes roved around, and they were forever fidgeting with their noses and elbows as if to make sure everything was still there.

"Poor frigging junkie," Durkin had said about Billy.

One of the nurses had said she'd seen tracks on Billy's arms. Cee had looked. Maybe there were and maybe there weren't.

5

*H*ALFWAY TO MARCY'S the gas gauge began twitching toward the E. Jason punched the seat in aggravation. He had the paints Marcy asked him to buy. Only one place had them, a tiny store in the mall that took forever to find. He'd promised to drop them off by five. But with a stop for gas he'd be lucky to make it by five-thirty. Marcy had told him not to be late because they ate at six. Marcy's family was the type that always did everything the right way—newspapers in the front hallway on rainy days for wet shoes, the windows opened to air out a room. And they always ate on time. Things sure were different at his house, especially with his mother working at that office. The laundry piled up, and his father put together their meals from cans on nights when his mother worked late.

Jason's fingers tensed around the wheel. The Sunoco wasn't far. If the lines weren't long he'd be in and out fast. The Payless was cheaper, something to consider, when gas went up a nickel every three days. But the Payless was on the other end of town, a good ten minutes there and back. Jason hung a huey, took Riverside to avoid Main, but he wound up hitting the Binghamton traffic anyway.

"Shit!" he shouted, punching the seat once more. He felt the spot on his hand where he'd broken the window.

It had begun to drizzle, a freeze-your-ass-off late February drizzle. The heater had conked out again. He'd fixed it once—faulty contact, no problem. But now there was a leak in the line going out of the radiator and damned if that was even worth doing anything about, considering the engine. What did you expect from a ten-year-old car? But there was no way that Big Bad Walter would spring for a new one. Poor Walter. Mornings he was up early for no good reason except out of habit, drinking coffee alone, sneaking a smoke after his wife left for work. Nights he wound up in front of the TV. He'd ask Jason if he felt like watching with him. Jason had his own set, but okay, throw the dog a bone. God knows why anybody'd want to hire the old fart to build houses, Jason thought, savoring his own maliciousness. Wouldn't get me to live in one of them. Big Bad Walter.

It was his mother who ran the show these days, not his father. It was her idea for Jason to get the car, too. "Give me one good reason why I should do the shopping when I have to work all day and there are two people living in this house who have more time than I do."

The clock on the dash said four fifty-seven.

He hung a left onto Laurel. Great, he thought, as he neared the gas station. The line began three blocks away, a good twenty-minute wait. He hoped to hell they weren't going to pull a pay-the-exact-amount number. All because the A-rabs were cutting off the oil. The government was afraid to attack them because we lost in Vietnam, his father said. The whole world was going to walk over America now, just wait. The needle quivered. Jason doubted whether he'd even make it to the pump. He was hungry. And he had to take a leak something bad.

He opened the bag beside him and looked at the tubes of paint. Prussian blue, cadmium yellow, burnt umber, a dollar-fifty a shot. He unscrewed the lid of one tube. A moist plug of chocolate filled the opening, smelling like turpentine.

You don't have to pretend we're boyfriend and girlfriend.

Marcy hadn't done it with anyone yet; she'd told him one afternoon. She'd spoken very matter-of-factly, as if announcing her college plans. She didn't intend to wait until she married, just until she found someone she liked and trusted. Trust was the most important thing for her.

Jason asked her if she trusted him.

Her answer had confused him. "In a way."

The lights of a car approaching down a side street hit the window of the passenger side. Jason had driven midway into a crossing and was blocking it. Well, let the guy in back of him pull out so this car could get through, he told himself. He sure as hell wasn't going to move and lose his place in line. The oncoming car honked. He gripped the wheel tighter. Someone got out of the other car.

"Hey, man, what you doing there?"

It was a black kid, who looked to be Jason's age. Jason ignored him. The kid went over to the other side. Jason sprang over and punched down the button. He didn't like blacks; they were always pulling a black power number on you, especially the ones with the poodle hair. They made you walk around them in the hall and acted like they were ready to slit your throat if you stepped on their foot by mistake.

The kid rapped on the window. "I'm talking to you, man!"

"Quit banging on my glass."

"You're in my lane." the kid said.

"I'm waiting on line, too."

He leaned over the windshield, directly before Jason's face. "I'm not gonna take your place, man. I got my gas. I just wanna get through, you dig?"

He really thought Jason was going to fall for that.

The guy looked familiar.

"You fucking little—" The guy leaned closer, trying to get a better look at Jason. His face shifted in surprise. "Goddamn!" he said suddenly. "God*damn!*" He ran back to the other car and got in.

In the instant Jason heard the car door slam shut he realized where he'd seen the kid before: at Nina's. Three more guys were getting out of the car and heading his way. Jason jerked the wheel around and lurched into the opposing lane—no one was coming, thank Jesus—hung a huey and tore ass down the road as far as Main Street. The other guys ran back to their car and gave chase. Jason was doing fifty, twenty over the limit, and he knew that if he had to brake he'd skid his ass into Kingdom Come. A silver ball of light seared his rearview mirror: They were right behind him. He reached Main. Good, they wouldn't be able to get him here—too many other cars on the road. Suddenly the light dropped away from his mirror. Had they given up? He considered turning around, but traffic was heavy. He couldn't go toward home—that meant heading back in the same direction he'd just come from. The safest thing would be to drive all the way out of town and then return on route 17. But what if he ran out of gas?

He made it to the end of Main and then almost to the highway entrance. The engine coughed and choked, the car did a little leap and then he began to slow. He pumped at the gas pedal, then floored it over and over again with frenzied stomps of his foot, as though pedaling a bicycle. The car refused to speed up and merely coasted calmly down the ramp. He braked and turned onto the shoulder. What the hell was he going to do now?

A car was coming down the ramp. Maybe someone could tow him back to a gas station. He got out of his car to wave the driver down.

Oh shit!

All four doors opened, and a bunch of guys piled out. There they were! He was trapped, not another person in sight. A sickly wetness had begun seeping down between his legs: He'd peed in his pants. He leapt back into the car and slammed his button down just as the black guys ran up. They went to the front and back of Jason's car and began heaving it up and down, a toy they were ready to flip over.

"Get off my car!"

They didn't stop. Something in the front of the car began to rattle. The engine seemed to be dancing on the trampoline of the block. Jason envisioned the block cracking, the radiator breaking free, the fuel line tearing out. He had to stop them. He got out.

"I said get off my car—"

An arm reached out and dragged him across the road. He was thrown against the freezing wall of earth. The wetness iced between his legs. A black guy pushed in close, his nostrils flaring, his skin gleaming dangerously in the headlight. The others locked in tightly around him.

"My man says you need to get the shit kicked out of you," the guy said in a self-assured tone.

Before Jason could say anything an iron weight of fist filled his stomach, then cracked against his face. Flinty sparks went off. His middle contracted into a painful chunk. He struggled to get away, but he was held fast.

Nina's son was coming up to him, a scared version of the photograph in the living room.

"Punch the gook, Reg," someone was saying. "Punch the fucking gook."

Reg gritted his teeth, trying to get ready. His cheeks shuddered with fear.

"Wait," Jason gasped.

"Come on!" one of the guys shouted.

"Reg—" Jason sputtered.

"Shut up!" Reggie said, almost tearfully.

"Reggie, I'm sorry, please—"

Reggie closed his eyes, hauled back, and slammed Jason in the face.

The ground went watery beneath Jason's feet. Everyone disappeared. He sank down. A little later there were sirens. A police car pulled up; its red light swung above him. A cop hoisted him to his feet. His stomach was bloated with pain. He was shivering.

"What happened?" the cop said.

Jason told him. They towed him to the Payless. He sat in the back of the cop car, imagining that the seat revolved. He kept seeing a light before his eyes that wouldn't go out. His head had begun to buzz.

He tanked three dollars' worth and went to the bathroom, and caught a glimpse of himself in the mirror. He almost looked drunk. His face was ruddy with bruises. A smudge of dirt below his cheekbone marked Reggie's punch and felt hard to the touch. He splashed cold water onto his face to stop the buzz in his head. He got himself a Coke from the machine outside and then suddenly remembered that he still had Marcy's paints. The station clock said almost five-thirty. He decided to drive to Marcy's house anyway.

Halfway up the steps he pulled the shirt out of his pants to cover the pee stain.

"I have something for Marcy," Jason said when her father opened the door. He offered the bag.

"I'll make sure she gets it," he said in a reedy voice. He went to close the door.

"Can I . . . can I just . . . is it okay if I talk to Marcy?"

"She's eating her dinner. I'll tell her you were here."

"Can't I just come in for a minute—"

"You should have arranged to get here earlier, young man."

Jason thought quickly. "It cost four-fifty plus tax." He'd laid out the money for Marcy and had figured to give her the paints as a present.

Her father reached into his pocket. "How's five?"

Jason took the money, and the door was closed. He stared at the bill, then at the shiny brass plate inscribed The Rands. He kicked the door and ran down the steps.

The door lurched back open. "That's right, you'd better run, you hoodlum," Marcy's father bellowed. "And don't come back, either."

Jason jumped into his car and burned rubber pulling out. He drove, hardly knowing where he was headed, feeling light with fear and satisfaction. He drove all the way out toward the state university, enjoying the long stretch of empty road. Slowly, he grew calm.

You don't have to pretend . . .

Jason arrived at an intersection, wondering for a moment where he was. Nothing but trees lined both sides of the road. He drove some more and then recognized his surroundings. Fitch Road. And there to the right . . .

He was about to pull off onto the shoulder as he'd done the night he trailed Richie, but this time he kept on, driving no faster than if he'd been on foot. Gravel split beneath the tires. The line in the middle of the road was cracked like bits of taffy. In the darkness above his headlight beams, the faces of the black guys glowered at him. His insides lit up with rage. "I didn't do what you think," he wanted to tell Reggie.

He pulled over, cut the engine, and got out, feeling fresh stabs of pain all through his body. A breeze buffeted the exposed peak of the bruise on his face. The buzz in his head had condensed to a painful weight. He crossed the road. The greedy mud sucked at his heels. Up ahead, the tops of the houses peaked up sharply, piercing the night.

Let me touch them.
Only if you tell me that I'm pretty.
Yes. Yes you are.
You don't think I'm fat and ugly?

Jason kept on until the houses came into view, black, cold-looking. He walked by each house slowly, as if to make sure all were still there. When he came to the last house he stepped up onto the porch. The soggy wood gave under his weight, the porch sighed. He tried the door, and it opened. The darkness inside was cool and silky, the air heavy with the sour compost of old newspaper. The walls receded like a cave's, marked by a shiny border of empty cans. He took a step, and his foot hit something dense and soft. He reached down to touch: mattress ticking, slippery and cold. The scar on his hand pulsed.

He went back outside, stood on the porch, hearing the slow lap of Davis Lake against the shore. He looked toward the road.

Without her shirt, Cee's whiteness had been blinding in the summer sun. And so soft. He'd kissed its powdery plushness.

Stop, you're tickling me.

He wanted to touch her and kiss her boobies where it was softer than the rest of her. At first she told him he couldn't because it was a bad thing to do, then she'd let him.

Now swear you won't tell anyone about it.

Afterward she told him to leave her alone. He didn't want to. It was fun touching her, poking her, poking in the soft places, the soft, fat places, her two fat water balloons. He wanted to sink his teeth into them, sink his teeth right in—

You creep! You stupid, shitty creep, I hate you!

She went for her shirt, but he snatched it away and made off with it.

You little creep, give me my shirt back! Give it back, do you hear?

But he was faster. The shirt trailed him like a wild bird. He ran and ran. Cee puffed and snorted behind him, tripping over the rocks and branches, trying to cover herself with her hands.

Jason, come back. Jason, don't go any farther!

He didn't listen. The bushes fled by, the bird flapped higher. He'd reached the road but couldn't stop. Skidding tires seared the road and he was hit by a hard noise that silenced everything.

There was a loud crack. Jason fell forward with a frightened cry onto the cold ground. He'd been holding tight to the wooden railing, and it had snapped.

He picked himself up and made his way back to the car. Each step tugged at the pain in his stomach. His parents were going to give him hell for coming home so late. Marcy's father would probably forbid her to see him again. By the time he was back behind the wheel, the buzz in his head had grown to a terrible noise.

6

"This is where I went to night school," Billy explained, opening the door to the windowless bar near the corner of Main and Allen.

The walls of Hadrian's Villa were papered with red and flaked gold. Lights with dusty, fringed shades hung from the ceiling, and dozens of framed head shots covered one wall like tile. The place made Cee think of a damaged jewel box, forgotten in someone's basement. The men at the bar met Billy with an appraising gaze as he came in; the bartender's nod implied acquaintance. Cee watched Billy's eyes darting back and forth among the customers, taking roll call. For those first few moments he seemed distant from her, as though he'd answer in a foreign language if she spoke to him.

"The Buffalo queer with a sense of history and tradition will go here and nowhere else," Billy explained. "The nouveau homo and the tourist frequent the Hibachi Room."

Cee found herself examining the men for what might betray their otherness. Hadrian's offered the usual assortment of fine-boned effeminate men she could have picked out on the street. Their faces looked so well cared for, their glance calculated and vaguely distant. What interested her were the average-looking men who might be loan officers or shoe salesmen, the Stanleys.

"Sew her up," a man wailed over the hammer of the disco music. He dug the heel of hand into his forehead with exaggerated distress. His sparse, threadlike hair had been teased up into a cloudy Afro, and his shiny, patterned shirt exposed a scraggly mat of greying chest hair. The glitter ball revolving above pricked his face with an unflattering sparkle. He made Cee think of an ill-tempered widow.

"What's his problem?" she asked.

"You mean the girl with the big mouth who could play 'The Heartbreak of Psoriasis'?"

"For God sakes, will someone please sew her up already!" the man persisted.

"Wayne, why don't you find somewhere else to wag your tongue, like an electric socket." Billy turned to the bar. "Two vodkas, Herbert."

"Would you mind telling me what he's talking about?" Cee said.

"If you insist: Knowing him, as I unfortunately do, what he probably wants sewn up is your . . . how shall I put it . . . genitalia. Only metaphorically, of course. He's one of those fags who doesn't approve of straight people patronizing gay bars. He's overreacting, of course. His glands won't permit him to do otherwise. But he does have a point." Their drinks came. "Here, take your medicine like a good girl. Herbert, say hello to my long lost cousin Janina from Czestochowa. She speaks not a word of English."

Cee glared at him.

"Chin chin!" Billy said.

Cee took a hefty swallow. "You talk about straight people as though they were termites."

"An interesting analogy."

"I wouldn't care if gays came into a straight bar."

"Well, that's very white of you. But first of all, there are others who would, especially if the queers didn't sit nicely with their hands folded in their laps but committed that most cardinal of sins, what my mother refers to as flaunting. Do you know what flaunting consists of? A queer acting like a queer. It's what you accused me of that night in the CPG."

"Well you were—"

"And second of all, Janina, straights can go anywhere. They can hold hands at a goddamn Howard Johnson's. They may osculate moistly in your everyday five-and-dime. And they *do*. So why should they come to a fag bar?"

"Don't look now, but here he comes again."

The man sidled over to Cee. "This is no place for women, only girls."

"Do relax, dearie," Billy said to him. "You've made your point. Now continue on your orbit."

The man kept glaring at her.

Billy groaned. "You're obviously dying to be introduced. Cee, this is Wayne Falk, the man who would be Viveca Lindfors. The only thing in Hadrian's that's been here longer than Wayne is the wallpaper. And Wayne, this is Miss Celia Gajewski of the Thompson City Gajewskis."

"Pleased to meet you, Miss Gajewski." His hand floated up for her to kiss. Most of his fat, wrinkled fingers bore rings.

Cee looked away.

"Well, well," he sniffed.

"Whew," said Billy. "For a moment there I was afraid you'd whip out your cock ring, too, and wouldn't that have been embarrassing for all concerned."

"As for you, you Sicilian runt," Wayne said, his leathery lips curled with derision, "I remember when the mere sight of a bus schedule was enough to make you drool." He returned to Cee. "I do hope you don't think badly of me. But surely you must know what kind of place this is. A temple of male perversion, a homo watering hole for those who crave to have their holes watered. In short, a phallocracy."

"How do you know I don't have a phallus, Liberace?" Cee said, warming up.

"She's more of a man than you think," Billy added.

"Well, my dear Celia, since you come to us accompanied by a bona fide cocksucker,—" he glanced Billy's way "—albeit of the lowest common denominator, I will give you yet another opportunity to enter into my good graces and kiss the ring of your choice—"

Cee gave his pinkie a tug.

"Watch how fast I get rid of him," Billy whispered to Cee. He leaned over, yanked down her turtleneck collar and planted a long hickey on her throat.

"Ooooh," screamed Wayne, a hand clasping his chest as he sailed away.

"See?" Billy said, winking. "It works like a cross before a vampire."

Cee took another swallow of her drink. "He's even more of a strain than you."

"Maybe. But I can tell that he liked you. And you must know that there are very few people whose existence Miss Wayne even acknowledges, let alone condones."

Cee watched as Wayne filtered back into the crowd. At first glance he seemed to be an older version of Billy, yet Wayne looked like he could be easily shattered, while Billy seemed indestructible.

"I wouldn't mind leaving now," she said.

"You want to go? Now? It's just after nine. The place doesn't get even remotely *amusant* until at least ten."

"I don't know if I can take any more amusement," she said. "But if I have to stay, then I'm going to need some help."

"Herbert!" he called. "Another vodka for Janina."

The place soon filled up until it resembled a cramped kitchen during a party. Around eleven the disco music faded, the lights began to dim, and people began moving toward the stage that was tucked into a far corner.

"Looks like we're in for a little enter*tain*ment," Billy said. "Well, we certainly did pick the right night, didn't we?"

The curtains parted. A tiny black man in a smoking jacket stepped up to the piano, waving to the applauding crowd in a halo of spotlight.

"Now I know you aren't making all that noise just for me," he said. He was answered with lots of Sure we ares and more applause. When he sat down at the piano his feet barely reached the pedals. He played some introductory chords as the spot retreated to the far side of the stage. "Let's hear it for the empress of Lemon Street, Miss Bernadette!"

Billy started to fidget.

"What's wrong?" Cee asked.

Before he could answer a tall black woman stepped into the light. The strapless sequined dress she wore barely contained her shelf-like shoulders and her arms looked capable of felling timber. Her hair was cropped short and great globes of rhinestones fell from her ears, framing her face like sconces. She walked on the frailest of heels, and her wrists clattered with jewelry. She acknowledged her audience with a modest smile. The piano modulated into the introduction of a song. She lifted the microphone from the stand, looked down for a moment, then began over the piano's tinkle:

> *Some folks they go huntin'*
> *where them moose go gruntin'*
> *and shoot them right between the—*

"Legs," someone suggested. The place broke up.

Bernadette motioned for Jake to stop. She planted a hand on her hip and her eyes narrowed. "You wish you had it so good," she snorted, then a moment later a smile broke through her mask of indignation.

"Now where was I? Oh yes—"

> *Some folks they go fishin'*
> *but my hobby is nutrition*
> *There's better things to do than exercise.*

She took a breath.

> *I like to eat*
> *a piece of cake, a piece of meat*
> *I like to eat*
> *in restaurants or on the street*
> *If I'm hungry or I'm not*
> *doesn't matter what they got*
> *if it looks good I'll stuff it 'tween my lips*
> *I hope it all fits!*

Her throaty song strutted across the accompaniment. With her arms outspread, she looked as though she could heave the whole place into the air.

"They say it's bad to eat just before going to bed," she added mischievously. "But what about after?"

> *I dine alone*
> *My table's got one chair*
> *just me at home*
> *but my kitchen's all prepared*
> *I never can stop looking*

> *but no one wants my cooking*
> *who'll help me eat the food upon the shelf?*
> *I sure can't eat it by myself.*

"I ain't built that way!" she hooted.

A second stanza ended with a piano solo, and Bernadette used it to shake her bangles at friends she recognized. Her bow at the end of the song made Cee think of an upside-down Eiffel Tower bending at the waist.

"Hello, all of you," she said.

"Where you been?" someone asked.

"I been busy."

"With what?" someone else shouted.

"Relaxin'."

"You lookin' good, Bernadette!"

"It's these earrings. They help the circulation."

Her next number was a slow, penetrating torch song, entitled "I'm Still Here." At one point her eyes found Billy's and held them in a steady glance as she sang the next lines to him.

> *I'm still here*
> *looking at you and remembering*
> *but I want more than memories to cling to*
> *late at night*
> *I'm still here . . .*

Heads turned to find out who she looked at. Billy's face tightened, as if he were trying to free himself from Bernadette's attention.

"Let's hear it for Jake Jamison!" Miss Bernadette said after the last number. She beckoned for the piano player to take her hand. He appeared tiny beside her, a baby she might pick up and carry. And then, to everyone's delight, she did, and planted a big kiss on his lips. The lights came on, and disco music began pulsing out of the speakers.

"I wouldn't mind her picking me up and kissing me," Cee said, turning to Billy. "Hey, where are you going?"

"I need a drink." He disappeared into the crowd.

Within a few moments a tall black man approached Cee. In his dark suit jacket and black turtleneck, he might have been an art collector: Miss Bernadette.

"Excuse me, I noticed someone standing next to you who looked familiar."

Cee craned her neck toward the bar. "If you mean Billy, he was just here a minute ago."

"I'm Vincent," he said, extending a hand.

Cee introduced herself. "Billy's told me about you."

"Don't believe a word of it. I am a responsible citizen who pays his taxes."

"Billy's only said nice things about you."

"Billy's 'nice' is everyone else's 'mean and nasty.'" He surveyed the crowd from his lighthouse height. "Where is that boy?" He shook his head. "You look like a normal person, Cee," Vincent said. "I mean, compared to Billy's usual companions. Are you a student?"

Cee told him what she did.

"You know, when I was your age I wanted to be a nurse. But in those days people like me didn't become nurses. Doctors neither. So I started dressing fancy and got in with a band. Why, my picture's up here somewhere. Let me show you."

The bar had filled to capacity by then and it took them a while before they reached the wall of framed photographs.

"Here," said Vincent proudly. He wore a sequined gown, his face and neck rising above the wave of a fur boa. "That was taken just before me and the band left for the coast. They were a swell bunch of fellas. We called ourselves Bernadette's Black Jack Boys. I'm too old to be touring around anymore, but once in a while Herbert asks me to come round and sing a little."

"Can I get you a drink?"

He peered at Cee's glass. "If that ain't water then it's medicine. Get me the same."

Cee squeezed toward the bar, searching for Billy. What was going on?

"Tell me how you and Billy met," Cee said, giving Vincent his drink when she returned.

"My, my, that was a while ago. You see, it was just around the time the Black Jacks were breaking up. I was returning from a string of engagements and was getting off the Greyhound bus with a worrisome load of costumes. I was all by myself because the rest of the band had gone down to New York, you see. Then I noticed this pretty little face nearby who looked like he'd be able to handle a suitcase of two." He leaned closer. "Tell me, is he all right? There are people in this city who do not like Billy as much as I do."

"Sometimes I don't know if I like him, either."

Vincent smiled uncomfortably, not sure that Cee had understood. "Look, what I mean is . . . you seem to be a new friend of his, a real friend, not someone out to get whatever you can from him. He needs people like that around him."

"You're his friend, too, aren't you?"

Vincent's eyes fell. "Yes, but we've moved away from each other somewhat. He doesn't come by all that much anymore. Sometimes I think he's a little embarrassed to."

"I don't think there's anything that could embarrass Billy."

"Maybe that's not the right word for it."

Cee turned her glass around in her hand. "How much of what he tells me should I believe?"

Vincent laughed. "No more than you absolutely have to. Oh, look, there he is! Yoo hoo!" He crooked a finger.

Billy had edged himself into the farthest corner of the bar, where he was talking to someone. His lips froze as if Vincent had caught him in the middle of a word.

"Why did you run off?" Vincent said when Billy came over. "You knew I saw you."

Billy looked down at his drink. "Just socializing," he muttered.

"And where have you been all these months? Whenever I don't see you for a long time I worry that you might have gotten into trouble again."

"What kind of trouble could someone like me possibly get in?" he said with exaggerated innocence.

"Should I go down the list alphabetically or by subject?"

"How come you never told me that Vincent was such a good singer?" Cee asked.

"Sometimes Billy forgets a whole lot of things he shouldn't," Vincent said, waving a finger.

"Guess I'm just a bad boy," Billy said.

"Well, this new friend of yours'll make you good. If you let her."

Just before leaving, Vincent approached Cee again. "How would you like to come over to my place one night?" he said. "Let me cook you up some of my spicy chicken." He produced a card. "Never mind that," he said, pointing to his stage name. "The phone number's right. You know where Lemon Street is, don't you?"

"In the Fruit Belt."

Vincent looked pleased that she knew. "You ain't afraid to come by, now are you?"

"I'd come even if I was," Cee said, going up on her tiptoes to give him a kiss.

※

CEE TRUNDLED DOWNSTAIRS barefoot, still in her bathrobe. Each step sank her deeper into the cold until her feet met the icy tiles of the ground floor. She opened the door and reached around to her mailbox. The curbside gurgled with melting snow.

"Sure you aren't overdressed?"

It was Don, flattening cartons on the street. She stuck her tongue out at him, grabbed what was in the box, and ducked back inside.

Three pieces of mail, a bonanza. Receiving mail was far more satisfying than getting phone calls, she thought, glancing at the envelopes. And how lovely it was to have a real street address instead of a dormitory box number. The wrinkled envelope came from Carl and was long in coming, to look at the tangle of cancellations. It had gone to the dorm and back to her parents before getting shuffled off to Buffalo. There was a letter from her mother. And a postcard.

She got back upstairs with a shiver and peeked into the bedroom to see if Jeanine was still asleep. She'd surprised Cee by arriving the evening before after visiting her sister in Batavia. The bed was empty, and Cee heard Jeanine singing in the bathroom.

They'd been friends since junior high school, although always very different from one another. Jeanine had never been part of Cee's outcast circle, and Cee had little interest in putting back beer after beer with Jeanine's friends. Somehow, they'd stuck together through the years. Jeanine was one of the few people Cee knew who always said exactly what they thought. She still lived in Thompson City and worked for Blue Cross.

Cee put up water for coffee, and then plopped down on Joel's spongy old sofa with her mail. Carl's letter answered one she'd written while staying at Marlene's. The three sheets were frail from the typewriter's hammering. He surprised her by remembering her birthday was approaching and invited her to come down and celebrate it with them. She'd considered a visit after leaving the hospital, but that was before she'd gotten her job. The remainder of the letter made her glad she hadn't gone. Since Thanksgiving there'd been only problems. The price of heating oil had skyrocketed. They couldn't afford to run the oil burner and used the wood stove instead, all of them sleeping in one big bed downstairs. They were prohibited from chopping down trees on the mountain and had to pay to have wood delivered. The house was drafty and never very warm. Melissa had gotten sick again—bills! And Elaine seemed impatient with him no matter what he did.

Cee imagined Melissa, sneezing and cranky under a pile of blankets and sleeping bags. If Carl mentioned money problems, it meant that Walter still hadn't relented about the trust fund. Or that Theresa hadn't spoken to him about it. One thing was certain: stubborn Carl hadn't, either. That would explain Elaine's impatience. There was more. A hearing had been held about rezoning the mountain for commercial use. The Mountain Coalition organized a picket line outside the county building. People testified against the project, and Larrabee's representative had been booed. The county voted to take no further action until yet another study had been made. Larrabee, eager to begin construction as soon as it got warmer, responded by upping the number of jobs from seventy-five to an even hundred, thirty of which would remain after the project was completed, for maintenance, groundskeeping, and security. He took out a full-page ad in the newspapers showing an Indian chief atop a mountain with one arm outstretched, under the headline "Conservation, Historical Preservation, and Economic Recovery." Another hearing was held. This time the county board voted to put the measure on the primary election ballot in June. No one could predict the outcome, Carl wrote.

The very paper of the letter felt heavy in her hands, so weighed down by problems was it. She imagined Carl sitting at the typewriter, bundled in sweaters, pecking at the keys with icy fingers—it almost made her want to jump into Ruby and drive right down there. Had his birthday invitation really been a veiled appeal for help? But a trip was impossible. The ER was short-staffed; the day secretary had broken her leg and was in a cast. Cee set aside the letter, needing a rest from its gloom.

She picked up the postcard. A night shot of Buffalo's waterfront and "Greetings from the Queen City," graced one side. The words "If the crown fits, wear it!" were scrawled on the reverse. It was Billy's credo, his response to closet queens, which he claimed Buffalo was crawling with. She was about to open the letter from her mother when the rumble of boiling water distracted her. As she went to the kitchen, she got a glimpse of herself in the living room mirror. She realized what had caught Don's attention more than her nightgown: the band of hickeys around her neck.

The hickey in Hadrian's had hardly been Billy's first. Nights when Billy came over and they didn't feel like going anywhere, Cee'd get out the BBQ potato chips and a quart of Diet Pepsi. They smoked, put on music, and then snuggled up. Soon they'd be into low-level cuddling, then active nuzzling. Billy's hands explored her clothed body tentatively, with a child's curiosity. One night he began kissing the side of her neck. She went to stop him but her hands fell away, and the hot circle of his mouth sealed against her. His tongue suctioned up her flesh, drawing it taut and thin as paper. His teeth perforated her skin, setting off a painful tickle. She heard herself gasping, his teeth retreated but his mouth clung, moist and pulsing, until he released the fresh wound to the cooling salve of the air.

The biting became a part of their closeness. She savored the pain that erupted each time he tore through one of the many maidenheads her skin possessed. Afterward, he lay with his head cradled against her breasts. Billy awakened acres of yearning within her, and it would have been the easiest thing in the world to sink into the chasm of her own desire, pulling him down after her. But she never returned his kisses, too conscious of what separated them.

Still, it was almost like making love, she thought. Almost.

"You ever have sex with a woman?" she asked one night.

"Are you crazy, you think I want to get my doodle chewed off?"

"I bet you never gave a hickey to that Kal woman."

"You're right."

"But you give them to me."

"You seem to like it. So quit complaining. Lie back and think of Poland."

Yes, she thought. She did like it.

Jeanine turned off the water in the shower.

Cee made coffee, poured herself a cup, and then tore open her mother's envelope. There was a large birthday card inscribed with poetry in flowery script, to which her mother had added a somewhat formal "To my daughter Celia" at the top and "from your Mother and Father" at the bottom. A chunk of folded notepaper fell into her lap: a letter. She read it eagerly.

Her mother loved her job at the Broome County Office of Parks and Recreation! "I don't think your father's crazy about it," she wrote. "Sometimes I think about quitting"—Cee's heart raced—"but I enjoy it too much."

There was some hope of Walter getting a part-time construction job in a county program for the chronically unemployed, but he was probably too old to be eligible. The union knew of openings, but they were all in the Sun Belt, out of the question. Then she mentioned a project being planned for Indian Mountain, which was probably his last hope.

Cee read that sentence over again.

Didn't her mother know what that project was? Even if she didn't work for the county it was no secret what the project would mean for Carl. To read Carl's letter, the whole town was up in arms. Cee scanned her mother's pages for Carl's name. It wasn't there. Were both letters talking about the same thing? Mailed from approximately the same place and written by people in the same family?

"Looks like real mail," Jeanine said, stepping out of the bathroom. "All I ever get are bills." She bent down, flung her hair over, and began wrapping it in a towel.

"I can't believe how long your hair is," Cee said. "When was the last time you cut it?"

"First year of high school. I'm not sure if I like your hair so short, Cee. It makes you look . . . tough."

"I am tough."

Jeanine finished tucking in the towel and pointed to Cee's neck. "You must be." She got herself some coffee. "Hey, let's see that wrist."

Cee held it up. Jeanine was one of the few people Cee had talked to about it.

"You're one crazy woman," Jeanine said, giving Cee's arm a squeeze. They sewed you up real nice, though. You should see the stitches my little brother got when he fell off his bicycle. It looks like there's a fish skeleton on his cheek. You must have had a Jewish doctor; they're the best."

She was about to ask Jeanine if she'd heard anything about the Indian Mountain project when the doorbell rang.

"Marlene!"

"Something from the hospital came for you, and since I was in the neighborhood I thought I might as well deliver it in person. Did you just get up?"

Cee felt conscious of the hickeys. "Sort of. Come on in. What brings you to these parts?"

"I'm going to the Real Meal for lunch," she said, handing Cee an envelope. "Feel like joining me?"

"Lunch?"

"It's almost one. Well, you've certainly fixed this place up," Marlene said, looking around. "It's so much brighter here without that awful wallpaper." She caught sight of Jeanine. "Oh!"

"Hello," Jeanine said.

Cee introduced them. "This is the nice woman I wrote you about who let me stay with her after I was in the hospital. You feel like going to the Real Meal to eat?"

"Sure."

Marlene looked a little disappointed, as though she'd hoped for time alone with Cee.

"I think I already know what this is," Cee said, opening the envelope. "Yup, just what I thought: a bill." She tore up the piece of paper and tossed it in the trash cheerfully.

"Shame on you," Jeanine said with a grin. "It's people like you who jack up the price of insurance."

"How's class going?" Cee asked Marlene as they walked into the restaurant.

"No men signed up. I was a little worried at first. I didn't want to teach a consciousness-raising group. But it's going so well now I think it's a shame that no men decided take it."

"Maybe it's going so well *because* no men signed up."

"Don't you miss being in school, Cee?"

"I don't go to school either, and I'm a decent member of society," Jeanine said.

"She didn't mean it that way, Neen."

"I know, I know. I was just giving your friend a hard time."

Marlene tried to smile.

"We have to go up to the counter to order," Cee explained to Jeanine.

"There's another reason I wanted to stop by," Marlene said in a quiet voice as they left the table. "I felt bad not having any time for you while you were staying with me."

"I understood. You had your work to do."

"Not only that. It was difficult for me having you there. You didn't put me out or anything. I was actually glad for the company. But you seemed on the brink of beginning over. I felt stagnant by comparison."

"Oh, I was on the brink, all right."

"Maybe. But I admired how you were so ready to push ahead. I wondered where you got the strength after what you'd been through."

"Have you spoken to Joel recently?" Cee asked, naming the name that seemed to hover above their conversation.

"No. I've written to him. But I've been so caught up with teaching my class that I haven't thought about him that much. I guess that's a good sign."

"Cee, this food reminds me of the stuff your brother used to cook," Jeanine winked, pointing to the menu board. "Tofu Lasagna, Soybean Casserole . . ."

Back at the table, Jeanine spoke about her job as a claims representative at Blue Cross.

"Some people call me up and talk to me as if I were their doctor. Or their psychiatrist. There's a lot of lonely people out there, that's all I can say. They start up about a bill, and the next thing I know they're telling me about their husband fooling around or their daughter getting pregnant. I don't mind talking to them, I figure I might be the only person they have who'll listen to them. But we aren't allowed to do that, and the supervisors can plug into my line and check."

"Did you say that supervisors listened in?" Marlene said.

"Sure. They switch into your line and hear what you're saying to the policy holders. For example, if a PH was getting on my case and I told them to kiss off and a supervisor was on the line, I could be booted out."

"And you like working there?"

"Well, the pay could be better, but the benefits are good, and the cafeteria's cheap. Cheaper than here," she said, smiling at Cee. "Anyway, I don't have too much choice in the way of jobs where I come from. You might have heard that there's a recession going on."

"But maybe if you got a degree you might—"

"Nope. No college for me," Jeanine said, plunging her fork into her quiche. "Who's going to pay for me to go to college, anyway? No one's in a hurry to give me a scholarship. I'm not brainy like Cee over here—"

"Knock it off, Neen—"

"And I hear Ph.D.s are driving taxis in New York. So what am I going to do with a college degree?"

"You might at least avoid a job where people spy on you," Marlene said with growing impatience.

"I don't know if you've heard, but most jobs in this country have one person telling another person what to do. That's what a job is all about. What do you plan to do with your Ph.D.?" Jeanine asked. "I mean, if you don't get one of those taxi jobs."

"Teach," Marlene said icily.

"If there's a spot open."

A spot, thought Cee, wincing. As if a teaching position were a job in a department store. Jeanine was unbelievable, Cee thought, wishing she could dive into her soup.

"Are you saying that I should drop out just because there's no guarantee I'll be able to find work? Maybe you think I should have majored in business or engineering just to make sure I'd have a job when I was done." Marlene sounded irritated.

"Engineers make good bucks, I hear," Jeanine replied. "And some places are even going out of their way to hire women these days."

Oh God, Cee thought. Jeanine and Marlene were at the opposite ends of the woman scale. "Okay, you two. Take it easy," she said.

Marlene finished eating quickly. "I have to be back on campus by two. Will you call me, Cee?"

"I don't think she went for me," Jeanine said afterward.

Jeanine wanted more than anything to see Niagara Falls, so they drove there. Cee began to notice things about Jeanine that disturbed her. It had started with Jeanine's comment about Jewish doctors. She tried to decide whether Jeanine's candidness had become crudeness, whether she was down-home or just provincial. Either way, she seemed stuck in a time Cee recognized as past, right down to her leather vest and cowboy boots. Cee suggested stopping at the women's bookstore; Jeanine said that, as far as she was concerned, they could pass on it. On the way home Cee took her on a tour of downtown; Jeanine commented on the large number of blacks on the streets. They stopped for groceries and bought what Jeanine wanted to eat: pork chops, frozen french fries, and beer. As Cee took out the skillet she realized how long it had been since she'd eaten this kind of food: not since Thanksgiving.

"How come you quit school, Cee?"

"It didn't seem to make much sense for me to be there."

"Watch out. You don't want to turn out like me, do you?"

"What's that supposed to mean? I thought you liked your job."

"I do. It's fine for me. But you'd go crazy doing it. My job isn't for anyone who thinks."

"Jeanine," Cee said.

Jeanine drove back to Thompson City early the next morning, right after breakfast. Cee yawned over her coffee, yet when she tried to go back to sleep afterward, she couldn't. Seeing Jeanine again showed Cee how far apart they'd grown. Saying good-bye to her that morning had seemed final.

7

It was a little past ten on Cee's night off. She had just gotten into bed with cup of herbal tea and the Virginia Woolf book Marlene had given her, when she heard a knock. She opened the door, and Billy trudged up the stairs without saying a word, pulled out a letter from his pocket, flung it into Cee's hand, and then flopped onto the sofa.

"Walking papers," he wheezed.

Cee read the letter, which had been typed. Stanley informed Billy that he never wanted to see him again. "Informed" was the word Stanley used. "Please understand that I'm simply not like you. I have a wife I love, two children, and a happy home. I don't want to put all that at risk."

"What is he risking?" Cee asked, returning the letter. She could see that Billy had been crying. "Does he think that he'll really turn queer if he stays with you long enough?"

"Turn queer? He already is." Billy threw the letter down. "Don't you see?" he said. "It's all bluff. Wifey must have dictated it to him under some dire threats."

She sat down. He put his arms around her and sobbed softly. "I hope you don't mind that I came here tonight, unannounced, I mean."

She reached into her bag and gave him a tissue. "You always come unannounced."

"I scared him away," he said, sitting up to blow his nose. "I was always putting on a show for him, trying to fascinate him, tantalize him. He never got to know me as a normal person who eats and sleeps and likes the smell of his own farts. The last show I put on went too far, and he freaked."

"You mean the light bulb—"

"That was just the tip of the iceberg, pardon the pun. We'd seen each other several days earlier. He'd given me my usual twenty dollars. But I really needed more. So I made a bit of a stink. 'Why don't you increase my allowance?' I said to him. 'You give wifelet whatever she wants. What about me?' I also let fall one or two uncomplimentary remarks about her in a rather loud voice. He can't take it when people yell at him, it reminds him of his clarinet teacher. The worst part was, we happened to be in the motel lobby at the time—"

"Billy—"

"I never even knew he played the clarinet. He certainly never played it—"

"Get to the point!"

"Regardless of what Stanley wrote in that letter, he knows he's as queer as I am, but he's convinced himself that as long as wifelet doesn't know about it, then it's okay. From what he tells me, their sex life is so minimal she would hardly notice when it stopped altogether. Anyway, it seems that Mrs. MacIntyre discovered a pair of my underwear in one of Stanley's suit pockets. She couldn't know they were mine, she only knew they weren't Stanley's, since they were women's underwear."

"You wear women's underwear?"

He gave his shoulder a shy shrug. "On special occasions."

"How'd they get in his pocket?"

Billy looked down and fluffed his tissue into the shape of a flower. "I put them there one morning after we'd spent the night together. As a kind of keepsake. So he'd find them when he went to pay the thruway toll. As you can tell from the letter, Stanley accuses me of wanting to wreck his marriage."

"He probably has a point."

"All right, I admit it. Maybe I did want to ... agitate things. But how else was Stanley ever going to get off his butt and take his life into his hands?" He threw down the tissue flower. "Now he hates me."

"But he did visit you in the hospital."

"The priests dropped in on Joan of Arc before they burned her, too."

Cee recalled the frightened man on the bench outside the ER the night Billy was brought in. "He didn't leave until you'd been transferred out of the ER, you know."

"Poor Stanley. I really scared him."

"What are you going to do?"

"Something useful. Like slitting my wrists, for example. Oh, I'm sorry, that was in poor taste, wasn't it?"

"You need money?"

"Yeah, but don't lend me any or you'll wind up hating me when I don't pay you back. But you may go with me to the CPG and buy me a beer."

Just as they walked in, the bar broke into a chorus of boos.

"Hey, it's Tricky Dick up there on the boob tube." Billy said.

The TV over the bar was tuned to a documentary about Nixon's career. He hovered over the cigarette smoke like an ugly angel peeping down from the clouds. The bad reception exaggerated his sunken eyes and furry brows. His rubbery jowls inflated balloonlike as he spoke. He was giving a press conference on the Watergate break-in.

"Watergate could have been something out of an old movie about vaudeville you might see on TV at four in the afternoon," Billy said as they sat down. "Nixon as Flo Ziegfeld. Ehrlichman, Haldeman, and Dean as the softshoe trio. Rose Mary Woods as the scheming meanie. Martha Mitchell as the good-hearted cigarette girl who dreams of seeing her name up in lights so she runs away from her puritanical father, Sam Irvine. Oh, God, now Dick's up there with Mao. Talk about Laurel and Hardy."

"By the way, how did you deal with the draft?" Cee asked.

"I told the draft board that I was afraid of men. Actually, to be more precise, I said that I would rather fuck with men than kill them, even though Orientals are notorious for having peanut dicks. The clown I spoke to said it pleased him to tell me that my words were going to be placed in my file just in case a prospective employer wanted to find out more about me. I asked him if that meant that I wasn't going to be drafted, and he said yes. Then I told him that was a pity since a recent scientific survey revealed that 37.9 percent of the generals in the United States army were closet queens."

"I watched Nixon resign with my brother Carl and Elaine at someone's house—"

"Who's Elaine?"

"Carl's wife."

"Those breeders," muttered Billy.

"Would you stop that? These people are family, for chrissake!"

"They're still breeders. Nixon's a breeder. All the men in the Pentagon are. Breeders make war, especially the male variety. What they really want to do is bugger each other but they're afraid to, so instead they play with guns, the bigger the better."

"I thought you said half the army was gay."

"I said they were closet cases. There's nothing meaner than a hard-up closet case."

"You always put people into pigeonholes."

"Who carved the pigeonholes in the first place? Who has been forcing men into one and women into the other for the past millennium, without a drop of lubricant, and who destroys those who don't fit?"

"I heard you the moment I walked in, Gizzi."

A blond-haired woman stood beside their table carrying a roll of posters. She looked somewhat severe in her boots and leather jacket. Her cheeks were red from the cold, and she exuded the energetic restlessness of a mountain climber in between peaks.

"Why it's Diana, the queen of the hunt."

"Look who's talking about queens," she shot back. "I only tolerate you because you're a eunuch," she said.

"That goes to show you how much women know about men," Billy sniped.

"Men? I don't see any men at this table," she said, smiling at Cee as though talking for her benefit. "Just a faggot with bad teeth."

"What brings you here, dearest Kal?"

"I was on my way to UB to poster for the Women's Day demo, and I saw you through the window." She turned to Cee. "And I was curious to see who you were sharing your table with."

"Allow me to introduce you two ladies. Miss Gajewski," Billy said, "this is Miss Katherine Lund. Miss Lund, Miss Cee Gajewski."

"Everyone calls me Kal. And I spell it with a K, like Kali."

"Who's that?" Cee asked.

"Goddess of fertility and destruction," Billy thundered. "My penis shrivels at the very mention of her name."

The famous Kal, Cee thought. She was tall and slender, with an angular face. Not pretty, but her eyes were a forceful grey, and it was hard to look away from her. She recalled Billy saying that Kal was around thirty, but she looked older. There was a tautness about her, a readiness to spring, to pounce and snap. Her hoarse voice had the scratchy warmth of a sweater.

"Have you decided whether you're coming to the demo?" Kal asked Billy.

"I'm trying to keep a low profile."

"You mean the one on International Women's Day in March, right?" Cee said, glad that she could show a little awareness.

Kal nodded.

"How come you're asking Billy about it?"

"There'll be a men's support contingent," Kal explained.

"All the way at the back, of course," Billy said. "After the revolution, the men will clean the women's boots and suckle their young. Have a seat, Kal."

"I should really get these put up tonight." She looked at Cee, then said, "Okay."

"I'm a widow," Billy said. "Stanley's left me."

"A pity," she said dryly.

"Kal never liked Stanley," he explained to Cee. "To Kal he was just another lowly privileged white male member of the bourgeoisie. Or was it a petty bourgeois lackey of the patriarchy?"

Kal sneered. "A closet case either way. From what you tell me, he's just another one of your father-substitutes. I think it's bad politics to sleep with people who aren't out."

"Love has no politics, Kal."

"And neither do you, evidently. I need something to drink." She turned to Cee. "Something to wet your whistle?"

"A Molson's."

Kal motioned to the woman waiting tables.

"The other day Cée got on my case for being sexist," Billy said. "Kal, tell her that I'm such a feminist I almost menstruate."

"Well you certainly can bleed, we've seen that," Cee countered. Billy stuck his tongue out at her.

Kal looked pleasantly surprised at Cee's dig. "Billy here would like to think that being queer frees him from his male privilege. How simple it would be if men getting fucked in the ass could undo the crud of centuries of woman-hating. If that were true, I'd line up all the men of the world, give them Vaseline, and tell them to take turns bending over."

"Keep talking like that and they'll never let you have your kid back."

"Leave Grant out of this, hear?" Kal said, suddenly stern.

Cee's gaze traveled from Billy to Kal. Their talk seemed more like scrutiny than chat, their barbs sharp and carefully aimed, as only those of people who'd known each other for a long time could be. Were they doing this for her benefit, spurred on by having an audience?

She sensed Kal studying her. The intensity of Kal's gaze was unsettling, as though ready to spark the moment Cee returned it. Cee wasn't used to being looked at that way. Men surveyed her in order to decide whether or not to keep on looking. Other women eyed her critically. Only some of them—those who didn't shave their legs, who carried backpacks instead of handbags—let their gaze linger like Kal's.

Just then Kal saw someone she knew at another table and went off to say hello.

"I think she likes you," Billy said.

"What's that thing she's wearing around her neck?"

"The double-edged axe? It's what the Amazons used to cut off men's nuts, or some such." He grinned. "You like her?"

"She looks a little unhappy. Something about her mouth."

"She's been through a lot."

Kal returned and drank the rest of her beer. "I'm going to split. Think you might come to the demo, Cee?"

"I work nights, so I have to sleep during the day."

Kal's eyes narrowed. "Well, you have to know your priorities. Maybe I'll see you around anyway. Let me give you my phone number and address." She wrote on a leaflet and pushed it into Cee's hand. "Best time to reach me is in the morning."

"There goes the revolution," said Billy when she'd gone.

8

*V*INCENT'S APARTMENT WAS a cosy museum of artifact and decoration. The many small lamps shed an amber glow through their heavy shades, and one wall was filled with almost as many framed pictures as in Hadrian's, except that these were all of Miss Bernadette. He'd prepared chicken in a spicy sauce, as promised, baked potatoes, and there was lemon meringue pie for dessert. He wore a long, dark robe that fell from his shoulders like a flow of lava. It was hard to imagine rambunctious Billy confined to such a tiny apartment. There was but one bedroom, hung with fabric like an emir's tent.

They smoked an after-dinner joint in the corner that served as a living room. Vincent pulled out his scrapbook of photographs, sepia and crinkle-edged, of train tickets and programs, even a silk opera glove whose mate was lost backstage in a theater in Louisville, Kentucky. "The one thing I regret," he said, after they'd reached the last, unfilled, pages of the scrapbook, "is that there are no tapes from the old days." His voice faded, and the silence seemed to contain all his unrecorded songs.

Then Vincent sat up abruptly, pushed the scrapbook to the side, and switched to the subject of Billy. Vincent talked about him the way a parent might, sorry about his mistakes, sad about a child who'd left him behind. One thing emerged: Vincent felt immensely guilty for having given Billy drugs. They hadn't been Billy's first, Vincent was quick to say. But unfortunately not his last, either. Vincent knew how to control himself. He'd smoked his first opium at fifteen and remained no stranger to it, but he'd always kept things under *control*. He spoke the word as a minister might. Billy lacked self-control; that was the real problem. And because of that other thing—Vincent never used the word "gay"—Billy had gotten himself into even more trouble.

"The worst part was when he started making a business out of the dope. It got him mixed up with a bad crowd. Now, I know there's got to be someone selling if there's someone who wants to buy. But why does it have to be Billy doing the selling? Why couldn't it have been some paper-brained dude with nothing better to do 'cause he ain't smart enough to?" A taut thread of regret pulled through his voice. It was clear how much Vincent had loved Billy, and still did. Suddenly his telling broke off, as if overwhelmed by the onrush of memories. He smoothed the folds of his robe, looking grandfatherly.

When it came time to leave, he sandwiched Cee's hand between his and said, "Now you look after him, okay?"

"Just tell me one thing," Cee said, standing in the doorway. "Does Billy still . . . sell?"

Vincent shook his head. "I could tell you yes, and I could tell you no, and both'd most likely be wrong."

Cee walked down the steps, her tongue working a bit of sour-tasting spice from between her teeth, her head a little cloudy from the dope. She paused to breathe in the air, which promised warmer weather. She felt sluggish, as if sediments of Vincent's voice had settled inside her joints.

A group of three black men sidled past. The neighborhood began to look less and less inviting. She thought of Billy mincing down these streets at all hours, the only white face for blocks. How had he survived? Yet wasn't survival one of Billy's biggest talents?

"I MISS YOU."

That Mickey Mouse voice.

"I miss you, too, Billy." She heard music in the background. "Where are you?"

"Oh, oot and aboot." Billy's pseudo-Canadian accent. "You doing anything tonight?"

"Working."

"Not until eleven. It's only eight. The night is young."

"Are you in Hadrian's?"

"Right for ten points. This accountant keeps trying to pick me up. You simply have to come rescue me."

"Accountants can't be much worse than insulation salesmen. Where the hell have you been for the past two weeks?"

There was a pause.

"Can I come over then? Just for tea?"

A moment later there was a knock on the door.

"I thought you said you were at Hadrian's."

"I was." He grinned. "But then I went to the Real Meal."

"Are you going to tell me what you've been doing since I saw you last?" she asked when they were upstairs.

"What have I been doing? Tending to affairs of state, you might say."

"I think we need to talk, Billy." She sat down and lit a cigarette. "Since I last saw you I've had some time to think. It occurred to me that if we hadn't run into Kal at the CPG I never would've met her."

"I'm sure you two girls would have bumped into each other eventually."

"That's not the point. She's a close friend of yours. You lived in her house for two years. You're always talking about her. Yet you never thought to have me meet her. Ditto for Vincent."

"I didn't realize that getting to know them was so important."

"You're ready to let complete strangers know you're a queer but you can't be open with your friends. And another thing: I don't see you for two weeks, then you show up, I ask you what you've been up to, and you say 'affairs of state.'"

"Go ahead and tell me to buzz off."

"You'd like that, wouldn't you? It would make things easier for you. It would keep you from getting your hands dirty." She exhaled impatiently. "Don't you think it's strange that I get to listen to hours of the most intimate aspects of your sexual life but you have nothing to say when I ask you how you've spent the last two weeks? Which still doesn't stop you from crying on my shoulder about Stanley. Why didn't you tell your good friend Kal your tale of woe?" She sprang to her feet and began pacing back and forth as she spoke.

"What does that have to do—"

"I'll tell you why you didn't: because you know she wouldn't listen. But you figured that Cee would—nice, dependable Cee."

"Celia, what's got into you all of a sudden?"

"I had this crazy idea that we were friends."

"Does that mean I have to sign a contract and give you a percentage of my thoughts?"

She yanked down her turtleneck, exposing a band of faint scarlet rings. "Why did you do that? Can you tell me?" She pulled the collar back up. "Know what I think? You love to have as many people as possible eating out of your goddamn hand. You love nothing better than for people to feel sorry for you—"

"That's where you're dead wrong. I don't want anyone feeling sorry for me. And if you were so worried about me you could have called."

"It would help if you paid your phone bill!"

"Stop shouting at me, will you?" he said in a tone of concession. "Look, could we go someplace? I could use a change of scenery."

Cee checked her watch. "Where?"

"How about a tavern in Lackawanna?"

She collected her things for work, and they got into the car. "I want people to level with me," she said as she turned onto 33. "For example. Is it true you used to deal?"

"Who said I did?"

"Vincent. I mean, I knew you shot up. I'd noticed your arms in the hospital. And I'd seen your medical history—"

"I haven't shot up in over two years. I suppose you've never done anything stronger than Ovaltine, Saint Cecilia?"

"No. But if I did, and you asked me, I wouldn't lie about it. So, answer the question. Did you use to deal?"

Billy answered slowly. "Yeah. Not far from the bus station. I'd already moved in with Vincent."

"Wouldn't it have been easier to hustle?"

"Vincent didn't want me to."

"Considering how much else you told me about your bus station days, it seems strange you didn't mention your little sideline."

Billy gripped his seat, as though holding on for dear life. He had two modes of reaction, she thought: The Swift Retort and this, The Bad Little Boy.

"Oh my God, what's that?" Cee pointed straight ahead.

A great floodlit stone colossus loomed up in the night. Two towers stood sentry beside the mound of a dome. Angels with stone wings stiffly spread held crosses as if to fend off some biblical beast.

"Our Lady of Victory Basilica."

"It's in the middle of nowhere."

"Almost. Lackawanna."

She pulled over and they got out. The air was spiked with the soot of the steel plant, which glowed like a sinister city in the distance.

"My mother and I went here on Easter Sunday," Billy said. "We had to take the bus, since my father didn't go to church. It took forever, like going on a pilgrimage. Inside it's huge, so that you feel appropriately small and insignificant. Lots of angels, lots of marble, and a God-fearing cleaning lady to dust it all. I was here just a few days ago. I got down on my goddamn knees and prayed that Stanley would come back to me. Then I prayed for my father's rotten soul and lit a candle."

"If you're so worried about your father's soul you should go over to his house and talk to him."

"I can't. The elder Mr. Gizzi is deceased."

Cee stopped. "I didn't know that."

"Welcome to Truth or Consequences," he said with some bitterness.

They walked toward the basilica and sat down on a bench.

"Vincent really is a very sweet man, Billy. He misses you. How come you never visit him anymore?"

"I can tell he has won your honkie sympathy." Billy clasped his hands in prayer and looked heavenward. "Pray for us, Saint Vincent, mother of grace and chitterlings."

She found his facetiousness irritating. "Maybe you don't call him up for the same reason you avoided him in Hadrian's—because you know he loves you. You don't want anyone to love you, especially if they run out of money to give you—"

"I stopped staying with Vincent only after he'd gotten me hooked, for your information."

"That's not the way I heard it. He tried to get you to control yourself. But you didn't listen."

"I didn't listen," he said, mimicking her.

"If a person doesn't shoot up more than once every three weeks they don't get hooked—"

"Just because we're in front of a church doesn't give you the right to play Father Confessor with me, which, if I may add, you have been doing all evening." He crossed his legs and looked away.

He was right, she thought. She knew why, too: because of every one of the days she'd tried to reach him and couldn't or waited for his call and it didn't come.

"I'm sorry," she said.

"Since you're so curious about me, then let me give you an account of Billy's early years with Vincent. It might surprise you to know that I was plagued with bouts of unhappiness at that time, which unfortunately occurred in less than three-week intervals, so that I needed to indulge in the big H more frequently than was good for me. Maybe it's not as glamorous being an eighteen-year-old cocksucker in Buffalo, New York, as one might think, especially when you suddenly find yourself with no place to live, no family, and no source of regular income. Maybe a teensy-weensy part of William E. Gizzi couldn't stand himself at all. Maybe he really hated the way his tongue hung out for whatever dick got thrown his way, not because he thought dick-licking was wrong, or because he thought that the men who didn't lick dicks were any better, but because of what he had to endure to find the dicks. And then, once he found them, he hated having to pray that the men they belonged to wouldn't hand his ass to him in a sling after they'd given Billy what he wanted. But the strange part is that even knowing they might hand his ass to him in a sling wouldn't have stopped Billy from going after them, not for one, solitary minute. In fact, Billy was even known to be turned on by it." He looked away. "And as far as Vincent goes," he said in an exhausted whisper, "I know he still loves me."

Cee's heart stammered. Billy, she thought, Billy—

Bells began to ring; ten o'clock. Suddenly the floodlights on the basilica went out and the building sank into gloomy shadow, as though the bells and the lights were hooked up to a timer. In the darkness the basilica seemed to be sneaking up from behind, as though ready to mug them, and the steel plant glowed even more ominously than before.

Cee pulled him to her and kissed him on the lips. His eyes flashed with surprise, and he almost looked ready to fling one of his retorts at her, but the rest of his face appeared peaceful. She kept on holding him, wanting more than anything to preserve the calm as long as she could.

When they were back in the car Billy produced a slender tinfoil packet from his pocket. "It's very mellow," he said, unfolding the foil to reveal a snippet of paper printed with two circles. "I don't know about you, but I could sure use some of this." He tore one of the circles in half, swallowed it, and gave the other half to her.

Cee shook her head.

"Come on. Take your communion like a good Catholic girl."

Cee regarded the snippet, which seemed to glow enticingly in the dark, and a moment later she held it between her fingers. "Hope we don't have any codes tonight," she said, swallowing it.

"Don't worry, you have a strong constitution. Not like some people I know who do windowpane before going to work at Bethlehem over there," Billy said. "They're the ones who wind up falling into vats of molten steel. It's sort of like throwing lobsters into boiling water. You ever hear the sound they make? Eeehhhh! Eeehhhh!"

Cee gulped, as if gagging on the acid. "Who was it?"

"No one you'd know. C'mon, let's drive back to the city."

They turned onto Main Street, where a crowd of people was milling around Buffalo Memorial Auditorium. They parked and walked over. Cee and Billy let themselves be pushed along by the crowds, and a moment later they were inside. The air was thick and yellowish and difficult to breathe. Drop by drop, Cee felt the acid beginning to trickle into the folds of her brain. A heavy sweat sheathed her. There were hundreds of people, mountains of faces, arms, and legs, wriggling limbs; it made her think of Carl's description of night crawlers in the bait can. She and Billy made their way around the long, winding outer hall. People pressed against her, hungry mouths feeding, the night crawlers turned to leeches. But she wasn't afraid. Let them touch me, she thought. Let them all touch me.

They reached a gate and soon were under a great, dark sky. On the stage, metal insects whirred and stung. Billy's face glowed like a firefly. They began to climb. Billy leapt lizardlike, slender and graceful. Her breath thundered through her mouth and ears as she strained to keep up. She swam in the sac of her sweat, buoyed up like an embryo. People spread out in a wide valley around her.

"I have to sit down," she told him.

"Not yet."

She thought of the hospital. They were climbing so far above it. How would she ever get back down in time? Stop, stop, she thought. But Billy kept pulling her along. People began to thin on either side of them; they were very high now, on the rim of a tornado whose center coiled fiercely far below. Drumming drilled through her skull, electric guitars flooded her brain with iridescence. Billy was slowing down. Finally they sat. He crouched beside her, a frog with black marble eyes. The air was warm flannel down her throat. The music stopped and started, and colors changed each time.

"How are you doing?" she heard Billy say.

He'd taken off his jacket, his shirt. His skin shone, the smooth stone of *The Pietà*, perfect. Touch his smooth skin, touch.

"Hey, you're tickling me, Cee."

Touch his belly, his wet arms, so smooth, so wet. She imagined water coming out of all the little holes he'd put in his arms. Smooth, wet arms, glass arms.

She kissed him, his mouth sponged against hers. His heart beat large inside him, she held him tight in her thick arms, her fat girl arms. She exposed her neck for him, her pure, white skin, smooth as the surface of a pond for him to rupture.

"Cee," he murmured.

His mouth dug into her, drinking her juices, her secrets. By the time he stopped, the music had stopped, too. Everything below them had begun pouring out through the bottom.

I have to go, she said. I have to go. She was shouting, but he didn't hear her.

"Let's wait before going down," he said.

Billy. Billy. I have to—

"Cee, you okay?"

She grabbed his arm. "The hospital. Tell them."

Billy gave her a funny look. He doesn't understand, she thought. It was hard to talk. "Tell them . . . in the hospital."

"Oh. We gotta find a phone."

They started descending. She feared slipping away from him. Finally they were on the ground again and began the trek along the outer ramp.

Without warning, Billy said, "C'mon, we gotta go this way!" He yanked her back in the direction they'd just come from. Everything seemed to fall, as if the whole Aud had toppled off its shelf. Just before turning around she caught a sight of a man in a fringed leather jacket who was headed straight for them. His mouth was beaklike, he swooped in close. The leather fringes quivered like the feathers of a preying falcon.

Billy's fingers felt wired around hers. He kept on dragging her against the swarm of bodies that lobbed against them from the opposite direction. She felt like a salmon battling her way upstream.

It was him, she thought, her thoughts slowly catching up to what was happening. Luke.

A moment later the Fu Manchu mustache appeared almost right in front of them. She could see that he held something shining in his hand. A knife, a gun—

"Shit," Billy said, pushing up a ramp that led back toward the rows of seats. Her body felt like it was bouncing away from her. "I can't, Billy. I can't."

A guard blocked them. "Aud's closed, folks. That way out," he said, pointing them back where they'd just come from.

Luke was closing in on them from behind. His eyes flashed mean and poisonous. Curt began converging on them from the other direction, red-faced as his little legs pumped. Billy picked a bottle off the floor and flung it at Luke. It hit him on the forehead with a round clunk, his eyes crossed, as if he were trying to see what had hit him, and then he toppled like a tree. Curt came at Billy, his knife gleaming dangerously. Billy kicked him, Curt let out a horrible wail, and Billy and Cee rushed past with everyone else all the way out to the street. They kept running alongside the building until they reached the loading docks in the back.

"Jesus," he said, leaning against the wall.

Cee tried to catch her breath. The cold air began to still the spin of her brain. "I knew them," she said after a while.

Billy gaped at her. "You knew who?"

"Those two guys. From Don's grocery."

"The store downstairs from where you live? What do they do there, stock the shelves?" He slumped over. "Jesus Christ. Jesus fucking Christ."

Roadies were loading amplifiers and big black speakers onto a truck.

"They look like coffins, don't they?" Billy said. "Maybe they have my size."

"Luke's brother Victor was the one who fell in the vat of steel, right?"

Billy's face spun around.

"I heard them talking one night in the grocery," Cee said, the slam of Luke's beer can jarring in her ears. "Wait a minute—are you the one who sold Vic the acid he took before he died?"

Billy looked away.

"So he was your . . ."

"Customer, yes."

"That explains why he wants your ass."

"Listen, I didn't know that acid was bad. Cee, you have to believe me," Billy said, agitated. "I'm no chemist. And while we're on the subject of Luke, there's something else you might want to know: He's Kal's ex."

"She was married to *him?*"

"Kal wasn't always her present, politically aware self, you know. She had her down-and-dirty days, too."

"Shit!" Cee said. "The hospital. I can't go to work now. Where's a phone booth?"

"Wait!" He peered around the corner of the building. "Okay, the coast is clear."

When Cee returned, Billy said, "Let's walk a little. My nerves feel like they've been through an Osterizer."

They headed down Main Street as far as the overpass. Before them lay a dark landscape of rubble and broken-down cars. A trail of lights climbed above.

"The Pulaski Skyway," Billy crooned. "Stairway to heaven and Fuhrmann Boulevard."

"This is where you go to . . . meet those truck drivers, right?"

"Picturesque, don't you think?"

They stepped off the road and began walking toward the water. The asphalt buckled, exposing veins of mud. Wrecked cars looked like the upturned prows of ships about to sink. At the water's edge a rank jelly heaved against the pilings. The city looked like a random muddle of light and shadow stretching along the water from the Marine Midland tower to the distant column of flame marking the steel plant.

"Down there is hell," he said, gesturing dramatically toward Lackawanna. "And there," he said, pointing to Canada, "is paradise. You and I, we're in purgatory."

She was shivering. Billy held her. The skyway rumbled with its weight of cars like the conveyor belt of a giant cannery.

"I wish they hadn't seen me there tonight," Billy said. "I've been trying to keep out of sight—that's the big reason I've been scarce. Well, now they know where they can find me." He looked around. "About five years ago I first met Luke here. He was a truck drivin' man then."

"What was he doing here?"

"Hoping to get his doodle sucked. Why else would anyone want to come here, for the view? After we'd finished our business I asked him if he could use a few white crosses. Truckers take them to stay awake. Luke copped, and that was the beginning of a wonderful business relationship."

"That must've been before he was married to Kal?"

"Oh, must it?" Billy shook his head. "After all I've told you about those unhappily married men I met at the Greyhound station, how can you ask such a question? Think of it: Not only was Luke unhappily married, but to a lesbian in the making. Even after I moved out, me and Kal and Luke continued to socialize, and I provided the refreshments. We made a charming threesome. We weren't big on conversation, but we had fun. I knew things between him and Kal weren't going to last. He'd married a dumb, skinny girl who wanted nothing more than to hold on tight to her man as he rode her around on the back of his Honda. But she'd turned on him. She started taking women's studies courses at UB, and the next thing you know she was going at it hot and heavy with a real, live woman.

"Luke did not like this at all. There were fights, and not all of them were verbal. One night he stumbled in on Kal and her lady paramour. He ranted and raged and pulled a knife on the woman, who hightailed it out of the house. She called the police. They came, but Luke convinced them that he and Kal were having a domestic quarrel. And they believed him. With unerring sense, I happened on the scene. Luke was just about ready to rape her. I snuck up from behind and conked him over the head with a frying pan, just like in the movies. He was out cold.

"Kal was raging. She was all set to cut him up in little pieces and feed him into the disposal, if she had one. She hit on an inspired plan that can only be called poetic justice. We stripped him, bound him up good, gag and all, lugged him into the back of Kal's car, drove to his mother's house, and dropped him off on the front lawn like a cord of firewood. To top it off, she tied this note to his big toe, telling his mother that she could have Luke back, because Kal didn't ever want to see him again."

Cee envisioned Luke piled, naked and skeletal, near the boxwood hedge of a Buffalo lawn. "No wonder Luke hates you," Cee said, letting Billy's story sink in.

"No, that's not why. And not because his brother wound up a piece of structural steel, either. Victor's brains had already turned to Silly Putty by the time he did my windowpane. Luke needs someone to blame for his life turning into dogshit, so he blames me for everything bad that's happened to him: his brother croaking, his wife turning queer and trying to get her kid back. Luke's like a horse with a broken leg who's waiting for someone to put him out of his misery."

Cee thought for a moment, then said, "How much does Kal know about you and him?"

"She knows that I used to shoot and sell. But she didn't know I was his supplier."

"Don't you think that's a little strange—selling dope to someone who was beating up your good friend?"

"Hey, wait a minute. I didn't tell him to trash her."

"But . . . you took his money."

"If he didn't get it from me he would have gotten it from somebody else—"

"I think the term for this is 'conflict of interest.' Maybe 'two-faced' is more accurate."

"But that's all over, don't you see? And I got back at him, too. You remember I told you about busting a guy around here? It was Luke. He was out to get me after the lawn party. Too bad for him that a cop happened to be cruising in the area. It's because of that bust that Luke had to stop driving trucks. I'm through with Luke."

"Too bad he's still not through with you. Now I'll have to look both ways before I leave my house. And Kal still has her kid to worry about." She kicked a stone into the water. "What I don't understand is, how did Luke get the kid if he's such a crud?"

"He had no record. The cop found just one joint in the glove compartment, and Luke used the same lawyer who'd won a big settlement for his mother from Bethlehem after Vic died. He convinced the judge that Luke's occasional joint was better than Grant being raised by a full-time lesbian."

They began walking back to the car. Billy touched her arm. "Cee, I don't think I can be alone tonight."

Cee took her nightgown into the bathroom to change, feeling a little like Stephanie. When she returned, Billy was already under the covers all the way up to his neck.

Cee left the light on.

"You will level with Kal, won't you?" Cee said. "I can't bear the thought of someone I care for being a shit. I'm referring to you, by the way."

She got into the bed, conscious of the squeal the bedsprings made. All of Billy's clothes had been piled on the chair. For a long time they lay in bed, awake, silent, listening to the distant rattle of a freight train. She reached over and switched off the light.

"I was a little scared being there in the Aud in the middle of so many people," she said.

"Aunt Billy took care of you, didn't she?"

"When I was peaking, I kept thinking of you as a frog."

"Was that why you kissed me, so that I'd turn into a prince?" He looped a wiry arm over her. His grasp was light but firm. He kissed her on the spot where he'd bitten her earlier.

Something inside Cee began to stir, as it always did when he touched her. Usually she held herself tight, but now her layers loosened and became slowly undone like the petals of a shy flower. She stroked his face. He turned onto his side, and his belly and chest slid taut against her. She felt herself pooling around him, sinking down, soft and unguarded. Billy's face hung above her in the darkness like a moon escaping clouds.

"Hold me," she said. She pulled him down to where she waited. At first, he struggled. But only at first.

He was gone when she awoke the next morning. A pain between her legs reminded her of what had happened, and a weight settled upon her heart.

Later that day she drove back to the basilica, took out her Konica, snapped several pictures, and drove back home. She wanted to record the place where she'd fallen in love for the first time in her life.

CEE THOUGHT ABOUT Billy incessantly. She grew forgetful at work. She knew she had to talk to someone about him. One morning she left work, wide awake, and eager for conversation. Vincent didn't live far, but he surely wasn't up at this ungodly hour. Cee recalled Kal saying that she was a morning person. But maybe she was angry at Cee for missing the women's march. Cee bought some doughnuts, an offering, then drove over. She knocked lightly, in case Kal was asleep after all, but the door opened without delay. Kal's hair was sleek from the shower. Strands of grey glistened, silver among the gold.

"Well, look who's here!"

"I brought us some doughnuts."

Kal's apartment was the top floor of what was once a gracious gingerbready house, subsequently divided up. A tiny kitchen had been built into a corner, crowded with shelves of dishes and thirsty-looking plants. Books and papers cluttered the table. A black cat, introduced to Cee as Elizabeth, curled near Kal's feet.

"I'm not much of a housekeeper," Kal said. "And Lara isn't either."

"Who's Lara?"

Kal's face went dewy. "A wonderful woman who is sleeping in my bed at this very moment."

She poured Cee's coffee, then grabbed a book from the pile and thrust it Cee's way. "You have to read this. It's about a tribe in Africa that has no rulers and is run collectively. A bunch of anarchists in the middle of Africa," she said with admiration. "The women's movement could learn something from that. Take the march, for example. Everything was going along according to plan, so hardly anybody in the city even realized there was a march at all, which is what the organizers and the police no doubt worked out beforehand. As we got ready to turn off Main and head toward Lafayette Square, I began to tell people to go the other way toward Niagara Square. That's where the city's center of power is, the city hall, the city courthouse, the county courthouse, even the fucking chamber of commerce. What's on Lafayette Square, except for the public library? A bunch of us broke off, but the others just kept plodding right along like sheep because there were cops all along the route. Big deal. There were more of us than of them. The marshals told me to stop messing things up and get back in line. Can you imagine, women telling other women to stop stirring things up?" Kal said with indignation. "What the hell were we doing there anyway, if we didn't want to stir things up?"

"Maybe people were afraid."

"Then they shouldn't have been marching in the first place," she thundered.

It was no later than a quarter after seven, Cee thought, but Kal was going top speed.

"Those are law books, aren't they?" Cee said, pointing to volumes as black as the cat.

"You bet. They're going to help me get my son back from the scum who is now his legal guardian."

"How often do you get to see Grant?"

"It's supposed to be once every two weeks. But his father always finds ways to get around it. He lets his phone bills go unpaid until they disconnect his phone so I have no easy way of reaching him. Or else when he pays his phone bill and I call up, he'll say that Grant is sick and can't go out, and he doesn't want me coming over. He can't legally prevent me from seeing my son, but he knows that I've set aside a certain time for being with Grant so that if it falls through I have to put off seeing him for another week. You should think twice before marrying a man."

The phrase struck Cee as odd. Who else would she marry?

"Do you really think you can get Grant back?"

"I'll be damned if I sit back and do nothing. The thought of Grant being under the control of a slime like my ex-husband makes me crazy." She looked down. "I can't believe that I was married to someone like him. I guess I was a different person then. I wasn't my own person. He wanted me, that seemed to be enough."

"Maybe you loved Luke without having a reason."

Kal's eyes darkened. "Where in hell did you dig that up from, some novel? As you can see, I don't have time to read novels. Yeah, I suppose I must have had my reasons. Luke wasn't always fried. When I first met him, he was just a kid who wanted to play drums in a band. There was something warm and homespun about him. He did leather craft and said he wanted to open a shop someday. He would have been good at it, too, but then came the chemicals, and by that time I'd pretty much decided that it wasn't a man that I wanted anyway." Her forehead furrowed. "How did you know his name was Luke?" Then she waved her hand. "Oh, Billy must have told you."

"Billy's sort of why I wanted to talk to you."

"What nonsense is he up to now?"

Cee looked down and saw Elizabeth's tail swiping back and forth. "I'm in love."

"Are you serious?" Kal said with a shout. The cat sprang away. "All I can say is, it's a mistake. A big mistake." She rapped her finger against one of the law books, as if to invoke a precedent. "I'm surprised at you; I thought you had smarts. I can understand why you might have grown fond of him. Everyone does when they first meet him. Billy is okay to be entertained by and to feel fond of, but not, I repeat, not to fall in love with. He tried to make me into a mother—the kind who gives her babies sleeping pills to keep them quiet."

"Kal, I didn't say I was going to run off into the sunset with him—"

"Sister, I can tell that you need to get seriously filled in about him. Billy spent the first fifteen years of his life having his father tell him what a pervert he was. Then, after discovering that he really was a pervert and liked being one, he dared the world to put up with him. It gave him the fuck-off attitude that he calls politics and permits him to be rotten to everyone except people he needs something from."

"I thought you guys were friends."

"We started out that way. At first I let him stay with me because he had nowhere else to go. We got closer. I'd just begun accepting my feelings for women, and I saw Billy as a kind of gay freedom fighter. He changed me. Before I knew him I was a good girl. Right after high school I went to Bryant and Stratton Business School for typing and bookkeeping, just like my parents wanted, and then got married and had a kid. Billy saw it wasn't right for me; he helped me see it, too, and for that I'll always be grateful. I still feel more for him than I do for any other man. And we've been through a lot together. But I've learned to keep Gizzi at a distance. There are people in this world, usually men, who make other people, frequently women, feel sorry for them. They want you to take care of them, which is bad enough. Only they don't really let you. You try and you try and wind up hating yourself for not being able to help."

"That's what you think is going on between Billy and me?"

"Go ahead, call me a man-hating cynic," she said, waving her hand. Cee was about to protest when Kal cut her short. "Before I say anything else, you should know that Billy was never one to worry about —how shall I put it—getting the facts straight. For example, I suppose he told you about his father kicking him out of the house. A very sad story. And it's true, except that his father kicked him out not only because Billy was screwing with the TV repairman but also because he had a needle in his arm. I can't say that throwing an eighteen-year-old junkie out of the house is any better than throwing out an eighteen-year-old queer. But notice which part of the story Billy chose to tell."

"Billy said he doesn't shoot up anymore. Is that true?"

"If it is, you can thank his terrible father, the ex-military man, who was able to get Billy into a treatment program for addicted Vietnam vets for at the VA hospital, even though Billy was no vet. Now, I know Billy didn't tell you that, either." She smiled sadly. "I once loved Billy very much, and maybe I still do. And I know that whatever he might have done, it wasn't to hurt me. But it hurt anyway."

"Like what?"

"Like selling dope to Luke even after he knew what Luke was doing to me."

"So you knew."

She gave an angry laugh. "Of course I knew. And it damn near killed me when I found out. I thought Billy understood what it was to get fucked over by men, and he knew how Luke had begun treating me. But then I found out something even worse." She sat back and crossed her arms grimly. "Billy was in love with Luke."

Cee set down her cup. "Billy? In love with Luke?"

"Don't look surprised. Billy loves talking Gay Is Good. He claims to hate going to straight bars. Maybe so. But Luke fits right into every one of Billy's sick fantasies." She tore off the words, syllable by syllable.

Cee remembered Billy talking about the Neanderthal men fucking him in the backs of their trucks.

"By the way," Kal continued. "Doesn't the fact that he's queer put a damper on your affection?"

"I didn't say he was in love with me."

"At least you're realistic." Kal ran a hand through her hair. "I think we've talked enough about Billy Gizzi for today," she said. She looked at Cee with the hint of a grin. "Remember that night in the CPG when Billy introduced us? I thought, 'Pity she isn't a dyke.'" She reached over and put a hand on Cee's shoulder. "You're an attractive woman, you know."

No one had ever said that to her, Cee thought, feeling the grey of Kal's eyes like warm flannel around her.

"But I'm glad I didn't fall in love with you," Kal went on. "Now we can be friends instead."

"That night I thought you looked a little mean."

"I am a little mean. These days it's healthy for women to be that way, don't you think?"

A red-haired woman appeared in the doorway, wrapped in a robe, her eyes still glazed over from sleep.

"Lara," Kal said, lifting up her arms to caress her. "This is Cee."

Lara's smile got stretched out by a yawn.

Just before leaving, Cee said, "Kal, are you . . . do you . . . I mean, is it hard for you, knowing that Billy and me—?"

Kal looked straight at her. "You should first ask yourself whether it's hard for you."

9

THE FIRST THING Stanley saw when he woke in his hotel room was the half-empty bottle of scotch on the night table. He checked to see if anyone was sleeping on the other side of the bed. No one was. He looked at his watch. It had been roughly twelve hours since he'd sat down to dinner with his family and told them that he was—

A homosexual.

The decision to tell them had come after he'd written that ridiculous letter to Billy. For days afterward, he felt nothing but shame. He punished himself with thoughts of Billy's chocolate eyes, which might be wild or calm as a forest. He thought of his smooth face, and most painfully, of that tight little bum, like two great ball bearings swiveling independently of each other in the socket of his hips. One weekend, needing more than ever to see Billy again, he'd even driven down to Buffalo—Audrey had been suspicious—but no one answered when he knocked on Billy's door, nor was Billy at Hadrian's. Stanley drove back, full of rage, and sadness. Something, as they say, had to give. He knew just what. The only question was when.

The signs had been clear enough, even if it had taken him long to notice them. Starting around age eighteen his throat dried to parchment any time an appealing man passed on the street, or when the momentary closeness of a jogger churned up an enticing whiff of manly exertion. He rarely left the public pool without an erection. The urges didn't disappear after marriage; wedded life merely obscured them, like wallpaper over a lump in the plaster.

Business had him on the road often, and he got into the habit of driving over to Buffalo any time he got down as far as Fort Erie. He stumbled onto a student place on Elmwood one evening, and fell into conversation with a group of guys. They were a good ten years younger, but he got on fine with them. When they said they were going someplace else, Stanley followed. The bar they went to was friendly, and he almost didn't notice that it was full of . . . men. He'd gotten drunk enough to make driving back impossible. When one of the guys offered to put him up for the night, he accepted. Later, when the man touched him, he let him, too drunk to push him away...

Early the next morning he crept out to his car, hardly able to face the sight of the naked man beside him. But he made a mental note of where the bar was: near the corner of Main and Allen.

Stanley's first night with Billy was much different. They had a long breakfast in the morning. They talked. Or rather, Billy talked and Stanley listened, entranced by the flow of effeminate patter pouring forth from the lithe, muscular young man sitting shirtless opposite him. Billy described the people he worked with at the restaurant (cretins who knew how to add and tie their shoelaces, but no more), and the customers (cretins with Diner's Club cards), swearing that one day he would go to New York and become the social secretary to a millionaire dowager who still wore pearls and pillbox hats, ate aspic for luncheon, and couldn't get into anything smaller than a size eighteen dress. He interrupted himself to peer out the window and declare, in pseudo BBC-English, "What a mahvelously blahnd day it is!" A moment later he'd started up again about seeing *Mrs. Miniver* on "The Late Show" with Greer Garson, his favorite actress, and was appalled when Stanley confessed to never having heard of her. ("What do you mean, she was Irish, that's almost Canadian, isn't it?") Billy asked Stanley what he did for a living, and when Stanley told him, Billy's chilly syllable of reply hit Stanley like a snowball: "Oh," he said. He assured Stanley that it needn't prevent them from getting together the following weekend, although, truth to tell, Stanley was in desperate need of a new haberdasher.

Was this how homosexual Americans talked? Stanley wondered.

Stanley surprised himself by keeping their date. After seeing Billy a few times, he was sure he'd break it off. He didn't. And later, when he realized that he liked Billy, he was determined to stop liking him. But he couldn't. Billy, once a recreation, a diversion, an outlet for frustration, had become a need. He tried convincing Billy that he really wasn't "that way." Billy had merely laughed. "Sweetie, if you weren't that way, it wouldn't hurt me so much to shit the day after I see you."

Yes, he liked Billy a lot. Perhaps he even loved him, even if he wasn't entirely sure that two men could love each other, and even if Billy was forever talking about coming out of closets, a ridiculous expression if there ever was one. (He rather had the feeling of being in a basement.) It just seemed a little strange to look down and see his cock crossed with Billy's as if on some coat of arms; to have Billy's red-nail-polished nails clutching his balls, or simply to have the person in bed with him be a man and not a woman. On the other hand, it didn't seem strange at all.

But the light bulb . . .

Sitting on that hard bench outside the emergency room, he kept thinking, Maybe it's true what people say about queers, that they're sick, perverted, and against nature. And no matter how you looked at it, doing what Billy did just wasn't . . . normal. After recovering from the initial shock, Stanley was furious that Billy had endangered his own life. But as the night wore on and Billy went into his second pack of frozen plasma, a brooding sadness filled Stanley. He feared for Billy's life. And he feared for his own. Each of Billy's screams accused him. Stanley felt as if he deserved to be in that bed as much as Billy, and to have lost as much blood and felt as much pain. Billy was far more honest and brave than Stanley had the nerve to be and was paying for his honesty in that hospital bed. Stanley could leave all of this behind and return to wife and house and insulation customers with nothing more than a motel bill to pay. And coward that he was, that's exactly what he'd do. But at least he'd had the gumption to give his name to the secretary. She asked what was his relation to the patient, pen poised over the admission form. A knot tied in his throat. "Friend," he'd stammered.

Once Billy was moved out of the emergency room and was asleep, Stanley left. He packed up his things at the motel, drove back to Toronto, and threw himself in bed, clinging to Audrey for dear life, wanting more than anything to believe in the rightness of being married to her. But he couldn't. "Tell me what's wrong," Audrey said to him. He couldn't do that, either, but knew that he would have to soon.

Driving home last night, Stanley had considered his choice of words. Would he say that he was gay? No, that sounded too political. Queer? Too insulting. Homosexual? A disease. As he neared his exit he grew jittery with stage fright. Perhaps Audrey's response would be to offer help. He stopped for a bottle of wine and a bouquet of flowers. It wasn't until he'd pulled into the driveway that he remembered that Audrey preferred potted plants to cut flowers. But there they were, wrapped and fragrant on the seat beside him, a dozen unnecessary yellow roses.

Anita, his pert eleven-year-old daughter, and Bonnie, the sheepdog, met Stanley at the door. Anita quickly took charge of finding a vase for the flowers, and Bonnie loped beside him as he went to hang up his coat. Stanley consumed most of the wine at dinner and felt somewhat dulled by the time they finished eating. The flowers overwhelmed the table and brought out the insistent yellow of the dining room, with its gleaming brass chandelier, cream-colored china, straw placemats, and wallpaper whose color, he recalled, was citrus. Stanley was about to refill his glass when he looked at Anita and Seth, who were eating their cake (yellow, too). Should they hear his little speech? He couldn't very well send them to their rooms; they would take it as punishment, and they'd done nothing wrong. On the other hand, he could simply say that he and their mother had something important to discuss. But that was always a signal for them to take up spying posts on the stairs.

Yellow, Stanley recalled, was the color of cowardice.

"I have something to say," was how he began.

And he told them. In a final, pitiful moment, he rejected the H-word for a silly-sounding Britishism. "I'm inclined toward men," he said.

"Children, I want you both to go to your rooms," Audrey said, without looking at her husband.

"They should hear this, Audrey."

"They already have," she said in an icy tone. She turned to Seth and Anita. "Do as I say."

Anita seemed anxious to hear more, but trotted off obediently. Seth looked Stanley right in the eye and said, "Does that mean you're gay?"

Stanley stammered, "Y-yes."

"I don't believe you."

"I told you to go to your room," Audrey said.

"It's true, Seth."

"Go to your room!"

After Seth left, they sat at the table without speaking. The presence of the children had made it easier for Stanley to say what he'd said. They made it . . . a family affair. Alone with Audrey, the issue had become a purely marital problem, more intimate. He yearned to hide behind the clump of roses.

"I suppose you have a good reason for all this," Audrey said. Her lips quivered. "I mean . . . do you have . . . proof? I haven't noticed anything different about you."

"Did you think I would suddenly start wearing dresses?"

"Don't make jokes, not now!"

"I have no proof, Audrey. Just my feelings."

"Your feelings," she said, a little smugly. "And you have no reason to believe that these . . . feelings of yours will change?"

It almost sounded as if she were referring to a nasty habit of his. He was tempted to see if Anita and Seth were hiding at the top of the banister.

"I don't think so."

She stood up. "Does your . . . friend's name happen to be William Guzzi?"

Stanley gasped. The evocation of Billy's name in that house was frightening. "Gizzi," Stanley said, in a daze. "How did you know?"

"This . . . person sent a package." She went to a drawer, retrieved a box addressed to MacIntyre. Inside were the house shoes Stanley had brought Billy. "I puzzled over these treasures for a long time before I found that a note had been enclosed, which explained everything."

Stanley dug into the box and found an envelope with a small card. "If the crown fits—"

He read no further.

"I suppose I shouldn't have been surprised after finding those panties. Of course, back then I thought you were carrying on with a woman. How naive of me." Her voice had grown unsteady. "Tell me, did you go for midnight walks with him, treat him to candlelight suppers, buy him presents? That is what one does when one is in love, isn't it?"

"Calm down, Audrey."

"And how long has this business with Guzzi—or Gizzi—been going on?"

"A year."

She began to sound worried. "Is he important enough to you to give up your family, your home, everything you've worked for?"

"Who says I have to do that?"

"What else can follow from this? Or did you expect me to invite your little friend to move into the spare room? I suppose you thought I would start each day with a smile to see you fixing his tea in those slippers." She pointed to the box with disdain. "What kind of man would send another man slippers like that to wear?"

"He didn't buy them, Audrey." He swallowed. "I did. For him."

Audrey stood back, as though he'd just told her he carried a contagious disease.

"Audrey—" He went to embrace her but she pulled away.

"I don't want you sleeping in the same bed with me," she said, her back turned to him.

"Because of the slippers?"

"Stop mocking me, Stanley."

"Are you throwing me out?"

She turned around, startled. "No, of course not. But... for the moment—" her voice grew thin, ready to pull apart "—it seems wiser that you find somewhere else to live. Maybe you can go to your brother Arthur." She remained with her back to him. Stanley could see her bra through her blouse. He yearned to hold her.

"Why did you hold onto those slippers for so long?" he asked.

"I was waiting for you to say something."

"But if you had an inkling about me, then why didn't you ever talk about it?"

Her shoulders shook. "Because... I hoped that there'd be nothing to talk about." The flutter in her voice had become a tremble. "I guess I was a coward, or else—" she glanced at the shoes "—I must have lacked imagination." She fled up the stairs to her room. "What are you two doing here!" she wailed when she reached the top of the stairs. Bonnie barked, there was a scuffle of feet on the landing, and he heard their bedroom door shutting.

Stanley picked up the shoes, whose color clashed wildly with everything else in the room. What had possessed him to buy them? He noticed Anita standing at the top of the stairs and motioned for her to come. She scampered down, and Bonnie lumbered after, her claws tacking on the floor.

"You were listening the whole time, weren't you?" he asked. Bonnie's bulky warmth fell against his leg. He put his arms around Anita and ran his hands through her watery-smooth hair. "I love you very much," he said.

"Mum's crying."

"I know," he answered. "I know."

"If you are inclined toward men does that mean you are declined toward women?"

It was an interesting way of putting it. "It means that I find men, I mean, I am attracted—" Stanley's mind rang with confusion. How could he explain it to her? There was no way of knowing how much she already knew about . . . the regular way. She hadn't even started her monthlies yet, had she? "Let's just say that I like men more," he said.

"I certainly don't like men, at least not boys. They're crude and silly and not at all smart."

"There are nice ones, too. Like your brother."

"You still love Mummy, don't you?"

"Of course I do."

"Oooh, whose are they?" She pointed to the shoes.

Stanley clutched the box protectively. "They're . . . they belong to a friend of mine."

He glanced upstairs, wondering whether Audrey would speak to him if he went up, then decided it was wiser not to disturb her. But his clothes were in the bedroom closet. He went down to the basement, found a small suitcase, and dropped in the shoes. A wash hung stiffly beside the water heater. He plucked down a couple of pairs of his underwear, socks, and T-shirts, and dumped them in. Back upstairs he spied a dry-cleaning ticket for his work shirts stuck to the refrigerator with a magnet; he folded that into his pocket. He'd have to make do with the suit he had on, but he'd have enough to wear for the next couple of days. On his way to the front door his eyes fell on the liquor cabinet. He took out a bottle of scotch and slipped that into the suitcase, too.

"Where are you going?" Anita asked.

"To Uncle Arthur's house."

"Why?"

Think fast. "Because your mother needs a rest."

Her face fell. "For how long?"

"I'm not sure. Not too long." His eyes fell on the vase of flowers. "Why don't you take some of the roses into your room. And tell your brother he may take some into his room, too."

"Seth?" Her face wrinkled. "Seth's a boy. Boys don't like flowers."

He smiled. "I'm sure some do. Tell Mum where I've gone." He glanced upstairs one last time. Audrey was still crying. "Give your daddy a kiss," he said, bending down. Anita kissed him. He gave Bonnie a tug under the neck and left.

As he got into his car it occurred to him that facing Arthur, his lovely wife, Carol, and their two wonderful children was more than he could bear. Their house reminded him too much of his own, right down to the living room on a mezzanine overlooking the entryway, to say nothing of the wife and two children. (How was it that so many middle-class Canadians of English origin resembled each other?) Instead of taking the turnoff for 401, he kept on going. He would drive into the city and find an inexpensive hotel.

After he was settled in his room, he called Arthur to tell him where he was, should Audrey call. "You in trouble?" Arthur asked.

Stanley assured him he wasn't. There was no need to say anything else, he thought. Audrey would would go to Carol, and the whole family would know the whole, sad story in a matter of hours.

That morning Stanley remembered a customer he had to see later in the day, reached for the phone, and rescheduled the appointment for the middle of the week. Only when he'd hung up did he notice how easily he'd done it; canceling appointments usually had him sweating and stuttering into the receiver. This morning he felt unusually calm. His fingers lingered near the dial; should he call Audrey? It was Wednesday: She was leading school groups through the Ontario Science Centre. He visualized her before a dinosaur skeleton. She was good at explaining things to children. Stanley recalled Seth's disapproving glare. Audrey would have her hands full of explaining now.

Should he call Billy? No, not yet, not until he knew just what he'd say to him.

He slipped out of his pajamas, ready to dress, then caught sight of himself, naked, in the full-length mirror. He couldn't remember the last time he'd taken a good look at his own body, except for the worried glance he gave his paunch every so often. There he was, big and pink, a froth of reddish chest hair, with reddish hair between his legs, too. ("We certainly are colorful," Billy had exclaimed, their first night together.) Today Stanley's penis looked smaller than usual, as if shrinking from the scrutiny. He'd always been able to satisfy Audrey all these years, hadn't he? They were never a wild pair, no toys, no acrobatics, but she seemed to respond. Would she go and find herself a lover now? A new husband? Stanley thought of Anita, of Seth, of Bonnie, even of the yellow dining room. And he felt very sad.

10

Cee turned on the ten o'clock news as she got ready for work.

The South Vietnamese government had capitulated to North Vietnamese forces. The communists had overrun Saigon. "To the very end, President Thieu clung to the belief that the United States would not abandon him," the announcer said in a flat, serious voice against a patter of teletype. The war in Vietnam, he said, was now officially over. There was a shot of an American flag being lowered, of planes taking off from a jungle landing strip.

Vietnam, she thought.

It was like yoghurt and Grauman's Chinese Theater and being cremated, which all seemed to come into existence the moment she first learned about them. It began for her after Jason was born, after John Fitzgerald Kennedy got shot, and after the astronauts rendezvoused and docked. Black kids had already started getting bused in from Binghamton. That South African man was on the cover of *Life* magazine, smiling after his heart transplant. Was it after the student nurses were killed in Chicago?

Vietnam displaced the fires and robberies in the *Sun-Bulletin*. The name of the country appeared like a word misspelled. (Veteran? Vitamin?) Where was it? Near China, flowery and full of dragons. Near Japan, where they made transistor radios. Boys in her high school called it 'Nam and talked of going there to stomp gooks. She'd just started high school when tropical villages began exploding into black-and-white flames on the news. A newscaster would read a report on the latest fighting, while behind him, arrows flashed on the map of Vietnam, a curled, stinging insect, or else they'd show soldiers firing into palm trees. Where was the enemy? she wondered. She found them on the pages of *Life* magazine: naked, screaming, Chinese-looking children fleeing the deadly fog of napalm, a man who stood stubbornly still as a gun was placed against his skull, its trigger about to be squeezed.

Your father can tell you from his own experience, Jason. Those Orientals aren't like us. They have no respect for human life, not even their own.

That's how they got those pilots to go on kamikaze missions in World War II. They have what you could call the killer instinct.

The kamikaze were Japanese, for chrissake!

Don't talk to your father in that tone of voice, Carl.

But Mom, he's filling Jason's head with lies.

Tell me, Carl, do you know what it's like to crawl on your belly through the jungle while some chink shoots at you?

And do you know what a baby looks like that's been hit by napalm?

I'll say it once more. You're turning eighteen next month. If you're not planning to register, you can just walk your fanny right over to the police station, because if you don't turn yourself in, then I will.

President Ford came on, speaking at a press conference. A reporter remarked that no one was expecting any ticker tape to be thrown on the soldiers returning from Vietnam as it was after World War II. What did the president think of that? People were already referring to the Vietnam conflict as the first war America lost, another reporter said. What was the president's response? A third reporter spoke of Vietnam as an American tragedy. What did the president have to say about that? Each time Ford responded in a multipurpose monotone Cee associated with politicians, one that could just as easily sell disposable diapers. "America can be proud of having fought to defend democracy," he said.

It was all over, she thought, about to leave the house. It had ended two years ago without being completely over. And now it finally was.

The streets seemed deserted, as if the war had been fought in the city and a curfew imposed. Cee felt tired. She knew why, too: Her period was late, and in this case, "late" was a euphemism. There were all sorts of reasons for a late period, and she obediently reeled them off to herself: a cold, stress, overexertion, change in daily rhythms. She had a bit of all of the above. Somehow, it didn't matter. She *knew* she was pregnant. Her fatigue meant something down there was slowly moving into operation. It was amazing what might happen in no more than three short weeks.

Cee hadn't seen Billy in all that time. She missed him, yet she was grateful at first that he'd left her alone. She'd felt only confusion after their night together; seeing him would only make things worse. But slowly she found herself needing to hear the nervous peaks of his voice and see the crazy flash of his eyes. Still he didn't call. She knew why: Billy was as scared as she was.

"Someone phoned and left a message for you," Anne said as Cee walked onto the unit, and Cee's heart raced as Anne handed her the note, hoping to see Billy's name. Carl's was written instead.

She called during her break. It was almost two in the morning, but he sounded wide awake.

"Cee, I'm so glad you called!"

It was still strange hearing his voice on a phone. "What's up?"

"The county approved the measure to lease the land. Larrabee signed an agreement with the board of supervisors." He paused. "We've been given ninety days to vacate."

"I thought they were going put it on the ballot in the primary election."

"That would have been necessary only if Larrabee wanted to buy the land. But the mountain will still belong to the county so there's no need for a vote. And that's not all. Guess who's getting one of the construction jobs? Dear old Dad. He was one of the first to be notified. A personal letter signed by Larrabee himself."

She struggled to take everything in.

"The bookstore's lawyer said that we might be able to prove that the plans violate state conservation laws. Larrabee'll have to file an environmental impact statement, and we can contest it. On the other hand, their lawyer has already indicated that he is ready to bring up the fact that I'm a draft dodger."

"But the war's over. Even the president said so," she said, hearing the irony in her voice.

"If it comes out, it won't look good," he continued. "You feel like driving down?"

"I have to work. I wouldn't be able to stay for longer than a weekend."

"I'm scared, Cee."

She heard him breathing.

"Let me talk to the head nurse about it."

Another pause. "Things with me and Elaine have gotten worse."

The door to the ER opened.

"Carl, I gotta go."

She hung up. A young black man was being rolled in. The bandages around his head were heavy with blood. No doubt he was yet another victim of one of the three Ss: street crime, substance abuse, or someone they knew—a family feud or lovers' quarrel. He didn't look good; his nose had that ominous pointy look.

"Anything for me?" Cee asked one of the EMTs, meaning ID, so she could do the Admit and get in touch with the "Person(s) to notify in case of emergency." The EMT shook his head. They pulled the drape. The defibrillator's jolt had the man hopping into the air and thudding back down. Some time later the doctors and nurses emerged, Durkin among them, making a thumbs down.

"Call downstairs," she said.

"We don't have any ID on him."

"Tell them that if they don't take him fast I'm going to step on their asses. I got living people here to worry about."

The morgue often took its time accepting what they called grab bags—unidentified corpses—in order to force the stations to do the tracking down. Cee went to the storeroom for a mortuary pack and set it beside the man. His face was covered. She had never seen a dead person before and lifted up the sheet.

Race. His face had a greyish tint to it, like old chocolate. One side of his mouth sagged low. She noticed that he'd grown a mustache—

Cee slapped the sheet back over him and returned to her desk. She sat down and rested her head in her hand. Then she reached for the telephone book. She vaguely remembered that Stephanie lived on Peach. There it was: Amalia Polite. Cee dialed.

"Hello?"

Cee recognized the sturdy voice of Stephanie's mother.

"I'm sorry to disturb you, Mrs. Polite. This is Buffalo General Hospital calling . . ."

"My dear Lord," Mrs. Polite said.

Half an hour later, Cee looked up from her charting to see Stephanie standing in front of her desk.

"You—" she said.

Cee thought she detected anger in Stephanie's voice, as if charging Cee with Race's murder.

"Hello, Stephanie."

She wore no makeup and looked weary.

"Where is he?" Her lips pressed together as though to keep herself from saying anything more.

Durkin put her hand on Stephanie's shoulder. "Cee here will take you to him."

"I didn't know you worked here," Stephanie said as they started for the elevator. "I thought you were in school."

"Not any more."

"Me neither."

It didn't sound like she wanted to talk.

The way from the elevator to the morgue was long. The cinderblock walls of the subbasement resembled those of a jail; they echoed the clack of Stephanie's heels and the stamp of Cee's clogs, a replay of their walks in the union.

Stephanie gasped when they showed her Race. "That's him," she said, looking away.

They started back to the elevator in silence.

"What happened to him?" Cee said at last.

"Race came over—I'm living with my mother again. She doesn't like him coming round. We don't go with each other no more, but he'd still come round. I let him; I didn't want to hurt his feelings. He still likes me and doesn't have no one else. Tonight my mother said, 'Can't you see the girl ain't interested?' Race said I made her say it. She said nobody had to tell her what to say. He got mad and left. He must have gone over to his friends' and got drunk and then who knows—"

"Someone stabbed him, Stephanie."

The elevator came. Neither looked at the other during the ride up.

Cee slowed her step to stretch out the time before they reached the ER, hoping Stephanie might say something about what had happened back in December—the stereo, the torn photos, Race—but she didn't. They stood for a moment outside the ER.

"That Race," Stephanie said, shaking her head.

"I'm sorry, Stephanie."

Stephanie shrugged and their eyes met for the first time that evening. She thought of telling Stephanie that she thought she was pregnant, as if that might establish some common ground between them. But Stephanie's glance told her that the events of the previous fall had been pushed to the side by the press of new cares, and that there was nothing for them to say to one another.

"I have to go. My mother's waiting in the lobby. Good-bye," she said, heading for the elevator.

"Were you two friends?" Durkin asked afterward.

Cee thought for a moment then said, "Yes," daring Stephanie to come back and disagree.

That morning after work she drove over to Kal's house.

Kal opened the door, still in her bathrobe.

"Kal!"

A thick ridge of purple rose from one side of her face. One eye was swollen and only half open. Scabs the color of faded rose petals shadowed her cheekbone. Her half-closed eye gave her a face a peculiar, childlike quality. Her face seemed hollow, like a house someone had laid waste. Cee thought of Race.

"Now you know what I look like without my makeup," Kal said, showing Cee in. "Coffee?"

Cee nodded weakly. The table was cleared of books and the lights were out. Kal moved between the table and the sink sluggishly.

"I didn't wake you, did I?"

"I would have had to have been asleep for that. These days I don't sleep too well."

"Tell me what happened."

"I ran into my ex-husband," she said, filling their cups. "Or maybe I should say that he ran into me. I assume what triggered him off this time was getting my letter informing him that I intended to appeal for custody of Grant." She lifted her cup to her lips as slowly as she'd walked. Her voice seemed thick and plodding. Everything about her seeemed weak and stricken.

Cee thought of the man hulking near Don's front counter, of the wasted Goliath who'd tumbled, bleeding, into the crowd of the Aud, struck by Billy's bottle. "It's hard to imagine a kid being so important to someone like him."

"He likes Grant, and Grant is about all Luke has to keep his world together, now that he isn't driving trucks anymore. Because of Grant he gets welfare and food stamps and SSI and AFDC and WIC and who the fuck knows what else. If it wasn't for Grant, Luke would shrivel up and die. He doesn't take care of Grant, of course; Linda, his girlfriend, does. And she likes Grant, too. It's probably what keeps her staying with Luke."

"If he's so worried about losing Grant, then why did he do something stupid like attacking you?"

"Because he's not very bright, and because he still can't deal with me wanting to be with a woman and not with him. Back in the old days, if I'd taken a new male lover, Luke would have challenged him to a duel. But a woman lover's not worth the effort, so I'm the one who takes it in the teeth."

Cee studied Kal's bruises. It was hard to look at her. In her bathrobe, a cup of coffee to her lips, Kal might have been just another battered housewife left alone to lick her wounds.

"When did it happen?" Cee said softly.

"Couple of nights ago. He was waiting downstairs with a two-by-four. It's a good thing Lara was here. She carted me off to the Meyer, and they bandaged me up." She paused. "I want you to know that I blame Billy for this," she said, pointing to her face. "In Luke's eyes, Billy and I are one and the same—it's guilt by association. But Luke can't get his hands on Billy, so he gets me. Maybe if he'd testified against Luke at the custody hearing I wouldn't be in this mess now." Elizabeth hopped up onto Kal's lap, as a corroborating witness.

"I thought you'd forgiven Billy for his involvement with Luke."

"I thought I had, too. This incident reminded me that Billy hadn't earned any forgiveness. You see, if I wanted to, I could find excuses for what Luke did. I know he's angry at the world, and there's no one for him to lash out at. Curt's too dumb for Luke's abuse to matter to him. Linda'd be out of there in a flash if he ever laid a hand on her. So who's left? The way he sees it, I'm fair game. After all, if one of my good friends is willing to two-face me, why shouldn't he? So I'm not giving Billy the benefit of any doubt. Billy knew just what he was doing the whole time he dealt with Luke.

"When the custody hearings began, I asked Billy to testify, since he knew enough to keep Luke from being appointed dogcatcher. But Billy said he was afraid to do it because of his dealing. I knew better. He just didn't want to say anything against Luke because, deep down, he was still in love with him. I asked my lover to testify that Luke had threatened her with a knife, but she didn't want anyone finding out that she was a lesbian. So they took Grant away from me and gave him to that scum, and I get a two-by-four in my face as I'm trying to go to work." Her face looked hollow. "My God, sometimes I hate men so much."

Cee knew that it wasn't just Kal's intention to reopen custody hearings that had made Luke go wild; it was Billy's bottle, too. But she couldn't tell Kal that, even though she sensed that she should. Something inside her pinched together.

"Kal," Cee said. She took Kal's hand, warm from stroking Elizabeth. She glanced at the law books stacked in a corner of the table like a mass of impregnable rock, too heavy for anyone to lift alone.

On the way home she stopped in Delaware Park. It was warm enough to leave her jacket in the car, the first morning that felt like April. She had the park practically to herself. The old trees graced her walk, guards of a seldom-visited museum pleased to see visitors.

Right after Stephanie left Cee got the results of her pregnancy test: She'd passed with flying colors. Would she tell Billy?

Not necessarily. She knew what he thought of "breeders."

Her mother? Oh God.

Next question: Would she keep it?

Elaine would advise her to keep the child and celebrate her woman's energy. She'd tell Cee to bring the baby up to the house and they'd raise it together.

Wonderful, especially now that they were going to be evicted.

What difference did it make if she told people or not?

Because she wanted someone to say, Now listen here. You march your Polish-American ass over to a clinic and get an abortion. Or else she wanted to be told, Keep it, keep it. You want nothing more than to be able to put your arms around someone and say, "You're mine, I'm yours, I love you." And what was wrong with that? It was why most people had children.

Cee headed for the lake and sat down on a bench, facing the templelike historical society building, a souvenir of the Pan-American Exposition. She'd seen pictures of the exposition: a miniature realm of domes and spires and palaces and canals. Then someone shot President McKinley on the grounds, attendance fell, and the exposition closed, bankrupt. Buffalo's rotten luck. All it took was one teensy bit of real life to bring the illusion toppling down. She imagined the kind of ladies who probably worked at the historical society: spinsterish crows in skirts and flats, wearing lockets. An American flag flew in front of the building. Her thoughts shifted to the news of the war ending. The fighting was over, and she was pregnant: a classic postwar scenario, a child born to a homecoming soldier and his long-estranged bride. But Billy had been no soldier, Cee was nobody's bride, and for years she'd heard one president after another claim that Vietnam was a peacekeeping venture, not a war. It seemed fitting that the official end of such a useless, lost non-war should occur alongside her mismatched union with Billy.

An abortion would have her in and out of the hospital on the same day. If you had to have a fetus sucked out of you, it made sense to have as little fetus as possible—

God, it was gross.

Just before leaving Kal's house she'd gone to the bathroom and peeked into Kal's room. Lara lay, her face a peaceful island, amidst the turbulence of her long red hair.

Women with women. Women without men.

Child.

Mother.

Cee repeated the words as she walked back to the car, until they became a mantra.

Something tightened in her groin. Please let it be a pre-menstrual cramp, she thought, in spite of all evidence to the contrary. Her cramps were like that Oriental torture where you ate tightly wrapped bamboo slivers that exploded inside of you and tore your guts to pieces. The first twinges had her praying to the Goddess Tampona for mercy. Now she hoped they might do their worst, if only it meant that she weren't pregnant.

But the twinge passed quickly. Too quickly.

A Coca-Cola truck was blocking her parking spot when she pulled up in front of her house. Don was talking to the driver. She honked.

"Relax, Cee. He'll be out of here soon. Oh, I saw your friend coming by just before." He rolled his eyes and made a limp-wrist gesture with his hand, grinning.

"Fuck you," she said.

Billy had come by. He'd finally come by.

She parked and walked upstairs. The telephone rang as soon as she stepped in the door. She pulled her key from the lock and ran up the stairs. The phone kept on ringing. It wasn't like Billy to be so persistent. She lunged for the phone.

"Cee?"

It was her mother. She had bad news: Jason was the prime suspect in a rape case. The girl had walked herself to the police station and had described Jason right down to the blink of his eyes and the scar on his hand. His car had been found near the old WPA houses. When the police came to the door in the middle of the night, her father had broken down and cried right in front of them.

"I'm going out of my mind," Theresa said. "We don't even know where he is."

After hanging up Cee pulled out her box of pictures and found the one of Jason she'd hung in her dorm room. On his back, his arms open, he seemed to be awaiting an embrace. She imagined him glistening infernally as he lifted weights in his room, and then she threw down the picture. Something had gone wrong, very wrong. It had been going wrong for a long time, but no one had noticed. People like Jason disguised their misery, lest it be discovered and used against them. They remained unnoticed, invisible, until they hurt someone else or got hurt themselves.

She reached for the picture once more. She saw Jason's image divided into face and torso; the first she recognized and cherished, the second threatened her. For a moment she thought she might tear the picture to bits, the way Stephanie had.

No. Before she did anything, she would have to hear the whole story. And she'd have to hear it from Jason.

Part Three

I

I'll ask you one more time, Elaine: Why did you set me up in front of the Coalition?"

He and Elaine had been to a meeting of the Mountain Coalition that lasted over three hours. Two dozen people had packed into Shera Hain's hot, low-ceilinged living room. Larrabee's lease had stunned everyone.

"I didn't set you up," she said, tensely articulating every syllable for emphasis. "I merely made a proposal."

"You already knew exactly how I felt about this proposal," he sneered. "Why did you bring it up at the meeting?"

"I wanted to see what other people felt about the idea."

"No!" he shouted. "You figured that if you asked me in front of everybody I wouldn't be able to say no. Which is just what happened. Now everyone thinks your idea is our last chance."

Elaine's mouth tightened. "I don't want to talk about it anymore."

"Well, I do."

"Not while I'm driving. You're making me nervous."

Carl sought a place for his hands, first on the seat, then on his lap. Finally one made for the armrest and the other gripped the seat belt.

For Carl, most of the evening had been a waste of time. One unrealistic proposal followed another. Someone suggested persuading Larrabee to transfer his project to the site of the abandoned sawmill, but who was going to buy luxury houses so close to a highway? A student from the state university declared that Larrabee's project violated the treaty of 1793, which gave the mountain to the Indians after they were chased up from the riverfront. Carl had practically expected someone to declare the mountain a free city, like those people in Copenhagen.

Toward the end of the meeting Carl found himself staring at the neon Dos Equis sign on the wall, which Shera's husband, Phil, had lugged back from a trip to Mexico. Carl wondered what it would look like lit up. Unable to resist, he plugged it in, and all the lights in the house went out. The meeting broke up soon after that.

Things had looked so promising only a month before, but Larrabee deftly turned each new development to his own advantage. An architect had published an article in the *Sun-Bulletin* that pronounced their house to be of significant architectural value, urging landmark status in order to prevent its being torn down. Larrabee responded by promising to restore the house as a museum. The local historical society claimed that the house had been a link in the underground railway during the Civil War. Larrabee cited this fact when he announced his intention of hiring a significant number of minority workers for the project. Finally, when a biology professor at the university reported that the mountain was an important refuge for two types of birds and an endangered mountain flower, Larrabee offered to accept a lease on the land instead of buying it outright. That ended the issue.

To celebrate his victory, the oldest men who'd been promised construction jobs had their pictures taken and displayed in the windows of the Broome County Savings Bank, an investor in the project. The sign above them read, Helping to Build Thompson City's Future. Larrabee announced a big fair on Father's Day to celebrate the occasion, complete with entertainment and a raffle. The proceeds of the raffle were to go to Wilson Hospital. First prize would be a deed to one of the houses. Walter Gajewski, who'd been unemployed the longest, had been named Father of the Year and was to receive a plaque during the fair, less than a month away.

The eviction would take effect the next day.

"I spoke with your mother," Elaine said, breaking her silence as they drove over Memorial Bridge. "We met in the city near where she works. She said that the job offer had perked your father up, but then the thing with Jason happened, and he's pretty down about it."

"I feel for him," Carl smirked.

Elaine gripped the wheel tighter. "Your mother also said that your father's worried about . . . the house."

"You mean he's having second thoughts about us getting kicked out? It still won't stop him from taking the job, Elaine, if that's what you're getting at."

She said nothing else for the rest of the ride. Rain began falling. Elaine switched on the wipers, and the monotonous slosh of the blades filled the silence.

I've snapped at her again, he thought. He hadn't meant to. But Elaine spending time with his mother made him uncomfortable. It reminded him of those women in political groups who were forever calling a caucus that excluded men. And the worst part was Elaine's secret agenda: a golden reconciliation between father and son.

Later, when Elaine was lying on her back in the lemon glow of the Coleman lamp, her breasts seemed unusually full, barely contained by her T-shirt. Carl sat on the opposite side of the bed, yearning to touch her. It was happening again: During periods of not having sex, there was nothing like a quarrel to make Carl absurdly randy. He turned to hide the erection poking through his drawstring pants.

"There's something else your mother told me that you might be interested in hearing," Elaine said, pulling the band from her hair and letting it fall free. "She said that the whole thing with Jason has made your father feel like he's lost yet another son."

"My father raised Jason to be what he's turned out to be," Carl said bitterly.

"Your father never raped anyone, for God's sake!"

"Don't yell, you'll wake Melissa."

"He takes what Jason did as a sign that he's made some terrible mistake, don't you see?"

"Well, he has. Like brainwashing Jason with his own backward ideas."

"I'm sure that your father never told Jason to go out and rape someone, either."

"Don't make excuses for Jason. That's what Cee used to do."

"The bottom line is your father needs to come to terms with you, especially now. Jason has gone too far out of bounds for him to deal with anymore. You're his only chance."

"To do what? Ease his guilty conscience?"

"No, Carl," she said, her voice strained with impatience. "To talk with you. Even your mother said she wished you'd do it."

Carl shook his head and went to the window. "I've already told you: There is nothing I want or need from that man."

"You both need something from each other."

"What?"

Elaine sighed. "To hear the other one say that you're not a monster."

A breeze, cooled and freshened by the rain, blew in the window. Carl clapped his hands around his bare chest and rubbed his arms. "I think it's kind of weird that you go around meeting with my mother without telling me."

"I tell you."

"Only afterward. You make a secret out of it."

"Maybe there are things that women can discuss better without men around. Anyway, I didn't think I needed a consent slip from you." She slipped her feet under the covers. "I like your mother," she said. "I think she likes me. And by the way, it's no fun talking to your back."

Carl turned halfway, reluctant to reveal his persistent erection. He heard how evenly she spoke, trying to avoid a fight at all costs, yet it was her evenness of tone that Carl found so unsettling. When they used to argue the valley rang with her shouts. Now she was as calm as a librarian. He sank into a wave of gloom.

"Tell me," he said finally, "where did Melissa get that stuffed toy elephant from, the one Jason used to play with? From the free box at the co-op?"

Elaine looked puzzled.

"And would you mind telling me how it is that Melissa knows about the *G* carved beneath the kitchen sink in my parents' house? I saw her going up to our sink and tracing the same letter there," he continued. "Did my mother happen to describe that to her when she gave her the elephant?"

"All right, Carl, it's true," she said, hitting the bed with her hand. "I admit it. I brought her over to your parents' house. Is that so terrible?"

"Even though you knew that I didn't want Melissa going there."

"Yes, Carl," she repeated in a tone of mock contrition. "Even though I knew you didn't want Melissa going there. But your mother called me at the newspaper right after she found out about Jason. She tried to reach you but you weren't here or in the bookstore. She was crying; she said your father was ready to jump into the car and drive it off a cliff. I said I would come over. Melissa was in the day-care co-op, so I picked her up. It seemed silly to drive all the way home and then back into town, and I couldn't leave Melissa in the house alone anyway. Your father looked terrible. Then he saw Melissa, picked her up in his arms, and kissed her. It was so good for him to see her. Don't be angry at me."

Where had he been? Carl wondered.

He remembered. It must have been one of those afternoons when he'd snuck away with Brigid.

"What did my father say about Melissa?" he asked in a low voice.

"That she looked like your mother. He was so happy." She paused. "He asked how you were."

"As if he cares!"

"Stop being selfish, Carl. Your family's falling apart, and you're feeling betrayed."

"My family fell apart long ago, Elaine. It fell apart because there was no good reason for it to stay together, and not because I never brought Melissa around for my father to gawk at, either. Tell me, what's all this sudden concern about my family?"

"Your mother seems to be on our side. Don't you think it's worth keeping in contact with her?"

"That's not the only reason you went down there, and you know it," he said, pointing at her. "You did it for the same reason you set me up tonight—"

"Stop saying that," she said, grabbing hold of the blanket. "All I did was to ask you to go and speak with your father and ask him to turn down Larrabee's offer."

"You tried to shame me into doing it!"

"All right! Maybe I did, but only because I'm really afraid that if we lose this house, we'll lose much more than a place to live." The lamp threw the contours of her face into relief; she looked careworn, and for several seconds, their eyes held each other.

"What do you expect me to do, crawl on my hands and knees and beg him not to tear our house down? He threw me out of his house, Elaine. And do you really think for one minute that he's not going to take that job? What chance does an unemployed fifty-five-year-old man have of finding another?"

Elaine's eyes fell to his crotch. Carl tugged at the drawstring, as if to yank his erection back.

"Carl, if we can just show that the money the county loses on Larrabee's tax breaks would equal the cost of the new junior high school, then they'd opt for the school and your father would still get a job."

"You know what my father's answer will be when I ask him what you want me to ask him? He'll give me a look that says, 'One of these days you're going to grow up and live in the real world.'" Carl could just hear his father's tone of voice, ringing with a clear-as-day rightness; calm, since only women and dogs lost their temper, and friendly, as though he were giving advice about a neighbor's weed problem. "If you want to talk to him so badly, then you do it," Carl said.

His erection showed no signs of diminishing. He dove into bed and under the covers. He wanted nothing more than to throw himself on top of her and make love until the house fell down so that there'd be nothing more to talk about.

Elaine stared at the ceiling, her hands on her chest.

"Should I turn out the lamp?" he said.

"If you want."

They lay in the dark.

"Why must you always be so unyielding, Carl?" she said, turning away from him onto her side. Her back rose up, broad and warm. The cover draped her rump enticingly.

Carl sensed her trying to keep to her side of the lumpy mattress, which otherwise funneled them together. The dark trail of her hair beckoned him. He longed to press himself against her inviting roundness. How could he seduce his own wife into making love? He didn't really know. He'd never learned how. He looped a cautious arm over her. She stiffened. He touched her breast.

"I don't think I can, Carl."

"Does that mean you don't want to?"

She lay still. Eventually Carl retreated.

He'd seen Brigid several times during the past few weeks. Each time he sensed her feelings for him deepening, all the while his remained the same. He liked her, and she was very attractive, but her zealousness wore on him, and he missed Elaine's cool-headed wisdom. Brigid had been at the meeting tonight, making sure to sit at a careful distance from him and looking especially earnest when Elaine spoke, as if out of respect.

He could tell she thought Elaine's proposal was a great idea, too.

"Elaine?" He rested his hand in the valley of her waist, the heel of his hand grazing the plump rise beyond.

She didn't answer. He knew he'd have to get high or else he wouldn't be able to sleep. He got up, pulled on a flannel shirt, and was about to leave the room.

"Carl?"

His heart knocked with hope. "Yeah?"

"Where are you going?"

"Downstairs."

"Oh."

And then she turned over.

He got the dope and headed for the belfry. He leaned back in his chair and propped his legs up on the ledge, breathing in the damp night air and taking thick, hurried tokes. The lights of Thompson City suggested an earthly constellation; farther away was the Milky Way of Binghamton.

Mountains were once considered the preserve of the devil so no one minded if Indians, fanatic fundamentalist Christians, or freaks lived there. Until Larrabee. Carl leaned farther back and surveyed the vault of the belfry's ceiling, where the four wooden panels had been fitted perfectly together, as though woven.

I'm really afraid that if we lose this house, we'll lose much more than a place to live.

Carl thought back to the coalition meeting, and his chest tensed. Elaine had spoken calmly. No wonder she'd been able to marshal everybody to her side. Carl detected her proposal's hidden message, directed to him alone: I'm going to ask you one last time to go and speak to your father, and if you don't do it, then . . .

He toked again with trembling fingers. A drop of water fell into his eye. He blinked, then stood up and stuck his finger into the apex of the ceiling. Wet. Damn, the roof of the belfry leaked. Which meant that water could get into the attic, too. As if he didn't have enough to worry about already.

"Wowert."

The voice from below scared him. "Melissa, that you?"

"Wowert," she repeated, tugging at the ladder as if it were a yoghurt tree.

He climbed down. "Come with Daddy," he said, giving Melissa his hand.

Elaine met them on the landing. "Where are you going with her?" she asked.

"She's a little hungry."

"She's not hungry, she just wants to eat. You saw how much she had tonight at Shera's," she said, giving Melissa her hand. "Come, back to bed, honey, nothing to eat now."

Melissa pressed her hands to her chest in resistance. It was impossible to promise a child food and then not come through with it.

"How about just a cookie, Elaine?"

After Melissa was back in bed Carl returned to the belfry. His house, he thought. He'd wanted to come to the house and the house had let him. Elaine had borne their child there. There was no other place for them. The floor knew his footprints and the walls his sighs. He needed it more than anything.

But when he thought of what Elaine wanted him to do, his heart darkened.

2

*P*LEASE DON'T *hurt me, please don't.*

Jason pushed awake from his dream, out of breath. The muscles of his arms tightened as if to grip. Bars, he thought, craning his head toward the window with its gates. Just like a prison, except locked from the inside. And books. Books and cockroaches, that's what this place was full of. Maybe the books attracted them. He lay on his back on the humid sponge of the foam mattress, wearing a pair of Aaron's underwear. The colorless morning sky was slashed by the diamond-shaped mullions of the gate. Every time a truck hit a pothole on First Avenue the building shook.

Nine-thirty-seven, the clock radio said. About an hour ago Aaron was stumbling through the tiny apartment, cursing, pulling clothes out of drawers and then stuffing them back in, unsatisfied. He bundled his frizzy hair into a rubber band, looking like an old-fashioned school-teacher. Just before leaving he kissed Jason on the forehead. Jason didn't kiss him back. Aaron was always trying to kiss him, even in the street. "Why not?" Aaron would counter. "They do it," *they* meaning normal people.

He rubbed his belly. The cords of his muscles had softened, even if it wasn't more than three weeks since he'd worked out last. Richie used to say that muscles got used to being worked, and the moment they felt you slacking off they slacked off twice as much, out of spite. Aaron wasn't very hard, but it felt good when he pressed against Jason. He liked wearing Aaron's clothes, too, especially his underwear.

Spanish music had begun blasting up from below. The streets of Aaron's neighborhood were like someone's living room. Men set up tables near the curb and played cards in their undershirts; people danced, drank, and ate in doorways. This city was crazy, and sometimes it scared him, but it was where the first car that stopped for him on the ramp to route 17 was heading. Getting away was the only thing that had mattered, getting away from where Marcy lay in that house, crumpled on that stinking mattress, from the dress he'd torn from her like a handful of grass, and from the terror in her eyes, as if she no longer knew who he was.

Please don't hurt me, please don't.

The man who'd picked him up drove a big two-door LeSabre with the AC turned up high. A large metal cross dangled from the rearview mirror. His voice boomed about sin and the wrath of God the whole way down. Jason sank into the icy, casketlike plushness of the front seat, shivering, his hands clasped around his chest.

The emergency fifty he'd taken from the Pontiac's glove compartment paid for three nights in a grungy hotel near the bus station where you got buzzed in through two doors. One night he went to a movie nearby. A man sat down beside him and pretty soon his hand had slid over to Jason's crotch. Jason had wanted to slug the guy. Except that he found himself getting hard. The man continued fondling him. Jason's head cleared, and he heard himself say, "Two bucks."

The man paid him.

He stayed in that movie the rest of the night, repeating the routine. One time Jason asked for money and a guy said, "Where are we, Tunis?" But Jason left with enough money for another night at the hotel. He went back to the movie the next night. A guy asked if he wanted to come home with him. Jason agreed to—for ten bucks. The guy had a set of weights in the living room and gave Jason a pair of gym shorts to change into; he changed into a pair himself. "Start lifting," he said. When Jason had worked up a sweat, the guy began playing with himself, the shiny gym shorts pulled down to his knees. "Lift those fucking weights," the guy said, stroking faster. "Let me see you lift them."

Jason learned about a street on the east side where guys waited to get picked up for money. One night an older man took him, soft and flabby, with gold bracelets and thinning hair. He asked Jason to take off his shoes at the door and made him shower beforehand. His bed had black sheets, and a little mean-tempered dog kept scurrying around. He cried like a baby when Jason fucked him and prepared a breakfast of foul-smelling cheeses and thick marmalade, which he ate in a fancy bathrobe. One guy wanted to do it to him. Jason wouldn't let him at first, but they smoked, and the guy paid him enough, so Jason turned over and closed his eyes.

The one thing he didn't do no matter what was take it in his mouth.

Jason would buy dope from a guy in the Village and spend whole days in his room, stoned and hungry, worrying whether the police were after him. What could they prove? It was his word against hers. But Marcy was cool-headed. They'd believe her. Her father had influence. Seeing girls Marcy's age on the streets of New York scalded his heart with fear.

He got down to his last couple of dollars and had to leave his room. He slept in the park, ate for free at a Hare Krishna place, or stole food off the stands along Ninth Avenue. One night he went to Washington Square Park, where people were clustered around a guy playing a saxophone. A joint got passed his way, he toked on it heavily, and then passed out on a bench.

He awoke to see someone standing over him. He thought it was a mugger and ran, but he tripped and fell. The guy helped him to his feet. "You don't look so good," he said. Jason asked him for something to eat, the guy got him a frank from a sidewalk vendor, Jason gobbled it down, pulled out the three crumpled dollar bills left in his pocket and said, "Please let me sleep at your house." That was the last thing he remembered. In the morning he woke up and there was the same fuzzy-haired man naked in bed next to him. It all seemed like ages ago, but it wasn't more than two weeks.

Jason got up and walked the few steps that separated the mattress from the kitchen, and threw some water on his face. A large board over the bathtub held a rack of drying dishes. He thought the frontier was the only place where people took baths in the kitchen. But here he was, in the middle of New York. Aaron looked like a canary in a birdbath washing in that tub.

Jason went to the refrigerator, where Aaron kept all his food, on account of the roaches. He found some oily peanut butter to spread on a slice of bread, and sat down at the kitchen table. Pushed to one side was a typewriter and folders full of papers. Aaron said he was a playwright writing his first play, about two men dressed as women who are plotting to bomb a bank. Aaron said it was political. On the wall were snapshots of Aaron in dresses, carrying signs.

The telephone rang.

Answer it?

It was Aaron.

"It's so nice to call and hear someone there," he said. Aaron spoke soberly: his work voice. "I forgot to tell you. I get out early today. You feel like taking a ride on the Staten Island Ferry?" He said he'd be back at the apartment at one, and they could leave from there. There was a rubbing noise on the line, as though Aaron were turning around to see if someone was listening.

"Hey, Richie," Aaron whispered. "I like you."

Jason hadn't told Aaron his real name. Just because.

He sat beside the telephone after they'd hung up.

I like you.

The guys who picked him up treated him like he was either a god or a piece of shit, but never like a regular person. Aaron did. He was different from Owen and the other guys from school. He never knuckled him in the biceps or slugged him in the chest. He didn't say things like "How you doin', asshole?" nor did he always want to go out and get wasted. Instead Aaron cooked them supper. He shampooed Jason's hair. ("You're my first dirty blond," he'd said. "And I mean dirty.") They took baths together, wedged into the tiny tub, their dicks touching. ("Like two uncles kissing," was Aaron's description.)

Jason kept staring at the phone. The whole time he'd been in the city he'd thought of calling Cee. More than Marcy's father or the police, it was Cee's bad opinion of him that he feared the most. But what could he tell her, except that everything had gotten out of control? And that it really didn't have much to do with Marcy at all.

It had to do with Richie.

Jason had missed him during those long November weeks after the incident at Nina's. Each time he worked out he imagined Richie's strength pouring into him. The leather gloves remained alive with Richie's grip, and they fed his fingers with energy. He kept hearing the bark of Richie's voice as he coached, or felt the burn of their bodies when they faced each other, each with a barbell high above their shoulders, when their triumph merged them. Jason had felt happier than ever before. His joy took root inside him, growing and threading through his muscles, until it had anchored itself so deeply that wrenching it free threatened to pull his very being along with it. Then Richie was gone.

Almost every day since coming to New York Jason saw guys who looked like Richie, with his build, his shiny, dark hair, and the same metal spring in his walk. He'd stumble on playgrounds with basketball courts full of guys stripped to the waist, their bodies ribbed with shining muscle, clambering against each other, and he'd yearn to tear off his clothes and throw himself into their midst.

Marcy's father had said she couldn't see Jason anymore after he'd kicked their door, but she told him that she was old enough to choose her friends. They went for walks to the old railroad yards, to the abandoned sawmill, her sketch pad always under her arm. Her friends thought they were going together, she told him, sounding dismayed. They just didn't understand: She and Jason were good friends.

Marcy had asked Jason to go with her to a dance at her high school. They were standing outside, almost at the entrance of the parking lot, when a new Olds pulled up. They watched as the proud, gleaming chrome of the car slid by. The car doors opened. A pretty girl stepped out. Jason tried to remember where he'd seen her before, but didn't have to think long. Richie appeared, in a shiny black jacket. The girl with him was the cashier from the supermarket.

At first Jason was happy to see him after all that time, but he sensed that something bad was about to happen. Richie slammed the door shut angrily, shouted something at the girl, and then stomped on ahead. Jason's heart chilled. Marcy asked Jason what was wrong, and touched his arm, but he pulled away. He hadn't said a word to her; how did she always know when something bothered him? He told Marcy he wanted to go home. Then the girl began coming toward them, waving at them.

"It's my friend Carol," Marcy said.

Jason had to get away. He headed for the track and began running laps. He returned, tired and sweating, but calmer. Richie had gone off somewhere. The girl was displaying an engagement ring.

"Welcome back," she said to Jason. "I'm Carol. You're cute."

Jason was so nervous that when he tried to say something he stuttered.

"Stuttering is a sign of sexual inhibition," she said. She dug a finger into his ribs. Jason jumped back. "Ticklish, too? That's another sure sign of inhibition—"

Marcy told Carol to leave Jason alone.

Richie appeared. His shirt was open, and he was sweating. Jason could smell that he'd been drinking.

"Where the hell have you been?" Carol asked Richie.

Richie caught sight of Jason. "Well, what do you know? It's Blink. That your girlfriend?" he said with a smirk, nodding in Marcy's direction.

"He's drunk, Jason, don't listen to him," Carol said.

"Well, is she?" Richie persisted.

"We're friends," Jason tried to say.

"Friends," sneered Richie.

Marcy took Jason's arm to lead him away but Richie blocked his path, his eyes ablaze and his lips silvery with spit.

"Get the fuck away!" Jason said.

"Get the fuck away," Richie mimicked, leaning over to Jason and blinking his eyes forcefully.

"Stop that!" Marcy shouted.

"Poor Blink can't get it up too good, can he?" Richie hissed. "You give it to your girlfriend yet, Blink? Have you? Have you?" He grabbed Marcy and began humping against her.

Marcy pushed him away. Richie fell back, laughing.

Jason's face filled with heat. "You c-c-couldn't get it up with Nina, either!" he said.

"Who's Nina?" Carol asked.

"Tell her, Richie," Jason shouted. "Go on and tell her."

Richie's face colored. "You shut the fuck up!" He grabbed Jason.

"Who's Nina?" Carol repeated.

Jason looked right into Richie's eyes. "Nina's some black bitch that Richie pays to fuck!" he blurted.

Richie shoved him, and they toppled to the ground. Jason flung Richie onto his stomach, grabbed hold of his hair, and pummeled his face into the asphalt with a wet smack. Carol screamed at Jason to stop. It took several guys from the dance to pull him off.

They got in the car. Jason drove off, a dizzy, hot glare before his eyes. The sound of Richie's face hitting the asphalt meshed with the throb of the car's engine. Why did he have to say that? Why? His foot pressed down harder on the gas pedal. They were speeding out of the town. He strayed to the middle of the road, headlights shot out from behind a curve, Marcy screamed, and he skidded to avoid a collision.

Marcy grabbed Jason's arm and told him to slow down, but he pushed her away.

"Jason, take me home. I want to go home—"

Jason kept on. It occurred to him that he'd wanted to kill Richie.

He realized where it was he had to go, and headed for Fitch Road, no longer aware of anything but the wheel gripped in his hand.

"I want to show you something," he said, swerving onto the broken road. The trees whipped by in a black whirr. He braked to a stop. "Let's get out."

"No. This place is creepy. There might be someone in one of those houses, some junkie—"

He pushed her out of the car.

Fright tore across her face. "What's the matter with you?" she cried.

He took her roughly by the hand.

"All right, Jason. All right. But just relax a little—"

They started across the road. He clamped his arm around her neck.

"Not so tight, you're hurting my shoulder. Jason, look at me—"

They stepped onto the mud on the other side and began walking toward the houses.

"Richie fucks any girl he wants. He fucks Carol real good. Bet you wish he'd fuck you, too, don't you?" His words pushed out of him like blood from a wound.

"Stop talking like that, Jason." She struggled out of his grasp.

"Don't you like me to hold you?"

"Yes, but it's too tight."

He went for her again, throwing his arm around her and molding the softness of her breast with his fingers through the slippery skin of her bra. He was walking them faster through the tall grass, holding her tighter.

"Jason, you're hurting me!" She pulled away. "What's going on?" she said, refusing to go any farther. "Tell me what's wrong!"

He grabbed her. "Don't you like me? Don't you want me to hold you?" He pulled her toward him and kissed her hard on the lips and thrust his hips between her legs. Marcy broke away and ran back toward the road. Jason pursued her, pulled her back, and scooped her up in his arms. She screamed, punched at him. He hauled her up onto the porch of a house. She punched at the side of his head, his face, anywhere she could reach.

"That's it, make like you don't want it, make like you don't, that's right." He kicked the door open. She began to cry and her body melted, helpless. "Okay, okay. We can do it, I'll let you. You can, but please don't hurt me, please don't."

Jason returned to his peanut butter and bread when he noticed a roach poised on a corner, its feelers aquiver. Enraged, he flipped over the piece of bread and squashed his fist down on it. He thought of taking a shower, but flopped back down onto the mattress, weak and miserable, anxious for Aaron to get there.

3

JASON'S CALL CAME at night just before Cee left for work.

"Cee, that you?" His voice sounded shadowy.

"Jason," she whispered, as though afraid someone might overhear them. Images tumbled through her mind and came to rest like figures in a slot machine: woman, dirt, blood. "Where are you? Are you in Thompson City?"

"No."

"Tell me where you are." She heard sirens in the background. A city, a large city. Syracuse? Albany?

There was a long pause and the smudging sound of the receiver moving against Jason's face. "New York," he said.

"Are you alone?"

"No."

"Who are you with?" God, this was exasperating. He was in a pay phone and who knew when he'd run out of money.

"This guy."

"What guy?" Cee looked at her watch and cursed. She'd have to leave in a minute. "What are you going to do?"

"I don't know. Stay here."

"Where is 'here'?" This was hopeless. She could talk to him all night and still get only half the story. "Listen, I want you to tell me exactly where you are and give me a number so I can reach you."

"You gonna call the cops?"

"No."

"Why do you want to call me?"

She couldn't explain over the phone. She had to see him before the police got him in their grip and turned him into just another creep on his way to Elmira or Bedford Hills.

"Because I have to speak to you."

"How do I know you won't call the cops?"

"I give you my word that I won't. Please tell me where—"

He hung up.

"Fuck!" She slammed the receiver down. What the hell was she supposed to do now? Go to work like nothing had happened and forget he'd called? And was she supposed to keep this wonderful secret to herself? But telling her parents would only make them crazier than they already were. She debated calling in sick and waiting, in case Jason called again. His phone call had been a confession of his guilt, a plea for help. He still needed it; he was bound to call again. But she couldn't wait.

He's lost, she thought, driving to work. He's already rolling down the road that led through rooming houses and prisons, from one of life's shitholes to the next, another faceless nonperson with matted hair and swollen legs who begged in front of office buildings, a Styrofoam cup in their hands. Her baby brother.

The rapist.

Durkin called Cee aside during her break. Cee's heart was pounding. She couldn't have been more than five minutes late tonight.

"Cee, let me be honest with you," she said. "You look terrible."

"Do I?" she asked, relieved.

"As if you didn't know it already. Now go on and tell Mama."

Cee thought of which crisis to name. Any would do: Carl's house. Jason. Billy. She chose the last. "I'm pregnant," she said.

Without missing a beat Durkin said, "That's no reason to look terrible. I'm sure your husband is very happy about it." Her icy tone let Cee know what she really thought.

"You know I'm not married."

"You're damn right I know," Durkin threw back. "So what are you going to do?"

Cee burst into tears.

"I'm going on the assumption that you're crying because you don't want to be pregnant," Durkin said, putting her arms around her.

"Yes," Cee found herself saying.

"If you were my daughter I'd brain you. But you're not, so we'll have to think of something else."

Cee looked up. "You don't have to do anything."

"I know." She reached into her handbag and gave Cee a tissue. "But let's look at this from a practical angle. You're a damned good floor secretary, no one's lining up to work nights, and I don't feel like losing you for the time it takes you to have this baby, which you have just told me you don't want. You work in a hospital. It's the place people go when they have your problem. I'm sure that someone could be prevailed upon to help you. Get my drift?"

"I don't know if I can go through with . . . that," said Cee.

"I couldn't either, but that's my Baptist upbringing. I'm not telling you what to do, but keep in mind that we can take care of you here, and no one has to know about it."

"I might have to take some time off to . . . think about it."

"Let me know as soon as you can."

"Thanks, Ms. Durkin."

"Mrs. Durkin. I worked hard for that Mrs. It's still making me work hard. But I'm not ashamed of it."

Jason called again two days later, early in the morning, right after Cee got home from work.

"Tell me where you are," she pleaded.

"New York."

"Where in New York?"

He didn't answer.

She was tired and in no mood for more of this. "Don't fuck around, Jason. I'm gonna find you no matter what, I swear—"

"You're gonna what?"

She quickly caught herself. "I mean, if you're afraid of going home you can come here."

"They're after me, aren't they? If I tell you where I am, you'll tell them, and they'll get me."

"If you didn't want me to know where you were, then why did you call up?"

There was a pause.

"I just called, that's all."

It sounded as though he were about to hang up. "Wait," she cried. "Don't do this to me." She was almost in tears. "Why won't you at least tell me where you are?"

"Manhattan. I don't know where exactly. Near this park."

"Central Park?"

"I don't know. They play bongos there at night."

"What's the address? Can you just give me the fucking address—"

"Why, you want to come?"

"Jason, you just said the police are out looking for you. If they find you—"

"Who said they will?"

"What do you think, you go out and rape someone and—"

He hung up.

"Goddamn!" she shouted. "God fucking damn!" Her head spun with confusion. She thought for a minute. When she had picked up the keys to Joel's place he'd given her the telephone of his apartment in New York. "If you're ever in the city, call up and say hello," he'd told her. She pulled out her address book, found Joel's number, and dialed.

"Joel," she blurted out, when he answered. "This is Cee from Buffalo, the one in your old apartment."

But someone else had picked up the phone. "Wait, I'll go get him," a man said.

Joel's voice came on, windy with yawning. "Hi," he managed to say. "You're certainly an early riser."

It was a quarter to eight in the morning.

"I have a little problem," she began, and told him what had happened. "I really have to find him."

"You said you don't have any address for him? And you don't want to go to the police?" It sounded too much for him to handle this early in the day. She heard him shifting in his bed as though sitting up. "If he really is in Manhattan, the park he means is probably Washington Square Park or Tompkins. They play bongos in Central Park, too, but he's probably not crashing with anyone who lives around there. Finding him will mean the needle-in-the-haystack routine."

"I want to try anyway. Could I possibly . . . stay with you for a couple of days?"

She heard more shifting. "It's a little tight here—I have two roommates—but I guess we can squeeze you in."

Cee told Durkin that she was going home to talk with her mother and needed as much time off as she could get. Durkin latched three vacation days onto the Memorial Day weekend for her. "It's strictly *verboten*, but if Nursing Service gives me a hard time I can tell them that you've only called in sick once since you started. I suppose I shouldn't mention the latenesses, though, should I?" she added, with a sharp grin. She counted boxes on her desk calendar with her pencil's eraser. "Six days."

"Is that the most you can give me?"

Durkin shot her an impatient look. "Rita, the weekend nurse, can jump in if I know that you're going to stay away any longer. But if Nursing Service gets wind of that, then you know where you'll be without a paddle."

The morning Cee planned to leave for New York there was a knock at the door. Billy stood downstairs, his left eye swollen and a cut across his cheek.

"I need some tea and sympathy," he said.

"Billy, what happened?"

"Luke," he said as they walked up the stairs. "He and Curt were outside Hadrian's last night. They were just as wasted as I was, but there were more of them than there was of me." He looked at himself in the living room mirror, gingerly touching the eye.

"What were they doing around Hadrian's, lying in wait?"

"They were probably on their way back from the Anchor Bar." He motioned to her backpack. "You taking off or something?"

"I'm going to New York."

"Why?"

She sighed, not sure she wanted to start explaining. What she really felt like saying was, "If you hadn't been so inaccessible for the past couple of weeks, as you so often are, you would know why I was going to New York." Instead, she said, "I have to find my brother." She told him what Jason had done.

"Your brother really did that? How old is he?"

"Sixteen. Wait. He already turned seventeen." She went for the photo of Jason. She had a vague idea of using it to make a sign about him. Lost brother. Sentimental value. Reward. "Here's my brother the rapist."

"Him? He looks totally harmless, more like My Brother the Raped."

"That's an old shot of him. He's so padded out with muscles now he probably wouldn't even fit in the picture."

"You once said that you'd kill any man who raped a woman," Billy said, returning the picture. "Remember?"

"Yeah, I remember, all right."

"Where in New York is he?"

"I—I already have a rough idea." She had no more of an idea than when she'd spoken to Joel.

She bustled around as she finished packing and made a thermos of gunpowder tea.

"Let me go with you, Cee. It'll be good for me to disappear from Buffalo for a while."

In the time since they'd slept together she'd missed him terribly, but she'd accommodated herself to his absence. Her talk with Kal had convinced her to approach Billy with caution, even suspicion, and she'd tried to place a slender but impenetrable partition between them. She knew it wouldn't be wise to see him again until she knew for sure what she would do about the baby.

"Can't you visit your relatives in Ohio?" she asked.

"Aunt Ida might have put up with me when I was a sweet eight-year-old, but I don't think she'd take a shine to me now."

Cee sat down opposite him, lit a cigarette, and inhaled deeply. "Do you know what happened to Kal?"

Billy looked frightened.

"The same thing that happened to you, only worse."

"Because of Grant," he murmured.

"And because of our little run-in with Luke at the Aud. She looked terrible."

He brought his hand across his mouth. "Jesus shit," he said, barely audible. "When did it happen?"

"About a week ago. Luke must not be very bright to pull this kind of thing right before Kal is planning to take him to court." She paused. "Unless he didn't think anyone who knows him would testify against him."

Billy's gaze shot up.

"Kal knows all about you and Luke," Cee continued. "Not just about the dealing, but about you being in love with him. Everything." She looked at him coldly. "And she found it absurd that you thought you could've kept it hidden from her. You're like a child who hides under a blanket and thinks no one sees him. I find it not only absurd, but a little low." She tapped her cigarette against the ashtray. "Is it really true that you were in love with him?"

Billy got up and began walking around the room. "Once upon a time Luke was long and lean and very hot. And though you might find this strange, what made him especially hot was me knowing that he did it with women. Luke wasn't gay, he was hardly bi. I serviced him. He let me. I wanted to. But it wasn't love, for chrissake. It was obsession. I knew it was twisted, and that got me off most of all."

"But with Luke—"

"Yes, with Luke, goddamn it," Billy said, picking up his jacket and throwing it back down. "Gross, disgusting Luke."

"You make things so hard for yourself," Cee said, snubbing out the cigarette. She leaned forward and rested her head in her hands. Within the dimness of her cupped palms, Billy's bruised face emerged like an image in a ruined roadside chapel.

"I didn't tell Kal about what happened in the Aud. I knew it would just make her blame you more. And somehow I didn't want that." Billy looked up. "But afterward I felt like a shit. I'd kept something from her. It was almost like you not telling her about Luke." She faced him. "When are you going to level with Kal, Billy?"

Billy took hold of her arm. "Sometime. I don't know when. Probably not next week. But listen. Let me go with you, please. I'll behave myself, I'm even paper-trained."

Cee felt his voice curling around her. Why had he become so necessary to her when she'd done without a man for so long?

Billy is okay to be entertained by, and to feel fond of, but not, I repeat, not to fall in love with.

It occurred to her that neither of them had mentioned having slept together.

He was pointing to her backpack. "You're sure I can't crawl in?"

Cee sighed. As usual, there was no stopping Billy. "I'll have to ask Joel if he has room for two."

THEY REACHED THE CITY in the late afternoon. Billy was so excited at finally being in New York that he whooped the whole time they were crossing the George Washington Bridge.

"Just go straight until the turnoff for Broadway," Billy shouted like a radio announcer. Cee did, forgetting that Joel had made a point of telling her to take the West Side Highway. She soon found out why: They were driving through Harlem.

"Great," Cee said.

"Well, it just goes to show you that Broadway isn't the Great White Way after all."

Joel lived near Columbia University on a dim side street. His house was a brick box, capped with a rusty metal cornice and shoehorned in between its neighbors.

"Hello, fellow Buffoons," Joel said, filling the doorway to his apartment. "Hope you didn't have any problems following my directions."

"No problems. We didn't follow them, thanks to Henry the Navigator over there."

"It's Henry Hudson, dear. We're in New York."

"This is my friend Billy."

"Home Sweet Home," Joel said, showing them into the living room. His beard had grown even bushier since the last time she'd seen him. "I inherited a sofabed from a neighbor since you and I spoke, so now you two won't have to sleep on the floor."

"Speaking of sleeping, Joel, would you mind if I crashed right now? I'm exhausted."

"You can go into my room; it's quieter," Joel said.

By the time she woke up it was dark. Cee crawled out and found Billy watching television in the living room.

"Hey, Sleeping Beauty."

"Where's Joel?"

"In the shower."

Cee found some bread and cheese in the kitchen. Billy followed her. "What did you do while I was asleep?" she asked, sitting down at the table.

"Do you want my version or Joel's? In my opinion, we talked. In his, I got on his nerves."

Cee groaned. "You promised me that you would behave. Joel was nice enough to let us crash here."

"That's no excuse for him to tell me that I'm affected."

"Well, you are."

"I know. I agreed with him, and he didn't like that, either. But I made up for it by cooking him *huevos rancheros.*"

"Feel like making me some?"

"Used up all the *huevos.* So tell me, Sherlock, what are we going to do?"

"Joel narrowed it down to two parks that Jason might have meant, and they're not far from each other. I showed you that picture of Jason; you know what he looks like, sort of. I think we should split up and start patrolling both those parks."

"And I think a snowball in hell has a better chance of staying frozen than we have of finding him."

"What else can we do?"

"Beats me. I'm better at losing men than finding them."

Joel appeared in the kitchen, shirtless and in sweatpants. Cee had never seen anybody so hairy.

"We were just discussing how to find Kid Brother, Joel," Cee said.

"I think I'll retire to the salon," Billy said, leaving.

"He doesn't like me," Joel said.

"I don't think you like him, either."

"You're right. I don't take to people who act as though they're in a movie. But he knows how to cook." He sat down next to her.

She was conscious of him not wearing a shirt and of the warm smell of soap that he gave off.

"I only have one lead to help me find Jason," she said. "A friend of his has relatives in New York. He might have gone there."

"What's their name and address?"

She bit her lip. "I can't remember it now."

Joel smiled.

"It's the same last name as someone famous, a political leader."

He kept on smiling.

"Oh, shit!" she said. Then she started to laugh. "What am I doing here?"

"Second question: What are you going to do with Kid Brother if you actually do find him?"

"I'd break his head, but he's stronger than I am. I want to find out what the hell made him do what he did. And I want him to march his ass into a police station and give himself up. It might make things a little easier for him in court."

"And what if he doesn't talk to you about it?"

"He called me up twice, so he must want me to know where he is."

Joel thought for a moment. "I have some women friends who say that most men are potential rapists."

"I know those women too," Cee said, a little impatiently. The familiar weariness swept over her as it did whenever she thought about what happened. "I could use a beer."

"Nothing in the fridge." He paused. "We could go out."

They went to a student place on Broadway.

"This bar reminds me of the CPG," Joel said.

"You know the CPG?"

"I used to live in Buffalo, remember?"

She'd almost forgotten. Since moving to New York Joel seemed to have changed. Her recollection of him had been of someone frowzy, overgrown like an untended lawn, friendly, but slow. Now he seemed sharper and more alert, even if his beard still made him look like a sleepy nocturnal animal. Perhaps going to Columbia and living in New York had perked him up. She noticed him looking at her and wrapped both hands around her glass, feeling self-conscious.

"Steely Dan," Cee said, when one of their songs came on. She wanted to divert his attention from her.

> *Rikki don't lose that number*
> *It's the only one you own*
> *You might use it when you feel better*
> *When you get home.*

"I heard their name is slang for a dildo," Joel said.

"I'll tell Billy; he likes to hear about things like that."

"What does your friend do?" Joel said.

"These days he's waitering. He's about the closest friend I have in Buffalo." *And the father of the baby I'm carrying.*

They ordered more beer. Cee looked around and was almost shocked to realize where she was. In a matter of weeks things had begun to pick up speed and get scary. Joel looked down at the table. Instinctively she slid her glass in front of the scar on her wrist.

"I meant to ask you if you'd seen Marlene," Joel said.

"I did toward the beginning of the year," Cee answered, purposely vague. She didn't want it to sound as though she was avoiding Marlene.

"Did she say anything about me when you saw her?"

"No."

"I feel a little bad about how things turned out between us," he began.

Cee felt him waiting for her opinion and recalled the stifled talk she'd had with Marlene about Joel in January. She grew restless, excused herself, and went to the bathroom. When she returned, the Steely Dan song came up on the jukebox once again. Cee said it was time to go.

"Just look at this kitchen," Billy said the next morning, waving his hands in despair. "Only heterosexual males could survive in a kitchen like this." He held up a plastic plate. "Melmac! Even my mother had Corning Ware."

"Quit complaining and get the coffee ready. And there happens to be a woman living here, too. You didn't see any Velveeta in the refrigerator, did you?" Velveeta was her favorite cheese.

Billy opened the refrigerator door but slammed it shut, closing his eyes in indignation. "I won't begin to describe what I have just seen. Of course, compared to that bathroom, it's the im*mac*ulate con*cep*tion."

Cee grabbed her bag. "See if you can bring yourself to make the coffee by the time I get back."

Downstairs, the grimy asphalt of Broadway pulled in both directions like a stretch of dirty licorice. She spotted a grocery store on the other side of the street and crossed to the middle mall. There she lingered. Noise welded the street together; the very air was bruised with shouting. Almost everything moved. Here was a place where people lived, she thought, not just where they wound up. Dank air rose through the subway grating to mix with the sweet poison of a passing bus. New York was a city of tunnels and subterfuges, the perfect place to get lost in and never be heard from again.

Most of the people in the store looked Hispanic and went about their shopping at an unhurried pace, as though the store were on a tropical island. She bought cheese, cigarettes, a bottle of orange juice, and a *Village Voice*. All the while her eyes darted down the aisles to see where Jason might be lurking.

Richie Castro, she thought, almost dropping the juice. That was Jason's friend's name.

"What took you so long?" Billy said, stretched out on the sofabed with his coffee.

"This city is intense," she said, setting the things on the table. "And I've only seen one corner of it. Me and my friend Jeanine always used to talk about hitching down here and going to the Fillmore East, but we never made it." Cee got herself a cup of coffee. "We have to talk business." She told Billy about Richie Castro.

Billy pointed to the phone. "Let your fingers do the walking." He plopped a phone book into her lap.

After an hour of calling, Cee had found nothing. "All of the Castros are at work." She threw book to the side, then suddenly grabbed the phone once more.

"Hello, Binghamton information? Could you please give me the number of a Castro in Thompson City? I don't have an address." Billy nodded his head in approval. "Thank you." She dialed a number and reached a woman who listened as Cee explained she was searching for her runaway brother, a friend of Richie's, who'd gone to New York. Mrs. Castro then gave her the number of Richie's aunt on Cornelia Street. But when Cee called the woman, she said she'd never heard of anyone named Jason.

"Let's go down to the Village anyway," said Billy, "so we can get a feel for the place." He winked.

They took the subway down and walked to Washington Square Park.

In one corner of the park a group of black men played a battery of steel drums. Their heads sprouted tangled gardens of dreadlocks, their shirts were off, their skin glistened.

"Kal says that men who go around without shirts are exploiting their male privilege," Billy said, gazing at them wistfully.

"Smoke, weed." A black man stood before them. "Nickels, dimes, whatever you want."

"No thanks," said Cee.

"Convenience shopping. Beats having to drive out to the mall," the man urged.

"He's got a point," Billy said.

"They don't have malls in New York," Cee said.

"My, my, a person could do a land-office business here," Billy said after the man moved on. He turned to Cee. "So tell me why you think Baby Brother went and did what he did."

"Answer that question and you'll probably find out why he put his fist through the front window of the house a couple of weeks ago."

The park thronged with people. She tried to imagine Jason there, blinking his way through the strange surroundings. She could stay there day and night, and even if Jason happened to stroll through, she'd miss him. He might be there right now. It occurred to her that she'd known from the very beginning the chances of finding him were nearly nil, but she'd come anyway. The truncated phone calls had been like the bits of a puzzle he'd challenged her to solve. His parents had long ago stopped responding to his bait; Cee alone did. Was she compassionate, or merely a sucker?

They walked around the Village and Little Italy, wandered in and out of record shops, Cee bought a scarf, and they went for pizza. When Billy announced that he wanted to do a little independent sightseeing, Cee headed back to the apartment.

Joel had just gotten in and was making supper with Peter, one of his roommates.

"Nothing in the lost and found for me today," Cee said.

"Hungry?" Joel asked.

"No," her reflex response. Actually she was starving. "I can help cook, though."

"Everything's just about done. But you can set the table."

They ate. Joel's roommate Peter was a quiet man with a thick beard and very dark eyes. He was a graduate student in the Russian department whose parents had fled the Soviet Union when he was young. He brightened when he heard Cee's last name, but she had to confess to not speaking a word of Polish except for *Jeszcze Polska Nie Zginiela*.

"I know it from a piece of embroidery my mother has," she said.

"The Polish people are not yet lost," Peter translated in a grave voice. "A quote from the work of the Polish Goethe, Adam Mickiewicz. Russian and Polish are both Slavic languages, of course," he continued. "But Polish is a West Slavic language and Russian an East Slavic language."

"My grandmother spoke Polish," Cee said. "I heard her; I remember hearing lots of shshes."

"My grandmother, too," Joel said. "But she refused to utter another word in Polish after leaving Poland for America. The Poles were not what you would call the best friends of the Jews."

"There's wine," Peter said, and Cee poured herself a glass.

"A friend of mine works for the Office of Social Services," Joel said. "He might know something about runaway shelters."

"I don't think my brother would go to a shelter. It's the first place the police would look."

"Your brother is wanted by the police?" Peter said, setting down his fork.

"Take it easy," Joel said.

"We can be arrested as accomplices just because his sister's here," Peter said, pushing back in his chair.

"You read too many detective stories, Peter."

"I'm not trying to help him escape," Cee said. "I want to find him and convince him to turn himself in."

Peter seemed relieved. He and Joel talked about their oral exams. What would her father have to say about someone studying Russian? Cee wondered. Or even nineteenth-century American literature, Joel's area. What would Kal say about it, as she pulled yet another law book down from the shelf, trying to decipher the child custody laws? Peter had the frail, carefully composed look of someone who spent most of his time in libraries. If his hands got dirty it was from dust or newsprint.

After supper Joel went to work in his room. Cee did the dishes, then she called up her parents but didn't tell them where she was. They'd had no word on Jason's whereabouts.

"I found out the name of the girl," her mother said. "I know her father from church. It's terrible."

"I'll get in touch with you next week," Cee said. She didn't want her mother to call her in Buffalo and find no one there.

Her mother's voice sounded fragile, ready to tear. The incident had stripped her of the new strength her job had given her. The talk left Cee in no mood for the verbal onslaught sure to accompany Billy's return to the apartment. She drank what was left of the wine, and decided to sleep in the room belonging to Regina, the third roommate, who wouldn't be returning for another day. The room was narrow and cramped. A mattress took up most of the floor space. Clothes were strung from a rope nailed up catty-corner. A large poster hung on the wall, a blown-up photo of people linking arms at a demonstration, with the words *Paris Printemps 68* at the bottom.

It was almost ten. Cee was mildly drunk. She lay down. Billy wasn't home yet. She imagined him stripped to the waist like the drummers in the park, his chest glistening under colored disco lights with a hundred other half-naked men. How easy it must be for men like Billy to go out and find someone. Gays didn't play this game of hunter and hunted. Among men and women, there always had to be a winner: the man. If the woman emerged victorious it had to be by cunning, stealth, or trickery.

But she hadn't tricked Billy. She'd wanted him, and she'd taken him. Why couldn't things have just developed from that? It was hard enough to find someone you really loved. So, when you did, why did it have to run along some fixed track, doomed to failure otherwise?

She picked up the book beside Regina's bed. *Knots,* by R. D. Laing. A packet of birth control pills serving as a bookmark slipped out. She pushed the book away, disgusted at what seemed like a bad joke, and reached for the book she'd brought. Jason's picture flew out. For some reason she thought of what that counselor in the Meyer had said to her: Maybe you had to hurt yourself in order to heal yourself. She'd taken a razor to her wrist. And Jason? A plate glass window.

No wonder she'd come to look for him.

When she awoke in the morning the photo reminded her about making the flier. She composed a bit of heart-rending prose to put under the picture, had the flier copied, and she and Billy hung it up around the Village, Columbia, New York University, and City College. Joel and Peter distributed copies among their friends and even chipped in for a small ad in the *Village Voice* personals. Several days later someone called to say that he'd seen Jason sucking off a black man in a public toilet, another claimed that he and Jason were planning to rob a bank together, and a third guy even claimed to be him.

"New York," Joel explained.

Billy found a paella pan buried in the back of one of the cupboards and volunteered to cook dinner. While they were eating, Billy noticed Peter staring at Billy's nail polish, a ringing blue.

"The shade's called *Cerulean,*" he said. "A dollar-ninety-nine at Bottom Line Cosmetics."

Peter frowned. "Why do you put that on?"

"Why not?" Billy said, spearing a piece of shrimp with his fork.

"Because normal men don't wear nail polish."

Oh God, thought Cee, fearing the worst. Peter had uttered the forbidden word.

"Well, tell me, Tolstoy," Billy said. "Just what are normal men like?"

Peter set down his fork, flustered.

"Billy," said Joel.

"Just because he's studying Russian doesn't mean he has to act like the KGB."

Peter pushed his chair back with a loud scrape, got up, and left the table.

"I think you owe him an apology," Joel said.

"Straight men think they have the last word on everything."

"You still didn't have to bite his head off," said Cee.

Billy shot her an enraged glance, pushed his plate away, and left the table, too. A little later they heard the front door opening and closing.

"I'm sorry Billy's being so difficult," Cee said.

"It's not your fault. Peter comes from a very traditional background. He even freaked the first time Regina had a man sleep over. And he's especially sensitive about the subject of the KGB. They hounded his parents for years before his father was able to swing a visa for them. Sometimes living with him is like walking on a tightrope, but I like him. He's just not used to seeing men with nail polish. I'm not, either, to tell you the truth."

"Peter sure picked the wrong thing to get on Billy's case for. Wearing nail polish is a political act for Billy. Now maybe I'll have two lost people on my hands."

"He seems like the type who can take care of himself," Joel said. He poured himself some wine. "You want a refill?"

"Sure."

When they finished eating, Cee began clearing the table, but as she was about to start washing the dishes, Joel said, "Let's retire to the library," and grabbed the bottle of wine.

They sat facing the window. A sliver of brilliant red sky shot through a break between the buildings across the street.

"What are you going to do if you don't find your brother, Cee?" He filled their glasses.

"If I don't find him, then the police will, and he'll wind up wherever they decide to send him so he can mix with the hardened lowlifes and learn from them." She had some wine. "Why don't you tell me a little about your family so I don't have to go on about mine."

Joel talked about his parents, who had been communists until 1956 and now put all of their energies into the family business, a small charter bus company. He had an older sister, married and settled down with a doctor "like good Jewish-American daughters are supposed to." A younger brother was still in high school. The wine rendered his soft voice even softer and fed the faint humming in the back of her head.

"Do you like living in New York?"

"It was good to leave Buffalo. It had grown a little too comfortable for me. In New York you can't get too comfortable. It won't let you."

"You know I never thanked you for letting me move into your place. I was having a rough time around then, and it made things easier."

"My pleasure." He refilled their glasses and they toasted. They sat for what seemed a long time. Cee assumed that at any moment Joel would announce that he had to get to work. She herself wanted to go for a walk. But neither moved. Joel's hand grazed her arm. She turned, he smiled, embarrassed. She found herself waiting for him to touch her again. She ran the tips of her fingers along his arm, a signal. He pulled them close.

"Cee," he murmured. Then he kissed her. Her mouth lost itself in the large softness of his. His hands rounded her shoulders, big hands, and very warm.

"I've never kissed a man with a beard before," she said.

"Kissing a man without a beard is like eating an egg without salt," he whispered, chuckling softly. She sensed him waiting for her to make a sign she wanted him to continue. They kissed again, longer this time. She inhaled the scent of his beard, heavily sweet. She was conscious of Peter in the next room.

"Come," she heard Joel whisper.

He led her to his room and closed the door, then lit a candle beside the bed. The light made the room feel rounder, smaller. Joel sat down on the bed and reached for her. The creak of the boxspring might have been Peter's staid reproof.

"I feel like a teenager," he said, "with these clothes on."

It was her cue. She rose, a little quickly, afraid of losing momentum. Her arm caught in the sleeve of her shirt as she took it off.

"Easy, easy," he said.

Joel shed his clothes unhurriedly, as though getting ready for a shower, letting socks and shirt fall where they would. He undressed like a man, she thought. Cee regarded the neat pile of her clothes with a certain tenderness, as might a bride. When they were both naked they slid into the bed together. She was conscious of looking only at his face, as if to draw his attention away from her nakedness.

"I'm not very experienced," she whispered.

He was a large, soft, warmth around her, a weight protective but insistent. She felt his hips pushing his hardness against her legs, for she still held them together. Not yet, she thought. His tongue was at her breasts, flicking and pursing her nipples until they stung with pleasure. She was conscious of his strength, his advantage. No, not advantage, she told herself, unable to control her mind's nervous babbling. Perhaps because of the wine, his movements started to take on a sloppiness that threatened to slip into hastiness, and it tensed her.

"Joel, wait."

He stroked her forehead, her arms. Slowly, she felt herself beginning to float. His hand found its way between her legs to that wonderful place inside her thighs. Her legs parted more. "Yes," she heard herself say, "touch me."

At some point during the night—or was it the morning after?—Billy appeared at the door.

"Oh," he mumbled, and retreated.

4

*B*ILLY COULDN'T DECIDE what made him dislike Peter more: his remark or his brooding eyebrows, long enough to comb. He'd fled the apartment, and soon was overcome by the same urgency he'd felt back in his bus station days, yearning for the feel of man's heft and for the wet pleasure of his mouth. His loins hummed at the prospect of downtown New York—and not downtown Buffalo—awaiting him.

The short time he'd spent in close quarters with Tolstoy and Yogi Bear had been taxing. Tolstoy needed some radical loosening up, and Billy knew just where, too. Yogi was one of those liberal types who tolerated homosexuals if they weren't too gay. To make matters worse, Billy sensed Cee getting moony over him. Billy could only shake his head and recall his mother's favorite phrase: That's why there are menus in restaurants. But still. Yogi had the flair of a chemistry teacher. And while he was on the subject—just because Yogi was studying Nathaniel Hawthorne didn't mean he had to look like him. Ditto for Tolstoy. What compelled so many heterosexual men to grow beards, anyway? The only thing less appealing to Billy than men with beards were men with beards who shaved their mustaches.

The first bars he hit that evening were uncomfortably empty and the music loud, as if make to the place feel full. As he went from bar to bar, the crowds grew larger, and the later it got, the more anxious were the faces of the men, eager to couple. New York had more types of bars than Baskin-Robbins had ice cream. There were bars for the well-kept and for the ratty and bohemian; bars with a pseudo-gruff cowboy motif and prissy lounges, complete with indirect lighting and a piano player; and there were wrinkle rooms and concrete dungeons. Buffalo fag nightlife was like shopping under communism: little choice and poor quality. New York's truly was a free market. Billy winked and flirted his way through the rest of the evening. His butt got pinched, he flicked his tongue at that man or this, but alas, no one he saw made him want to lift his petticoats, throw up his legs, and forget tomorrow.

By four in the morning Billy had hardly tired himself out. He remembered someone in Hadrian's describing in hushed, awed tones a place in a cellar deep below the wholesale meat market district near the river. Billy had no address, but when he caught sight of men in police hats and leather pants heading down the grimy cobblestone streets west of Ninth Avenue, he followed.

Halfway down the length of a building whose blood-smeared loading docks were hung with ominous rows of meat hooks, an unmarked door opened to a dimly lit subterranean city. It swam with men. The air dripped with a pungent brew of male sex. Bare-chested men sidled past him like figures on a frieze. Others lurked in corners, crouched in bathrooms, or writhed in leather slings. It was part bullfight arena, part Colosseum, and part bazaar.

Billy let himself be fondled, stroked, explored by dozens of tongues and lips and unmatched hands. His fingers wandered across acres of flesh, smooth and hairy, muscled and flaccid, black, white, and varying shades of beige. He grabbed hold of a catalogue's worth of penises and testicles enough to repopulate the world many times over. Yet every so often he'd disengage himself from this squirming Medusa of naked limbs and think, Is this really happening? People were doing what wouldn't get done in any bed on the Niagara Frontier, even with the doors closed, the curtains drawn, and the lights turned out.

He wandered over to the circle that had formed around a young man on his knees. Everyone's fly was open, their erect cocks hung about his head like a ring of satellites. Billy edged closer. What was this, a bargain table at AM&A's? The boy—he couldn't have been more than seventeen—was sucking off everybody in turn, eyes closed, mouth afroth. The next in line held his member at the ready, his face slack with need. The boy flung his swollen lips between the pair of legs hungrily, as though the cock were a teat of mother's milk. One by one the men came, folding like ducks in a shooting gallery as their loins convulsed around the boy's head. Billy's hand had migrated to his own distended crotch, when he noticed a man directly across from him. His pants were unzipped, revealing a soft drape of flesh just above his pubes, and his thinning hair did its best to cover his scalp.

Stanley . . .

Billy went limp. What would Stanley have said to all this? Butter-faced Stanley, his knight in shining polyester. What would he think of the men crouched in the bathrooms, or the butt-slapping boys humping two feet away, and what would he say to the sling, he, Stanley MacIntyre, who never engaged in anal intercourse except under cover of near-darkness. Sticking a light bulb up your ass was romantic compared to what went on here.

What was Mr. MacIntyre doing at that moment? Billy wondered, as his dick slunk back into dormancy. Considering the hour, he was probably asleep, which meant he was snoring: night-long squalls that filled billowing sheets of mucus stretching like sails within his nose. A night of it was almost enough to make Billy seasick. But it would have sounded like a lullaby just then. How he missed the faint smell of milk that clung to Stanley's flesh, and his endearing ritual when getting undressed: He'd stand in his underwear and socks, pull out the elastic band of his jockeys, and peek down to make sure everything inside was still present and accounted for, before letting the band snap back.

A pair of naked buttocks had begun thrusting at the boy faster and faster. A man gripped the boy's head like a saddle's pommel. The boy held the man's ass as if he were inflating a beach ball . . .

Billy left to get coffee upstairs.

He sank three cubes of sugar into his cup and stirred. Something about the scene one floor below disturbed him. Not the craving for dick, certainly; that was fun and good for the circulation. But afterward, when the blood had ebbed away from the groin to more respectable body parts, he knew what more than one of those men felt: shame. How well he knew that compulsive grab for tissues, the nervous zip of the fly, the hasty departure from the car/bush/toilet stall, all of which comprised the furtive blow job's afterglow. Wasn't that why fags wound up in places like this?

Of course, one might reel off any number of explanations: There were offspring-demanding mothers, intercourse-demanding wives, neighbors who snickered, schoolmates who slugged, bosses who fired, and judges who jailed, not to mention the menacing hordes of pasty-faced priests in basic black. Sex guilted straights, too, which was why *post coitum omne animal triste est*. But for queers, it definitely could be *Bonjour Tristesse*. Billy sighed. Time was, when fags got painted onto Greek vases. Now they fucked in basements.

"Cup of hot water, please."

A man with a ponytail stood beside him.

Billy watched as he produced a tea bag from the pocket of his jeans. With his large nose and the bush of hair banded at his neck, there was something birdlike about him.

The bartender set a Styrofoam cup filled with steaming water before him. "I'll have to charge you the same as a coffee."

"Thought you'd save yourself something for a rainy day, did you?" Billy said.

The man glared at him. "They don't have tea and I don't drink coffee except when I work," he answered tartly and turned back to his cup.

Well, we've obviously both won the Good First Impression Award, haven't we? Billy thought. He sipped his coffee, feeling tired. One hour down in the depths had worn him out more than a whole evening of above-ground carousing. It had to be almost five in the morning. His gaze drifted back to the man with the tea. Nose or no, he was kind of cute, and his serious strain piqued Billy's curiosity. Who drank tea in a place like this? Even more intriguing: What kind of man would bring his own tea bag along?

"Say," Billy said, trying again. "What is someone like you doing here?"

The man shot him an irritated glance. "Looking for a variorum edition of William Butler Yeats."

"Me, too. But still, it's no place for a nice Jewish boy to be—"

"How do you know I'm Jewish?"

"It's written all over your cute nose—"

"That's almost anti-Semitic. And by the way, Jews aren't the only people who have large noses." His eyes narrowed. "Italians do, too."

"Italians don't have *large* noses, they have *Roman* noses. Okay, okay. So you guessed my ethnic heritage. But say what you will," Billy said, tapping his nose. "Yours ain't the junior miss size. I'm Billy."

The man smiled. "Aaron."

"My, how nice you look when you smile, Aaron. I'm sure your mother used to tell you that all the time."

"She also told me that I shouldn't talk with my hands and that I should walk like a boy."

"How did you walk?"

"Like my best friend, Florence."

Billy moved closer. "I kind of like you," he said. "Can I buy you another hot water? Straight up and with a twist, right?"

When the Styrofoam cup arrived, Billy went for his wallet. Aaron's eyes fell to Billy's fingers.

"If you run the brush along the edge of each nail after you finish putting on the polish they won't chip like that," he said, reaching for another tea bag.

Billy spread his hands before him and sighed. "A rush job. But seriously, what do you think of this place?"

"I go for its rugged, Carl Sandburg Chicago-y quality. Otherwise I only come here when I'm feeling desperate."

"Desperate for what?"

"Desperate to feel less desperate."

A wail rose from a man strapped into the sling.

"I understand exactly what you mean. You want a husband, don't you?"

"I thought I'd found one. A crazy one, maybe; someone who would have pronounced Yeats as Yeets. And who claimed not to be gay. But I knew better."

"Do you always talk about Yeats in places like this?"

"What shall we talk about instead, the Fag Three *F*s? You know: food, fashion, and furniture?"

"All right. So tell me what happened to your husband."

"I haven't seen him for days. No phone calls. Nothing."

From the sling came more yells and gasps.

"Say, did you happen to see the guy downstairs in the middle of that circle-suck?"

"Oh, you mean Robert."

"You know him?"

"He carries on like that all the time. You'd think he'd never seen an erect penis except in one of his med school textbooks."

"Med school? He looked like he was still in high school." Billy gave Aaron's arm a squeeze. "Know what? I'd invite you to my place except that it would take too long to get there."

"Oh yeah? Where do live?"

"Buffalo."

"Buffalo, New York?"

"No wisecracks now. Somebody has to live there."

It was already beginning to get light outside. They took a crosstown bus to Aaron's.

"With more than two people here it must get crowded," Billy said when they were in the apartment. "What's that you're typing?" He motioned to the Royal on the kitchen table.

"A play," Aaron said.

"So, you're a writer. That explains why you were talking about Yeats. Say, is that you?" He pointed to a picture of Aaron in drag.

"Taken at last year's Stonewall march," he said with a touch of pride.

"Pardon my saying so, but why the lackluster attire? I think you're the type for a low-slung—"

"I was Eleanor Roosevelt."

They undressed and lay down on the foam mattress.

Billy yawned. "It's nice to be horizontal." He kissed the side of Aaron's face. "With you."

Aaron lay on his back, hands behind his head. Billy began stroking Aaron's belly. Aaron giggled a little, then settled, still.

"Penny for your thoughts," Billy said.

"I guess I'm a little tired."

"We'll fix that." He flung his mouth at Aaron's neck and sank his teeth in.

"Hey!" Aaron rubbed his neck.

Billy began stroking Aaron's chest, but when he took Aaron's dick into his mouth it stayed soft.

"Nothing personal," Aaron said. "But I don't really think I'm into it." He glanced at the clock. "Shit, it's almost six. I have to be at work in three hours." He looked over at Billy. "How about a little nap?"

They cuddled up. Some time later there was a knock at the door.

"Who's that?" Billy said.

"Probably some bum who got into the building," Aaron mumbled into his pillow.

"Hey," said a voice in the hallway. "Hey, Aaron, you there?"

Aaron crept to the door, naked, and peered through the peephole. "Jesus, he said. "It's him," he whispered to Billy. "My ex-husband."

"Hope he's not the jealous type."

Aaron opened the door. Jason rushed in, breathless, as though being chased. His eyes swung over to Billy. "Who's that?" he said.

"A friend," Aaron said, flustered. "Where have you been all this time?"

Jason kept staring at Billy, distrustful.

"Sit down, Richie," Aaron said.

Billy kept looking at him. "What did you say his name was?"

Jason shot him angry glance. "Who the fuck are you?" he said.

"Jason," Billy said, a hand to his mouth. "You're Jason."

Jason's hands jerked forward, as though ready to land a punch in Billy's face. Billy jumped back, springing naked from under the sheets. Jason surveyed Billy, infuriated by the merry swing of Billy's dick, then his glance darted back to Aaron, as if seeking an explanation. For a moment it looked like he might pick something up and throw it at them, but he turned and ran from the apartment, charging down the steps with a rhythmic thud.

"Richie!" Aaron was about to go after him when he realized he had nothing on. "He's gone," Aaron said weakly as he shut the door.

"Was that the husband you were talking about in the bar?"

Aaron nodded.

"How long have you known him?"

Aaron looked down. "Two weeks."

"He lived with you?"

"Yes."

Billy came over to him. "Don't get scared, but you were sharing your humble abode with a police suspect." He pulled out a copy of Cee's flier from his jeans. "Not as professional as what they hang up in the post office, but it'll do."

Aaron stared at the paper. "Jason Gajewski," he read. "Where did you get this?"

"From his sister. She's looking for him, too."

"What did he do?"

"Rape someone." His tone sharpened. "A girl."

Aaron slumped down on the mattress, bewildered. "He didn't look good. He probably wanted to take a bath and sleep."

"Can I use your phone?"

Aaron stood up, suspicious. "Why? Are you going to tell his sister that you saw him?"

"She'll want to know."

"And then what?"

"And then we'll pack him up and take him home, I guess."

"What do you mean?" Aaron sounded angry.

"What do *you* mean, sweetie? Are you considering hiding him? There are laws against that. He pulled some pretty nasty business back there."

"According to what you say, I was hiding him for the whole time he'd been here."

"You didn't know. But now you do." He put his arms around Aaron's shoulders. "Wisen up. You meet a stud, he fucks your brains out. What more could a girl want? But exactly how long was your married life—two weeks. I know that's the equivalent of two years in heterosexual time but it's still a maximum of fourteen days, Aaron. Fourteen." He counted on his fingers. "Onetwothreefourfivesixseveneightnine—"

"All right!"

"Losing him sure beats being a sitting duck. Which is what you'd be if the fuzz found him here with you. Not only that, but from what Sis says, he sounds a little on the hotheaded side, so who knows when he might turn on you."

Aaron slumped back down onto the mattress. "I think I need to be alone right now."

Billy dressed. He kissed Aaron on the neck where he'd bitten him. "So much for my night of passion," he sighed. "I'll give you my number if you give me yours."

Aaron smiled and scribbled on a piece of paper.

"Mine's on the flier," Billy said.

CEE WAS AWARE of no more than a careful perforation in her sleep as Joel got up to leave that morning. When she opened her eyes again it was almost ten. God, it was wonderful waking up in a man's bed! Last night after making love they had talked and talked and then made love again. She told Joel about Carl and the house, about her mother, about Thompson City. Even the most unexciting story was fun to tell lying naked beside someone.

She made coffee. Peter appeared in his bathrobe, on the lookout for Billy. Cee smiled at him, but he barely reciprocated; he'd lumped her together with Billy, and the hint of a scowl on his face told her that he'd heard them in Joel's bed the night before. With the water on the stove, she hopped back into Joel's bed with a *Village Voice* and flipped to the concert pages. Everybody was playing in the city that week. She imagined moving in with Joel, doing her errands on Broadway, and then coming home to him. She was aware of a wetness creeping out from between her legs. Just before entering her, he'd murmured something about whether he had to use anything. She said it was okay, leaving him to think she was on the pill. She didn't feel like telling him that a person couldn't very well get pregnant twice at once.

Images of diapering, the greedy nibble at her breasts, baby carriages, and teething interrupted her reverie. Lord knows what it was going to look like—Billy's button eyes, her own limp, blond hair . . .

She was already thinking of having it.

The key turned in the front door. She looked up, heart aflutter—was Joel back so soon?—then heard a woman's voice.

"Hello? Anybody home?"

Cee put on one of Joel's shirts and stuck her head out of the bedroom door. A woman with curly hair and a blazer was setting down her suitcase.

"Oh," she said, noticing Cee.

"I'm Joel's friend," Cee explained. "I—I mean, I'm crashing with Joel. You must be Regina, right?"

She nodded. Cee felt her trying to decide what to make of a half-naked woman in Joel's bedroom.

"I have my stuff in your room," she said. "I'll get it out."

"Great. I've been on a bus all night, and I'm exhausted."

Cee dressed and moved her backpack into the living room, wondering where to stow it. There wasn't much room, but something stopped her from putting it in Joel's room, so she lumped it on top of Billy's stuff.

"Regina, you're back," Peter said, leaving the bathroom. He smiled broadly, as though pleased to have reinforcements against Cee and Billy.

Someone began ringing the doorbell over and over again.

"Who can that be?" Regina said.

Cee went for the door. Billy flew in right past her.

"Can't talk, gotta pee," he sputtered.

Cee saw Regina's surprise. "Oh, that's just Billy," she said. "He's crashing here, too."

"Doesn't he have a key?" Peter said, glaring at Cee as if holding her responsible.

"How come you didn't use your key?" she called after Billy, to make Peter feel better.

"Lost it," he shouted back.

Cee felt Peter looking at her. "Don't worry, I'll get a new set made up," she said.

Regina went into her room. A moment later Billy emerged from the bathoom. He was about to charge past her again but she pulled him by the arm. "What the hell is going on?"

"You balled him, didn't you?"

Cee was so surprised she couldn't answer right away. "So that was you last night."

"This morning, you mean. And the answer to your question is, Yes. What a pair you made, Bacchus and Venus." He spoke with the testy authority of a tattletale.

"What were you doing snooping on me?"

"I didn't snoop. I witnessed. And the only reason I came into your little lovenest was because I was ravenous and wanted to steal some money from your bag for eats. Strange, I had the keys then. I must have lost them on the way—"

"You're actually jealous!"

"Whyever would I be?"

"You are, aren't you?" She began to laugh. "Oh, how sweet." She stroked his cheek. "Tell me more as I drink my coffee." She went to the kitchen. "Well, it looks like Peter must have done the dishes."

"The hell he did!" Billy said, selecting a mug from the rack. "I did, early this morning. I decided to be big about being dumped on last night."

"By the way, where were you all night?"

"Don't change the subject. I want to know what's going on between you and him—"

"Knock it off." She poured their coffee.

"Those are bagels," Billy said, pointing to a paper bag on the counter. "The dark ones are pumpernickel and the others—"

Cee extracted a ring of keys.

"Oh that's where they were hiding," said Billy, taking them.

Cee halved a bagel and went to butter it. Billy snatched it away. "No one in New York eats bagels without toasting them, don't you know that? For a Catholic you can be such a WASP."

"As far as Joel goes, I just slept with him once."

"I know this sounds weird," Billy began. "But after we . . . you know, when we did it, it left me feeling a little . . . elated." He picked up the keys and slid them along the ring like worry beads. "For days afterward I walked around feeling completely confused. I wasn't sure who I was anymore. I suppose I should tell you that . . . it was my first time."

"Billy!"

"With a girl, of course. I felt like I'd proven to myself that I could do it, me, a fag." He stuck his head through the doorway. "Oh, hello, Peter."

Peter looked flustered. He'd been in the living room the whole time pretending to be looking out the window.

"Sorry about last night," Billy said. "If you've changed your mind we can have your nails looking splendid before you can say Catherine the Great."

Peter charged back into his room.

"I still don't understand what all that has to do with me and Joel sleeping together?"

He gave her a shy smile. "You'll laugh if I tell you. When I walked in and saw you with him I thought, Well, I guess she's found someone else. See, isn't that dumb?"

"It is. But sweet."

Billy said, "It really is okay, you and him. I have a weakness for chubby men myself."

"Aren't you going to tell me where you were?"

"Sodom. Or maybe it was Gomorrah. South of Fourteenth Street anyway."

"By yourself?"

"Sometimes. But I saved the last dance for someone named Aaron. I spent the night over at his place." He looked away with deliberate detachment. "Oh, by the way, Jason showed up, too. Hey, something's burning!"

A thick plume was spewing up from the toaster. Before either of them could do anything, Peter had already run into the kitchen. He pulled the cord from the outlet, fished out the burned corpse of the bagel and flung it into the sink.

"Use the toaster oven next time!" he scolded.

The phone rang. Peter picked it up. "Oh," he said, setting it down, looking annoyed. "It's for you."

"Hello?" Cee said. "Mom! How did you know I was here?"

"Where's Jason?" Her mother sounded out of breath.

"Jason?" Cee looked at Billy. "I—I don't know. That's why I'm here. But how did you get this number?"

"From Carl. I called you up at home, no one answered so I tried the emergency room. The woman sounded surprised that I didn't know where my own daughter was."

"I didn't want to worry you."

Great, she thought. Now Durkin knew she hadn't gone home to her mother.

"Well you did. Jason's not with you, is he?"

"No."

"If they find you with him, you'll get into as much trouble as him." Her voice raced.

"Mom, have you spoken to the police? Have they contacted you?" Get her to be factual, she thought.

"It wouldn't have been so bad if he hadn't run away," Theresa said. "This way it really makes him look guilty. Your father won't talk about it. He sits in the living room in front of the TV set and doesn't even put it on. It scares me. He said that maybe if I wasn't away at work all the time something like this might not have happened."

"That's a crock of—I mean, that's ridiculous, Mom. Jason's not a little kid anymore. And Dad stays at home all the time. He might have done something, too."

"But maybe he's right, Cee."

"Mom, don't even think that! Listen, did the police say anything about Jason?"

"They're out looking for him, if that's what you mean. Holy Mother of God, this is like a nightmare!"

After she hung up, Cee said, "My mother is one freaked-out woman. Hey, wait a minute. Before the phone rang, you were saying that you saw Jason."

"This morning. At that guy's house."

"How come you just let him get away?"

"What was I supposed to do, stick him in a sack and bring him back uptown with me on the subway? You obviously haven't seen your brother in a while." He flexed his bicep.

"Is he all right?"

"A little the worse for wear, but I wouldn't kick him out of bed, as they say. Of course, I probably wouldn't be able to."

"Where did he go? Tell me everything! And cut the jokes."

Billy told her what he knew, then pulled out the piece of paper with Aaron's number.

"Let's go over to that apartment this afternoon. Jason might have gone back there." She picked up her coffee cup and was about to take a sip when a coil of pain sprang open in her groin. The cup left her hands and fell onto the linoleum. She stared at the broken bits of beige ceramic in the dark puddle of coffee, looking like bones in a tar pit. She waited for the pain to subside. Her period, charging through her uterus with the power of a thousand buffalos? She braced herself against the edge of the counter until the spasm passed.

"Cee, you okay?"

She stood up. Nope, she thought. No period. There was something inside her that was making room for itself. After ten weeks it already had legs. She was losing time. The other day when she'd walked by a huge hospital, she'd almost felt like checking in under a false name, flashing an empty wallet, and throwing herself at the mercy of the man who ran the suction machine.

"I, um, it's all right," Cee managed to say. Wipe it up, she told herself, looking down at the spilled coffee. Wipe it up before Ivan the Terrible comes and makes a stink.

But Peter was already there, glowering.

AS SOON AS Billy left, Aaron saw what time it was and realized that he had exactly one hour and twenty-one minutes before he had to leave the house for work. He thought of the impending seven hours of typing in that windowless office, surrounded by women whose faces were glazed with makeup thick as marzipan and watched over by the owlish supervisor in her glass cage.

No. Not today.

He called in sick. His eyes fell on Billy's flier. There he was, younger, looking somewhat out of it, his hair shorter, but still Richie—or Jason.

Raped. A woman.

Aaron massaged the pain on the side of his neck. What a viper that Billy was.

All things considered, the revelations about Richie weren't that surprising. Hadn't Aaron been a little suspicious of Richie's story? To explain why he had no place of his own and no clothes except those he wore, Richie had said only that he'd just gotten into town. Still, what had people thought of Aaron as he traipsed through Europe, backpack and long hair, a hippie of threads and patches. "We are all children in transit, moving along the lines that connect us," he'd written in his journal at the time.

But at least Aaron had had a backpack, a change of clothes, and used his real name.

He opened the refrigerator, peeked into the swamp of plastic containers, then closed the door. He'd go out for breakfast.

His underwear drawer was empty. Richie'd taken to wearing his stuff; everything was dirty. He pulled his jeans on over his bare buttocks, and stuffed a ten-spot into the pocket without the hole. He took the flier, too. To have something to read, he told himself.

It was barely nine o'clock but the heat was already tropical. Such weather always brought out hordes of good-looking young men in skimpy attire, leaving Aaron weak with longing after walking a block or two. His ardor seemed fated to remain long-distance. The city teemed with unattainable, perfectly chiseled homos who took pains not to need anyone else. Their beauty was that of the distant peak or, more precisely, the iceberg. It was with tense romance language majors or frowsy Lefties that Aaron hit the foam. Men he found truly attractive or interesting eluded him, or, if by chance they deigned to grace his hovel, there was always a string of heart-thumping thresholds to cross in the morning: Would the man stay and drink his coffee? Eat his breakfast? Would he give Aaron his number? Accept Aaron's? No wonder Aaron had become addicted to Richie in a matter of days, having so much pleasure at his disposal, as well as the chance to satisfy Richie's transparent need. What a pleasure it was to have a guy waiting for you after seven hours of paid nothingness, even if you couldn't kiss him on the lips.

Aaron headed for Vaselka's and got a seat at the window. A man passed by outside: tall, very skinny, a lean white face. Musician, Aaron thought. A woman was with him. Black pants, black top, sunglasses. Artist. Everybody made art in the East Village. It was sickening. By reflex he took a pen from his pocket and went for the napkin. He'd taken to writing in public places to prevent his work from becoming insular. But it was too early to feel inspired, so he began to pen in the napkin's embossed pattern.

He'd been writing the same play for three-plus years with no sign of finishing it. These days it seemed its sole purpose was to supply him with an answer when people asked what he was working on. Despite corrections and reworkings, the play remained a series of unconnectable fragments reaching out toward each other across the typing paper without ever meeting: bits of stained glass that didn't quite fit their frames, letting light leak in. His breakfast came. Aaron set down the pen, unfolded his napkin and punctured the glistening sunny-side-up egg with his fork.

One day he had come home to find Richie clad in a pair of Aaron's underwear, arranged in an appealing sprawl of legs and torso on the mattress, reading *Black Elk Speaks*.

"The Indians were powerful people," Richie said. "They were proud, which is why the Americans beat them down. The place where I grew up was holy for them."

"Where's that?"

"Quaspeck."

Was this person really a rapist the police were looking for? But why else would he give a false name? (Aaron had looked up Quaspeck in an atlas but couldn't find it.) He took out the flier. So, I've housed a real, honest-to-goodness felon for the past two weeks, he thought. Maybe I can write my next play about Jason-Richie after the success of my first. With his pen he gave Jason more hair, then drew in the sweatband Jason always wore, and muscles. His pen poised over the paper, then he drew a feather, and another, until Jason sported a complete headdress. Big Chief Body-of-Death, Aaron said to himself. Big Chief Lying Asshole. He crumpled up the paper and threw it onto his plate when he was finished eating.

What should he do for the rest of the day? he thought, back on the street. A whole, uninterrupted day stretched before him, the perfect opportunity to hammer away at act two. But the thought of returning to his stifling apartment, his fingers sweating on the typewriter keys as he changed the mother's lines for the umpteenth time, sent him hopping on a bus in the direction of Central Park.

Jason was sitting in front of Aaron's door when he returned later that afternoon.

"Hi," he said, a little sheepishly.

"How come you took off so fast this morning?" Aaron said when they were inside.

"That guy was here." Jason looked down. "Is he coming back?"

"No, Jason. He isn't."

"Why'd you call me that?"

"Because it's your name." Aaron shook his head. "Now listen—" he took a breath. "Billy told me everything. I don't think it's real good that you stay here."

"I never saw that faggot before in my life."

"Jason," he said wearily, "in case you didn't notice, I'm a faggot too. And incidentally, so are you." He went to the refrigerator and poured himself a glass of cold water. "Thirsty?" Jason nodded. Aaron cut off a piece of lemon and squeezed it into a glass.

"I'm no faggot."

"What do you call what we did every night and every morning you've been here? Wrestling?" He gave Jason his water. "If you think that you're a real man as long as you don't kiss me, fine. But I'm worn out and I'm not in the mood to hear it. I also want you to leave, but before you do, I'd like to know one thing: Is it true that you raped someone?"

Jason nodded.

"Why? Were you so horny?"

"No. I was . . . mad."

"At her?"

"No. At everything."

Aaron's voice darkened. "But why did you rape her? You said you weren't horny, you were mad. You could've called her names or hit her or—" his gaze fell on the knife he'd just cut the lemon with "—you even could have stabbed her. But you didn't. So if you didn't rape her to have sex with her, then you must have raped her for some other reason."

"You talk like there's a reason for everything," Jason shouted, trying to free himself from the tangle of Aaron's interrogation. "You think everyone always knows why they do something."

"Maybe not while they're doing it, but afterward."

"I don't want to talk about this."

Aaron thought for a moment; then he said, "You went off and raped a woman. You piece of shit."

"You think you're so smart, you with all your books," Jason exploded. "You think you have all the answers, don't you? Well, you don't. You only think you do. Your answers are either made up or they're somebody else's. You tell them to yourself long enough until you believe them."

Aaron remained calm. "Your sister's looking for you."

"Let her."

Aaron shrugged and poured himself more water.

"Listen, Aaron," Jason said. His voice shifted down abruptly. "Can't I stay here? Just for a while? Look," he said, fumbling in his pocket for some crumpled ten-dollar bills. "I made some money while I was away. On that street." He tried to give Aaron the money, but Aaron wouldn't take it.

"Jesus!" Jason shouted, hurling the bills on the table. "Even if the cops come here, couldn't you just tell them you didn't know about the whole thing?"

"Right. I could hide you in the wine cellar and when the police come I could say, 'Well, officer, considering how we used to fuck like bunnies I can't imagine him doing anything like that to a woman, but you're free to search every single nook and cranny of the entire house, including the grounds.'"

"How do you know for sure there are cops looking for me?"

"Isn't that what usually happens in a case like this?"

"They don't know I'm in New York. If I just keep out of sight, they'll give up, won't they? I mean, I didn't even hurt the girl. I didn't use no gun or nothing. She couldn't have gotten pregnant from that one time, or else she could get an abortion." His words came in uneven bursts. "People do a hell of a lot worse things than I did. They plan them, and then get away with it." He began pacing back and forth. "Whose side are you on? You sound like a judge, ready to throw my ass in the can. But you don't know how it is. You and your goddamn books, your goddamn faggy-assed way of talking. You don't know how it is to worry about important things like getting a job. My father was laid off and hasn't worked in months. He might never get another job for the rest of his life. And you . . . you live in your own world, sitting at the typewriter, typing out what no one's ever gonna read—"

"I think you'd better go," Aaron said.

Jason turned to him, his face damp with worry. "Where?"

"Go home." He looked right at Jason. "Go to . . . Quaspeck."

"Please. Let me stay here with you. I'm sorry. I didn't mean the last part about your writing."

Aaron shook his head.

Jason swept the knife off the table and held it in front of Aaron. His eyes seemed to shake from their blinking. "I'll . . . I'll . . ."

Aaron didn't move.

"Jesus!" Jason thrust the knife into the table. Then he ran out of the apartment and down the hall.

Aaron waited in the doorway as Jason's steps thundered lower and lower. Then he went inside and pulled up the knife from the table. He left the money where it was.

Later that evening Aaron heard the door buzzer. He pressed the Talk button, expecting Jason's voice to flood the speaker grille.

"I'm Cee Gajewski, Jason's sister. Could Billy and I come up and speak with you for a moment?"

He waited for them in the doorway. He was in no mood for company and decided that he would say as little as possible.

A heavy woman arrived at the door, out of breath. The viper was with her.

"We meet again, William Butler," the viper said.

"That's quite a climb," the woman panted. The man kept looking at him. Aaron could tell they were waiting to be asked in, but he didn't move from the doorway.

"We were wondering if you happened to see Jason again today," the man asked.

"No, I haven't." Aaron was conscious of the money on the table, evidence to the contrary. "I told him I didn't want him staying here," he added, to be a little truthful.

"I have to leave the city the day after tomorrow," the woman explained. "So if you hear from him before then you'll let me know, won't you?"

She seemed nice. He felt bad about lying to her. "Sure," Aaron said.

She turned to go. The viper lingered for a moment. "Nice seeing you again, Yeats," he said, winking at him.

Only after they left did he realize that he'd thrown away the leaflet with the phone number. Well, that took care of that.

He picked up the file folder containing his play and opened it. Each line was choked with cross-outs. The typed letters were embedded in layers of correction fluid. He got as far as the second page, then closed the folder and pushed it to the side of the desk. He leaned back, deafened by the sirens and trucks on First Avenue.

5

"You must be the only person I know who doesn't have their mattress on the floor," Cee said.

"I'm no longer an undergraduate," Joel explained.

They were finishing a bare-assed breakfast in bed. Joel showed signs of once having been well-built and athletic, but his body had thickened to an undefined, if attractive, bulk. With his beard and fullish face, he made her think of King Solomon. At first she'd retreated back under the sheet after making love, reluctant to expose too much of herself, but after a while it just seemed silly. She discovered that if she sat up so that her breasts cascaded but not high enough to crease her belly fat, she might be quite appealing without clothes.

"I've given up hope of finding Jason," she said. "I called that Aaron guy up this morning in case he'd seen Jason since last night. He said no and told me that he'd made Jason leave. I think he was even less happy to speak to me today than he was yesterday." She ran her fingers across Joel's chest. "Maybe I should stop trying to find my brother and leave him here with that Aaron. Maybe that's what my brother needs most of all, someone to love him."

"What do you say we raid the place tonight and kidnap Jason? Just like Patty Hearst." Joel took her hand and began fingering the scar. She went to pull it away, but he held it. "Looks mean," he said, and his eyes waited for an explanation. When Cee said nothing, he kissed the scar and released her arm.

Cee found it more and more difficult to hide her feelings for him, yet he seemed more reserved. He'd stopped mentioning Marlene, and she never brought her up, but anytime a silence in their conversation parted one sentence from the next, Cee imagined Marlene's presence filling it. She felt uncomfortable seesawing with another woman over the fulcrum of a man; she wanted Joel for herself.

It was past one before they got up, and Joel suggested a short jaunt up along the Hudson. Before she knew it they were setting the breakfast things onto the floor to make love for the second time that morning. Afterward, feeling soft and careless, she asked whether he thought he might get together with Marlene again. Joel turned from her abruptly.

"What do you want me to tell you?"

She cursed her own lack of poise, her inexperience. Her whole body prickled with regret. She drew the sheet over her. Joel got up and began putting on a pair of shorts.

Just past Tarrytown Joel said, "Let's check out where I went to summer camp as a kid. Take a right when you see the sign for the Taconic."

"Is this place just for Jews?" she said, pointing to the sign, as they entered the grounds.

"Naw, it's just run by your typical Jewish liberals. They let everybody in, even people like you." He winked.

Joel showed her around the camp, the lake, the outdoor theater, the cabin where he got laid for the first time.

"You probably had a hell of a lot more fun than I did as a kid," Cee said. "We usually got to stay with my grandmother for two weeks. One summer we drove to the Thousand Lakes, mostly so my father could go fishing. We ate fish every day. I hate fish."

It was getting late. They'd arranged to meet Peter for dinner in the East Village where an Eisenstein double feature was playing. Cee had grown to like Peter. His studying Russian made a little more sense to her once she found out that his father had been a professor in the Soviet Union, narrowly avoiding Stalin's jails. Peter's goal was to translate the works of exiled Soviet writers into English.

They got back to the city ravenous.

"How about a slice of pizza to tide us over?" Cee said as they double parked in front of the theater. There was a pizzeria across the street.

She got back to the car with their slices just as the movie let out.

"Here," she said, getting in. "Be careful, it's hot." Joel went to take it. Cee screamed. "Look, there's that Aaron guy!"

"Ow!" The pizza had slipped out of Joel's hands and landed, cheese side down, on the bare skin of his thighs.

Aaron heard the scream and turned around. Cee thrust her face down.

"Who?" Joel said, in misery, scooping the hot cheese off his leg.

"Jason's boyfriend. Let's follow him. He might be going to meet my brother."

"What makes you so sure?" Joel said.

"It's worth a try. Why don't you drive. You know the area better." She got out.

Peter appeared just then.

"Wonderful film," Peter said when he got in. "I had forgotten just how masterful that scene on the steps was—"

Joel started the car and zoomed out.

"What's going on?" Peter said, going for the arm rest.

"We're following that guy on the other side of the street with the frizzy hair," said Cee.

Aaron had walked to First Avenue and was stopping at a grocery store.

"I'm famished," said Peter.

Cee offered him the rest of her pizza.

"No thanks. I'm allergic to the preservatives they use in the dough."

"What's Aaron doing now?" Joel said.

Aaron emerged with a container of yoghurt and a banana and began eating the banana as he walked toward East Ninth Street.

"Listen, if the two of you don't feel like eating, could you take me to Astor Place so I can catch the subway?" Peter said, irritated.

"Wait, it won't be long. He can't wander around forever," Cee said.

They raced down to Avenue C, narrowly missing the gush of a fire hydrant turned on full blast. They sighted Aaron as he turned the corner, heading south.

"Where the hell is he going?" Joel said. "This isn't the neighborhood for a stroll."

But there Aaron was, walking slowly, oblivious to his surroundings, face turned to the pavement, looking sad. When he finished the rest of his banana, he found a garbage can to toss the skin into, then opened his yoghurt.

At the next corner two tough-looking Puerto Rican men surrounded him and edged him against the wall.

"They got him!" shouted Cee.

She jumped out of the car.

"Cee, wait!" Joel shouted.

"Oh my God," said Peter.

"Leave him alone," Cee said to the men.

The men turned, startled. Joel leapt out after her.

"Look out, he has a knife!" shouted Peter from the car.

A man was coming at Joel from behind, Joel spun around and stomped on the man's toes. Peter began honking wildly; a crowd formed. Joel and Cee hustled Aaron away toward the car.

"Drive," Joel said to Peter as they all piled in.

Peter put the car into gear, and they lurched forward. "I—I haven't driven in two years," he said.

"You're doing fine," Cee said, adding a measure of insistence.

"My God," said Aaron, staring ahead of him in a daze. He noticed Cee. "You came over last night with the viper, I mean—"

Cee shot him a confused, but knowing glance.

Joel introduced himself. "You sure picked a great place to go for a walk."

"I feel like I'm driving a getaway car," Peter said, grinning.

"We were hoping you'd take us to where my brother is," Cee said.

Aaron's lips tightened. "I haven't seen him. I told you that already. Twice. You can let me out here," he said when they reached Saint Marks Place.

"Feel like joining us for something to eat?" Cee said.

"I already ate," he answered quickly.

"Only a banana," Joel said, humoring him. "And you lost your yoghurt."

He smiled and said okay.

After they'd parked Peter mopped his forehead with a tissue.

"You really did fine," Cee said.

The Ukrainian Restaurant—Peter's idea—was closed for renovations. Joel suggested Dojo's.

"I never get full on Japanese food," Peter said.

"Try the tempura," Aaron advised.

While they were waiting for their orders Cee went to the bathroom. Joel asked Aaron how he'd met Jason.

"On the street," he answered.

"Did he say where he'd come from?"

"No."

"Anything about where he was going after he left your place?"

"What is this," Aaron said, annoyed as he had been in the car, "an interrogation? I thought we were going to get something to eat."

Peter turned to Aaron. "Say, weren't you in the Eisenstein movie?"

"Both of them."

Peter looked impressed.

Cee returned just as their orders came. She tore open her chopsticks and ate, conscious of Joel's silence. Was he still thinking about her hapless remark that morning? Perhaps mentioning Marlene had set something into motion that couldn't be stopped. He ate nervously and dug his fork into the mound of rice as though wishing it were mashed potatoes. The meal became tedious.

Cee turned to Aaron. "Can I ask you a personal question? You were . . . in love with my brother, weren't you?"

Peter waited to see what Aaron would say.

"I guess so," Aaron said.

"So you're like Billy," Peter said, almost like an accusation.

Cee heard the waver in his voice. Poor Peter, she thought.

"Actually, I think we're quite different from one another."

"You really have to leave tomorrow?" Joel said to Cee.

She was about to answer when she saw Jason walking by the window. "That's him," she gasped, pointing. She lurched out of her seat.

Joel grabbed her arm. "Wait, maybe Aaron should go first. Jason might make a run for it if he sees you."

"I don't know about you but I'm staying right where I am and finishing my meal," Peter said, gripping his fork.

Cee turned to Aaron. "Go out there after him, talk to him, invite him up to your house."

Aaron scowled at them. "You both just want to trap him! You want to turn him over to the cops!"

"How come you're defending him, Aaron?" Joel said. "I thought you kicked him out of your house."

"I did, but I don't want him thrown into jail."

"He's already halfway down the fucking block," Cee said, pushing up out of her seat. Joel followed her.

"What's going on here?" Peter asked Aaron. "Do you know?"

Aaron bit his lip to keep it from trembling. Then he sprang out of his seat and left the restaurant.

A waiter appeared beside Peter. "You pay?" he said.

Joel and Cee had already reached Third Avenue when Aaron caught up with them.

"I really feel that tempura," Cee said, panting.

"There he is," Joel said, pointing down the short block to the corner of Fourth Avenue.

Jason stood over a sidewalk display of magazines. Nearby a man's guitar chugged out heavy metal from a portable amplifier, beside a sign that read Music Forbidden in Poland. The light changed, and a thick belt of traffic blocked Jason from view. When the light changed again they were about to cross the street when a screech of wheels knifed through the air, followed by a hollow-sounding explosion. Two cars had accordioned into one another. The spray of broken glass over the asphalt made it look as though they teetered on an iced-over pond. Traffic pooled around them, and moments later an ambulance siren began snarling their way. Police appeared and began pushing people back to make room for it. Jason was nowhere to be seen. Someone was being ferried into the ambulance on a stretcher.

"We're never going to find him in this crowd now," Joel said, straining on his toes to see above the people.

"He probably kept going along Eighth Street," Aaron said. "Let's head that way."

They crossed Astor Place just in time to see Jason making for the subway entrance.

"Jason!" Aaron cried, running to him.

Jason turned, but when he saw Cee, he took off, heading north, then cutting east down Ninth Street.

"This way," Cee yelled, leading them back toward Astor Place. But the crowd had grown, police had put barriers along the curb, and they weren't able to get through.

"Officer, I'm a nurse," Cee said, flashing her Buffalo General ID card. The cop let her through but blocked Joel.

"Wait for me back at the car," she called to them, starting up Third Avenue. Her legs seemed barely able to carry her; she felt like an engine about to shake itself apart. Just before Twelfth Street she spotted Jason resting against a parked car. She crept toward him, keeping as close as she could to the building fronts. Jason looked up and down the block, as though unable to settle on a direction. The bluish street light made his face look pearly and curiously peaceful.

Just as she was about to approach him, he caught sight of her. He made a run for it, and she flung herself upon him with every molecule of force in her body. He fell, and his head hit the pole of a No Parking sign with a heavy twang. He let out a confused cry, then crumpled to the ground. Blood spread across the side of his head.

A man walked by. "Get me a cab!" she shouted to him, pulling a scarf from her bag to press against the wound.

When a cab came, she and the man huddled Jason into the back seat, and they drove the three blocks to where Joel was waiting.

"Richie!" said Aaron.

Jason's eyes fluttered.

"Give me a hand with him, Aaron," Joel said. They deposited Jason in the back seat.

"Get ice, Joel." He ran into a coffee shop and returned with a bulky package wrapped in a towel. Cee placed it against Jason's head.

"Do you want to come with us?" Joel said to Aaron as they got inside the car.

Aaron could only stare at Jason. Then he shook his head. "Goodbye, Richie," he said.

Cee held Jason in her arms all the way uptown. Every so often he stirred, mumbling.

"It's okay," she whispered to him. "It's okay." You asshole, she thought, holding him close. You goddamn asshole.

Part Four

I

Walter Gajewski stood by the living room window and checked his watch. Dan Washington wouldn't be driving by to pick him up for another hour. Dan was from Binghamton, another long-term unemployed case Larrabee'd given a construction job to, a colored fellow, but, as far as Walter could tell, just as nice a guy as you'd ever want to meet. Married, four kids, a house with a mortgage to pay off, just like everybody else. Dan was a good ten years younger than Walter, but most of the men on the job were, too. Pops, they called him. To hell with Dr. Kraus, he thought, Pops is going to work today.

It was barely six but the sun was already strong. Shallow grey craters in the path marked where flagstones had broken loose during the winter. The grass looked faded, but what was the use of worrying about new seed when you weren't sure if you could make next month's mortgage? He felt a surge of defiance. Maybe the place wasn't more than a cinder-block cheesebox in a subdivision built on a drained swamp, but it was his. Right after moving in he'd proudly carved that *G* under the sink. He'd put up shelves, hung cabinets. Everything had been done well, the sockets sunk, the wiring hidden, the wall plugs snug. Now the place had begun to look shabby, neglected. It needed a paint job but good. With a regular paycheck coming in, he'd make the place shine.

They were going up to Indian Mountain for the first time. He'd been too excited to sleep, like a schoolboy before a class trip. But when he shaved he saw how his eyes swam in red, and the hollow feeling in his bones meant that his tail was going to drag all day. He considered going back into the kitchen for a second half-cup of coffee but decided to try and do without. He blinked, urging alertness into his eyes.

For the past couple of months sleep had come stubbornly. It started back in January, when Theresa announced she'd gotten a full-time office job. He made a scene. Why hadn't she talked about it with him first? And how the hell did she get a job when he hadn't worked in half a year? She told him: The caseworker in the welfare office helped her get it. What welfare office? What caseworker? Then it all came out. They'd been on the dole for months without him even knowing it. She'd worked out everything—papers, bills—in secret. "But welfare?" he'd said. "That's for the colored."

He ran his finger along the weather stripping. He'd gotten that done last winter and tacked rubber strips along the doors, too. Each time the heating oil truck came, the bill was like a telegram of bad news. He saw the cheap cuts of meat Theresa brought home, the way her wallet bulged with coupons she'd clipped—anything to save a few cents here and there. What good did it do? Hours after a shopping trip Jason had hacked away half of the pound cake or peeled off most of the bologna slices.

Walter kept peering out the window until he realized it was the glass itself he looked at, the glass Jason had put his fist through. Without having to shift his gaze he could see the faint brown splotches still left on the carpet by the blood. He'd heard the smash, jumped out of bed, expecting a burglar, then saw Jason stumbling against the wall, his arm spurting blood like a garden hose. Jason's eyes had that strange, empty look they'd had as a kid.

Walter clasped his hands together, as if to keep himself from doing as Jason had done. Theresa had told him to spend more time with his son. *You're his father; do something else besides watching television with him.*

My son, he thought.

Walter felt the noise his heart made in his chest, closed his eyes, and willed calm. It was the coffee. Kraus had warned him. "A cup'll turn your ticker into a time bomb, Walter," he said. He went outside to get the paper. The air was chilly but the cold felt shallow; it wouldn't last. Back inside, he glanced at the headlines: "Green Light for Larrabee." Below was a picture of that house. The caption read, "Hell no, we won't go!" People clustered before it, their fists in the air. He examined the fuzzy outlines of the picture and found Carl, holding Walter's granddaughter. He stared until the dots grew blurry.

"You're ready to throw your own son out into the street again," Theresa had said, "this time along with his wife and his child."

Walter put down the paper. Where was Dan? The foreman had told them to leave extra time to get to the site, in case there was trouble. Just the other day some of those kids from the university sat down in the middle of the road to block the trucks. Where do they come off doing what they're doing? Do they know what it's like to live on what they earn? And to think the county almost gave in to them. Good thing the board of supervisors came to its senses. What a waste —a hundred jobs out the window, ninety-nine plus his.

And Christ Almighty, if Larrabee hasn't been fair to Carl, offering him a house with a full quarter acre of land to boot. Who ever got more than an eighth of an acre around a new house these days? How much was that house going to cost him? Nothing, not a penny. And what did he and his friends say to Larrabee? They gave him the finger. So to hell with them.

"Who are you talking to?"

Walter spun around, startled. Theresa stood in the entry to the living room in her bathrobe. She'd had her hair cut short, and for a moment, he almost didn't recognize her.

"Jesus, you scared me."

She checked the water kettle and left. He poured himself a glass of orange juice. A piece of paper with the number of the police station had been fixed onto the refrigerator door with a magnet. How long had Jason been missing? Two weeks now? No, longer. What was happening to his family? He didn't understand jack shit about anything anymore. When he was growing up, life wasn't easy, but there was a logic to things. Children were born, they grew up and lived with their families, they married. There were always lowlifes and corrupt politicians, but everyone seemed to have the same basic idea of how things should be. Crooks did wrong, but they'd have given anything to be better than they were. The corrupt politicians got exposed, McCarthy got booted out. Nixon, too. Vietnam, well that turned out to be a bad deal all around, but who could have known that beforehand? If America hadn't stuck out its neck in forty-one, who knows how far Hitler might have gone. But Vietnam was over. Things were getting better; you could see that when guys like Dan Washington landed a construction job, and he had a nice car, too, a whole lot nicer than Walter's beat-up Pontiac.

The police had found it on the side of the road where Jason left it. They'd called them up in the middle of the night; he couldn't believe it was happening to him.

The window had been a warning. "Go talk to him, he's your son," Theresa had said. But he hadn't. He hadn't been able to, he'd never known what to say. Jason had a spark to him when he was little, different from Carl and Celia. But it went out after the accident. He became someone else. Mostly it was that look in his eyes, that blinking stare. It scared Walter. He was ashamed to admit it, but it did. His own son scared him.

Walter set out cups and saucers and plates. Since Theresa got that county job it seemed she lived in the office. Overtime, she explained. So Walter took turns with Jason doing the shopping. Going to the A&P was worse than going to the public library, which is where he'd often pass the morning before they started cutting back on the hours. The library was usually empty, but he was bound to run into someone he knew in the A&P who had a word or two of sympathy ready for him.

The kettle sent up a plume of steam. As he turned off the gas he caught sight of the wall calendar, a red circle around Father's Day.

"You look tired," Theresa told him as she came in.

"I didn't sleep well last night."

They sat down. Theresa buttered a melba toast and read the paper. Walter poured her coffee.

"Thanks," she said without looking up.

Did she see the picture? Did she see their granddaughter?

He went to pour himself a cup.

"You know what Dr. Kraus told you about your heart," Theresa said, barely looking up.

These days they didn't have much to say to one another. They didn't quarrel, but if you didn't talk, you didn't quarrel. They used to talk, didn't they? What about? The children? The house? Money? Anything else? Anything else? There must have been other things. He surveyed the table: low-fat cottage cheese, diet margarine, low-salt Muenster cheese, all because of his heart and her weight-watching. They might have been living in an old-age home.

"Maybe if I had someone to converse with I would drink less coffee," Walter said, filling his cup.

Her eyes lifted briefly. "This is my only chance to read the paper."

"Couldn't you read it in the office? You certainly spend enough time there."

Her eyes narrowed. "The office is where I work." She turned a page crisply.

"You think I'm a creep for going to work up on Indian Mountain, don't you?"

"You have to do what you think is right, Walter," she answered, her voice carefully controlled.

She'd brought home a bakery cake and made a big supper when his job came through. But then Elaine started talking to her. Elaine was the only woman he'd ever seen with more hair on her legs than a man. One day in the winter he'd walked in and found them both sitting at the kitchen table, drinking coffee, as though Elaine lived next door. After that Theresa began coming at him with questions. Did he really think the developers had a right to build expensive homes and a hotel in the middle of a recession? Did he think it was an accident that the county suddenly approved a rezoning plan that made it easier for private developers to build on publicly owned land? How could the county support the construction of vacation homes when a new junior high school was desperately needed? Last night at supper she went too far and said the project was sure to upset the water table. "What in God's name do you know about the water table?" he'd thundered.

It had been a stupid thing to say. She got up and went to their room. He followed, expecting to find her crying. Instead she was talking to someone on the telephone. When he came in, she put her hand over the receiver and waited for him to leave the room. Before they went to sleep she asked him if he planned to go to the site. It sounded like a challenge. Who in their right mind would turn down a chance to work after living like a pauper for so many months? "You bet I am," he said.

"I didn't mean to sass you last night," he told her.

"That's all right." Her thoughts seemed elsewhere. She gulped down the rest of her coffee, got up, and took a piece of meat from the freezer which she set out to thaw.

A car honked outside. Walter started to get up.

"It's Sylvia," Theresa said, grabbing her cardigan. "See you tonight." She left.

He sat there thinking. She hadn't kissed him good-bye.

It didn't mean anything, he told himself. She was in a hurry.

But she could have at least kissed me.

Last night she hadn't kissed him good-night, either, like they were brother and sister. Was that what happened to people who'd been married as long as they were?

The worst thing was that she'd stopped wearing that thing. Right after the operation she was so afraid of him seeing her that she made them give her something temporary before the permanent thing was ready.

Now she looked . . . uneven, lopsided.

Seven o'clock. Where was Dan?

The phone rang. Dan, saying he had car trouble?

It was Elaine. She wanted to speak with Theresa.

"She's already left for work."

"Oh, I'm sorry." She sounded ready to hang up.

"Wait—" Walter took a breath. "Maybe I can help you."

"Um, no, that's okay," she said. "I just needed to ask something . . . about Melissa."

"Is everything all right?"

"Yes. Don't worry. Tell Theresa that I called."

A car pulled into the driveway. Walter took his lunch box from the refrigerator and headed for the door. He got as far as the front steps, expecting to see Dan leaning out of the window wearing that English-looking cap of his. Instead a small burgundy-colored foreign car was mounting the driveway. Three people got out: his daughter, a skinny man, and Jason.

Jason.

Walter ran to his son and grasped him in a clumsy hold, then stepped back to look at him, almost giddy with relief.

A moment later Walter heard another car honking.

"Walt!" shouted Dan, waving at him from behind the wheel.

"Celia," Walter said, stumbling over to her. His hands fidgeted. He sensed she didn't want him embracing her.

"Man, we gotta get a move on," Dan said. "Hey, is that your boy?"

Billy stepped forward and offered his hand to Walter. "Gizzi's the name."

Walter shook it weakly, still looking at his son and daughter. "I'll be back a little after five," he said, walking toward Dan's car. He turned to his daughter once more. "Celia—"

"The man's waiting for you," she said.

"Do you always have to be a wiseass?" Cee said, once they were inside. "Gizzi's the name," she mimicked.

"Your father was no doubt wondering who I was, so I saw fit to introduce myself," Billy replied. "You certainly are in a foul mood."

"Jason? Where are you?"

"In the kitchen."

"What are you doing?"

"Eating something."

"What are you going to do afterward?"

He stood before the open refrigerator. "Quit playing jail warden."

"I have got to lie down," Billy said.

She showed him to Carl's room. "There's bedding in the hall closet. I'm still buzzing from all the coffee I drank." She paused. "Sorry I snapped at you."

"You feeling okay down there?" He nodded toward her abdomen.

"I guess." She went downstairs. She'd driven all night, and the black stripe of route 17 kept flickering before her eyes.

Yesterday at this time she was still in bed with Joel.

A little later the phone rang.

"Mom!" she said. "Oh, it's good to hear you. How did you know I got in?"

"Your father just called me. How are you?"

"Exhausted. When will you be home?"

"A little after five. I'll ask Sylvia if she'll let me get out a little earlier tonight." There was a pause. "Your father told me that Jason's there."

That was all she said about him. Afterward Cee went up to her room and closed the door. Her shelves still held high school books and paperbacks, but the upholstered chair she'd dragged home from a yard sale was gone. Jason had commandeered the old TV Jeanine's brother had given her. The room felt too orderly to be hers anymore; aloof, it recognized her only as a visitor. She lay down. The bed seemed so small after Joel's.

SHE'D JUST WOKEN UP when Billy knocked on her door. He swam in wearing a turquoise chiffon ball gown.

"What a town you've got here—so authentically A*mer*ican! How on earth could you bear to leave it? I've been everywhere—Woolworth's, the Seven Layer Bake Shop, and, as you can see," he said, lifting the folds of the gown to make a deep curtsy, "Amvets."

"Oh my lord—"

"I found just the right things to accessorize it, too. The woman in the store was very helpful."

"She saw you in that?"

"Of course. How else could she have picked out these?" He hoisted up his gown and lifted a leg to display his high heels.

"What time is it?"

"Around four."

"Already?"

"I notice you haven't asked me why I was driven to such lengths of fashion inspiration," Billy said, lips pursed in annoyance.

"Why, Billy, I didn't think you needed a reason."

"Since you insist, I'll tell you. The gay group at the state university is having its summer prom this Saturday. How's that for timing?"

"Just don't model it for my parents. By the way, have you seen my brother?"

"He went out for a walk before I left."

"And you let him?"

"Do you think I could stop a brute like that? We don't exactly get along, you know. He wouldn't listen to anything I'd say."

"I was hoping you'd at least keep an eye on him. Who knows, he just might decide to hitch away again. I need a cigarette." She groped for her pack.

The back door opened and closed with a thud, followed by the thick plod of steps up the stairs.

"Here comes the hairy ape," said Billy.

As they went downstairs, the phone rang.

Cee got it. "Hello? No, this isn't—Elaine? Elaine!" She let out a little shriek and pulled the receiver into the living room to talk.

Billy was making coffee when she hung up.

"Remember I was telling you about Carl's house?" she said. "After the county gave the developer the go-ahead for the project, a bunch of people barricaded themselves inside and are refusing to leave until the bulldozers pull out. The developer threw up a fence around the place, and the cops aren't letting anybody in. Elaine said they've stored up food and there's a big garden so they'll be able to hold out for a while, but not indefinitely. Ron, their lawyer, is in touch with the district attorney, and he's trying to work out some kind of deal." She spoke in a breathless rush.

"Since you've mentioned getting back to Buffalo, when did you plan to get back to Buffalo?"

"There's no way I'm leaving here while that house is under attack. I'll call up Durkin, give some sob story about my father, and beg her to let me stay here until the beginning of next week."

Or I could simply tell her what happened to the baby.

The back door opened again.

"Mom!"

"Oh, Cee," her mother said, pulling Cee close. She began to cry.

"Mom, everything's okay. This is Billy."

Theresa smiled at him. "Is Jason here?" Cee nodded. Her mother set her pocketbook on the table, then faced the stairs as if trying to decide whether or not to go up to Jason's room. Weariness collected in her face. "Is he okay?"

"Yes, except for the lump on his head he got trying to run away from me."

Theresa kept looking, then turned abruptly toward the kitchen. "Your father will be home in an hour," she said. "I have to get supper—" She put her face in her hands and began to cry again.

"Mom," Cee said, going over to her.

"I'm all right," she said, avoiding Cee's embrace. "Just let me get supper started." She looked around. "Where's your friend?"

Billy had left the room. Cee silently thanked him for letting them alone.

Her mother stood before an open kitchen cabinet. "Corn or peas?" she said, thinking out loud. "Elaine told you about what's going on with the house, didn't she?"

"Yes. I want to be there with them, Mom."

Her mother's voice grew stern. "You won't be able to get through, Cee," she said, taking down a can. "And your going up there might make things even more complicated than they already are."

Cee watched her mother grind the can open. They'd seen each other for barely ten minutes and they were about to argue. "What does Dad say about all this?" she said. "Doesn't he realize that Carl's going to be kicked out?"

"Cee, please, let's not start that now. You don't know what it's been like, living with him the whole time he was out of work. I'd wake up in the morning and see him sitting at the kitchen table like an invalid without a clue of what to do for the rest of the day. Recently he went for his checkup, and Dr. Kraus told him that his heart wasn't looking any better than it had in the fall, so you can imagine how that made him feel. Here," she said, pushing an onion and the cutting board her way. "Slice this thin for me, will you?"

"Why did he take the job if his heart's not so great?"

"Because he wants to prove that he can still work, which I understand."

"Let him do volunteer work, push people around in wheelchairs, read to the blind—"

"Cee, it's your father you're taking about, not some rich lady with time on her hands." Theresa poured off the pinkish water from the bowl the meat had thawed in.

"Dad should tell Larrabee to stick the job up his ass."

"It's not so simple and, anyway, your father would never do that. The way he sees it, he has every right to have a job. You act as though it was his idea to build the houses. Well, it wasn't. And would you mind watching your language?"

"Do you remember how he used to tell us how great this country was because everyone had the chance to make something of themselves?" She sliced, and the knife hit the board heavily. "It turned my stomach but I was never sure why. Now I know: The only people who believe things like that don't have to worry about money." She set the slices before her mother.

"You forget he lived through the depression."

"Did he ever let anyone forget it? You lived through the depression too, but you never carried on like him."

Her mother set the onions in a pot to brown, stirring them, her face drained of expression.

Cee regretted having come on so strong. "I heard Dad is getting some kind of award," she said softly.

"Yes. He's become something of a local hero. Everyone knew how long he'd been without work, so now they're happy for him. And they also think that Carl and his friends are a bunch of loafers getting in the way of a good thing."

"Is that what you think, Mom?"

The sweet smell of the onions filled the kitchen. "Cee, I don't know what to think anymore." She dumped the meat into the pot and an angry sizzle rose up. "The whole drive home I was dreading seeing Jason again," Theresa said in a low voice. "I kept thinking that ever since Jason was little he's done things that made me feel sorry for him and want to throw him from a moving train at the same time. This new escapade is too much for me, I admit it." She paused. "When the police told me that he'd run away I thought . . . I felt . . . a kind of . . . relief. I prayed nothing bad would happen to him. But after what he did, I thought that maybe the best thing would be for him to just go away. Your father blames that Richie kid for turning Jason into a hoodlum." She took out a large glass bowl. "Help me with the salad."

"Since when do you guys eat salad?"

"Everybody eats salad these days, for crying out loud."

Cee stoppered the drain, let the cold water run, and began washing the lettuce. She watched her mother tending to the meat. Pot roast, she thought. How many pounds of it had she consumed at her mother's table? The heavy smell of the meat collected in the air, weighing on her like a blanket that was too warm. Her mother bustled around the kitchen as she always had. Something in Cee weakened.

"Mom, I have something to tell you," she heard herself say.

"Now what?"

Cee didn't answer right away, unsure of what should come next. "I'm fine, nothing's wrong. But I was . . . pregnant."

"You were pregnant?"

"I lost the baby."

Theresa clasped her hands to Cee's cheeks and held her face, as if searching for traces of what had happened. "We've got to get you to a doctor."

"I'm fine, really I am."

Her mother kept her hands on Cee's face. "Did you want it?"

"I wasn't sure."

Her mother released her and turned toward the wall, her arms clasped around her chest. The front door opened.

"Theresa?"

Walter Gajewski strode into the kitchen, a big bouquet of flowers blocking his face.

She flung her arms around him, as though reassured at seeing what was familiar.

"What's the matter?" he said. "Cee!"

But she'd already left the room.

That evening Cee called Joel. The calm of his voice soothed her, but she was aware of a certain distance. He was buried under work, he said, and Cee wondered if that meant that he'd neglected it too much on her account and now regretted it. He and Peter had quarreled after the incident at Dojo's; Peter had moved out. Joel sounded a little sore about it. He mentioned running into Aaron at a poetry reading, but that was the last reference he made to her having been in New York. He said he planned to come to Buffalo in the beginning of July.

"Oh," Cee said, brightening.

"I'd like to see Marlene again," he said, as if to explain the trip. "But I really do hope we can see each other also."

All right, Cee thought, hanging up. Joel's life seemed to have closed seamlessly over her departure, as though she'd never been there. Yet that night at Dojo's he'd seemed sorry that she was going, hadn't he? It was hard to know what to make of the conversation. She didn't have too much time to think before a cramp hit her. The pain was more or less bearable and not, thank God, the insistent torture of the night before. It subsided, but she didn't trust the calm. Who knew what absurdities this huge body of hers would stage next . . .

She had sensed something wasn't right while she was in New York. It seemed she hadn't stopped going to the bathroom the whole time. And those cramps. If you don't have the decency to menstruate, she'd told her ovaries, then knock it off. But the cramps only worsened. Last night, just outside of Middletown, she pulled over, ready to pee out the last of her bottomless cup of coffee. But as soon as she stepped out of the car the pressure inside her began to pulse, as if motorized, and she made a run for the toilet, frantic.

Would the door be locked? They usually kept them locked, oh God, don't let it be locked. She thrust her hand at the door. It opened. Inside it was as brightly lit as a hospital. Urinals. Christ, she was in the men's bathroom. Where were the normal toilets? She needed a plain, old fucking toilet. How come men got their own special toilets? They could pee anywhere. She pushed a cubicle open and held on as she swung down onto a hard rim of wet stone. The goddamn seat wasn't down. She tried to heave herself back up, but her legs went dead. Pants, pull down my pants. She went for the snap of her jeans, for the zipper. Her fingers hung like strips of felt from her hand, useless. Pull it down, pull it down. Why am I so fucking fat? Get the pants down, pull, rip. The zipper finally gave. She got her jeans down as far as her knees and thought of medieval torturers flaying their victims. The pain began expanding within her, oh Jesus, she started to pee, sheathing her legs in a stinging heat. There was blood on her skin. My period, she thought, but her insides kept on blustering and bulging. The pain was too big for her to hold, she had to let it out, let it out. It pressed and pressed, her cunt yielded, too much, too much . . .

Then it was over.

She slumped forward and sat for a long time. She felt her insides closing up, pulling together. My period, yes, it's okay. She surveyed the plump landscape of her flesh, the fjords of her thighs dropping to the cold depths of the toilet. She parted her legs, peered into the water. Under the shadow of her monster thigh, floating in blood soup: a little doll, a one-eyed fish-baby, no larger than her fist, with tiny hands and tiny feet, cabled to a lacy anemone of afterbirth—oh Mother of Jesus, a *baby!* She kept looking. A baby, *which may or may not have still been alive.* She began to shake as if her body were ready to heave forth another horrifying surprise. She looked closer. A face, a nose, even what looked like a penis. It was all there. A curl of pubic hair floated alongside it, not hers, she was sure, some man's, a fucking man's, they were everywhere, deep into a woman's most private moments—

She squelched the rage in her brain. A baby, she thought. Hers. No larger than her fist. A person's heart was the size of a fist. Her heart, her baby. A boy.

Someone was coming in. She reached behind her and did what seemed utterly necessary: She flushed. No one to see it, no one to take it away.

"You okay, Cee? It's me, Jason."

She froze. His voice, his killing, stabbing voice, his evil body, his evil, dicked body. I've birthed the child you forced on that woman, she thought, the woman you left, dirty and bleeding. I've received it instead of her, been midwife to it. She's free now, free of your poison, I've flushed away what you did to her. I got rid of it without them, without their instruments, their corkscrews, without their white coats, white as toilets.

"Cee?"

He tried the door to the cubicle. She'd locked it. His boots pointed like spears under the door.

"Get out," she was finally able to say. She heard him leave.

She hiked her pants up to her knees, waddled to the sink, grabbed a fistful of paper towels, wet them, and returned to her cubicle. Carefully, she cleaned herself. The paper felt as rough as a cat's tongue. The towels were stained beet-red, blood-red. She dropped them in the water, shapeless, soggy flowers. She flushed, sending them off to her progeny, tumbling forward in a universe of water, flowers for her baby, another little Moses bound for a river where he'd never be found. Then she began zipping herself up.

She stared into the white ceramic quarry of the toilet bowl. Disinfectant like a squid's ink stained the water blue. She unlocked the door. Everything was as it had been: still, clean, lifeless.

2

T̲HERESA GAJEWSKI FACED a stack of green-and-white-striped computer printouts on her desk. She looked over to Helen Frank's desk, crammed with framed snapshots of children and grandchildren, Snoopy figurines, and a plastic miniature cherry tree. Theresa's desk looked bare by comparison, but Helen assured her it would fill up the longer she worked there. Theresa was grateful it hadn't. Seeing the faces of her three children every minute of her working day would be just too much for her.

She looked at her watch. It was almost nine. She'd been in the office for nearly twelve hours. Her neck felt imprisoned in a collar of steel from sitting so long. She would go through everything just one more time, she told herself. And then she would make the call. She tapped the edges of the printouts into line with a pencil, and then went for a drink at the water cooler. The terrazzo floor felt especially hard through the soles of the house shoes she'd slipped on after five. Being alone in the large office, with its strong geometry of desks and file cabinets, felt far different from being at home alone. You were never alone there anyway, even if no one else was with you. The kitchen where you'd peeled potatoes for years knew you, the draperies whispered when you took them down to clean, and your skillet complained when you burned the eggs. Offices were about territory. The more powerful you were, the more you got. Women's allotments were small: the space behind a counter, the tiny room off the kitchen for the maid, her own secretary's desk.

She filled her paper cup and went to the window. Hawley Street was deserted. The fluid calm of summer had begun to set in. As a child growing up in a town even smaller than Thompson City, she found summer was when time hardly moved, when days curled up and browned in the sun, one just like the other, followed by evenings still as stone. She sipped her water. The office had been an oven today, with fans only blowing the hot air around. They couldn't put the AC on because of austerity measures. The people in the new building were lucky; their windows were sealed, the rooms climate-controlled. Still, the old building was nicer, everything rounded and muted, strips of brass in the black floors, cream-colored ceilings. From the thirties, like her. But—speaking of the thirties—hot as a dustbowl.

She tossed the cup away and returned to her desk. It had taken several weeks to receive all the printouts. Theresa asked for no more than one item per week to avoid suspicion. Sylvia Dewer, the office manager, who had to approve all requisitions, appeared at her desk one morning and asked why she suddenly needed records from the Office of Budget Planning. Surely not for anything having to do with Parks and Recreation, Theresa's department. Theresa had explained that she was curious. Sylvia peered at her over her reading glasses and said, "Women over the age of fifty don't have to play games with each other. What's up?" So Theresa told her. Sylvia answered, "Okay, you want to play Watergate investigator, fine, but not on office time. Stay after school to poke around." Then she added, "You really think it's going to make one iota of difference, Terry?"

She liked Sylvia. Divorced, no children, she'd constructed a career for herself at a time when women married and had children—or else.

The civil service had been the logical route for Sylvia, too lazy to sweep floors, too smart to just type letters, but short a college degree. Theresa told her what she needed, and a week later Sylvia plunked a stack of printouts onto Theresa's desk just before quitting time. "Courtesy of the Freedom of Information Act," Sylvia said. "But just remember, if anyone asks, it's your freedom, not mine."

Theresa had first noticed the coincidences after spending a week in February filling in for a secretary up at the planning department. Larrabee had just begun negotiating with the county for the right to build on the mountain. Each day batches of letters went out to different construction companies. As she typed, she noticed that certain names kept cropping up on letterheads and invoices. At first she thought she'd mismatched addresses. But no, it was an old name with a new address. Of course, that didn't mean anything, necessarily. But she remembered it. When she checked further she discovered that the contracts for the new firehouse, the water main, and the repair of the obelisk commemorating the battle fought against the Quaspeck Indians had all been awarded to contractors whose bids also happened to be the highest. The companies had different names, but they shared some of the same higher-ups. She hauled out business directories for the county and for the state, compared boards of directors, and made a diagram of her findings. The result was a family tree: construction company executives, government officials, and presidents of boards of directors branching off one trunk or another and interwining. *And nearly all of them were linked to Larrabee.* But what did that prove? Money attracted money. Larrabee had his fingers in more than one pie, no surprise to anyone. And the mere fact that the county executive's brother happened to be on Larrabee's payroll—which she'd also discovered—was hardly cause for scandal, either. But the connections threw a different light on the county executive's line about the Indian Mountain project being a joint venture for the economic welfare of Thompson City and Broome County. When she confided her suspicions to a man from the comptroller's office, he sounded scared and hastily said the question lay out of his jurisdiction.

Sylvia asked Theresa who she was doing all this for. She had to think.

For Carl, her moody, overcomplicated son? Was helping him keep his house a way to make good after Walter had kicked him out of theirs? For weeks after Carl had left she pulled herself out of bed in the morning, weak with worry. When she visited him in the bookstore, she found him bundled in a frowzy wool sweater, not drop of color in his face, and her heart would break. But slowly, she realized that Carl, stubborn, pigheaded Carl, was living the way he wanted to. No, she wasn't doing this just for him.

For Melissa? The first and only time Theresa had been up to the house was for the child's . . . ceremony. She had fretted the whole night before over whether she could bring herself to go, knowing the child wouldn't be christened, knowing Carl didn't want Walter to come. The worst part was seeing the baby lying in a crib hammered together out of scrap wood. Elaine gave Melissa to her to hold, and for a moment Theresa wanted to run away with her and bring her back to civilization. Then Melissa began to cry; Elaine took her back, opened her blouse, and fed her. Carl looked on, and an expression of simple joy that Theresa had never seen illuminated his face.

The winter before, Melissa had gotten sick. Carl called up, saying he needed money to pay the doctor. Walter refused, hoping it might persuade Carl to come and talk with him. Carl didn't come. Theresa knew he wouldn't. She thought of Melissa in that drafty house, wearing the patched clothes plucked from a bin at the food co-op, and knew that if anything, anything happened to the child, Carl would be crippled. She withdrew money from their joint account, and arranged for Max from the bookstore to give it to Carl as a loan from him.

So perhaps she was doing it for Melissa, or for Elaine. Or maybe because she'd decided that it simply had to be done.

Her eyes fell on the painting on the wall showing a large sailing ship on the Susquehanna about to put up anchor. Aboard was William Thompson, a fur trader, looking like George Washington in a long, dark cape and tricornered hat. A band of Indians stood on the shore, painted and feathered, lead by a chief holding a peace pipe, his arms outstretched to welcome the new settlers.

She opened her address book and found the number Elaine had given her of a man from the *Sun-Bulletin* who was interested in exposing Larrabee. Then she set the book aside. Without the help of the comptroller's office, she could prove little. Not only would she get laughed at, she'd lose her job, and Walter his. They'd be right back to worrying about the mortgage and counting nickels. Walter would install himself in the club chair, aging by the minute. What would she have gained? Maybe it was time to stop playing detective.

Yet something about the whole thing didn't sit right with her. One of Larrabee's men had come over to the house to promise Walter that he'd be kept on after the project was built. There'd be other projects, too, he said. Walter believed him. She didn't. Their line made sense only if they were looking for some good publicity—and the best way to empty Carl's house.

She flipped through the printouts, watched the numbers dance like figures in a deck of movie cards. She stopped at one item: five thousand dollars for the cleaning and restoration of the bronze plaque on the obelisk. The sum was broken down into the cost of removing the plaque, transporting it to a restoration studio, cleaning, and remounting. Why couldn't they just have paid a weekend car simonizer to go over there with a rag and a can of polish? What good did the plaque do anyone, cleaned or not? But the town was going to have to shell out for its cleaning anyway.

She pulled out two large maps. One was of Larrabee's project. The road leading up the mountain branched off into a hydra's head of smaller roads with names like Timber Trail, Pinewood Lane, Forest Grove. The houses looked like toys scattered over the terrain around an oblong patch of blue, Quaspeck Lake. Where Carl's house should have been there was nothing.

Nothing.

Sylvia had dug up the second map, which covered the same area, drawn up in the year the mountain had been incorporated into the county, 1862. A lacy border framed it; the large lettering was fancy, the small, nearly illegible. Brown water stains blossomed over the stiff paper. Thompson City—still called Thompsonville—was hardly more than a widening of the road between Syracuse and Scranton; Binghamton was a cluster of tiny squares. A cross in a box marked Carl's house. A pair of dotted lines indicated the route of the old water conduit, starting at the lake and leading toward the house before dropping down to houses along the road where that man and his mother lived. Her eyes returned to the blank space on the new plan, and her fingers clenched tightly around the paper.

She decided to call Ron, the Mountain Coalition's lawyer, first, and ask him what he thought about it.

Ron's wife answered. He was up at the house, she said, which meant no one could reach him, since the county had ordered the phone disconnected. Theresa said she'd try him in the morning. She hung up and stared at the old map, the house, the lake, a fanciful letter *N* curling atop a directional arrow. She'd been told that no deed existed for the house, but if she knew her fellow county employees, they probably had gone through only the records stored in the new building, which dated from 1867, the year the city of Binghamton was incorporated. Anything earlier would be here. If there was an old map of the area, chances were there were documents related to it, or else how could the map have been drawn up?

With a start she pushed out of her chair and hurried to the hall. Was Willy still there? She'd seen him with his cleaning trolley other nights when she'd worked late. She'd have to search for him floor by floor. She took the elevator to the top floor, and heard his radio as soon as the elevator doors slid open.

"You still here, Mrs. G?"

He smiled, and his face dissolved in wrinkles. She judged him to be in his fifties, but when he smiled he looked ancient.

"You wouldn't happen to have the keys to the archives office, would you?"

"How else would I get in there to clean it?" He motioned to a heavy-looking key ring on his belt.

They rode the elevator down. She was conscious of being taller than he was. It occurred to her that he might be Walter's age. Since Walter had been laid off she'd grown aware of the ways men grew old: their ears becoming leafy and sprouting wads of hair, their gait sinking into a waddle, their middles thickening. She didn't let Walter buy knit slacks in that nondescript old-man's color between beige and grey, and she made sure he didn't bring home a pair of white loafers. She didn't want to be married to an old man.

Willy opened a heavy door that led into a windowless, dampish room, like a library except for metal cabinets instead of open shelves.

"I can't get into those," he said, motioning toward the shelves. "But that gadget can tell you what they got." He pointed to a microfilm reader.

"Willy!" She nearly cried with joy. "You know how to work that?"

"My son probably could, he knows about those kinds of things."

Theresa looked closer. She'd figure the thing out, so help her.

Willy left, and the door boomed shut behind him. She pulled open one of the wide drawers where the numbered rolls of microfilm lay nestled like eggs. Where to begin? There had to be some kind of index. There was: a small wooden cabinet beside the microfilm reader with drawers of file cards. After she found an entry for title deeds she extracted a roll and began trying to thread it. It took some doing, but soon tangles of writing emerged on the reader's screen. She turned a knob, and the writing slid away like the credits of a movie. The deeds seemed to be arranged by year, starting with 1834. But who knew when the house was built? After a while she found herself turning the knob idly, too tired to read.

Tomorrow, she thought. For now, she'd go upstairs and call the man from the *Sun-Bulletin*.

JUST AS EDGAR began to speak Melissa started crying.

It shook Carl out of the tired daze he'd sunk into during the long meeting. He was about to get up and check on Melissa, but Elaine motioned for him to stay put. He watched as she made her way toward the stairs. Her overalls were rolled up to her knees, and the muscles of her calves flexed with each step.

It was almost eleven. The second jug of iced tea was empty. The pauses between speakers grew longer. Edgar alone seemed to have the energy to talk. He was the oldest among them, a stalwart Lefty from New York, a one-time union leader who'd landed in Thompson City in the fifties to work in the shoe factory after being blacklisted. He was a familiar sight at rallies and demonstrations, and people usually indulged in his penchant for long-winded accounts of the strikes and sit-ins he'd helped organize. It looked as though Melissa's crying might cut Edgar's talk short, but he continued. "What we're experiencing is a classic battle between the propertied class and the propertyless," he said. Anytime he used the word classic it meant a lecture was coming.

Carl wasn't in the mood for it. Edgar's comradely attitude got on his nerves. He worried about Melissa. Last week the house awoke in the middle of the night to a convoy of cars pulling up in front and honking their horns. They had disappeared by the time everyone reached the porch, but it was clear what had happened: A backlash had developed against the house. People wanted Larrabee's jobs and didn't care about anything else. Since then a night didn't pass without Melissa waking up crying, as she had just then.

The day after the county gave Larrabee the go-ahead, the Coalition put out a call for people to come up to the mountain and live there for as long as they liked—house-sitting, it was jovially referred to. Someone used topographical surveys of the mountain and the price of Larrabee's lease to determine the cost of the county's deal—per tree: seventy-nine cents. The first day, people from all over the county showed up, along with students from the state university and the odd Sierra Club member. A hat was passed around each day, and everyone dutifully tossed in their seventy-nine cents to buy food. A street theater troupe showed up and performed a piece entitled *The Tape Recorder of Rose Mary Woods*, ending with a chorus line of people contorted to imitate Nixon's notorious secretary. Once again the floors were lined with sleeping bags, and dishes got done by a jolly assembly line. Then the police ordered everyone to vacate the house within twenty-four hours or risk arrest. The number of revelers winnowed down to those at the meeting: Max from the bookstore, Edgar, a close friend of Elaine's named Alyce, and a family: Phil, a teacher at the alternative school, Shera, who taught at the state university women's studies program, and their four-year-old son, Benjamin. With Elaine and Carl—and Melissa—there were nine people all together. "Almost enough for a minyan," Elaine had joked during their first meeting. "Of course, people like you and me wouldn't count," she said to Melissa. "We're only girls."

Their telephone had been cut soon after. Visitors were searched by the police. Finally the sheriff's office blocked their road entirely, letting people leave the house but not enter. The question discussed that night and the night before was how to use the upcoming Father's Day Fair to their advantage. The action would have to be a final effort, since anyone leaving the house couldn't get back in.

Edgar showed no signs of ending his monologue. Ron, the only person permitted through the police line, began putting his papers into his briefcase. "I have an early day tomorrow," he said.

"It's late, Edgar," said Alyce gently. "I think we should try to pull things together."

Edgar motioned with his hands. "I'm just trying to make the connection between—"

"I'm too tired to do any more connecting," said Max, a little brusquely. "And anyway, we already know which side of the fence our asses are on."

"I still think we should exploit Walter Gajewski getting that award," said Shera. "Carl has to confront him directly."

Carl sat up. He didn't like Shera, a loud woman with an Afro-style haircut and a penetrating voice. She was on Elaine's side. Their argument repeated itself in his brain like catechism: Larrabee claimed his project would enable the men of the town to do what all Americans sought to do—support their families. The Coalition would show that he was about to break up a family, and not just any family, but precisely the one whose father the developers had singled out to receive their Father of the Year award. The plan was to get Walter Gajewski to refuse it in front of everybody and announce that he wasn't accepting Larrabee's job offer.

And they wanted Carl to convince him to do it.

"Maybe we should talk about it tomorrow," said Phil, glancing sympathetically at Carl. "When we're not so tired."

"We don't have that much time," Shera said.

"There'll be a lot of publicity for the Father's Day thing," said Alyce. "We could put Larrabee on the spot, and he'd have to be careful about how he responds, since the media'll be there."

"Putting somebody on the spot is one thing but expecting Larrabee to back down is another," said Phil.

Shera turned to Carl. "Why haven't you said anything about this during the whole meeting?"

Carl looked down at the floor. "I've already said all I have to say at other meetings."

Elaine rejoined the circle.

"We were just discussing Carl speaking to his father—" Shera told her.

"We weren't discussing anything, Shera," said Carl. "You were trying to force me into doing what I said I am not prepared to do."

"Carl, maybe you should say exactly what it is you have against the idea," Alyce suggested.

"This whole thing is unfair," Carl shouted. "I feel like everything's on my shoulders now because we haven't come up with any other ideas."

"But we have," said Alyce. "We collected signatures. We tried to get the youth hostel people interested. Our plan for building the houses near the old sawmill was rejected. And the Native American group we spoke with said that we wouldn't have a chance using an Indian treaty in a New York state court. The county felt free to go along with Larrabee, especially after he agreed to find another place for you and Elaine."

Ron stood up. "At this point the only way we can stop Larrabee is by offering him a concrete alternative to the saw mill property, period." He looked around for his jacket.

"Are you saying you've actually accepted that he'll build those houses?" said Shera with a hint of contempt.

"I spoke with Steve Polikoff in the district attorney's office. He said that legally speaking we don't have a leg to stand on anymore. The environmental impact statement was our last chance. After yesterday's article in the *Sun-Bulletin* about Larrabee's connections I was hopeful, but there's going to have to be an investigation before the county takes any action. And an investigation is the easiest way to push the whole thing out of the public eye, which is just what will help Larrabee the most. If you want my honest opinion, this idea of yours sounds pretty shaky."

"That's not the word for it, Ron," Carl said. "More like pie-in-the-sky and just plain naive." He turned to the others. "You're all banking on the idea that a little *Life with Father* routine is going to make the county back down on its deal with Larrabee. Even if my father did refuse the job, everyone would assume that he'd done it to keep his son's house from being torn down, and for no other reason. But that would imply that he really gives a fuck about my house getting torn down. I'll wager he'll drive the first bulldozer over it. He's the reason I came here in the first place. He's been waiting all along for the chance to show me that father knows best. Don't think he's not going to use it." His voice pulled with strain, and for a moment, no one spoke.

"You always refused to bring Melissa to him," Elaine began. "You told me that if he really wanted to see his granddaughter he could drive up here."

"Elaine, what does that have to do—"

"I wanted to go down there. I didn't like him any more than you did, but I felt it was wrong to deprive him of the chance to see his grandchild. So I brought Melissa there myself. And he was beside himself with joy at seeing her. Maybe you don't know your father as well as you think you do."

"Carl, if you're so sure of what he thinks why don't you confront him?" Shera said. "Go ahead and call him on his power number—"

"Oh to hell with that, Shera!" shouted Carl. "You haven't spoken to your own mother in five years. And to hell with all this talk of my family getting broken up. I don't have a family anymore!"

"What about us?" said Edgar.

Carl turned to him. "I—I didn't mean it that way, Edgar." He looked around the room, then stopped at Elaine. "I just don't think I can do it," he said, almost in a whisper. "Don't you understand, Elaine?"

Edgar put his arms around Carl's shoulders. "Maybe he's waiting for you," Edgar said. "Maybe it's true that your father wants to bulldoze your house. It would give him a chance to get back at you. But it would also give him a reason to come here and see where you live."

"And then destroy it."

"It doesn't have to be that way." He paused. "I know a little about those things. I have a son of my own, you know."

"What?" said Max. "I didn't know you were married."

"I'm not. Nor was I. But that doesn't mean I can't have a son, does it? He's about your age. I haven't seen him in a good ten years; I don't get to Crete that often. But he's still my son, even though he'd be the last one to admit it. Which is one goddamn shame. I miss him sometimes. Maybe that's why I like being around you folks so much. Carl, the son-of-a-bitch might spit in your eye when he sees you. But maybe he won't."

Carl remained in the living room after the others had left. Elaine said she was going for a walk out back. When he asked if she wanted company, she told him, without malice but firmly, that she'd rather be alone. He turned down the lantern and leaned back in his chair. The troubles with the house had borne down on their relationship for several months until it was shot through with a hundred tiny fractures. The eviction threatened to crack it wide open. Elaine had tried talking to him about it, he knew, but he always felt himself clamped shut. Everything seemed to hinge on one issue alone: Would Carl be willing to break the silence between him and his father? Elaine was using this same question as a final test of their relationship. She did it for the sake of the house, yes, but tonight he realized that much more lay in the balance. She had charged him with heartlessness, even cruelty, for the way he'd treated his father all this time. The charges would stand even if Larrabee wanted to build his houses in Brazil.

Carl rose and went out back to look for Elaine, but he reached the lake without seeing her. Where could she have wandered off to? He returned to the house and lay down in their bed, thinking to wait for her, but he fell asleep. He awoke to the sound of shouting from outside, where a pitched battle was raging between the people from the house and the police. Elaine was shouting to be let back in; the police claimed she'd overstepped their line and were now blocking her way, standing with clubs at the ready. Shera lost her temper and threw a rock. It struck a police helmet. They grabbed her and trundled her into the van. When Phil attempted to pull her back, they took him, too. Carl ran down just as the van pulled away. He spent the rest of the night beside Melissa, shaking under the covers from a chill that wouldn't subside.

They were down to three people and two children. And the day after tomorrow was Father's Day.

3

I CONFESS.

Jason sat on his bed, shirtless, his door open to catch any breeze that found its way up to the attic. On nights like this the hot air in his room was almost too thick to breathe. But there was nowhere else to go. He couldn't even walk down Main Street without people gawking at him. He finished a beer, tossed it onto the pile beside his bed where it landed with a playful ting, and pulled open another. It usually took him three beers to start floating pleasantly free. Tonight he'd gone through five and his head was still tight from all the things on his mind. Well, there was another unbroken six pack in the refrigerator. He took a swallow and savored the beer's iron taste, glancing at the empties with satisfaction.

Cee took him to the police station that morning, and he signed the confession. A date for a juvenile court hearing was set, and he was released in Cee's custody and ordered not to leave the county. "Ordinarily we'd have held him, since he was a runaway," they told her, but they knew her father.

You spell confess with one s or two?

Jason rubbed the bump on his forehead. He could've gotten away from Cee if he really wanted to, he thought. As long as he knew Aaron wanted him back. But Aaron didn't, so what difference did it make what happened to him?

The policeman's lip had curled as he read the confession. Everyone was so angry at what Jason had done. But this world was full of people who were just after what they wanted. He'd met plenty of them in New York, and they were prepared to pay for it. If you could pay, and if no one found out, anything was acceptable. Those same men who had Jason tie them up and beat them would have condemned him right along with everyone else in Thompson City. What gave them all the right?

Even Aaron condemned him.

Across the room, as if to match the beer cans, lay his weights, looking like a pile of heavy playthings. The first day back he'd put on the gloves, screwed on a pair of twenties, and began to lift. His muscles felt sluggish, as if woken from a long sleep. He pushed the bar into the air, lowered it down to his chest, and the familiar heat started to rise in his arms and legs, but he grew weak, and the weights came rattling to the carpet. He hadn't touched them since.

There was a sharp knock at the door. Cee came into his room and said, "You and I are going to have a chat."

Jason shook his head. He'd told her the same thing he'd told his father: Forget about talking about Marcy; what's done is done.

"I've signed that paper. Leave me alone."

"I didn't spend a week traipsing around New York looking for you to make like nothing happened."

"You didn't have to look for me, I was doing fine by myself. Why didn't you just leave me alone?"

"I went after you because I want to understand. Because if I don't understand I might hate you."

"You can hate me if you want. Mom already does." He helped himself to a generous swallow and felt a slight fuzziness beginning to spread across the back of his head.

She said, "Okay, it's my turn to talk." She started in about how her friend Jeanine got raped five years ago and still woke up screaming in the middle of the night. There were cases of fathers raping their own daughters, uncles raping their nieces, did he know that? Husbands rape their wives and no court of law convicts them. There have even been cases of men raping the corpse of a dead woman. Men didn't rape for the sex, there were prostitutes for that. They raped to show that they could do what the hell they wanted to do with women. They rape because they hate women.

Her voice grew raw and tinny. He couldn't listen to it anymore. "I don't hate Marcy!" he shouted.

If Marcy had yelled right away, Jason thought, if she'd put up more of a fight as soon as they got out of the car he might have realized what he was doing and stopped. But she'd tried to act calm at first, she tried to go along with him so everything would seem normal, and not out of control. She'd waited too long to fight back. But it was done, and there was nothing anybody could do about it, not even Cee.

He didn't say another word and thought she would leave. Instead she asked him about Aaron. "He liked you, right?" she said. He knew what she was getting at—to admit that he was queer. "Know what I think?" she said. "I think you raped Marcy to prove to yourself that you're not gay."

Jason finished off his beer with an angry gulp and then threw the can across the room. "Why do you always come at me with your questions? You're always trying to open me up and make me tell you things. You did it when I was a kid, too. But it's none of your business. It's you that you got to worry about, not me," he shouted, giving his chest a thump. He pulled into a tight ball, his knees against his chest, his arms like barrel staves around them.

His eyes had turned glassy, almost mirrored, and Cee saw only herself, broken by his blinking.

People should learn to mind their own business, Stephanie had said.

Cee watched a trickle of beer ooze out from the can. "How does your head feel?" she asked softly.

"It's okay."

"I'm sorry I hurt you."

He told her not to worry about it. Then she said, "Remember the time we were down near Quaspeck, the time you stole my shirt?"

He looked up. She had a scared expression on her face.

"I couldn't stop thinking about it the whole time we drove up from the East Village," she said, "when I held the ice against your head. I was so worried that I'd hurt you. Like you got hurt before."

He kept looking at her.

"Say something," she said in a dry, whispery voice.

"It's all right," he told her. "Don't worry about it."

THE NEXT DAY it was just as hot. In the morning he did the shopping. Walter couldn't come with him as usual since he had to work. Jason missed his father being along. He would complain about the prices and say how much cheaper things were in his day or else make jokes about the women's hairstyles.

In the afternoon Jason put on a bathing suit, grabbed a can of beer, and sat out in the backyard. When it grew too hot, he went back up to his room and switched on the TV. Two guys were going at each other, one in regulation trunks and shoes, the other wearing horns like a Viking and furry boots: It was the fixed wrestling from Washington, D.C. Jason lay down to watch.

I, Jason Gajewski, confess to having forced Marcy Rand . . .

When it came to the part about filling in Marcy's last name on the police form he'd had to ask; he'd forgotten it. That made him feel bad. It was something about her he should have remembered. Jason Gajewski. Marcy Rand. Their two names together, almost like they were getting married.

Gajewski. That's your father's picture they put in the bank, isn't it? And your brother's the one holed up in that house on Indian Mountain?

In New York nobody cared what you did. Here they could tell you the color of your toe cheese. Jason felt like asking him if he knew whether or not he'd scratched his ass last night.

The Viking had grabbed the guy from behind and held him around the neck. He heaved him up, the guy's legs flew into the air like a rag doll's and then hit the ground with an exaggerated stamp. The Viking flipped him over, and mounted his back until the count was up and the match was over.

Another match began, this one between a Chinese guy and someone with war paint and a headdress . . . an Indian. The headdress teetered back and forth as he stomped out of his corner. They were both big guys: muscled arms, beefy necks and shoulders, big thighs. The two men locked together with the usual constipated grunting. The Chinese guy held the Indian's head under his arm and was walking him around the ring as though displaying a prize dog. And the Indian was letting him, goddamn it. This stuff was so stupid, Jason thought. But he felt himself getting hard.

The Chinese guy tightened his hold around the Indian and was pressing up against him from behind, his crotch buried in the Indian's ass. Jason got harder. He turned over onto his stomach and started pushing against the mattress. The Indian suddenly freed himself and went at the Chinese guy full force. He threw his arms around the other guy's chest, hoisted him up, then thrust him back onto the floor of the ring like a sack of laundry. The Chink tried to get up, but the Indian heaved him up in the air, and threw him down again. The audience went wild.

Marcy trusted me. She liked me, she never thought I would hurt her. Didn't she know I was a piece of shit, why didn't she realize—

The Indian was sitting right on the Chink's crotch. Jason was pushing faster against the mattress.

I didn't want to hurt her.

The Indian held the Chink's head to the ground with his knee while the Chink twisted in agony. Each time the Chinese guy bucked up the Indian lobbed him back down and held him there by wrapping his legs around the Chink's middle—thick, muscular legs. That Chink couldn't get the hell away now, no way, those legs had him. Jason kept pushing.

Someone knocked.

Jason froze. "Who is it?"

"Billy."

Jason slipped under the covers. "What do you want?"

"Mind if I borrow a pair of your underpants?"

"Don't you got your own?"

"All dirty."

"Yeah, okay."

Billy came in.

"What the fuck do you have on?"

"Blue chiffon, what does it look like?"

"You're wearing a fucking dress!"

"A gown, dear. A floor-length evening gown, if you please. I'm going to a party tonight. You don't think I'd doll myself up like this to go bowling, do you? So which drawer has your unmentionables?"

"You got that from my mom?"

"How could I? We're entirely different up here." He clutched his chest. "What are looking so surprised for? You mean to tell me you've never seen illusion sleeves?" He opened a drawer. "Oh, here we are. Will you take a look at these," he said, pulling out a pair of briefs. "Genuine American Fruit of the Looms!" He pressed them to his nose. "And so lemony fresh!"

"Just take them and leave. Why'd you come here anyway?"

"I happen to be a guest of your sister's. We're both relaxing after chasing you all around New York."

"Nobody asked her to."

"She did it because she cares about you."

"The fuck she did. She just wanted to tell me to my face that she thinks I'm a piece of shit. Okay, you got your underwear, now go."

"You're mad at me for making it with your boyfriend, is that it?"

"He wasn't my boyfriend!"

"All right, your girlfriend. Anyway, we didn't get past the basics. It was you that Aaron wanted, if that makes you feel any better."

"Get out, you faggot."

Billy threw the shorts into his face and turned to leave.

"Pick them up!"

Billy gave him the finger.

Jason threw back the covers and jumped out of bed and grabbed Billy before he could leave.

"Help! Rape!" Billy shouted, playful. "Oh, I'm terribly sorry—"

"I'll beat that smile off your fucking face."

"Get away from me—"

Jason went for Billy but grabbed the top of the dress. The fabric ripped down the seam with an angry snort.

Billy stared at the torn fabric, unbelieving. "You ripped it! Why'd you rip my dress, you asswipe!" He stepped out of the torn dress, naked, and began folding it.

Jason kicked the door shut with his foot. Billy looked up, startled.

"I've been wanting to slug your face in ever since I met you."

"Here," Billy said, grasping his dick. "He's what you really want, don't you? Even if you're too fucking scared to admit it."

Jason's mouth twisted with rage. They circled.

"Come on, Champ," Billy said, wagging his dick. "Beat up the faggot. Come on, come the fuck on!"

Jason lunged, delirious. Billy sidestepped him nimbly and sank into a crouch.

"Hey, check out what's between the Champ's legs, a one-hundred-percent genuine American hard-on. Another Fruit of the Loom. My my."

Jason threw himself at Billy, and they fell onto the bed. Billy pushed himself back up. Jason shoved him against the wall and slugged him in the stomach. Billy gasped and doubled over, his mouth drawn to a circle. He staggered toward the door but Jason pulled him back.

"I'm not finished with you yet," Jason roared. He stripped off his bathing suit and threw himself at Billy. "I'm gonna goddamn show you, you—" He locked his arms around Billy's waist, pried his legs open and thrust deep into his ass. Billy's head shot forward under the shock of entry. Jason began heaving and grunting, his groans grew broad and windier. Just before he reached his peak, Billy rammed his ass backward forcefully, toppling Jason over, and a jagged line of his sperm piddled into the air. Billy staggered out of the room, leaving Jason on the floor. From the TV came the sound of applause and a bell. The Indian strutted around the ring, hands clasped above his head, the winner.

Billy's hand reached in a moment later, snatched up his dress, then slammed the door, as if determined to have the last word.

AFTER PULLING HIMSELF away from the monster homo, Billy slipped on a bathrobe and went to look for Cee. He found her in her room, stuffing clothes in her backpack.

"Are you really going up to that mountain?" he said, trying to sound calm, but the next moment he was falling into her arms and crying. He told her what had happened. He cried so long and hard that he almost didn't notice that she'd begun crying, too.

"Hey, what's the matter with you? I'm the one who just got raped."

"Remember when we pulled over to the Arco station," she said. "It was a baby, Billy." She waited for him to say something.

"And?"

"Think, Billy. The night we tripped."

He'd sensed her pushing closer to him that whole night and for days before that, a wind slowly building. It had been enough to make him avoid her. But that night's haze of confession, acid, and steeplechase left him open. With Joel, the wind had changed direction, leaving Billy in the calm. Cee's news stirred up the storm once more. This time it raged inside him, tearing down houses and uprooting trees. Their baby, he thought.

"You sure?"

She nodded. "Billy Junior."

For the first time he could remember, there was nothing he could say, not a word. He kissed her, picked himself up, marched into the bathroom, and locked the door. Their baby, he thought, his, William Ernesto Gizzi's. He was a less-than-prodigal son who'd been a father for a time but hadn't known it, whose son—Cee said it was a bambino—never knew his father, whose father knew his father but wished he hadn't. Billy began to cry once more. If things had been different, if he and Cee had been... like other men and women—and that didn't mean Billy wanted them to be, he wouldn't change so much as a chromosome—but if he and Cee were, and if the child had lived, then wouldn't that have been sort of, well... nice?

He did what he usually did after nights of bus station debauchery: He drew himself a scalding, purifying bath and tubbed for a good half hour until the pulse of his bruises subsided. Then he toweled off, opened the medicine chest and—did they have it? Yes!—found some Ben-Gay to rub in.

Theresa looked uneasy when Billy asked her if she thought she could mend the dress. She fingered the material, as if to say, You're really going to put this on? But when she learned that it was Jason who'd ripped it—Billy didn't give all the details—she ran it through the Singer, and repaired the tear expertly. She handed it back to him with a shake of her head, and said that a man wearing a gown for one night wasn't all that much stranger than a woman strapping herself into a girdle for much of her adult life.

He returned to the bathroom, taking along the cache of Mary Quant cosmetics procured from Woolworth's. He unsnapped the little container of twilight-blue eye shadow and got as far as finishing one eye before there was a knock on the door. It was Musclebrain. "Use the downstairs john," Billy told him. Musclebrain said he didn't want to pee, he wanted to say something, and could Billy please open up. "Tell me what you have to say," Billy told him. There was a silence, a shuffling of feet, some hesitant breathing. Then Musclebrain walked away.

Billy shrugged. My ass still feels like the Wreck of the Hesperus, and he wants to have a conference, he thought. He examined his finished eye, outlined in black, shadowed with blue, and tailed with a thick, curving line, the eye of a surly chatelaine with a ringful of keys to an echoing chateau. He was about to start on his second eye, when he thought of the baby and started to cry once more. A black rain of makeup coursed down his cheeks. He sat down on the edge of the tub, surprised at his own reaction, and waited for his sobbing to stop. Then he washed his face, and started all over again.

Billy crept downstairs in full dress, heels held in his hands to avoid the sound track. Who should he meet in the kitchen but Musclebrain, sitting in a chair, legs apart, in that Suck My Dick slouch that male teenagers favor so much. Father was there, too: a cross between Captain God and Stonehenge. He was fiddling with a fishing rod, the way real American fathers are supposed to do. When he saw Billy his mouth actually dropped open, just like in comic books. Meanwhile, Musclebrain looked ready to sound off. Say one word, Musclebrain, Billy thought, and I'll tell Daddy exactly what you did to me no more than two hours ago. One syllable, Musclebrain. To Musclebrain's credit, he held his tongue. Not only that, but Billy could see that something about him was different. The wild sheen in his eyes was gone. He looked confused . . . even scared.

Dad put down his fishing rod. "What in hell are you doing in that?" he said.

Billy sensed that humor would be wasted on him, so he answered factually. "It's Saturday night," he said. "I'm going out."

Musclebrain got up. Billy jumped back, fearing a reprise of their recent tryst. "Wait," Musclebrain said. He left and came back with a pair of jockeys.

"You forgot these," he said, tossing them Billy's way.

Dad's gaze traveled from Jason to Billy back to Jason, also like the comics. "What is going on?" he said. "What the hell is going on?" It almost looked like he was ready to grab those briefs and tear them to shreds.

Billy smiled. "Thanks. I guess it could have gotten a little nippy without them," he said as he stepped into the briefs. He smoothed his gown back down, slipped on his heels, and klatch-klatched his way down the flagstone path to the bus stop.

4

CEE CUT RUBY's low beams and slowed her to a crawl when Junior's house came into view. She turned off the ignition and sat looking at the windows of the house, stubbornly domestic with curtains and potted geraniums. Inside, Junior sat immobilized before the television set, a can of beer wedged between his legs. He seemed too big for the chair. His face was expressionless, dense as moist plaster. Junior's mother kept to one end of the sofa, eyes to her knitting, like a chaperone who didn't realize that the girl had already left or had never shown up. It looked like they'd been sitting that way for hours and might remain if no one shut the TV off.

The lights of the police checkpoint flickered through the leaves. The ominous bulk of the bulldozers rose nearby. Cee had avoided the check by making a wide loop through Conklin instead of driving directly from Thompson City. "If they catch you, they'll charge you with trespassing," people who worked at the bookstore warned her. Trespassing, she thought. The mountain was still in public hands; the transfer wouldn't go into effect until the day after tomorrow. Cee got out of the car and flung her heavy pack over her shoulders. The cans of food rattled inside. She'd tossed them in, hardly looking at the labels. (Would anyone up at the house really eat the Spam?) It was chilly; she wished she'd worn something warmer. And she had to pee.

Celia, what in God's name do you want me to do?

Tell Larrabee to stuff his job.

It's fine to change the world but not when you're hungry from not eating the night before.
I don't remember you ever waking up hungry.
You're not old enough to.

Earlier that morning Cee went to Shera's house, where Elaine was staying. Everyone who'd been arrested the night before had been released soon after being booked. Elaine looked very, very tired. For the first time Cee could remember, she smoked a cigarette. "You can tell my boss is a liberal," she'd said, exhaling a little too forcefully. "He called me up to say that he'd still keep me on even though I have an arrest record." She said she didn't plan on returning to the house, figuring they'd only bust her again. Shera wanted to, mostly because of Benjamin. Elaine tried to dissuade her; Ron could get him the next time he drove up there. When Cee told them that she planned to join the blockade, Shera asked to come along. Cee thought for a moment. She didn't know Shera very well, but her excitable nature made Cee uncomfortable. "If it's okay with you I think I'd rather go by myself," she said.

"Give Melissa a kiss for me," Elaine said. She pressed Cee's arm. "It's good you're going up there," she said as they hugged. "Carl needs you."

Cee began walking down the road. She thought about the baby, the product of her frightened body and Billy's frightened heart. Cee had been wary of Billy even before Kal's warning, but he had gnawed at her resistance until she set aside her suspicions. He roused her from her thick, unsatisfied yearning and made her want him even though she knew Billy's affection was unstable. Maybe she'd struggled against giving the baby up because she knew it meant breaking her surest tie to him. Now the baby was gone. A part of Billy seemed to have gone with it, and her heart blistered.

Her mother had taken her to a gynecologist, who pronounced her out of any danger but said that the miscarriage had not been complete. (What was left, Cee'd wondered: An eye? A finger? The fragment of a soul?) The rest would have to be removed as soon as possible. "Can it wait?" she'd asked. "What in God's name for?" the doctor wanted to know.

Because I'm joining the blockade on Indian Mountain.

She planned to follow the chute all the way up. It couldn't be far, but everything was so overgrown, it would be hard to navigate with a flashlight. Which she'd forgotten. She had to pee real bad now. She considered going into the woods but taking two steps away from the road was like stepping into a jungle. Doing it so close to the barrier would be insane because—she felt herself grinning—she could be caught with her pants down. But since losing the baby it hurt not to pee when she had to. If anyone came around she would say she was hiking the Appalachian Trail and had gotten lost. She looked both ways, undid her pants, yanked her undies down—Jesus, they fairly glowed in the dark—and lowered herself. Ahhh. Her piss struck the ground loudly, as though hitting glass. The leaves deflected a hot prickle back against her thighs. Guys sure had it easier when it came to bodily functions. The cool air tickled her cheeks. It hurt to squat; women who gave birth this way must be in better shape than I am, she thought. Suddenly something down there twitched, as though her body still wasn't sure what had happened in that rest room. She half-expected another strange, unstoppable whoosh from inside her.

Afterward she felt light with relief, her head cleared, and she quickly discerned the dark band of the chute. Close to the road the path was no more than a gentle incline. She imagined the icy mountain water rushing down through the wooden conduit on its way to kitchens below. Could Carl and his friends have rigged up such a system? Highly doubtful—they often forgot where the compost heap was. Farther up she felt the grade of the ascent increase, as if the mountain were an animal arching its back. Cee clutched branches and roots, determined not to be thrown. Here was where she and Melissa had flown into the November afternoon. Her calf muscles complained. The rush of her breathing was almost loud enough to see. Twigs snapped underfoot, dead leaves crunched—the police would have to be deaf not to hear her. She took another step and then slipped. She teetered, grasping wildly at a knobby tree root. A beam of light was thrown just over her head, and the rusty bark of dogs tore through the night. No one at the bookstore had said anything about a K-9 patrol! The light hovered closer, stubbornly close, threatening to drop down and expose her. The dogs kept on. Her grip began to weaken. Her fingers felt made of chalk, ready to snap. A moment later she fell, pulled down by her pack. She whipped past a whirr of leaves and branches and toppled onto a prickly ball of bush. Light flew in her direction as if she'd tripped a switch. She lay helpless as a turtle on its back as the dogs yelped with excitement, sounding no more than ten yards away. She expected the clamp of their teeth at her ankles any moment. Scratches threaded her face with fire. The whole mountain shook with the pounding of her heart. Voices approached and branches snapped. Policemen were filtering through the woods toward her.

Then everything stopped. A car door slammed shut, an engine started. One of the policemen shouted to another. The dogs' barking retreated, and a moment later, the light fell away. She peered through the woods. The police were still down there, vans and all. So what was going on? It didn't matter. She pushed herself up on her feet, adjusted her pack, and headed back to the road, abandoning the idea of climbing all the way up the chute. By a second miracle she would find the path that led the long way around up to the house and take it.

"You got through!" said Edgar, opening the door and giving her a hug. "Carl was sure you'd try to come."

Max and Alyce were in the kitchen. Alyce got up and kissed her. "Look at your face!"

"I fell."

"Reinforcements, at last!" said Max.

She unloaded her pack onto the table. When she took out the can of Spam, he said, "Mmm, some down-home food."

"What was going on out there?" Alyce said, returning.

"The weirdest thing happened," Cee began, turning her face as Alyce dabbed on the aloe vera. She told them about her attempt at the chute. "They knew someone was there," she said. "You could have heard me in the next county."

"They probably held off while Ron left. Whenever he's around they're careful. They don't want him to catch them doing anything that wouldn't look good in the papers."

"Have you seen Shera and Elaine and Phil?" Max said.

"This morning. They're fine." Cee looked around. "Where's Carl?"

"Upstairs," said Alyce softly.

Carl was lying down when Cee came in. Melissa sat cross-legged on the floor, working a wooden puzzle.

"Ceewee," Melissa said, running over to her.

Cee caught Melissa and they went to Carl. To her surprise, he put his arms around her and hugged her tightly.

"Oh, Carl," she said. "If anything happens you can all come to Buffalo and live with me."

"Ron was just here. Larrabee's lawyer told him that he hoped all his clients were in good standing with the IRS. I haven't filed a tax return in three years. Larrabee can simply have the feds move in and do their dirty work for them. And there's more. It turns out that Larrabee's son was killed in Vietnam, and he's very proud of him. You can imagine what he thinks of people like me."

"Who told Larrabee about you not registering?"

"His name begins with *W*."

"Dad wouldn't have done that."

"Not on purpose. But one of Larrabee's men was over to the house for a little chat with the Father of the Year. Wouldn't you know he asked about Walter Gajewski's three lovely children? And can't you just picture Walter pouring out his heart about his eldest? I certainly can."

"How come Larrabee's stepping up the pressure? I thought the deal was already signed."

"Yes, but that was before people found out that the Father of the Year's younger son is a rapist. Every newspaper article that has mentioned Jason has mentioned dear old Dad, too. And vice versa. Someone spray-painted Castrate Rapists on the window of the bank where they hung Walter's picture. One of Larrabee's men went to the father of the girl Jason raped, offered his sympathy, and then asked if he would consider dropping the charges against Jason. In return for a little token of their appreciation, of course. But not only was the father not interested, he also made his disinterest known in a statement, which the paper published today. Legally, Larrabee still has won, but people have begun to talk. Larrabee wants us out before things get any worse and someone starts calling for an investigation." He paused. "Have you seen Elaine?"

"This morning. She's all right, but she looks very tired."

"She didn't mention anything about . . . me?"

"No. But that might have been because Shera was there."

"That Shera!" said Carl, with sudden anger. "She's wormed Elaine onto her side. She and everyone else are all hoping I'll go down and ask my wonderful father if he'll consider quitting the job on principle. But they're deluded if they think that's going to stop a seventy-million-dollar project." Benjamin appeared at the door. Melissa slid off the bed and ran over to him.

"You're still so afraid of Dad, aren't you?" Cee said. "He's just a fifty-five-year-old frightened man with a bit of a heart murmur—"

"I'm not frightened of him!"

"So why haven't you talked to him all this time?"

Carl turned to her, his face looking blank. "Do you really think it would change anything now, even if I did?" He sank down into the bed. "By the way, I saw him."

"Larrabee?"

"No, Dad. Earlier this week. They came up the mountain to do some measuring. I was out on the porch. The trucks appeared like conquistadores landing in the New World. They yelled up 'Hey, you hippies!' Then I saw him, looking rough and tough in his boots and work clothes."

"Did he see you?"

"I don't think so, he was too far down. Cee, my whole world is coming apart. And all because of a handful of assholes."

Cee took off her shoes and lay down on her side next to him. Carl produced a joint and held it out to her.

"Sure," Cee said.

Carl lit it and toked. "I know that the person I always feared and hated and ran away from is just a simple, scared man. But that doesn't make it any easier for me to see him again." He passed the joint her way.

"He was always much more afraid of you than you were of him, and probably still is. In that way you're no different from Jason. You're both so scared. You're scared of Elaine, too, aren't you?" she said. "Scared to let her love you."

"She told you that?"

"No. But I know you."

Carl stretched out beside her. "It's hard for me to imagine Jason being afraid of anyone."

"Remember the time he broke your slides, and you hit him? I was furious with you, I'd never known you to be so cruel. Then Dad beat you. I heard it all the way in my room, each time the strap hit. You cried and cried, and all I could think of was, Please, stop hurting him." She stroked Carl's arm. "Some women compare their lovers with their fathers. I think I compare them with you. You were more interesting and more intelligent than anyone else I knew."

"But a nerd. An overcomplicated, self-absorbed nerd."

Cee sighed. She thought of all that had happened to her in the past couple of months that he knew nothing about: Stephanie, Billy, Joel, the baby. Now wasn't the time to talk about any of it. She would get around to telling him most of it eventually. She couldn't hold important things inside her. Carl could. It made Elaine crazy. "Carl thinks that talking about himself is a sign of giving in," she'd once told Cee.

Cee recalled her resistance to talking to that psychiatrist at Meyer Memorial after she cut her wrist. Like brother, like sister, she thought. Except that something had changed inside her since then. If she suddenly found herself back in that dingy office, she could have gabbed away a month of sessions.

Carl snubbed out the joint. "Maybe one of the reasons it's hard for me to realize how close we were is because nothing like that has happened to me since."

"Elaine once said she thought I loved you more than she ever could."

Carl took Cee's hand. "Maybe she's right," he said.

5

WALTER AND JASON were nearly the only ones on the road winding out of town, headed for Davis Lake for a little night fishing.

It had been Walter's idea; he told Jason he felt bad seeing him pent up at home for so long with nothing to do. Technically, the lake was out of bounds for Jason since it was over the county line, his father explained. But he wouldn't tell anyone if Jason didn't. Big Bad Walter's sense of humor.

Jason hadn't wanted to go. The fight with Billy left him with a sullen, sickly feeling. Jason had knocked the wind out of Billy, he'd humiliated him. But Billy had won. He hadn't tried to; he didn't even realize they were opponents. The fight had been in Jason's mind alone. And he'd lost. But he couldn't say all that to his father when it came time to leave.

Jason looked into the back seat. "Where's the beer?"

"In the trunk, where it'll stay. I don't believe in drinking and driving. You know that, Son."

"Should've gotten more than just one six-pack. What else is there do while you're fishing but drink?"

"Fish."

"That's for the fish to do. How come you like fishing anyway?"

"Gives me a chance to think. There's nothing nicer than a lake at night."

It was just dark enough for headlights. Jason crooked his elbow out the window, and adjusted the side vent so that warm wind hit his face. He wished he could drift away somewhere. Things seemed to be closing in on him. There was no place he could go without being watched or asked questions.

His father shifted in his seat, the car swerved a little. "Too much damn play in this steering wheel. I should get it looked at. Bet you could fix it easy, Son."

"Why is Mom giving me such a hard time? She always bosses me around and gives me things to do."

"She's upset about . . . the whole thing."

"I came back, didn't I? I signed the paper. What else does she want me to do, walk around with a sign saying Guilty? She's worse than Cee. She said that what I did was about the lowest thing she could think of." He paused. "You think that, too?"

"Jason, it's not so easy—"

"Just answer."

Walter looked away. "It was . . . a bad thing you did, Son. But listen to me. No matter what happens, I'm going to stick by you."

"How come you call me Son all of a sudden? You never used to."

Walter's face grew taut. "There's a lot of things I do now that I never used to do."

The moon set a silver circle rolling on the asphalt. The turnoff to Jim Maynard's came. Walter took it a little too wide, and they skidded along the shoulder before he righted the car.

"Hey!" Jason shouted, grabbing the door.

"It's this steering wheel," Walter said, a little shaken.

"If you can't drive, then let me."

"It's because of you, you're making me nervous!"

"I didn't want to go on this little trip. It was your idea."

"All right, all right, it's okay now. Everything's okay, just relax."

The road was narrow and bumpy. "Jim sure is one funny guy," Walter said, to put the incident behind them. "He's lived out here as far back as I can remember, all by himself." A pair of lighted windows emerged from the trees.

"I'll wait here," Jason said. "Could you give me the keys to the trunk?"

Jim appeared at the screen door, a tall man with a slender face. "Hello, Walter. Come on in."

"I can't stay too long. My son's waiting out in the car."

Jim glanced over toward the car. "Oh," he said.

"Guess you know what I'm here for."

Jim went to the back of the house and returned with a coffee can heaped with black earth.

"You should hook yourself some nice lake trout tonight," he said, snapping on a plastic lid. "You remember where the boat is?"

Walter nodded, took the can, and gave Jim a ten-dollar bill.

"Ready for the big day tomorrow?" Jim asked, somewhat coolly.

"You bet."

"Afraid I'll have to miss it. I'll be with my sister and her family over in Vestal. And, to tell you the truth, Walter, I don't like what Larrabee's got planned for Indian Mountain, so I don't think I'd want to celebrate it, either. I hope you won't take this personal, I know it means a job for you. But it's how I feel."

"That's all right, Jim," Walter said, switching the can from one hand to the other.

Jim glanced at the car where Jason sat with his knees up, drinking a can of beer. "I guess you're glad to see your boy again," he said without much conviction.

Lacey Park was bright as daylight with activity as they drove by. A ghostly looking ferris wheel towered above. From the far side came the sound of hammering where a stage was going up.

"What's happening tomorrow?" Jason asked.

"We're all going down to the park here for the Father's Day Fair and a barbeque. Your old man's going to get up on the stage so the mayor and a bunch of other important people can shake his hand and tell everyone what great guy he is. How's that sound?"

"All that just because you got one of those jobs?"

"Don't you think your old man deserves it?"

Once past the park the road sank back into darkness. The moon sailed swiftly across the lake. They passed a sign that said Entering Tioga County. Jason threw his can out of the window and it rattled behind them. Walter gripped the wheel grimly. The sky grew darker. He felt as if they were leaving behind everything he knew and held dear.

Jason picked up the rods and gear box, and stuck his father's seat cushion under his arm. The shore was deserted. He felt like a thief on a night job.

"You don't have to carry all that at one time, Jason."

"I'll manage. You just bring the beer."

The boat was tied to a short wooden pier. Their feet clomped on the planking.

Jason threw his father's seat cushion into the boat, then stepped down the ladder. His father followed, lowering himself ponderously. Jason could hear his breathing. Suddenly the six-pack fell from his hands.

Jason cursed. "I'll row," he said.

"Let me get settled here first."

"If I row we gotta change places so I can sit toward the back of the boat."

Walter was about to ease himself down in the seat. "If you wanted to row so bad how come you got in first?" He straightened himself back up, and they began edging toward each other. The boat pulled against its moorings with a storm of shallow waves.

"Easy," Jason shouted. "You're making the boat rock like crazy." His father's gut rubbed against him, dense as upholstery.

"You dumped all the things right in the middle here," Walter shouted. "There's no place for me to put my foot." He grabbed Jason to steady himself.

Jason went for a can of beer as soon as he sat down. He felt a ring of dampness around his bare upper arms where his father had grabbed hold of him.

"Jason," Walter said, facing him, "I want us to enjoy ourselves tonight. Can't we just enjoy ourselves?"

Jason pulled the ring off the beer with a low hiss and flung it into the lake.

Walter frowned. "The fish don't need that," he said.

Jason brought the can to his mouth, then spat into the lake. "Jesus, if there isn't anything worse than warm beer."

"Let's go as far as Smuggler's first," Walter said with a sigh of resignation. Smuggler's Island was an acre of trees poking out of the water, where the county line bisected the lake. According to local lore, bootleggers of the last century avoided the tax agents in one county by burying their illegal wares on the other side.

Jason began rowing. The water felt smooth and dense against the oars. The shore receded into a dark blur. He watched the rolling flex of his arm muscles with each pull. Then Billy came to mind again, and Jason's sullen feeling returned. His loins still ached. He'd wanted to hurt Billy. He'd felt the poison building up inside him with each thrust, and he'd thought, I want it all to come out of me at last, all of it, every drop, every drop of my strength, my poison strength. But Billy was indestructible, like those punching bags at the gym that sprang back after each slug.

After Billy left, Jason had waited for his limbs to subside. His foul smell funneled up around him. Someone was mowing the lawn on TV. Jason looked at the underwear, still crumpled on the floor where Billy had thrown it, and a wave of shame broke through him. He picked it up, and Billy's cackle sounded in his ears, as if the underwear held Billy's voice. Jason put his bathing suit back on, took the underwear, and went downstairs. Billy was in Cee's room, crying and telling her what had happened. She comforted him as she'd once comforted Jason. He stood outside, his fingers knotted around the underwear, unable to go in. Later, when Jason tried to talk to Billy in the bathroom, Billy wouldn't open the door.

Walter felt the breeze against his neck and let his eyes close. He breathed in the air gratefully and enjoyed the feeling of being carried. "You sure are taking us along at a good clip, Jason," he said. The gunwhales made a pleasant rattle with each stroke, and a tugging sound issued from Jason's chest. Walter imagined his son's pack of angry muscles, the serious look his face took on when he lifted those weights, or his eyes, soft in color as Theresa's, but so restless. The first night after Jason returned Theresa lay in bed crying. "He should have stayed away," she said. "He doesn't want anything from us. And there's nothing we can give him." Walter said she was wrong. He'd nearly wept in relief to see Jason stepping out of Celia's car that morning. It seemed like a chance to make good between them, a last chance.

The trees of Smuggler's Island came into view, massed together like a castle with many turrets.

"Take a breather," he said. "I'll row." They changed places again.

Jason leaned back. The beer had saturated his head unhampered by food. His father's rowing was slow but even, dependable and steady. It was how his father did everything. The rhythmic splash of the oars into the water was like a clock ticking.

"How about some fishing," Walter said after a while. He opened the tackle box and reached for the coffee can. "Here are the crawlers. Help yourself. I got some new floats. They light up in the dark like the numbers on a watch. Here, I'll show you." He took out one of the floats, shone his flashlight on it, then held up the tiny glowing ball. "Like magic," he smiled.

They baited their hooks. Jason swung his line in first. It hit the lake with a twang, and the float came to rest on the surface, a tiny lantern set adrift.

"I can't believe that friend of Cee's," Walter said. "It was bad enough listening to the way he talks and watching him walk but when he put on that dress . . ."

Jason studied the float. The morning he walked into Aaron's apartment and saw Billy there, both of them naked, he felt as if he'd stumbled into a corner of a vast, secret society, as though behind every door of Aaron's building there might be other pairs of naked men just like them. He reached for another beer.

". . . and just walking out of the house," Walter continued. "Out of my house. You'd think he'd be embarrassed to be seen like that."

Jason could tell his father was working up to mentioning the underwear. Billy could hardly believe his eyes when Jason gave him the briefs. His father had scowled, like any minute he might grab Jason by the scruff of his neck and pull him away.

"Cee's gone up to Indian Mountain," Walter said, as if realizing that Jason would say no more on the subject of Billy's dress. "Did she tell you anything about . . . the house?"

"No. Just about Marcy. She doesn't talk to me unless she has to. She hates me just like Mom does."

"Mom doesn't hate you. Cee doesn't, either. They just don't understand why you did what you did. And frankly, neither can I."

"So you hate me too, right?" he snapped.

"I didn't say that, Jason," he said wearily. "Your mother and sister hardly talk to me, either, you know. They blame me for what's happened with Carl's house. Your sister thinks I'm happy about it getting torn down. But I'm not, believe me. They could have had a new house, better than the shack they're living in now. Guess we've both become the black sheep of the family." He pulled in his line a little. "You know, I once thought that Carl was . . . like Billy. Carl was always so soft, so weak."

His father was starting with that again.

"Carl has a kid now, so you don't have to worry anymore," Jason said. "Speaking of babies, did Cee tell you about hers?"

"Cee had a baby?"

"On the highway, coming from New York. It sort of slipped out in the toilet when she went to take a leak."

Walter jerked around, his line tugged out of the water, and the float danced into the air. "What in God's name are you talking about?"

"I swear. She went to take a leak, and blubb! It slipped out like a fish!"

"That really happened . . . to Celia?"

"Didn't Mom tell you about it? I'm sure she knows. She and Cee haven't stopped talking to each other since Cee got here."

Walter studied Jason's face, as if searching for a smile to signal a joke. "How did you find out about this?"

"I heard Cee and Billy talking."

Walter pulled in his line. "I don't feel like fishing anymore. Give me one of those beers, will you?" He took a long swallow. He set the beer into his tackle box, looked downward, and belched loudly. Why hadn't Theresa mentioned any of this to him?

"But that ain't the best part. Guess who the father is."

Walter gave him a helpless look.

"Billy's the father. Billy the fag."

Walter shook his head. "Jesus," he said.

"You didn't think fags could have kids, right?"

"Stop using that word, will you?"

Walter began taking the float off his line. He dumped it into the tackle box, closed the lid, and sat there without moving. A breeze stirred the surface of the water, whistling faintly.

"We're drifting," Jason said.

"So let's drift. Everything seems to be drifting these days. The whole goddamn world's drifting. Tomorrow I'm going to get up on the stage and say how tickled I am that every frigging thing in my life has turned out so wonderful." He crouched over, as if burdened by the moonlight on his shoulders.

"Tell me," Walter said without looking up. "Is it true about you and that boy you hooked up with in New York?"

Jason's glance snapped forward. "Who told you?"

"Your mother. Cee told her." He faced Jason. "Then it's true."

Jason's limbs tightened. It infuriated him to hear his father ask him that. Jason grabbed the oars, jabbed them into the water, and began stroking wildly, sending the boat forward with powerful strides.

"Hey, what's up?" said Walter, holding onto the sides. "Where are you going?"

Jason kept on with his furious rowing.

"I said where the hell are you taking us?"

"I don't know, goddamn it!"

"You're headed the wrong way. The car's on the other side."

"So that's why you started talking about Billy just before, isn't it?" Jason shouted, biting off each word.

"I just want to know what's going on with you. I feel like everyone around me has secret lives that I don't know anything about—my son, my wife, my daughter—"

Jason rowed faster. "You're just worried because I turned queer on you."

"Don't you talk to me like that. I'm still your father. I might never have understood you since the day you were born but, God Almighty, I have to now. Stop rowing, for chrissakes. Jason, stop!" He lurched across the boat and gripped Jason's forearms. The oars jerked up from the water. The boat rocked, and little waves licked up around the sides. Walter's can of beer fell with a lopsided thud. "Christ!" he shouted, seizing the can and throwing it into the lake. The silver crescent of its rim bobbed on the water until the can began to fill and it sank, taking the silver with it.

"Now listen to me. There's a couple things I want to know, Jason," Walter began, breathing heavily. "And you're the only one who can tell me. We've hardly talked since you've been home."

"We hardly talked any other time, either, so why start?"

"Maybe . . . maybe because I'm afraid that if we don't talk now, it might be too late."

"Too late for what?" Jason sneered. "For everyone in the family to live happily ever after?"

"You hole yourself up in your room with those barbells and hardly say a word to anyone, you put your fist through a plate glass window one night and bleed like a pig, and then you do what you did to that poor Rand girl—"

"I already told you, I'm not saying anything about Marcy."

"Oh, yes you will." Walter's face was glistening with sweat. "You will because I can hardly walk down the street anymore, because the town's full of people like Jim Maynard who've known me since I was a little kid and who can't understand why Walter Gajewski's son raped a sixteen-year-old girl. I can't either, Jason, and you better make me understand soon, because I'm going out of my mind."

"They all know you're kicking Carl out, too."

"Are you comparing one thing with the other? You— What gives you the right . . ." A sputter of rage flamed in his eyes, but the mention of the house crippled him, and he sank back. "I don't understand anything," Walter said, looking out over the water. "Not a goddamn thing."

The spurt of rowing had left Jason tired. His body felt immobile, as if his blood had become heavier. The beer left behind a vast buzzing in his brain. The boat had drifted to the far side of the lake; the lights of Lacey Park had all but faded. Jason stared into the darkness until he could discern the roofs of the houses.

"You know what's over there?" he said, pointing to the shore, about a hundred yards away.

"The wrong side of the lake," Walter mumbled.

"What else?"

"Fitch Road?"

"Going the other way."

"You mean River Road?"

"Remember what happened there?" Jason mimicked the screech of tires.

"Jesus, you scared me!" Walter shot up in his seat.

"Afterwards I used to think that it was you who'd been behind the wheel of the car that conked me. Isn't that something? Wonder what that means. Cee probably knows. She loves figuring out reasons for everything." He spoke in a distant, dreamy voice.

"Let's get back," Walter said, sounding exhausted. "Are you going to row or should I?"

"You used to say I wasn't right in the head, remember?"

"I never said—"

"Not to me." Jason continued in a trancelike tone. "But I heard you say it anyway. You and Mom used to talk in the kitchen early in the morning. I could hear real good after the accident."

Walter sat very still.

"You know what else there is along that road?"

"Nothing. It's just an empty stretch—"

"Between the river and Fitch Road, on the left side if you're headed toward the river, on the right if you're going toward town. Damn, Dad, I thought you lived here all your life—"

"The cabins, those old WPA houses! I know what you're talking about, for chrissakes. I told you I didn't want you going there, I told your sister, too, but you went anyway. A strong wind could have blown them down. You could have been crushed by a falling beam. And I told you hundreds of times not to run into the street without looking, the way you used to. But you wouldn't listen—"

"So I had nobody to blame but myself—"

Walter grasped the edge of the seat, as if he'd been struck. "I didn't say that, Jason. I'm sorry. And I'm sorry I said those things. I didn't know better back then. Now can we go? It's getting chilly and I want to get some sleep." Weakness veined his voice.

Jason stared toward the shore as if he hadn't heard. "I did it to her in one of those houses, the one closest to the shore. Look, there. Hey, why aren't you looking?"

"Because I don't want to see. You drank too much beer, you're talking crazy, and I want to get back home."

"Toward the end she kicked and screamed but I did it to her anyway." His words grew choppy with the force of his breath.

"My God," said Walter, finally drawn into the scene.

"I bet you were just a little proud when you heard about what happened."

"Your mother and I didn't bring you up to do such a thing!" Walter shouted.

Jason smirked. "You used to tell me about you and those Philippine women who'd let you do it for cigarettes."

"That was different! It was during a war. And we didn't force ourselves on them."

"Be honest. When you got the news about Marcy, didn't you think, Well, thank God, the kid can't be so crazy after all if he goes after pussy—"

"Jason, keep a civil tongue in your head!"

"—especially now that you know what he really is."

"I already told you: You're still my son—"

"C'mon, Dad. If you had a choice between me doing what I did to Marcy and me being a fag—"

"I never used that word about you."

"I bet when you heard about me and my little friend in New York you got worried, didn't you? And when you saw Billy you got even more worried. You thought anything would be better than having a son like that. Anything would be better than having a son like Billy who wears dresses and lets another guy fuck him in the ass, right?"

Walter slapped him across the face. The boat rocked back and forth. The tackle box slid off the middle bench and hit the bottom with a crash like breaking glass. Jason threw himself at his father and flung his hands around his neck. He pulled Walter's face close, as if to get a better look at him. "You wanted to talk, but you didn't want to listen, did you? You really didn't want to know!"

"You're hurting me!" Walter's eyes were blank with terror. His breath came in wheezes.

Jason pushed his father backward. Walter hit the rim of the boat with a heavy thud. He gasped, his legs swung up, and he tumbled sideways into the water with a cry like a wounded animal. His white arms cut through the water as he splashed to the surface, struggling to stay afloat.

"Jason!" His voice sucked into a gurgle.

Jason watched the heavy, helpless fish his father had become. "Come on, war hero. Get into the boat. It can't be more than six feet deep here."

"I—I can't."

Jason reached over and held out his hand. Walter grasped it, sputtering water. "Hold onto the side, I'll get us to the shore, and you can climb out there." He rowed until the weeds clogged around the boat, then stepped into the muck and heaved his father up.

"Put your arms around my shoulders."

"Jim's boat," his father murmured.

"It won't go anywhere. C'mon, try to walk."

Jason slogged through the silt near the shore. Walter's legs dragged along, nearly useless.

"I can't, I can't," he gasped.

"Just a little farther."

They reached the muddy bank of the lake. Jason set his father down, his heavy limbs pooled around Jason's legs. Jason knelt beside him. "Just take it easy," he said. Walter's breaths came in shallow shudders. Jason leaned over closer. "You okay, Dad? Dad! Say something!"

A wet bubble formed between Walter's lips, but he remained silent. Jason couldn't tell whether or not his father's chest moved. His hands pressed against the wet flannel of Walter's shirt, feeling for the reassuring message of a heartbeat. He jumped to his feet and began running, passing the houses one by one. The road was deserted. He ran down the broken asphalt, searching the darkness for the pair of headlights that might bring help.

6

CARL WANTED TO go on talking but Cee dozed off, clothes and all. He was too edgy to sleep. He thought of going down to the kitchen to talk with Alyce. He liked her. She had a quiet but sensible way of framing her opinions. She realized what was going on between Carl and Elaine. After Elaine had been carted away, he'd sat with Alyce. "What have I done?" he'd said to her. She took his hand. "Go to her," she advised. "Go to her and spill your heart out to her at last."

Now he started for the steps, then heard Edgar's voice. He was in the kitchen, too. Carl decided not to go downstairs. Edgar often waxed melancholic at this hour and could be depressing to listen to. He remembered that the roof of the belfry needed repair. He'd go up there and have a look at it.

From up in the belfry it looked like the lights in the state university stadium were on. But at eleven o'clock at night? He reached up and pressed at the ceiling. One panel, spongy with fragrant rot, gave easily. He kept poking until half of the ceiling had fallen away in damp chunks. He noticed something lodged against the inner wall of the cupola, stood up on the chair, and groped with his fingers until he eased out a blackened metal case, as deep as a shoebox but wider. The lid appeared to be soldered shut. He climbed down the ladder and went into one of the small upstairs rooms. It took an hour to dig through the melted lead with the point of a screwdriver.

A leather folio lay inside, white with mold, brittle and breathing mustiness. He tried opening it, but its two halves clung to each other like frightened animals whose nest had been discovered. The binding was as tight as a coil. He wedged his hand between the two halves, the crease groaned and cracked, and a moment later the two halves lay separated in his lap. Each held a pouch with a thickness of folded, waxy paper. The paper resisted the pry of his fingers; at first he discerned no more than a fanciful letter *N* enclosed in a star-shaped border: a map. After some cautious bending he was able to ease it open a little farther, all the while the paper emitted warning creaks. Each panel revealed wavy threads of elevation lines, the crisscross of intersecting roads, an airy spread of letters spelling out a place name. When the whole map lay spread out on the floor he saw the words *Quaspeck Lake* spread across a faded greyish patch that might once have been blue. Lower down, within an elaborate frame, were written Indian Mountain, Thompsonville, New York. His eyes fell to a rectangle with a cross inside it. The house. And the road. That broken line—the route of the water conduit?

He refolded the map, his hands light with excitement and almost too shaky to work. He extracted the second document from its pouch. This one was thinner, more fragile. It bore a stiffly lettered heading in gothic script: "This Indenture."

It was a title deed. It was the title deed.

What was the deed doing in the belfry? He'd heard of builders depositing the plans of a house in the belfry. But not deeds. Unless the congregation feared losing it or—worse—having it destroyed. Which they had good reason to. They knew they were outcasts, even heretics. Destroying their deed would have been the easiest way to oust them. So they'd kept it in the family. He read on, his chest breaking with excitement:

> THIS INDENTURE, Made this Twenty-fourth day of May in the year of our Lord one thousand eight hundred and sixty-four between The Church of the New Evangelist of the Village of Thompson, Broome

> County, State of New York, of the first part, and Thomas McDowell, of the second part, Witnesseth, that the said party of the second part, in consideration of the sum of six hundred and fifty dollars to him duly paid, has sold and By these Presents does grant and convey to the said party of the first part his heirs and assigns ALL that certain piece or parcel of land situated in the Village of Thompson aforesaid partly in Great Lot No. 7 and partly in Great Lot No. 8 . . .

Finely wrought letters described the property's exact border:

> Beginning at a post of stones on the westerly side of the road leading from the town of Conklin to Thompson thence North eighty-seven degrees west along the South line of land occupied by John W. Williams . . .

He ran downstairs to show the others, but Alyce and Edgar had already gone to sleep. He sat down at the kitchen table and read the rest, his eyes tripping over the tight knots of script.

> In the event that the Church shall cease to exist, then the aforesaid property shall be duly divided equally among those who wish to remain and live on it.

Carl read the names—members of the congregation? Mr. Josiah R. Tyson, Mr. Hubert Hampton, Mr. Orville Richardson—all of them sturdy WASP names, nary a Goldstein or Rodriguez among them, nor was there an Emma or a Polly or a Hermione. But there had to have been women if there were children. Unless it meant that women were not to inherit any property. His eye stopped at one name: Mr. Bradford Ellicott Dowling.

Dowling.

Carl rubbed his eyes. Deep inside the house Benjamin whined. He'd cried for a solid hour after Shera and Phil had been taken away and, like Melissa, rarely went through a whole night without waking. A moment later Carl heard footsteps; Max or Alyce was going to comfort him.

Carl went out onto the porch. The police brooded in their little encampment. The pair of bulldozers looked like sleeping prehistoric beasts. A little farther away, almost endearing by comparison, were the lights of Junior's house. Where was Elaine? Cee said she was with Shera and Phil. Would she move in with them, together with Benjamin and the wonderful Dos Equis sign? He'd seen Elaine growing closer to Shera all during the weeks the Coalition had met, and he imagined Shera magnifying each of Elaine's doubts about him into a battle cry.

Tomorrow was that fair, he thought. And the day after tomorrow . . .

By the time he slipped into bed beside Cee he knew exactly what he would do in the morning.

He rose very early, and dressed as quietly as he could, so Cee wouldn't wake up. He went to the large storage closet that Melissa had claimed as her warm-weather bedroom, cushioning its floor with a mound of blankets and sleeping bags people had left behind in the house. Benjamin was curled up beside her. The air inside was musky and sweet. The two looked like stowaways in steerage. Just before he reached down he paused. Waking Melissa was the first step in carrying out what he planned to do that day. She turned over, taking most of the blanket with her, and nestled into the abundant comfort, leaving Benjamin in nothing but his father's University of Oregon T-shirt. In the past year Melissa had grown from a toddler, a shapeless conglomeration of her parents, into a child who could walk, who had preferences and her own way of doing things. Their child, he thought.

He gave Melissa's shoulder a nudge.

Benjamin's hand sought the blanket immediately, as though alerted to having lost it. Carl prayed for him not to wake up; if he did he'd rouse the rest of the house, too. Melissa's eyes opened. Before she could say anything he lifted her up.

"Caw," murmured Melissa.

"Come with Daddy." He crept back out into the hall and closed the door, feeling like a kidnapper.

"We're going to town," he said, setting her down. "Elaine's in town, too. We're going to see her." They walked down to the kitchen. "You wait here, okay?" he said. He scampered back upstairs for her clothing. Melissa was waddling naked toward him when he returned, her nightgown trailing from one leg, her feet flapping against the floor. "Caw," she cried, pleased at having gotten undressed by herself. The children's crusade, he thought, fitting her into her overalls, as though they were a suit of armor. When she was dressed, he made himself coffee and poured granola and milk into a bowl for Melissa. Her grip on the spoon was sure, but most of what it held splashed back into the bowl before reaching her mouth. Carl knew better than to try and help her; she insisted on eating by herself. When she was finished he dabbed her face with a damp towel and went for the papoose, an old backpack he'd cut holes in to carry Melissa when she got tired. He checked the pocket of his overalls where the deed was, and they left through the back door. He didn't feel like seeing any cops first thing in the morning.

The sky was a thin blue. He knew from the height of the sun that it couldn't be much later than six. The chilly air felt like peppermint down his throat. His eyes were watery from having slept so little. He led Melissa toward the path to the lake, wanting to see it one last time. The water was the color of cobalt, stern and uninviting, as if it sensed intruders about to approach. Carl imagined Larrabee's houses rising around it, he heard the pling, pling of a tennis ball being bounced around a court and the roar of cars.

A bird arched across the water. A cardinal? In the four years he'd lived here he'd learned precious little nature lore. Junior knew where the strawberries and huckleberries grew. People crashing at the house returned from hikes with armfuls of herbs to hang up and dry. But Carl couldn't identify more than a couple of trees. Maybe that showed that he didn't belong here.

But would the rock stars buying Larrabee's houses know where red bergamot grew any better than he?

Pling, pling.

At Friday night's meeting of the Coalition he'd felt like a Jonah who'd brought a storm upon their ship, but whenever he thought of seeing his father, Carl's heart resisted. That morning in June four years ago when he dumped his things into the back of the VW that jiggled its way up to the house, he sensed his father slipping farther and farther away from him, a boulder fallen off his back. When he got to the house, he sat for a long time on the back porch, listening to the cheerful clatter in the kitchen, the hum of someone chanting, the barking of a dog in the woods, and all he could think was, I've gotten away, I've gotten away.

Today he was going back.

"Come, Melissa. Time to hit the road."

As they neared the clump of police he took Melissa's hand firmly.

"I'll be here later," he said as he walked through the line. "My daughter and I live here, and we're coming back."

One of the troopers gave him a snide grin. "Happy Father's Day," he said.

A man with a portable tape recorder strung around his neck approached him. "You're one of the people living up there, aren't you?" he said, pulling out a pen from his shirt pocket.

"Who are you?"

"I'm with the *Herald-Examiner*. Is it true that the county plans to evacuate the house tomorrow? The district attorney's office has given notice that the house is to be evacuated by tomorrow morning at eight o'clock."

"You got the story wrong. We're here to stay."

"Move along, Johnny Appleseed," said the policeman.

Carl spun around. "You fucking pig!"

The trooper raised his stick. Melissa shouted. Carl pulled her behind him. The reporter stood watching. The stick was lowered.

"Baby," she cried. Baby was the name she'd given to the doll Cee had brought her. She ran back. A policeman blocked her path.

"We'll get Baby later," Carl said, taking her hand.

"No!" She wrenched away and wrapped her hands around her chest.

"Melissa, please." Carl felt everyone looking his way, the troopers, the cops, the newspaper reporter. "Baby has to stay and watch over the house so no asshole takes it while we're away," he said, speaking loud enough so that everyone heard him.

Melissa's face grew serious as she thought it over, then she let him take her hand.

When he reached the road he searched for Elaine's car but didn't see it; she'd picked it up. He headed for Junior's house. Just before he knocked he glanced at the *D* on the door.

"What do you want?" Junior's mother stood, her face veiled grey by the screen.

"I'd like to speak with Junior."

"He's asleep."

"Would you possibly be able to tell me where he—"

The door closed.

Thank you very much. Mrs. Dowling. Thank you for being the creep you truly are.

Dowling.

It had come to him just before falling asleep last night. Carl couldn't be sure that the Dowling on the deed was related to the Dowling who drove a Ford pick-up and lived with the person who'd just slammed the door in his face. But if that turned out to be true . . . Well, that was one of the things he was headed into town to clear up.

They started down the mountain road. The trees were a glistening green. The road curved gracefully, russet-colored and smelling of clay. The first time he'd seen it in winter, flanked by snow on either side, the colors had reminded him of the sweet potatoes and marshmallows of Thanksgiving. Melissa took short steps, leaving bits of words behind her. If she were better able to talk she might ask him why they were going to town, he thought. Sensing his uneasiness, she might assure him that he'd made the right decision, that his father—her grandfather—would be happy to see him.

And she would tell him not to be scared.

"Waine?" she said.

"I already told you," he said, irritated. "She's in town. We'll see her when we get there."

Melissa frowned because he'd raised his voice to her, and then evaded the conciliatory hand he went to place on her shoulder.

It occurred to Carl that no one in the house knew where he'd gone. Why hadn't he told anyone? Because by the time he'd made up his mind everyone had gone to sleep.

And . . . also because he didn't want it to look as though he'd given in.

When they reached the county road, he stuck out his thumb. Melissa, grinning with the prospect of playing this new game, did the same.

A car full of teenagers swooped by and nearly drove them off the road. Melissa screamed. Carl yanked her out of danger, but she kept crying, so Carl set her in the papoose and carried her. Usually he liked hitching. The idea of sticking your thumb out beside a road and landing almost anywhere was exhilarating. It was a tangible bit of freedom, a glimpse into infinity, for wasn't freedom a kind of infinity? But that morning he felt anything but free. The house had been his freedom. Elaine and Melissa and the people who'd lived with them were part of it, since freedom implied the freedom of those around you. He fought for his small piece of freedom. It had been a good struggle, but perhaps he'd fought for the wrong reasons. Elaine accused him of coming to the house to escape his father. Maybe when he said *freedom* he really meant *flight*.

A Beetle was stopping. A woman wearing a bandana leaned out the window and apologized for not taking them; two children sat in the back, and a laundry sack was stuffed in beside her.

"You know what time it is?" Carl asked.

"Just after eight. You should get picked up soon. Plenty of people will be heading into town for the barbeque," she said, driving off.

He decided to go the rest of the way by foot and turned off at the old county road. He outlined what he'd do when he got into town. He'd drop by Ron's office and deliver the deed right away. Then he'd go to his father. After that he would look for Elaine. He would try to talk, as Alyce had advised. And then? Could he say to Elaine that he was sorry? What could he apologize for, if the purpose of an apology was to set things right? Everything hadn't been right between them. "You're just too far away from me, Carl," Elaine had said. "Maybe you always were." But did that mean it would stay that way? Didn't she believe he might change?

Melissa was flapping her arms, as though ready to fly the rest of the way to town.

"THAT'S QUITE a contingent you have out there," Ron said, as Max opened the door. "The sheriff must have called for reinforcements from Binghamton."

Max told them that Carl and Melissa had left.

"What? That's impossible. I didn't see anybody walking along the road. Maybe they got a ride. I heard that Cee's here."

"Upstairs," Max said. "She's still asleep. Coffee?"

He nodded. "Her father's in the hospital. He had some kind of boating accident last night."

"I'll get her," said Max.

Edgar put a cup of coffee in front of him.

"Shera and Phil and Elaine were each given a summons," Ron continued. "They could have been held overnight. The fact that they weren't shows the county is trying to go as lightly as possible. They don't want trouble, especially not today." He drank some coffee. "I spoke with the district attorney's office, and Steve Polikoff said that they would be willing to drop all charges against the three of them if you guys signed a paper saying that you'll pull out of here within a week. But if you don't—"

"We won't!" said Edgar.

"—I can't predict what they'll do, but one thing I know is that the Father's Day Fair nonsense in Lacey Park is great cover, if the sheriff should decide to move in ahead of schedule—"

"You mean they might try to evict us today?" Max said.

"That's illegal!" Edgar shouted.

"It'll be moot once they get you out. If you folks agree to leave, then all you have to do is sign the paper they gave me and they'll call off the dogs out there."

"Ron," said Max, shaking his head no.

"Okay, I didn't expect you to sign it," he said, "but it's my responsibility to deliver it. Now that we've settled that, let me show you this." He produced a yellow folder from his attaché case. "Theresa has been staying after work night after night, digging through the county archives, and she's found something that might be very useful to us. This is a copy of a legal notice printed in the *Thompson City Sun* of April 1864, about land being bought by a religious community. It's not a title deed—none seems to exist for the house—but it might help us trace the owners."

Cee walked in, rubbing her eyes.

"Morning, everyone." They turned to her. She looked around the room. "Where's Carl? Where's Melissa?"

"We don't know," Alyce said. "We think they went into town."

"What? We were up talking until late last night and he didn't mention going— That means he can't get back in, right?"

"Listen, Cee, there's something else," said Ron, shading his voice. "Your father was taken to Wilson Hospital last night. I don't know why, but it had something to do with a boating accident. Your mother's with him."

"A boating accident? What was he doing out in a boat? Is he okay?"

"I don't know." He looked at his watch and went to the phone. "I told the district attorney's office I'd let them know about the paper as soon as I could."

"You forgot?" said Alyce, making a pair of scissors with her fingers.

"Oh, right. I'll do it when I get back to town. Do you want to come with me, Cee?"

She looked at the others.

"Go and see your father," Alyce said, touching Cee's arm. "We'll be all right."

"Shera's worried about Benjamin. Let me take him, too."

By the time they were back outside, more troopers had arrived, standing in silent rows. Behind them, students from the state university had assembled, cheering Cee and Ron and Benjamin as they emerged from behind the police line.

MELISSA LET OUT a little shriek in her papoose. Carl turned around, stopping shortly. Coming down the road was an entire house, right down to the rain gutters, riding on a long trailer, towed by a cab. Plastic warning flags fluttered from the cables tying it down. It looked as if it had just been bought at a cash-and-carry place, ready to be set down on a sixteenth-of-an-acre lot. Melissa clapped her hands with delight and grabbed onto Carl's shoulders, urging him to follow it. The driver gave them a friendly honk. Carl was almost tempted to stick out his thumb. How many people could say that they'd been picked up by a house?

Melissa motioned to be let down. Carl realized why when he noticed the dark stain on her pants.

"Oh, oh," he said. He'd forgotten to bring along a clean diaper or an extra pair of underpants. Melissa had almost graduated from diapers; every so often there were slip-ups.

"Come on, let's get out of those pants and take a little dip, Melissa." A creek ran parallel to the road, a spillover from the lake, which Larrabee planned to channel through a cement trench to flow under ornamental wooden bridges. Melissa ran bare-assed toward the creek, giggling and stomping into the water. Her laughter flitted like birdsong through the woods. As he washed her pants he began to hear music, the doodle of a marching band. Central High? Too far away, and it was the wrong season for football. Then he realized: Lacey Park.

The town lay under a Sunday morning pallor, not calm, but listless. The day had grown very hot; his overalls felt heavy, and the back of his neck was damp beneath his hair. He headed for Ron's office. It was closed. He walked by the bookstore and noticed there were people inside. Today they were taking inventory.

"Brigid," he said when they walked in.

"Oh!" She turned around, carrying a stack of books, which she set down on a stool. "I didn't expect to see you here." A pencil was propped behind her ear. Melissa ran off to the yard behind the store. "You look tired, Carl."

Elaine had dubbed Brigid Herbal Essence because of her sweet face and perpetually sunny disposition. Today her pleasantness seemed almost painful; he was ready to fall into her arms and weep. As the situation with Larrabee—and Elaine—had worsened, he found himself thinking about her more and more. It had been easy enough to stop by her house for an hour or so, even if he knew it wasn't a good idea to keep on seeing her. Somehow, he'd needed to.

"Have you seen Elaine?"

"No, but I heard she was released along with Phil and Shera."

A moment later Melissa was running toward them.

"Watch out!" Carl said. But the stack of books had already toppled over from the stool.

"Don't worry about it," said Brigid, going to collect the books.

Carl went to the back and called the newspaper office. Elaine wasn't there. He thought of calling his parents but decided it would be better to simply head over to the house. The clock in the store said ten to ten.

"Come, Melissa, we have to go." He looked at Brigid, and then leaned over and kissed her.

After the lush randomness of the mountain, the rectangular lawns before each house on his parents' street looked stiff and drained of color. Melissa scampered ahead; she'd been to the house often enough to know the way. The house seemed to retreat with each step he took, as though he were on a treadmill. He went up the flagstone path to the front door like a visitor. It was locked. No one answered his ring. No car was parked in the driveway. The back door was locked, too. He peered in through the screen of the kitchen window and saw the G below the sink, the knotty pine paneling of the dining area, the Black Madonna. Everything looked the same.

"Carl? Is that you, Carl?"

He turned around. Mrs. Winograd from next door stood on her back porch. She had the same blue-grey hair he remembered, looking metallic in the dull sunlight.

"I can't remember when it was I last saw you. How have you been? You know, I've been reading all about what's happening up on Indian Mountain. Oh, hello, Melissa!"

Carl had to pee but hesitated asking to use Mrs. Winograd's bathroom for fear she'd snag him into a long conversation. "Have you seen my mother and father?"

Her face went taut with surprise. "You don't know? They brought your father to Wilson Hospital late last night."

"What? What happened?"

"I don't know. I'd drive you over but Howard took my car into the city."

He started to go.

"What's happening with that house of yours? I think it's a shame that Larrabee can just come in here and boss everybody around, all because of his money."

"A shame, yes. I have to go, Mrs. Winograd. Nice seeing you again. Come, Melissa. Come!" She looked tired out from all the walking. Church bells began ringing. He'd heard them all his life but today they took on an ominous tone. Wilson was too far away to go by foot. He'd return to the bookstore, drop Melissa off with Brigid, and take a bus—

Just then a car pulled in the driveway. He recognized it: Elaine's. And Elaine was driving it.

JASON HADN'T BEEN able to sleep after bringing Walter to the hospital. He kept thinking of his father lying heavy-looking and still on the grass like a bum who had fallen asleep. Around dawn he left the house and began walking to the hospital. Is he still alive? he thought. Is he still alive?

Last night he'd run until his legs felt ready to give out without seeing a car on the road. The moon shed a brittle light that pursued him, accused him. When he finally spotted a car on Fitch Road he took off after it. Nails sank into his chest. Jason shouted at the car. It slowed. Jason threw himself against it.

"Help me, please help," he gasped.

The car braked. The driver, a young guy, shot him a frightened look through the window but wouldn't lower it.

"Please!" Jason cried. "It's my father!"

They drove back and pulled off the road where Walter lay in the weeds. He mumbled weakly as Jason put his arms around him to lift him. They heaved him into the back seat. His body shifted limply within his clothing as though it were a sack that held him.

"Keep his head up so he doesn't choke," the guy said.

Jason cradled his father's limbs, studying the tiny broken vessels in his noise and the freckled scalp that showed through his thinning hair.

Walter's head slumped to the side.

"Hey," Jason shouted. "He's passed out!"

"Slap his face," the guy shouted. "Slap him! Hard!"

"I can't!"

"Slap him!"

Jason's hand sounded like it hit water as he struck his father's cheek. Walter's eyes fluttered, he mumbled, and saliva bubbled at his lips. The guy clutched into fourth and floored it. Jason held Walter to keep him from sliding off his lap, amazed at his father's weight and the bulk of his muscles. The town flew by at a frightening pace—Lacey Park, Jason's school, the bus station, the monument.

I can hardly walk down the street anymore.

After Walter was admitted to the hospital, Jason called home from the emergency room but no one was there. Where was his mother? He had to sign all the papers himself. Would the police see this report? Would they be able to tell that he'd violated the conditions of his release by leaving the county?

My father and I went fishing on Davis Lake. The boat tipped, and he fell in, he'd written.

Jason called the house every ten minutes. It was almost midnight before his mother picked up the phone. She'd just returned from the office. He had to tell the whole story over again to her. She said hardly anything. By the time she arrived, Walter had been moved from the emergency room to a regular room and was sleeping.

"Who knows if I can even believe the story you told me," she said, shaking her head.

"You can believe what you want to believe."

Her eyes widened. All the anger he'd felt from her since returning looked ready to spill out. She slapped him across the face, right there in the room, in front of a nurse. She hit him so hard that he fell against the wall. Then she hit him again. "This is for what you did to your father," she said. "This is for what you did to that girl. And this is for what you did to Billy. And this is for what you've been doing to me."

"Mrs. Gajewski," the nurse said.

She didn't stop. "Cry, for God's sake," she screamed at Jason. "Why aren't you crying?" She went at him again. He backed into a corner, knocking things off a nightstand. A bottle crashed.

That morning Jason reached the hospital sweating and faint.

His father was asleep. His skin was white and chalky. Tubes ran to his arms and into his nose. His gown seemed too small for him, his arms and neck bulged out of it almost comically. Jason sat for a long time watching the rise and fall of his chest, making sure it didn't stop. Then he noticed his mother's jacket on the back of a chair and panicked but was too tired to get up. He dozed off sitting up.

"Jason, is that you?" It was his father, shifting in bed. He spoke in a windy voice. Each word sounded creased. "Let's . . . have a look . . . at you."

Jason rose, stiff from the chair, and approached the bed. He caught sight of his own face in the mirror over the sink: two splotches the color of raw meat marked his left cheek where his mother had hit him.

"Your face?" Walter whispered, pointing.

"Dad, you okay?"

"I'm . . . okay. So stop that blinking, will you? You're . . . making me . . . nervous."

Theresa walked in. She glanced at Jason coldly. Jason pulled back from the bed.

"When did you get here?"

"Just before."

She turned her back on him to adjust Walter's blanket. She seemed to stand between them on purpose.

Elaine came into the room with Melissa. "Oh," she said, when she saw Jason. "Hello."

"That was fast," Theresa said. "Did you find the things I asked you for?"

She pulled Theresa aside. "Carl's here. He was at your house when I got there. He stopped off to go to the bathroom."

Jason looked at Melissa. She was his niece, he thought. The first time Elaine brought Melissa over to the house Jason kept looking at her, as if meeting a lost sister.

"Say hello to Grandpa, Melissa," Elaine said.

Melissa seemed puzzled, as though she didn't understand why someone would be in bed in the middle of the day. Walter touched her hand but she pulled away, unsettled at the way her grandfather looked.

"Has she eaten?" Theresa said.

"Carl gave her some cereal at the house."

"She must be famished. I'll take her down to the cafeteria." She took Melissa's hand. "Come, sweetheart. Come with me—"

Carl came into the room. "Mom—"

Theresa put her arms around him and held him.

"I didn't even know Dad was here," Carl said. "Mrs. Winograd told me." Theresa released him. He nodded uncomfortably at Jason, then turned toward the bed. The room grew very still. "Hello, Dad," he said.

Walter's head turned, and he looked at Carl. Then he started to gasp.

"What's wrong?" Elaine said, shooting up out of her chair.

He was crying. He pushed the canula from his face, and it began hissing.

"Walter, leave it," said Theresa.

He motioned for Carl to come closer.

Carl leaned over stiffly. One of Walter's hands rose up to touch his arm. "Carl," he said in a strained whisper.

A man appeared at the door with a tape recorder strapped around his neck. "I'm from the *Herald-Examiner*. Would you mind if I had a few words with Mr. Gajewski?" he said.

Carl turned around, recognizing the man's voice.

"We're not holding any press conferences," Elaine snapped.

"It won't take long," he said, stepping up to the bed. "Mr. Gajewski, Lacey Park is already full of people waiting for you to accept the Father of the Year award—"

"He won't be there," Elaine said. "Now would you please leave?"

"Is it true that your boating accident had something to do with your youngest son, Mr. Gajewski?"

Walter kept looking at Carl, uncomprehending.

"Anything you have to ask him you can ask me," Theresa said to the reporter. "I'm his wife."

"Don't talk to him," Elaine said. "Larrabee's paid him."

The reporter turned to Elaine. "You'd better be careful, Miss. There are laws against slander. Now Mr. Gajewski—"

"I've seen you before," Carl said. "You were up at the house this morning, weren't you?"

"Just doing my job," he answered. "Now Mr. Gajewski, do you have anything to say to the hundreds of people in Lacey Park?"

"Get the nurse, Mrs. Gajewski," Elaine said. "Mr. Gajewski, don't say a word to him. He'll write what he wants anyway. They've been against us from the very beginning—"

Walter turned to the reporter, as if just realizing that he was there.

His hand hadn't left Carl's arm the whole time.

Cee and Ron walked into the room.

"Dad?" she said, approaching the bed.

Walter smiled at her weakly.

"Ron, help me," said Elaine. "This creep from the *Herald* won't leave us alone."

Cee went over to Jason and pulled him to the side. "I want you to tell me right now what happened last night."

Jason said nothing.

"I'm waiting."

"It was his idea to go fishing, not mine."

"The family would like you to leave," Ron said to the reporter.

"Leave me alone, Cee," said Jason.

"Cee," Elaine said, motioning to the reporter.

"Did you forget that you weren't supposed to leave the county?" Cee said sharply.

"That's enough," said Theresa.

"And I sure don't understand why you bothered coming here."

"I said that's enough, Cee." She turned to Jason. "Why don't you just go back to the house and wait there?"

Jason's face darkened with anger. "Why should *I* go? Why not you? Dad told me you've hardly spoke to him during the past couple of weeks."

"Jason," said Theresa.

The reporter scribbled on his pad.

Jason stepped backward, as if to take a group picture of them all. "Come to think of it, I'd like to know what all of you are doing here. Like you, Cee. Or you, Carl—you haven't spoken to him in years. What are you all doing here playing one big happy family?"

From Walter Gajewski's bed came strange, sucking sounds. The mask had fallen into his mouth. He'd fallen asleep.

Jason left. He walked and walked, waiting for the shaking inside him to subside. He felt weightless and unsteady from hunger and lack of sleep. He stopped at the intersection where the monument was. Except that it was . . . gone. Hadn't it been there last night when they drove past? Behind the border of flowers, in the middle where the monument should have been, was a bald block of stone. It looked so strange that way.

The welt on his face burned. It was the first time his mother had ever hit him.

He followed the people heading toward the park. Would Marcy be there, too? His heart began to race. If he saw her, if she didn't run away when she saw him—and if her father wasn't there—he'd try to talk to her, he'd try to explain . . . By the time he reached the park, his mouth was dry as paper. He got himself a soda, then headed toward the field. A guy with long hair was arguing with a cop to be let in behind a barrier that had been set up. The cop waved Jason through. Not far from the entrance, a house stood on a trailer, surrounded by potted plants that were supposed to look like shrubbery. A plastic picket fence ran around it, there was even a fake flagstone path and a mailbox. A house on stilts, just like ours, he thought. The sun was very strong and bounced off the white siding, painful to look at. A sign said that the house was air conditioned, so he went inside to cool off. People were filing through the rooms, opening the closet doors, peeking into the bathroom. A girl played trampoline on the bed until her mother caught her. A woman wearing an apron was giving out crackers and cheese in the kitchen. Kids ran barefoot over the shag carpeting, turned on the faucets, puzzled when no water came out. Jason sat on a couch in the living room, drinking his soda, and eating a cracker. He realized that it was the first thing he'd eaten all day. The woman gave him seconds but no more.

He went back outside. A table selling raffle tickets had been set up near the house. A big rotating drum held them, like a sudsy depth of water behind the glass of a washing machine.

"Buy a raffle, young man?" the woman behind the table said. "Fifty cents, three for a dollar. You might win a house for you and your family." She held up a roll of tickets.

"We already have a house."

"Well, what about when you get married and have kids? A nice-looking boy like you is sure to find someone you want to marry and settle down with."

Jason kept on. Toward the lake a stage had been built. Several men in suits were shaking hands to the side of it. Country music twanged from the loudspeakers. He'd never seen Lacey Park so full. All the picnic tables had been taken, and people had brought their own. Dogs raced through the crowd as if on a slalom course. Barbeques smoked with charcoal, and the garlic of hotdogs sweetened the air. More and more students had massed behind the police barrier. Several carried signs saying Our House Isn't Your House and Larrabee? No siree!

He spotted Richie sitting on the ground on a blanket. He appeared to be alone. He had on a pair of swim trunks and sunglasses, nothing else. His skin was tanned and his muscles shiny with lotion. Jason's chest tightened, and he walked away to get something to eat. As Jason passed through the crowd he heard his father's name mentioned. What if he told them what had happened? What if he said his father was in Wilson wearing an oxygen mask, looking like death warmed over?

And all because of him. That's what his mother believed.

It was getting hotter by the minute. A folksong duo mounted the stage, picking banjos, and singing a song about a coal mine and then another about the prairie. People turned up their portable radios. Jason got a hotdog and sat down under a tree. The park was as noisy as a supermarket. The students in the parking lot had begun chanting loud enough to be heard above the singing.

Larrabee, no siree!
Larrabee, no siree!

After the folksingers left the stage, a line of white-robed figures began moving across the park like a carpet unrolling. There must have been at least fifty of them, all of them black. The crowd grew quieter as rows of people filled the stage. Even the chanting died down. A black man stepped forward and announced the group: The Liberty Street Baptist Church Gospel Choir. He turned and lifted his hands, and a moment later the park filled with heavy-sounding music that swept over the crowd like a deep wave.

Jesus, Jesus, I ain't got no husband
Jesus, Jesus, I ain't got no husband

By the end of the song the tempo had increased. The music bounced up and down, with the singers clapping and bobbing on the stage, airy as marionettes. Their faces were oiled in sweat, but they appeared not to notice the heat.

Jason glanced over to Richie. A girl now sat beside him. Jason recognized her—it was Carol, Marcy's friend. Her face was an angry, sunburned pink. She wiped her forehead, looking uncomfortable. Richie kept to one end of the blanket, staring off into the distance. Carol seemed to be trying to figure out what he was looking at. Jason realized that she was pregnant.

> *Woman, woman, you got five husbands*
> *Woman, woman, you got five husbands*

The choir picked up the pace, clapping all the while, but the audience responded only halfheartedly, worn out from the heat.

Reggie.

There he was, shaking his head and clapping his hands as he sang. The wound on Jason's face flared. Nina was probably in the audience, too. Jason wanted to leave but he felt immobilized by the heat, and the choir seemed to be making the air hotter. He was relieved when everyone finally began to file off the stage. The park sank into a humid daze afterward, as if everyone had eaten enough and heard enough and just wanted to wait for a breeze.

Men began to set up chairs on the stage. The drum with the raffles was carried up and placed on a table. Several men in suits mounted the steps and sat down. Every so often one of them would look at his watch, wipe his forehead with a handkerchief, and peer out into the crowd. Finally a man Jason recognized as the mayor stepped up to the podium. He welcomed everyone to the annual Father's Day barbeque, quickly correcting himself by saying that he hoped it might become an annual event, since so many people had shown up for it. When he finished, a heavy man with a block-shaped face said he was proud to represent the construction workers of the Triple Cities area, men who never shied away from hard work, who were prepared to do an honest day's work for a day's pay. He glanced behind him to the mayor, as if not sure how to go on.

"Where's Walter?" someone shouted. Others joined in with the question. The union president assured everyone that the guest of honor would be on hand any moment, and hurriedly retreated from the podium.

The high school band began trooping over to the stage for a squeaky version of "You Are the Sunshine of My Life." After the pomp of the gospel singers, the band looked like a confused army, their instruments clumsily held sabers.

"And now, ladies and gentlemen, citizens of Thompson City," the mayor said, after the band left the stage, "it gives me great pleasure to welcome a man who is about to do so much for our community, the president of Larrabee Construction Corporation, Mr. Gerald Larrabee!"

Larrabee, no siree!
Larrabee, no siree!

A man strode to the podium in a suit as blinding white as the shingles of the house. He stood before the crowd as if he wanted to embrace it, a smooth, durable smile on his lips. The flash of his tie bar seemed to be giving signals.

"I am proud to be embarking on a new project, which will be the start of a new era in Thompson City history, a fusion of ecology and good business." He spoke calmly and very clearly, like someone on the radio. The students responded with a drone of boos and shouts. His smile never lost its shape. "It will show that the answer to a recession is not resignation but action—"

Larrabee, no siree!
Larrabee, no siree!

"You, the people of Thompson City, have shown your support for this project, and, in doing so, have made a commitment—"

Larrabee, one's thing's clear:
We don't want your houses here!

The chanting grew too loud for him to continue. His smile pulled to a tense line, and he gave an angry glance toward the students before turning back to the audience. "Ladies and gentlemen, those rabble-rousers you hear think that progress is a dirty word. They would live on nuts and berries and cook their meals over an open fire. I say, that's fine for them, but I myself have nothing against modern technology, and I'm sure that you don't—"

Larrabee, Larrabee,
You don't know ecology!

He cleared his voice and starting describing the house that would be raffled off, speeding up his delivery to get as much in as he could before the next onslaught of chanting. "Three bedrooms, air conditioning, wall-to-wall carpeting, a washer and a dryer, even a dishwasher—"

> *Larrabee, one's thing's clear,*
> *We don't want your houses here!*

"—and I'm sure you're all waiting for the raffle—"

> *Larrabee, we won't stop,*
> *Till you're off the mountaintop!*

For the first time during his speech he began to look nervous and moved to the table with the raffle urn as though wishing to end the spectacle as soon as possible. He rolled the drum, placing the microphone near it, so everyone might hear the cascade of tickets inside. Just then a loud grinding sound rose from the far end of the park. An alarmed hum spread through the crowd, and people began turning around. Several policemen were seen running from the barrier toward the house. The students used the chance to break through the barrier and stream into the park. They quickly spread through the crowd, throwing handfuls of leaflets as they went.

Jason had just picked one up one of the leaflets when slowly, very slowly—he couldn't even be sure it was happening at first—the house began to wobble. The potted plants and picket fence fell away. The house looked ready to slip off onto the ground. Then it began to move. It rolled slowly but steadily. Jason ran closer and saw what was happening: A pickup truck parked in the lot was pulling it. A lamp fell out of the window of the house. Things were heard crashing inside. The mailbox was uprooted. There was an explosion: the air conditioner?

"What in God's name?" Larrabee said, not realizing that he spoke into the microphone.

The house had begun to press toward the crowd. There were screams as picnic tables turned over. Dogs yelped and children were picked up and carried away. A patch of grass caught on fire where a grill got knocked down. The house rolled halfway to the parking lot before the police halted its progress and ordered the driver out. A large man wearing overalls opened the door of the cab and emerged, smiling and raising the clasped hands of a champion. The students cheered. Most everyone in the audience had turned around to look. The marching band was called back for an especially loud reprise of "You Are the

Sunshine of My Life" as if trying to capture the crowd's attention, but some people had begun packing up their things and leaving. The students were herded back into the parking lot. The leaflets remained scattered through the park, like ticker tape after a parade. Larrabee stood watching what was going on, a grim expression on his face. His white suit hung heavily, as though he'd been caught in the rain.

"Ladies and gentlemen, I just received word that today's guest of honor will be delayed," he said. "You know who I mean: a man who is willing to work hard so that he might live in dignity and support his family." He smiled, but the smile threatened to sink into the choppy waters of his voice. "He was born in this town and has lived here all his life; he built a home here, married here, and raised a family here—Walter Gajewski: a good neighbor, a friend to many, a working man. He's the reason we made this fair; for him, and all the other working people of this town. We wanted to show our appreciation to everyone in Thompson City for the support you've given our project."

Jason watched Larrabee's Adam's apple slithering over the knot of his tie as he spoke. What was he saying about his father? He didn't even know him. He caught sight of the reporter who'd been at the hospital, now standing at the far end of the stage, talking to the mayor. The mayor stepped up behind Larabee and said something to him.

Larrabee, we won't stop . . .

"I was going to wait until Walter Gajewski arrived so that he could pick the winning raffle himself, but I have just gotten an update that he's been called away on urgent family business. That shouldn't surprise anyone: We all know how devoted Walter Gajewski always was to his family."

A rumble arose from the crowd. "Where's Walter?" people began to shout.

What was he saying? Jason thought. What the fuck was he saying? What were all of them saying? The heat and the echo of the loudspeakers had turned them into one, blustering, senseless voice. No one in the audience was listening, but everyone sat there. They didn't give a shit about his father, either, they'd come to pig out and see if they won one of those cardboard houses Larrabee wanted to unload on them. They didn't know anything about his father in his too-small hospital gown, who sounded like a crankcase full of sand every time he took a breath.

Larrabee, one thing's clear...

"Walter Gajewski's family is the chief reason he's working on this project," Larrabee continued, raising his voice to drown out the protesters.

"You don't know shit about my father," Jason yelled.

People sitting near him turned around.

"When I spoke to Wally Gajewski and told him about the raffle, he said it was a wonderful way of showing appreciation to the people of Thompson City for supporting the project."

Larrabee, Larrabee...

"You're lying," Jason shouted.

More people looked at him.

"You don't know a thing about my father!" Jason said as he made his way through the crowd.

Larrabee turned toward him.

"You just picked my father because you figured he was a loser," Jason said, pushing his way toward the stage. "Everything you said about him is a fucking lie!"

He had just reached the steps to the stage when two policemen blocked his way. Another threw him against the side of the stage and began frisking him.

*Larrabee, Larrabee,
That's police brutality!*

Larrabee shouted for the policemen to release Jason. "We have a young man here and I believe he would like to say something to you all." He turned to Jason. "Here, young man. Step up to the microphone."

"Get on with the raffle!" a man in the audience shouted.

Jason mounted the steps. The crowd hushed into near-silence. Jason looked out, transfixed. Outside in the parking lot students were trying to block the police from taking the truck driver away. The gospel singers had folded the leaflets into fans and were fanning themselves. The marching band stood in clusters with their instruments, looking like heaps of shiny scrap metal. Jason found Richie in the crowd. He'd taken off his sunglasses and was staring right at Jason.

Several people began shouting, "Rapist! Rapist!"

"It's all lies," Jason began, but his voice fell away as if deflated.

"Rapist! Rapist!"

Jason tried to speak but could only stutter. He felt a tap on his shoulder. He spun around, it was Larrabee.

"Take it easy, now, Son—"

"Don't you call me that!" He glared at the man. Up close, he could see the lines across Larrabee's face, the dangerous flash of his tie bar, and how he was sweating. Jason's eyes fluttered, out of control. "You're all a bunch of liars. You don't know anything about my father. And he doesn't need you!" His voice boomed through the park. "He doesn't need any of you or your fucking job—" Jason threw down the microphone; a bruising high-pitched squeal jolted the crowd. He grabbed the raffle urn; its little door opened, and raffle tickets sailed into the audience. Two policemen sprang up to the stage and went to grab him from behind. "You're all liars!" he cried, hoisting the urn high above his shoulders, his voice white with hoarseness, a blinking Atlas. With a grunt he heaved the urn into the audience. There were screams. The urn landed with a rusty groan on the grass just before the police locked their arms around him and pulled him away.

7

*T*HE WHOLE WAY hitching back to Buffalo Billy tried to decide which had been stranger: Joel's little dormitory in New York or the Polish-American Ozzie Nelsons in T-City. Either way, he had to agree, travel certainly was broadening. Cee's mother was just about the only sane person *chez* Gajewski, probably because she was too busy to play *Good Housekeeping*. But that Jason—he was nothing less than a mutation of hormonally induced manhood, homosexuality gone amok, perversion perverted into menace. Still, never was menace more attractively packaged.

After the dance, Billy went home with someone named Simon, a French major. Pretty though he was, Simon fluttered with literary quotations, which only reminded Billy of Aaron, and that in turn made him long for Stanley. Simon offered to loan Billy clothes to wear going back to Thompson City but Billy demurred. "The dress is made of cool 'n' carefree Dacron," he sang. And what was wearing a dress in the streets of Thompson City compared to being ravaged by a psychopathic closet queen at home? He freshened up his makeup, kissed an astounded Simon good-bye, and began walking across the campus.

Billy kept thinking of the one thing he'd wanted to do in New York but either (1) hadn't gotten around to; (2) put off; (3) hit upon reasons not to do; or, most importantly, (4) hadn't had the correct change for when the mood hit *and* he stumbled on a pay phone that actually worked—calling Stanley up. Stanley hadn't given him a number, but it had been easy enough to copy the information off Stanley's luggage tag. Billy had carried the number around with him at all times like a magic formula, too powerful to use except when absolutely necessary. He ordered a small Coke at a Kentucky Fried Chicken, paid for it with a tenner, and asked for his change in quarters, which the astonished cashier took a long time to count out so he could gawk at Billy. By the time he found a phone booth, dialed, and heard someone answer, Billy was so anaesthetized with fear that he switched on his low voice without stopping to listen to the person on the other end.

"Hello, my name is William Gizzi, I'm calling from Niagara Falls Construction Company, and I'd like some information about the new fiberglass-free insulation—"

A young girl's voice broke in and told him to hold on while she called her mother ("It's for Daddy!"). A woman's footsteps click-clicked over to the phone, and Billy knew in an instant who was approaching: the woman in the picture Stanley dutifully set out in the motel room, a solemn reminder of faith and obligation in a dress with a scoop neck, her hair in a page boy.

"My name is Billy Gizzi," he blurted out, forgetting his spiel.

"Oh." Her voice disappeared into a void for a few seconds. He expected to hear the sharp click of the receiver being hung up. But no, she had put her hand over the mouthpiece for a moment.

"Would you happen to be the person who sent the slippers?" she said at last.

His throat caught on a mouthful of air. It shocked him to hear a total stranger casually making reference to what he thought no one else in the world knew about. But when he regained his calm, he realized that it wasn't unlikely for her to have found out about the slippers. On the contrary: Hadn't he planned it that way?

"Yes," Billy said in a small voice.

"And you're the one who's . . . been with him?"

His throat did another whirligig. How much did she know? Was there anything she didn't already know? He looked at the receiver, barely able to face its next utterance. "Yes," he said.

"Well, Stanley's . . . not here. He's moved out."

"Holy fu—"

"That was about a month ago," she continued, discreetly sidestepping his interjection. "Not long after that he was arrested at the border. He had an unpaid parking ticket, and they found a marijuana cigarette on him. He was let out because I posted his bail money—" he heard her stumble over this vocabulary "—and now Stanley faces a trial."

Billy felt like he was in a comedy act, being thrown one ball after the other and expected to catch them. What? Told Audrey? Moved out? Busted? Trial? Was she really talking about his Stanley?

Billy hesitated offering sympathy; she might turn around and blame him for everything that had happened. He asked if there was anything he could do. He made a point of calling her Mrs. MacIntyre.

"No," she said. She assumed that Stanley would get off. First offense. Domestic problems. The lawyer handling her divorce had agreed to take on the case, and he was very competent.

"Divorce?" Billy gulped.

"Why, of course."

"Of course," he repeated, in a daze.

She gave him the address and number of a hotel in Toronto. Just as he was ready to hang up she said she had to ask him a question.

"Do you really love Stanley?" she said. The even tone of her voice grew ragged. "Maybe if I knew that you did it would somehow make this whole thing . . . easier."

Billy caught sight of his reflection in the chrome of the pay phone, his eyes fierce with mascara, his lips alarmingly red. Makeup gave him a frightening look. Did Stanley really trust him enough to do all he'd done?

"Yes, Mrs. MacIntyre. I do. I do." I do, he repeated to himself, Stanley's bride.

As he went to leave he noticed a line of people on the street who'd been watching the whole time. "Phone's free," he said as he left.

His heart fluttered with fear, with joy. While speaking with Mrs. MacIntyre he'd made a decision: He wouldn't call Stanley or even write to him. He would go to him.

"WHAT BRINGS YOU here?" Kal opened the door but showed no sign of letting Billy in.

"I . . . just wanted to say hello."

Kal nodded. "You've said it."

"And I thought that we might see each other again."

"Okay. We've seen each other."

"Kal, don't be like this."

"Grant is coming over in a half-hour, and I want to get the house straightened up before he gets here."

He followed her into the kitchen. Elizabeth sat on a chair, eyeing him as he came in.

Kal remained standing.

"Cee told me what Luke did to you."

"You have some rather violent friends."

"He's not my friend, Kal."

"Excuse me. Business associate, maybe? Client?" Her tone chilled. "Ex-boyfriend?"

"Kal—"

"I think he was looking for you. Too bad he ran into me first."

"Please sit down. I feel like I'm under interrogation." He gave Elizabeth a gentle push and the cat let out a hiss of protest as she hopped down.

"Are you trying to say it was my fault?" he said, motioning to the chair.

She sat down. "No one should try to tell you anything, Billy."

"Look, if it makes you feel any better, Luke got me, too. Right before I left Buffalo."

Kal's expression hardly changed.

"Did Luke say why he was after you?" he asked.

"We had a long discussion pro and con prior to him picking up that two-by-four." She shook her head in disbelief. "I know why he did it, and so do you."

"Because you're taking him to court about Grant?"

"And because of whatever shit he thinks you pulled on him. Ever since we delivered him onto his parents' lawn we're linked forever in Luke's twisted psyche. But even if he had all the reasons in the world, it's you I hold responsible for Luke's attack. You took his money, you kept him in drugs, and you kept carrying on with him, even though you knew what he did to me. This little love tap was hardly Luke's first," she said, pointing to the faint mark on the side of her face.

"That was long ago—"

"Not for him, as you can see. What else does he have to fill his time except thinking of ways to get back at me?"

"So why do I have to take the rap? I'll tell you why. Ever since you discovered your woman-loving-woman-ness it's embarrassed you to have a man as a good friend. Your hyperlesbian separatist comrades don't approve."

Her eyes widened. "That's the line you've always used to explain to yourself why you've been cut out of my life. But it's your line, chum, not mine. You know as well as I why I decided to stop having anything to do with you. Should I tick off the reasons once more?"

"You kicked me out because I reminded you of your good old used-to-be, when you were still a skinny girl with long blond hair from well-kept Kenmore who liked tough boys on motorcycles like Luke Wilms. I reminded you of some not unpleasant times with me and Luke, some of which included getting very, very drunk or very, very high and when we were all high enough, winding up in the same bed. Which happened more than once, may I remind you. That was the real reason why you threw me out, Kal. I was just one politically embarassing memory after the other."

"Yes, yes," she said, her voice climbing. "I won't deny that it made me sick, actually physically sick, to think of how I'd shared my body with someone like Luke, and knowing you had, too, made you repellent to me." She pulled her hands together in her lap as if to gather her thoughts, and began again calmly. "But I'd gotten over most of that when I threw Luke out of the house. And I wanted more than anything to forget what had happened between you and me because I cared for you so much. But I couldn't. I felt so betrayed. And then, when you refused to testify at the hearings . . ." Her voice grew grittier. "Have you any idea how humiliating it is to have some self-satisfied male judge tell you that a junkie makes a better parent than you? Where were you when they told me that Luke would get custody of Grant—bending over behind a truck somewhere?"

"That's not fair!"

"And it was probably the same place you were right after the trial when they took Grant away! Let me tell you something, Gizzi. There were times you don't know how close I came to calling up the Buffalo Police Department and telling them where they could find you and what you were selling. And you know what stopped me? Not politics or ethics or any of that. It was Vincent. I assumed you had your stuff in his apartment and I didn't want them finding it there. Because if they did, and if they had to choose between busting an old black queen and some kid whose father was a retired army asshole, I knew who would get what. So tell me," she said, crossing her arms across her chest. "Why did you come here, anyway?"

Billy didn't answer right away. "To talk about something else I did that I knew I couldn't tell anyone else except you. It has to do with Cee."

"Is she all right?"

Billy nodded. "She was pregnant." Kal's mouth opened. "She lost it." He looked away for a moment, as if to avoid the sharpness of her glance. "The baby was mine."

Kal sat forward, her chair squeaked against the floor, and Elizabeth darted from the room. "What?"

He nodded. "I felt so strange after she'd told me. I even started having fantasies about being a father. But the strangest thing was that it got me thinking about us, about how we were, back when you just started getting wild. I knew I had to see you and try to sort things out between us." He shook his head. "We were the perfect anti-couple, fag and dyke."

"That's a long time ago," she said, her voice a little milder. "I was ashamed of being married to a man and having his child. I wanted to turn everything inside out, just the way you did." She offered Billy a crooked smile. "And I haven't forgotten any of it. I know that I was a Barbie doll before I met you. You helped me become the raving lesbian I am today. But losing Grant turned me bitter. I had to pay for being a dyke, and pay dearly, while the men around me got off free. Maybe I really don't have a reason to blame you any more than Luke. But I expected more from you. You used to say that queers were better than straights for the same reason that women were better than men or blacks better than whites, remember?"

"Gizzi's Theory of Relativity of the Oppressed," Billy said.

"For a while I believed it. And it helped me. And it certainly had me making allowances for you."

There was a knock at the door.

Kal rose with a start. "That must be him."

Billy got up. "Listen," he said, almost in a whisper. "Let's talk again."

"We'll see," Kal said. She gave his hand a squeeze.

The knocking grew insistent. Kal opened the door.

Grant rushed in, hardly looking at either of them. He wore jeans and a baseball jacket. He had auburn hair, and hints of Kal's face. He was tall for his age, and Billy knew where that came from. Grant gave her his cheek to kiss, but his face hardened in a moment of impatience; in a year or so he wouldn't tolerate his mother's affection.

Billy watched, and a lump rose in his throat.

He left, taking each step slowly. Kal had loved him, she'd trusted him, and he'd betrayed that trust. Cee had come to mind more than once during Kal's litany. Like Kal, she had seen through the Billy Gizzi Repertory Theater. Billy served up a character *du jour* like the Statler restaurant's businessman's lunch. Waif, dandy, street kid, faggot anarchist, intellectual, victim, stand-up comic, street revolutionary: Billy might be any of these at any given time or place. Cee had fallen for it, but only for a while.

He spent the rest of the day meandering around the homey West Side. Parts of Elmwood Avenue in the summer had a dreamy, southern quality. People might be found sitting on porches they forgot they had the rest of the year. Children in flip-flops walked down the street licking ice-cream cones; neighbors called to each other from open windows. He was about to buy an ice-cream cone himself, when he reached into his pocket for change and pulled out the slip of paper with the address and number of Stanley's hotel. He stared at it, hardly aware of the people passing by around him.

A bus came along. He rode it to the Greyhound station. He bought a ticket for the six-o'clock express to Toronto. It was almost four.

The Dog House's ambiance was midway between a public telephone and a public convenience. Its customers always seemed to be sitting before empty plates. It was hard to know how long either had been there. He chose a seat by the window and took a chance on the tuna fish platter. While waiting for his order, he looked at the slip of paper once more, wondering what the Prince of York Hotel was like. It sounded so British. Hopefully the bedcovers weren't of the plastic plush variety offered by the Towne House.

He considered his trip. The bus would get into Toronto just after eight. Would he call from the station, or simply arrive and have the desk call up? The former was the more sensible choice, the latter, the more dramatic. To listen to Mrs. MacIntyre, it sounded as if Stanley had had enough drama for a while. The most sensible thing of all would be to call before leaving the city. But if he did, Stanley might tell him not to come.

He surveyed the other patrons. Buffalo certainly wasn't Paris, where artists and writers congregated in smart cafés and brasseries during the day. Here, people who had better things to do did them, instead of letting cups of coffee grow cold in places like this. As he expected, he was the only one who seemed to be there to actually eat. Perhaps these were the chronic unemployed, given pocket money in exchange for showing up so that the place still looked like it was in business. He glanced outside the window with its majestic view of Main Street—

Wait a second . . .

Billy checked again to make sure whether the lanky-looking person with the midget sidekick really were who he thought they were. The sight of Luke and Curt felt like an ice pick through his chest. He considered holding up a menu as camouflage. But these menus were way smaller than those in that Tonawanda diner he and Cee had gone to, and he'd just stand out among the zombies that way. No, he would remain as still as everyone else and hope they didn't see him.

His tuna platter arrived: a cheesy, fish-smelling mound resting on lettuce whose main function seemed keeping the tuna from dirtying the plate. Pale-colored tomato slices drooped close by. He thought of the nights in the stale-smelling plush of Luke's truck, his yellow eyes gleaming down as Billy worked between his legs, breathing Luke's close smell, hearing his goony drawl of pleasure, and waiting for the hot shot of mercy to charge down his throat. The night outside

Hadrian's when Luke grabbed him, Luke's face had veered up against Billy's for a terrible moment, a topographical relief map of a physically diverse region: faults, craggy mountain ranges, dusty arroyos, even craters and evidence of strip mining. It was the closest Billy ever came to seeing a ghost.

A fly had alighted upon the tuna fish, as though sensing that Billy would do it no harm. It planted itself shamelessly in the goo, its feelers and greedy mouth parts working furiously to take advantage of this bonanza. Well, why not, if that's what made it happy, Billy thought. It was just getting what it wanted.

He thought he was going to be sick.

Luke and Curt began crossing the street in the direction of the restaurant. Billy's eyes darted around the place: no means of escape, and for all he knew, the restaurant might even lack a bathroom to hide in. There was nothing to do except to reach behind the counter for the knife that had just sliced his tomatoes. But they kept walking, and soon they were gone. They looked almost comical from behind—Big and Little. Billy noticed how hard Curt's legs worked to keep up with Luke.

The fly was still there, clinging to the tuna fish even as he pushed the plate away.

8

*S*HE LAY ON *her back, naked, on sand as white as her skin. Her belly was round, smooth, the ivory dome of a mosque in the desert sun. The light fell thick and heavy. Billy was somewhere nearby, though she could neither see nor hear him. Any moment he would rise like a moon beyond the horizon of her girth.*

She grew aware of pressure around her wrist, a bracelet of persistent discomfort. It was being wound tighter by a mechanism of gears and rachets. Slowly, the pain intensified until the bracelet reached bone. Her wrist was ready to splinter, to snap. She wanted to cry out for someone to stop the gears.

But the one thought that ran through her mind was, Don't let him see. For it was Billy who had clamped the band around her wrist, and Billy turned the wheel to tighten it, and she knew she mustn't let on to him how much he hurt her.

Cee's eyes broke open. Bars of chrome ringed her bed, bottles hung above—where was she? Then she remembered: Meyer Memorial. Outside the window, cars rumbled along on route 33. She imagined them spilling downtown as far as the Genesee Street exit with the sign saying Expressway Ends, as if Genesee Street marked the edge of the world.

"Rise and shine," someone said.

The woman in the next bed. What day was it? She'd done a double shift on Wednesday—the day before yesterday?—to help make up for the time she'd been away. ("This had better be your last miscarriage this year," were Durkin's words.) She'd gone home and slept until waking up in the middle of the afternoon, feeling as though a dull knife had been lodged in her cervix. The sheet was soaked with blood. She fished the phone over to the bed by the cord and dialed the Meyer ER—she knew the number by heart. She recalled being carried through the apartment and down the steps, while the knife lodged deeper inside her.

"You know what time it is?" she asked the woman across from her.

"Seven-oh-eight."

From the television came the sound of laughter. Ann Sothern. Ann Sothern at seven-oh-eight in the morning. Well, that's when the program came on. Cee rubbed her wrist. Why did they have to make the ID bands so tight? She always asked patients whether theirs felt all right. Further up her arm was the focused sting of the IV site, ringed by purple blotches, like the dough around raisins in a cake. Why did they send new techs down to the madhouse of the ER instead of a calm place like maternity? She sympathized with whoever it was who'd had to dig through her fat to reach a vein, but if you don't know what the fuck you're doing then you shouldn't be doing it. A thick band of gauze held the butterfly in place, also too tight, so that it tugged at her skin. Were they trying to save on gauze? The Meyer was a public hospital, not some cost-cutting Catholic one.

She tried to lean over and willed her pelvis to shift, but it remained anchored into the socket of the mattress. Then she saw: Strips of dirty canvas crisscrossed her front like a cat's cradle.

"Hey!" she shouted, suddenly enraged at her condition. She groped for the call light. A few minutes later a young woman with dark hair who reminded her a little of Marlene appeared. "They tied me up."

"You left us no other choice. You pulled out two IVs last night, and you'd already lost so much blood we didn't want you pulling out of the plasma." She began loosening the restraints.

"Oh," Cee said meekly. "Do I get food?"

The nurse looked at her watch. "Should've been here by now. Everything's slow because of the holiday."

"What holiday?"

"Today's the Fourth."

Cee looked at her.

"The Fourth of July."

"Any news about when I'm going to get out of here?"

"You just got in here. Don't you like us? Or do you think Buffalo General's so much nicer?"

"How did you know I work at Buffalo General?"

"You told us. Last night. You kept reminding us to call the ER there and let them know you wouldn't be in. You seemed pretty worried about it. So I called, and who should answer but Janet Durkin."

"You know her?"

"I did my surg rotation with her. Glad she's *your* boss and not mine."

"If you were on last night how come you're still here?"

"Because just as I was getting morning report a patient started yelling." She smiled.

"Sorry. Do they know what's the matter with me?"

"Some kind of infection. The doctor ordered a whole series of tests on the blood we stole from you last night. The seven-to-three people'll have the results."

There was a rattle in the hall.

"Chow time," the nurse said. "I'll see you tonight."

A paper American flag had been planted in the sweet roll on her tray. She held it up. "Happy Fourth of July," she said to the woman across the room. The woman nodded, more interested in her breakfast. A real live wire, Cee thought. Or maybe she was freaked by seeing me tied up. The woman looked to be a little younger than her mother. What was she in for? No tubes or bottles, no special diet, she wore her own pajamas, a sign that she'd been here a while. Post op, perhaps.

Kidney stones, what fifty-year-old women got. Cee twirled the flag between her fingers, and the colors swam into a blur. She drank the coffee but pushed away the rest of the tray. She wasn't that hungry after all. A big anti-Fourth of July demonstration was planned for that day. Cee'd wanted to pop over for some of it but it didn't look like she'd be doing much popping today.

"Excuse me, are you going to eat your cereal?" the woman asked.

"No, you can have it. The milk too."

"They sure had a field day with your arm," she said, emptying Cee's tray. A moment later she was back in her bed, the box of cereal opened to form a bowl, crunching away before the television screen as though they'd never spoken.

After the trays were removed, two orderlies appeared, pushing a platform scale.

"We have to weigh you, Miss," one said, exchanging a stifled grin with his partner.

"Couldn't I use the floor scale?"

The first man pointed to his clipboard. "You're down for the platform," he said with authority. He explained the procedure to her, then asked her to roll onto the scale.

"What about the curtains?"

He'd forgotten to draw them, shot an embarrassed glance at his partner, and yanked them around her bed with impatience.

Just before she crawled back into bed, her hospital gown became undone, exposing a great white chunk of ass. The second guy, who looked to be new on the job, was clearly fascinated, but the first seemed annoyed, as though a wonderful opportunity had been wasted on someone like her. He gave the scale an irritated push out of the room.

"Those people," the woman across from her said, after they'd left.

"What do you mean?"

"Them." She nodded to the door. She meant the weighing guys. Who were black.

Cee looked puzzled on purpose. The woman frowned. She'd counted on Cee aligning with her.

"Don't get me wrong," she said. "I don't have nothing against them, but sometimes they get on my nerves."

The news came on. The woman pushed the set away without turning it off. "By the way, I'm Betty," she said. "Are you a student?"

"No, I work in a hospital."

"That's how come you gave those two a hard time."

She seemed determined for Cee to come out on top.

A voice on the TV was giving the holiday death toll predictions.

"I'm not very patriotic," Betty said, by way of commentary. "When they told me that I wouldn't get out until after the Fourth it didn't bother me none except that it meant that I couldn't go to the Saint Agnes church picnic."

"I don't feel like celebrating the Fourth of July. I'm not sure I have a reason to be proud of being an American."

"I wouldn't want to be anything else," Betty said sharply.

Well, to tell you the truth, I've always wished I'd been born in Upper Volta, Cee thought. Why was it that people over a certain age could always be depended on to give the same mindless answers to certain questions. She could almost predict what would follow: how bad it was in Russia (always Russia, never the Soviet Union), the depression, immigrants from all over the world coming here, and so on.

Betty drifted off into sleep, the television still on. She was one of those people who needed it as background noise. When Cee read *1984* she found the idea of a television you couldn't shut off unbearable. Well, Betty was paying for the set by the day and wanted to get her money's worth.

Cee thought of Kal, a true morning person, and decided to call her. They'd seen each other only briefly since Cee returned from Thompson City. She asked for a roller for the bottles, pushed her way down the hall as the bottles swung precariously, and fumbled in her bag for change.

"I'm in the hospital, Kal."

"Another double shift?"

"No. I'm a patient. In the Meyer. It probably has something to do with losing the baby. I'm okay. It hurts a little but I can get out of bed and everything. Feel like visiting me sometime?"

"You poor thing. You need anything?"

"Everything. They came yesterday and took me away like the Gestapo."

"Can you wait until after the demonstration? Then I can come for your keys."

"That'd be great. I was wondering. I haven't seen Billy since I've been back. Vincent hasn't either. Have you?"

Kal gave an impatient sigh. "Not for about two weeks since he came over and confessed to me. What is it about Catholics that makes them think they can do shit but if they apologize afterward everything will be wonderful?"

Cee called Marlene later that afternoon.

"I heard you were in New York," Marlene said.

Her tone of voice told Cee that she knew everything. Cee hesitated answering, as if any utterance would incriminate her. Did it have to be this weird between two women when a man was involved? Then she remembered: Marlene always reacted seriously. Cee told her she was in the hospital. Marlene asked what had happened, sounding nervous. "It's not . . . I mean, you didn't . . ."

Cee laughed and explained about the baby. "No razors this time. It just felt as if there were. Come and visit me," she said. "For old times' sake."

She waited for Marlene to mention Joel; he'd talked about coming to Buffalo around now. But Marlene said nothing. There wasn't anything to tell, Cee thought. She'd had a little vacation in New York with Joel, which was nice, but it wasn't going to change things between him and Marlene. And maybe it was better that way.

"Bring me something to read when you come, Marlene," she said.

Cee dug into her purse for more change to call up her mother. Several days ago, Theresa had called and filled Cee in about what had happened since she left Thompson City. The title deed that Carl had found had been declared authentic, and a judge ordered a halt to any further work on the project until ownership could be proved. Carl and Elaine and Melissa returned to the house. Larrabee would be permitted to build on the land, provided the owner agreed to it. Since the deed had come to light, two people claimed to be descended from congregation members listed on it, including Junior. The county had offered Larrabee a parcel by the river, but it looked as though Larrabee's days in the county were numbered. The *Herald-Examiner* printed a shrill account of the incident in Walter's hospital room, which painted Elaine as a violent radical and hinted at her connections to the student demonstrators who had disrupted the fair. The *Sun-Bulletin* story mentioned Theresa's discoveries about Larrabee.

Both papers printed pictures of Jason being dragged away.

Theresa had gone for her checkup. The tumor showed no signs of metastasis, and Dr. Kraus said that, after five years, a relapse was improbable. "It means that I'm considered cured," she said. But she didn't sound especially happy. Walter's condition hadn't improved. The police found out that Jason violated the terms of his release the night he'd gone fishing, and she imagined the incident at the barbeque wouldn't help him. His confession remained the sole factor in his favor.

Now Cee slipped a bunch of quarters into the slot and dialed her mother's number. No one was home. Her coins tumbled back out as though she'd hit the jackpot on a slot machine.

A group of people stepped off the elevator. The visitors—a middle-aged man and two boys—turned out to be Betty's. The boys lumbered by, embarrassed at seeing a woman in a hospital gown. Cee followed them back to the room.

"Why aren't all of you at the picnic?" Betty said.

"We took a break," the man said. He leaned over and kissed her. "We would have gotten here earlier but they closed off Delaware on account of an accident or something."

"It was because of a protest," the older of the two boys corrected him.

The man ran off the names of all the people they knew who were at the picnic, told about so-and-so's grill catching fire, and someone's dog going crazy from the heat and biting someone.

Families, Cee thought. She would have liked to read but it was too noisy to concentrate with all the talking and the babble of the television, even if she'd had a book.

"What's that?" the younger boy said to his mother, pointing to Cee's pack of plasma.

"Blood," Cee said.

The boy looked horrified.

"How come?"

"Because I lost so much of it last night," Cee explained.

"How?"

"Don't ask questions like that, Ronny," Betty said.

A moment later Billy appeared in the doorway.

Cee didn't recognize him right away—he was was dressed as the Statue of Liberty, in a long white gown, complete with torch, crown, and a big black eye drawn with eyebrow pencil. A man wearing a sport shirt and jeans was with him.

"Happy Fourth of July, everyone!" he said, waving the torch. "Say hello to Ms. Liberty and her new husband."

Betty and her family stared.

"Billy!"

He flew over to her bed with a noisy flounce of fabric.

"How did you know I was here?"

"When you didn't pick up your phone I tried Buffalo General's ER. Oh, hello!" Billy called to the people across the room.

"Meet my roommate, Betty," Cee said, a little flustered.

Betty smiled, sort of.

"Who are you?" the older boy said.

"I'm the future of America," Billy answered brightly.

"She's a man," whispered the younger boy.

"You must be Stanley," Cee said, wrestling the conversation back onto their half of the room.

Stanley smiled uncomfortably. "I remember you from that night . . . in the hospital."

"I want you to know that Stanley here risked being arrested at the border for leaving the country after having been accused of drug trafficking."

"Billy, you really don't have to—" Stanley said.

"Well, that's what happened, didn't it?"

Betty shut the TV off and listened.

"You both came from the demonstration?" Cee said, changing the subject once more. "How was it?"

"The cops said there were only five thousand, but they're full of shit. Niagara Square was packed." He looked over to Stanley. "Tell her which contingent we marched in." Stanley shook his head, embarrassed. "Go on, tell her. And you better not use that H-word, either."

Stanley looked down. "The . . . gay contingent," he said.

"His very first demonstration," Billy said, beaming, as though Stanley were his son. He took hold of Stanley's hand. "I'm so proud."

"You see, I told you it was a demonstration that caused the traffic jam," the older boy said.

"Mind your own business," his father shot back.

"Now Stanley's a public queer, just like me," Billy said.

"Stanley," Cee said, noticing Betty's stare.

"Oh, you don't have to worry. Now that he's officially come out, Stanley's no longer afraid of people knowing that he's a cocksucker, are you?"

Stanley blushed quite deeply.

Cee swallowed. "Was Kal there?"

"Of course. Would she miss a chance to piss on the patriarchy? Lara, you know Lara, her girlfriend, she was marching right next to her. Pretty little thing, isn't she? She said, 'If you really want to do something decent, then come to Kal's custody trial and testify that you've sold Luke drugs.'"

Betty's mouth was hanging open, literally.

"What are you going to do?"

"If I do that, it might mean my own hide. I mean, no court in New York State'll hear what she wants me to tell them and then say, 'Well, that's really honest of you, Mr. Gizzi. And just because you've been so gosh-darned honest we're not going to prosecute you according to Nelson Rockefeller's drug law.' You know what they'll do?" he said, gesturing with the torch. "Set me up in an efficiency apartment somewhere in, say, Elmira or, if I'm really lucky, Attica."

"It probably depends on how much Kal means to you," Stanley suggested.

"He's right, Billy," said Cee.

Billy sighed. "I'll do it if Stanley wants me to," he said, touching Stanley's face. "Look how much he's giving up for me: the respectable life of a devoted husband and father of two children—" he flashed a look over at the two boys "—all for the sake of—"

"Jesus, Billy," said Stanley.

"What's all this about you and drug trafficking, Stanley?" Cee said.

Stanley explained.

"All that for one joint?" Cee said.

"And an unpaid parking ticket," Stanley added.

At some point Betty's family left, and she walked them to the elevator. Her husband glared at Billy on the way out.

Billy winked at the older boy.

"He winked at me," they heard him say in the hall. "The man in the dress winked at me."

"Serves you right for looking at him," the father said.

Later that night a nurse told Cee that she had a phone call in the nurses' station.

"Hello? Mom!"

"Cee, what's wrong? I called Buffalo General and they said you were here."

"It's because of the baby. I've only been here since last night. But I'm all right."

"It was such a shock when they told me—"

"I said I'm all right," she said, getting edgy. "How's Dad?"

Theresa began to cry. "This morning," Theresa mumbled. "In his sleep."

Cee stared at the receiver, at the grille clogged with particles of dirt. She was hearing about her father's death through all this gunk.

"Mom . . ."

It occurred to her that her father's death was the very last thing she'd expected, even though she saw how weak he was. She thought Jason might run off again, or that someone might set fire to Carl's house, but somehow she'd expected her father to pull through.

"Everyone was there," her mother was saying. "Carl, Elaine, even Melissa."

"Was it because of what happened on the lake?"

"Who knows? And what difference does it make now? Dr. Kraus said that he had no business working on those houses. He had no business working on any houses."

"But pneumonia—he came into the hospital with pneumonia."

"They took care of that. It was his heart . . . I know what you're thinking, Cee," she said, sounding almost angry. "But it was an accident. Accidents happen. It was an accident, for the love of God!"

What does she want me to say? Cee thought. That Jason had nothing to do with it? Yes. That was exactly what she wanted to hear.

Her mother blew her nose. "Carl's taken it the worst. You know, I never believed that he'd come to the hospital the way he did."

"At least Dad saw him again before . . ."

"Cee, listen. I have some things to tell you." Her voice suddenly cleared. Cee imagined her mother motioning with her hands for attention. "First: Elaine's going to Syracuse. Neither of them have spoken of divorce, but I'm afraid that's what it's going to amount to."

"And Melissa?"

"She'll stay with Carl for the present." She sighed. "He's broken. He feels like he's failed. I didn't know what to say. I like Elaine." Theresa hesitated, as though trying to see how she might have prevented what had happened. "But at least he'll be able to stay in the house," she continued. "It turns out that a great-great-grandfather of that neighbor of Carl's was a member of the church, so it's possible that the house and land will go to him. He's already said that if it does, Carl can keep living up there as a tenant. He said he won't let Larrabee build on the mountain, although he's thinking of building a small house up there for himself."

"What about Junior's mother? She hates Carl. She'll never let him stay in the house."

"The house would go to Junior and not her. It appears she isn't Junior's real mother."

Cee remembered a snatch of conversation with Carl about that a zillion years ago.

"If all that works out, I'm going to sell the house here and move up there to be with Carl and Melissa."

"You really want to do that?"

"I don't think Carl will pull through this any other way. It'll be good for Melissa. And I don't want to be here alone. I'll have to learn to drive, of course, and it'll take me another twenty minutes to get to work in the morning. But I'll get a dog. I'll have a garden. I've already told Junior that I would help him pay his fine with the money from selling the house."

"What fine?"

"For the damage he caused with the truck the day of the fair. They're talking about thousands of dollars."

"You certainly have thought everything out to the last detail."

"I had to, Cee. I'd go out of my mind otherwise."

"You haven't said anything about Jason," Cee said.

Theresa's voice lowered. "There's nothing to say now. They postponed the hearing on account of Walter. Everybody here now thinks Jason's crazy and dangerous."

"Is he going to live up at the house, too? With Carl?"

Theresa sighed.

Cee began to cry as soon as she got back into bed.

"Cee?"

Betty came over to Cee's bed and put her arms around her.

"Cee," she said. "What's the matter?"

"I don't really know, Betty. I don't really know."

Her father, she thought. It was hard to imagine that lumbering, self-satisfied hulk of a man with nothing more to say. He'd always been a figure on a distant podium, easy for her and Carl to take potshots at. As far back as Cee could remember, she and her brother had set themselves squarely against him. He'd stood for everything there was to break down, cast away, and start over from. They'd disapproved of him, condemned him, and finally abandoned him for all sorts of ideological reasons; they hadn't been satisfied with simply disliking him for being pigheaded and domineering. Now he was gone, leaving them to shout their indignation into the empty air. What had someone written in the UB student newspaper after they announced the end of the war in Vietnam? *Now that the war's over, who is there to fight?*

Betty changed channels.

Cee sat, staring at the blank landscape of her cover sheet. "I don't know," she repeated to herself. *If you don't know, then who's going to know?* She heard Elaine imitating her Yiddish-speaking mother. But Cee really didn't know. So much in the past couple of months had been dumped into her lap without an explanation, specimens on a scientist's desk that no one else could identify.

In the middle of it all was Jason, getting yanked along this way and that, an arrow spun during a board game, round and round it goes and where it stops, nobody knows. She thought of how he'd looked on the evening news as they dragged him away from the stage in Lacey Park: helpless, yet strangely triumphant.

Betty had fallen asleep. The television was still on.

photo: Dirk Wolter

About the Author

Eric Gabriel Lehman was born in New York City. His first novel, *Waterboys*, appeared in 1989. He currently lives in Berlin, where he works as a musician.

Editor: Thomas Christensen
Text designer and typesetter: Philip Bronson
Copyeditor and production coordinator: Zipporah Collins
Proofreaders: Catherine Cambron, David Sweet, Teresa Castle
Printer and binder: Haddon Craftsmen